I0746823

HELL TO PAY

BOOK TWO OF THE HARVESTERS SERIES

LUKE MITCHELL

Copyright © 2017 by Luke R. Mitchell

All rights reserved.

No part of this book may be reproduced in any form or by any electronic or mechanical means, including information storage and retrieval systems, without written permission from the author, except for the use of brief quotations in a book review.

Cover design by Yocla Designs

Cover illustration by Hokunin

Editing by Lisa Poisso

Proofreading by Dj Hendrickson

PROLOGUE

Haldin Raish leaned forward, steepled his fingers in a decidedly masterly pose, and surveyed the two combatants before him. Elise arched a raven black eyebrow at him. He ignored it.

"Again."

Elise dipped deep into her personal vat of sarcasm and threw him the salute she found there. He hid his decidedly unmasterly smile behind the steeple of his fingers. Elise turned, all grace and deadly beauty, to square off against her opponent, a slim man with suave features and dark hair peppered with gray.

Alton Parker looked to be in his early forties. He wasn't.

"Begin," Haldin said.

Elise rolled her shoulders, sank into a ready stance, and raised a hand to Alton in invitation. For several seconds, Alton only watched, unmoving. Then he sprang forward to throw a sweeping punch at Elise's head. She sidestepped the blow then ducked the follow-up backhand, wasting nothing with her movements.

She really was a sight to behold, especially in the heat of combat.

Alton threw a series of jabs, and Elise handled those just as fluidly, turning each one aside with crisp precision—always redirecting, never outright blocking. Just like they'd practiced.

She stepped outside of the last punch, pushing the blow past her. She yanked the dark polymer practice knife from her belt and plunged it at Alton's face.

Alton twisted and dropped his head out of harm's way, then swept a kick at Elise's thigh. It wasn't a particularly well-aimed kick, but coming from Alton, it would still be plenty dangerous.

Elise turned through a tight aerial that took her over the kick and left her face to face with Alton.

He darted forward before her boots touched the deck. Elise only barely managed to throw herself aside in time to avoid his grab.

Too close. That was his cue.

Haldin plucked the clunky pistol from his lap.

Ahead, Elise pulled out of her evasive roll in a ready crouch, wary blue eyes fixed on Alton.

He pointed the gun at her and pulled the trigger.

Elise's hand was already flying up when the gun gave a sharp, cracking puff. There was a blur of motion, and then a squishy blue dart pulled to a halt a few inches from Elise's open palm, hovering in midair.

Haldin almost laughed at the surprised expression on her face, but then Alton lunged for her with a low growl.

Elise's other hand shot up like a striking viper. Alton's charge slowed as if he'd suddenly been plopped into a chest-high pool of thick honey. His growl deepened, rumbling in his chest, and his pale eyes came alive with fiery red light, whites and irises both. He took another step forward against the resistance. Then another.

In front of him, Elise was down on one knee now, her fair, creamy skin a few shades paler and shining with perspiration. She began to shake from her exertions.

Haldin was opening his mouth to call them to a halt when the squishy blue dart hovering next to Elise's hand reoriented itself and launched toward Alton seemingly by its own accord.

The dart struck Alton right between his glowing red eyes with a defiant little squeak. Elise looked up, clearly strained but grinning nonetheless.

Haldin couldn't help it this time. He laughed. "Okay, good, good. Both of you."

Alton relented his forward march, the fire draining from his eyes. Elise blew out a long breath and plopped down to the deck.

"Not bad," Alton said, frowning down at the squishy blue dart by his foot. "You're getting stronger."

"Was that full power?" Elise asked between heavy breaths.

A satisfied smirk curled the corners of Alton's mouth. "Hardly."

"Wonderful." Elise shook her head, clearly disheartened.

"It actually was," Haldin said. He reached for the dart and it flew from the deck to his open hand before he'd thought twice about focusing his mind or channeling the requisite energy. By now, telekinesis required little more mental involvement than using his own hands, which wasn't so surprising. Alpha knew they'd had enough time to practice over the past months.

Elise gave him one of her looks.

"It was," he said. "You're doing amazing, Lise."

"Good news, everyone!" came a voice from the corridor outside. A moment later, Johnny walked into the room in all his flame-haired glory, holding up a single finger exactly as Haldin had known he would.

"You've been watching that show again."

Johnny gave one of his full-body shrugs. "Gotta bone up on the references somehow, broto. Don't want people to think I'm a weirdo."

"But Johnny," Elise said from the deck, "who could ever think that about you?"

Johnny waggled his eyebrows at her and turned to Alton. "I think the jumper-thingies are all done with their space nap. Or whatever it is that they do."

Alton nodded and strode past Johnny and out of the room.

"Space nap?" Haldin said.

"Yeah, man."

"You're such a space sap," Elise said.

"Nice," Johnny said, offering her a hand.

She took it and allowed herself to be hauled up. "Thanks."

They both turned expectant looks on him.

"What?" He stood and slid past them to follow Alton. "I don't wanna space rap."

"Ooo!" Johnny said.

"Eh," Elise said. "I've heard better."

Haldin paused for a three count then spun and made a grab for Elise. She was already moving, not that his extended senses hadn't already told him that. He could have grabbed her as she whirled past, but then he would've missed the chance to see her darting off down the hallway with one of her adorable little giggles.

When you're stuck in space for months on end trying not to lose it, it's all about the little things.

They arrived in the large cockpit to find Alton at the main console, eyes closed in concentration. Ahead of him, the round walls of the front half of the room were in their transparent viewing mode, granting an open view of the star-dotted void their last jump had landed them in.

It was a truly breathtaking view. Or had been, at least, the first hundred or so times he'd seen it.

The others trickled in slowly: Phineas and James, Therese and Franco, all gathering to watch the daily ritual unfold.

Alton stirred from his trance and glanced over at the assembled audience.

"How many more?" Haldin asked.

Alton shook his head, just like he did every other day.

Haldin let out a sigh, and they all gathered in front of the enormous view port.

"Everyone ready?" Alton said.

"You know it, Red," Johnny said, just like he did every other day. He must have enjoyed the irony.

"Five seconds," Alton said.

Elise took hold of Haldin's hand, and they all held their collective breath, just like every other day. The customary hum ran through the hull, and the usual tingling sensation crawled over his body. The ship shuddered, and for a second, the world outside went dark. Not outer space dark, with stars and everything, just… dark.

A few silent seconds crept by, just like they always did, and then, just like every other day, the darkness of normal space snapped back into sight, and—

Haldin's mouth fell open, shock smacking him like a tall wave.

"Holy space crap," Johnny muttered.

"Sweet Alpha," Elise whispered.

A giant blue planet filled the view port, covered with swaths of green-brown land masses and swirls of wispy white cloud formations. Haldin stared at it in a stupor until the pressure of Elise's grip on his hand tugged him back to reality.

After all this time, they'd made it.

CHAPTER ONE

J arek Slater stood tall and unflinching before the scrutiny of the three Resistance commanders, wishing they'd get on with it. For the moment being, though, they appeared perfectly content to sit back and wait for god knew what. Certainly not for the rest of the council to arrive. Not a single soul had been late to this particular gathering. They'd piled through the doors in force, jockeying for position to secure good seats for what was sure to be the event of the year: the chastising of the Soldier of Charity.

And now their stares bored into him from all sides like a hundred prodding fingers goading him to lose his shit.

Entitled pricks.

They were going to have a long wait if they wanted to see him squirm. Especially since he was wearing Fela. If this dragged on much longer he could close the exosuit's faceplate and take a damn nap standing up.

He never should have let Al and Pryce talk him into this olive branch bullshit. Hell, the way things were going, he was starting to wonder if he shouldn't have just stayed at Pryce's shop and enjoyed a nice whiskey instead of flying off to the port and duking it out with the Red King's army to save the day for the Resistance. Which he totally had, by the way.

Apparently someone had forgotten to tell that part to the two dozen glaring a-holes in the council chamber.

Finally, by some imperceptible cue that Jarek could only assume involved divine right, Commander Nelken deigned it the appropriate time to begin and leaned his paunchy bulk forward on the commanders' head table.

"Mr. Slater." His voice was heavy. Solemn. Freaking theatrical. "You know why we're here. Twice in the same day you endangered the lives of our men and women. First when you raided our armory and committed what would reasonably be construed as an act of war against us. Then again when you knowingly brought an enemy combatant—and a raknoth, no less—into this base only hours later. It's unacceptable."

Nelken was right. It was unacceptable. And he could take that unacceptable pile of bullshit and shove it—

"Easy, sir." Al's smooth English accent was crisp and soothing in his helmet earpieces. "Control."

Al was right. That would drive the bastards crazy.

He spread his hands wide and put on his best carefree grin. "Okay, you got me. I'm trouble. A real loose cannon. Maybe even a terrorist. But let's not stop there. I think we missed a few parts. Like where I stopped said raknoth from killing everyone and saved actual shiploads of your people."

At the head table, Commander Sloan's creepy slender form straightened and he opened his mouth to speak.

Jarek silenced him with an armored finger. "Plus, on a scale from no-no to act of war, I'd put the business here somewhere around stealing from the cookie jar. You know, aside from the part where it wasn't actually stealing on account of this suit belonging to me and everything."

Murmurs. Murmurs everywhere.

If they were going to try to take him into custody or make him pay for his "crimes," he wished they'd whip 'em out and get to it. But they wouldn't. Of course they wouldn't. Because this was how it went with outfits like the Resistance, wasn't it?

They putzed around, babbling about their cause and fighting the good fight until someone came along and actually got shit done, and then they all lost their heads over the audacity of the thing.

Who the hell did he think he was to swoop in and right their sinking ship?

How dare he take back what was his? How dare he be his own man, follow his own compass? Who'd given him permission?

Jarek had met more than a few freedom fighter types since the Catastrophe and remained woefully unimpressed. Most were just as afraid of upsetting the status quo as everyone else. And those who weren't, in his experience, tended to be goddamn psychopaths.

There was a reason he'd steered clear of organized tomfoolery like the Resistance since a catastrophic hiccup with one such psychopath in his teenage years had earned him the ridiculous nickname Soldier of Charity and nearly cost him his life to boot. And as good as saving the day at the ports had felt last night, there was an even better reason he couldn't wait to get the hell away from all this.

A couple dozen reasons, actually. And they were all still staring at him, muttering back and forth behind raised hands as if Fela's sensors didn't allow Jarek to hear every word they said.

Commander Sloan's disturbingly green-eyed glare was particularly ferocious as he whispered to Commander Nelken that they could not—repeat, could *not*—just let Jarek walk away from this fiasco without punishment.

Jarek kind of wished they'd try to stop him.

"Fine," he called.

The room snapped silent at the sound of his voice.

"It's unacceptable. Don't accept it. Was there something else you fellas wanted?"

Nelken's perpetual frown darkened. Sloan looked like he was actively trying call bright green death rays from his eyes to smite Jarek down.

Beside them, Commander Stacy Daniels gathered herself to speak, her expression mostly neutral, if maybe a bit stern. "I think it's safe to say our time would be better spent calling it even and moving on to the matter of the nest device's activation and what it might mean for us."

Jarek gave her a grateful micro nod. Compared to the rest of these jackals, Daniels didn't seem so bad—even if what she'd just proposed was an exercise in futility.

The truth was that they knew jack crap about the raknoth device that had blasted a holy Jesus beam into the sky last night, aside from the one cryptic tidbit the Red King had given them between his maniacal raknoth giggles.

Retribution, he'd said. The nest had raised the call for retribution. Whatever the hell that meant.

There was a decent chance it was nothing but pure, grade A bullshit—a fun little threat the defeated King had spun in the moment to keep them afraid and guessing. But something told him it wasn't.

Jarek clearly wasn't a people person, but he did like to think he could read them fairly well, and the Red King's little meltdown had felt sincere enough to make him wonder what the hell could frighten a raknoth like that.

He'd been hoping to shake the red-eyed bastard until more answers fell out, but the Resistance had unsurprisingly taken quite strict custody of their raknoth prisoner the moment he'd entered HQ—never mind the fact that Jarek had been the one to capture him, thank you very much.

From what little he'd heard, the King had been monk-like in his commitment to silence since they'd brought him in. Jarek wasn't sure he could do much better, but that didn't make him any less irritated at the territorial shutout.

Either way, if they weren't going to try to slap him in the ol' irons, he wasn't about to sit here and listen to the council try to extract a meaningful conclusion from a single itty-bitty clue.

"I'll leave you guys to it then," Jarek said, turning for the door. "Wouldn't want you to have to slow everything down for me."

Nelken's voice was heavy with threatening authority. "Slater."

Jarek kept walking.

Sloan must have been close to conjuring up those death rays after all, because Jarek swore he could feel the glares pelting into the back of his head as he pulled open the double doors and slipped out to the narrow hallway.

"Masterfully handled, sir," Al said. "Glad to see all those communication self-help books are paying off."

"It's the strangest thing. I wiped with every single page, and I feel like I just didn't absorb anything!"

"Charming, sir. And you have company."

He'd already heard as much. Fela's auditory sensors were a work of art, but even without them, he would have heard Commander Nelken's approach easily enough. The man wasn't exactly light of foot, and his normally heavy breathing was clearly elevated right now. Anyone's guess why.

"You arrogant son of a bitch."

Jarek turned to watch Nelken close in at a spry power walk and didn't try overly hard to hide his amused grin. "Don't hold back, Commander. Tell me how you really feel."

"Like I'd take great pleasure in ordering my agents to rip you out of that suit and hog tie you in the brig if I didn't think the fight would wreck half the base."

"That"—Jarek cocked his head and nodded—"is actually fair enough. You know, wild injustices aside and whatnot."

Whatever else Jarek could say about Nelken, it took some stones for the commander to march straight up to Jarek and prod him in the armored chest. "All you had to do in there was half-ass an apology. Order could have been restored, and we could have gone back to peacefully disliking each other. Was that too much for your pride to swallow?"

Jarek wrinkled his nose at the strong waft of aftershave and what he could only assume was pure, distilled anger. "I dunno." He glanced toward the council chamber. "I think I really nailed the half-ass bit."

"Dammit, Slater," Nelken growled. "This is an unstable time for us. For all of us. These people need to know we're steady and afloat here."

By what looked to be a considerable force of will, Nelken took a step back and let out a sigh. "Look, I know it was… uncouth of us to try to keep your suit, especially once you helped Carver escape from the Fortress, but we're not the villains here. I don't need to tell you how uneven this fight is for us. I'm not asking you to sign the dotted line and give me a 'Sir, yes sir,' but I can't have you around here if you can't at least act like you give half a damn about Resistance authority."

"That's the thing, Nelken. I don't give a damn about you or your Resistance. I came here to get my exo back and I stayed to help my friends. That should've been the end of it. But now that crazy raknoth bastard in there"—he pointed toward the holding cells—"the one I captured, by the way, tells us some kind of retribution is about to rain down on our heads, and I kinda wanna know what the hell he's talking about before I go gallivanting on my way. So you can give me back my prisoner, or you can suck it up and let me at him. I don't really care. Just don't go thinking I've joined your fight. I'm not your soldier—not to command, and sure as hell not to reprimand."

They held locked glares for a good ten seconds, Nelken's eyes stern and unyielding. Finally, the commander's expression relaxed by a hair's breadth. "I did say *act* like you give a damn."

The crack in Nelken's domineering exterior took Jarek by genuine enough surprise that a huff of a chuckle escaped him. His surprise doubled when Nelken returned a thin smile of his own.

Guy was probably going to pull a muscle if he wasn't careful.

"Fine. Maybe I can steer clear of blatant disrespect for a day or two, assuming no one tries to steal my suit in the middle of the night."

Nelken tilted his head. "All right then."

Jarek gestured toward the holding cells. "He really hasn't said anything yet?"

"Not a word. And he doesn't seem to particularly care about any physical discomfort." Nelken hesitated before adding, "If he keeps this up, we might have to ask Rachel to take a crack at, you know." He tapped at the side of his square, buzzed head.

"I don't know much about telepathy, but as far as I understand, that kind of thing is dangerous to toy with, and Rachel isn't exactly clear of mind right now, what with Michael having been touched by a Jesus beam and everything."

Nelken nodded. "I'm aware. But we need to figure this thing out soon. The King is healing disturbingly fast."

"Huh. Creepy."

Nelken looked exasperated. "There are reasons beyond pride that we were upset about you bringing a raknoth here. I don't see how he could break out of his restraints, but I'm not interested in taking chances."

"Well, as a rule, I stay away from the real sadistic shit, but if we need to trim him down a few limbs"—Jarek patted the hilt of the enormous sword strapped to Fela's back, the one he'd dubbed the Big Whacker—"all we need is a good chopping block."

Nelken's brows crept upward. "And that doesn't fall into the category of 'real sadistic shit'?"

"I've seen some stuff, man. And some things."

Nelken studied him for a long moment. "I don't doubt that. Now would you be willing to talk to Rachel? With Carver's current condition… Well, you know her better than anyone else who's currently conscious. I can see to it you're updated if anything happens with the prisoner. Otherwise, it's probably better for everyone if you stay on your ship."

"Yeah, well, I was gonna do all that anyway, so…" Jarek turned back down the hall and threw the most sarcastic two-fingered salute he could manage over his shoulder.

"So glad we cleared that up," Nelken muttered behind him. Then, more loudly, "Slater."

Jarek paused and turned his head just enough to show he was listening.

"Don't go thinking this little talk means you're off the hook. I might be a commander, but if you give my people reason to come calling for your head again, I won't stop them."

Jarek grinned.

Maybe Nelken wasn't the worst jackal on the planet. Jarek wouldn't pick the guy as a drinking buddy or anything, but at least the stern bastard seemed to be playing things straight with him now.

"Understood," he said. "You know, assuming any of us still have the luxury to worry about whose is bigger at that point."

Nelken frowned. "You really think something's coming?"

"Eh." Jarek shrugged. "Above my pay grade."

"No one's paying you."

"Exactly."

With that, he continued down the bland hallway, enjoying Nelken's silence behind him. His grin faded soon enough, though.

In truth, he had no idea what to think. He hadn't been lying to Nelken. If it weren't for the nest exploding and the King's cryptic warning of impending doom, he probably would have made for the hills that morning—dropped Alaric back in Deadwood and taken several hot showers to wash the traces of the Resistance's mangy mitts from himself and Fela.

Hell, maybe he would have even offered Rachel a ride home and seen where that went. As a rule, he pretty much avoided anything outside of casual, fleeting engagements, but after the string of mishaps they'd muscled through together over the past couple days...

It didn't matter. And not just because she would've said no (okay, probably *hell no*). It didn't matter because the nest *had* exploded, and the King *had* warned them that retribution was coming for them. The best laid plans of Jarek, as they so often did, had gone and gotten royally cocked up, and now here he was, tied up in what was almost certainly someone else's problem.

"This is why we don't get involved," he mumbled.

"You're right, sir," Al said. "I'm sure this will all resolve marvelously if we fly away now and pretend none of this ever happened."

"Yeah, yeah. Keep it up, Mr. Robot. We'll see who's laughing when I hand you over to Pryce for parts."

Al didn't deign to respond with any more than an indignant sniff, an utterly unnecessary affectation for a bodiless construct.

Jarek reached the end of the dull hallway, started to turn toward medical, and paused. As far as he knew, Rachel hadn't left Michael's side since they'd arrived last night. She'd be hungry. Peace offerings never hurt.

He turned for the mess hall, tromping from one dull hallway to another. From what he'd seen, every room and hallway of HQ was nearly identical: gray cinder block walls, smooth, slightly-darker-gray concrete floors, yellow lighting that had a sort of plastic feel to it.

Before the Catastrophe, it would've been the kind of place people made Soviet prison jokes about. Now, though, those same people would look at the place and see safety, security.

Jarek just felt cramped.

No matter where he was, he seemed to be hunkering down to avoid smashing his head into the ceiling. The hallways were narrow enough that everyone felt the impulse to go chest-to-chest passing by one another, even if it wasn't strictly required.

And that was just the physical stuff. It had been a long while since he'd spent much time in such a densely populated space, especially one where everyone wasn't actively trying to kill him.

It made him antsy.

The sooner he figured out what the hell that giant beam-shooting egg had actually done, the sooner he could confirm whether it was safe to leave this circus behind and go back to the good life. And if it wasn't, and the Red King wasn't just blowing fear-mongering smoke in their eyes…

Honestly, if the sky was about to fall, he wasn't entirely sure what the hell he was going to do about it, but it was pointless to speculate before they knew more. Answers first.

But before they got to that, he had a pair of sandwiches to find.

CHAPTER TWO

Rachel laid her brother's still hand across his torso and leaned back in her chair. She blew out a long breath and stretched, arching her back and neck until she could see the wall behind her. It stared right back, bland and depressing and utterly uncaring about the suffering going on just a dozen feet from its cool surface.

She'd always rolled her eyes at the people in stories who'd sit at the bedside of a comatose loved one and just wait, accomplishing nothing when they could be doing anything. If they wanted to help so much, why not at least get up and go take care of that person's affairs? Why not scour the country for a second opinion? Or a fourth or a fifth? Why not find other options? Hell, why not go find someone else they could help and hope the universe was paying attention?

Why the hell would someone just *sit* there?

She hadn't understood.

And now here she was—sitting, waiting, accomplishing nothing when she could be doing anything.

She could have left. Could have started trying to find out what the hell that damn egg had done to Michael when it went off. She needed to eat, to sleep, to shower. And she could have done all those things.

But what if he woke up and she wasn't here?

What if he went the other way, and she missed her last chance to see him drawing breath?

She couldn't risk it—couldn't even think it without wanting to scream. So she'd sat here all night. And now all day, according to her comm.

"Trying to see things from the other side?"

Rachel whipped upright in her chair to find Jay Pryce watching her from the doorway. The sight of the paper plate and sandwich in his hand elicited an immediate and violent rumble from her stomach.

"What?"

He looked at the ceiling and turned his head sideways. "You never just...? Never mind—forget I said it. How are you holding up?"

She shrugged and looked at Michael's dark, silent form as if that should say everything. Pryce acted like it did. He came to offer her the plate. She took it gratefully and began savaging what turned out to be a peanut butter and jelly sandwich. Pryce occupied himself with checking the few monitors they'd hooked Michael up to.

HQ's medical facility consisted of two rooms and sported a grand total of three permanent beds. It wasn't exactly up to the gold standard of pre-Catastrophe times, but it was a hell of a sight better than nothing. The Resistance even had a pair of doctors and a couple of nurses living on base, though no one had been able to divine anything about Michael's condition beyond the fact that he was indeed comatose—for all the good that did them.

"No changes," Pryce said. He took a little penlight out of his pocket and proceeded to open each of Michael's eyes with thumb and forefinger and shine the light in them. Apparently satisfied, he pocketed the light, cupped Michael's head, and gently tilted it left and then right. Lastly, he took Michael's left wrist in one hand, laid his other hand over Michael's biceps, and worked the arm through a short range of motion.

Despite everything, she felt the ghost of a smile hovering near the surface as she watched Pryce at work. There didn't seem to be any limit to the disciplines the guy dabbled in. From mechanic to chemist to engineer to medic, he just kept getting more eccentric.

She swallowed a mouthful of peanut butter and jelly. "Is that your professional opinion, Dr. Pryce?"

He set Michael's arm down, looking abashed. "Sorry, I'm not helping. I just get curious."

"I don't think Michael minds."

Pryce tilted his head as if to politely say, *No, probably not.*

She shifted her sandwich, readying the next bite. "Any interesting tidings from the world beyond?"

"Not really." Pryce started fidgeting with his hands. "Although Al and I did talk Jarek into appearing before the council, so..."

"Be ready for gunfire and explosions?"

"Would that I could joke about it. I just hope Al keeps him centered in there." He frowned down at his restless hands and jammed them into his pockets.

The poor guy was clearly itching for a project—probably to cope with the stress of the past couple days. Too bad he couldn't return to the workshop that was his pride and joy. Not right now, at least. The Red King's men would almost certainly be watching it, waiting for anyone who might know something about their missing boss to come along.

She felt partially responsible. Sure, Jarek had been the one to lead them to Pryce's shop after their escape from the Red Fortress, and it wasn't really her fault the Reds—or rather, the Red King—had tracked them. But that didn't make her feel any less bad that good, kind, brilliant Pryce had gotten dragged into this mess because of them.

"We need to get you out of here," she said. "I'm pretty sure this is how good scientists go mad."

Pryce didn't say what he was thinking, but his bushy gray eyebrows managed to convey the gist of the message: like she was one to talk, sitting here all night and day.

"Alas," Pryce said with a wan smile, "it seems my only hope is to find ways to use my powers for good here for the time being."

"Speaking of which,"—she nearly jumped at the sound of Jarek's voice from the doorway—"I could use some help patching up the ship. She's got more holes than a… Eh, never mind. But point is I've got me some holes that need pluggin'." The last part he said in what she had to assume was supposed to be a pirate voice.

Jarek scooted around Pryce and caught sight of the last bit of sandwich in her hand. "Ah, dammit!"

She spotted the sandwich-laden paper plate he'd been about to offer her and almost laughed out loud at the mental image of Jarek's massive armored figure shuffling around in the kitchen with a jar of peanut butter and a tiny little butter knife.

"Maybe you can plug it in one of your holes," she said.

"Ha!" Jarek scooped the sandwich off the plate and glanced at her. "You sure you don't want seconds?"

She started to say no, then reconsidered and held her hand out.

"Gah." Jarek plopped the sandwich down and handed the plate over. "You tease."

She arched an eyebrow.

"What? I was talking to the sandwich."

"Uh-huh." She ripped a large bite out of the sandwich in question. "I hear you're making friends in high places around here?"

"Oh yeah. Everybody loves me."

"I think you're confusing an absence of gunfire for fondness again, sir," came Al's voice from Fela's speakers.

"Ahh, right. Okay, no one tried to shoot me. Yet. Nelken even smiled." He cocked his head. "Almost."

All things considered, Rachel was actually mildly impressed the bullets hadn't flown. Jarek and the Resistance both had plenty of reason to be pissed at one another right now, and Jarek wasn't exactly a diplomat.

"Any news from our scaly friend about Michael?" she asked.

Jarek shook his head, all jokes bleeding out of his expression. "Sorry, Goldilocks. Sounds like they haven't gotten a word out of him yet. Guy runs his mouth while we're fighting then clamps down like a nun in a sex shop when we actually want him to—what?" he asked at her incredulous stare, a stare she saw Pryce was mirroring.

"You're gonna call someone else out for talking too much in a fight?" she asked.

Jarek waved the question away. "Totally different. He was all doom and gloom. I like to think I'm more fun and fresh. Plus, I also talk to people after I'm done trying to remove their entrails, so point for Jarek."

"Uh-huh."

She took another bite.

Pryce stroked his chin sagely.

"Anyways." Jarek's expression sobered again. "It doesn't sound like Stumpy's about to flop and spill the beans easy." He rubbed at the back of his helmeted head in a gesture Rachel was starting to realize was a kind of nervous tick for him.

He was about to say something he didn't want to. And, without fail, "We might have to consider other options."

She swallowed her bite and allowed a moment for the flare of irritation and the underlying rush of fear to sweep through her chest and settle in her stomach. "Other options like me trying to drill into a raknoth's mind, you mean?"

Jarek gave an apologetic shrug. "Let's talk theoretically."

She set the remaining half of her sandwich down, closed her eyes, and rubbed at her forehead. "Theoretically, at full strength and under perfect control, I have no idea if I have a prayer of punching into his head. Less theoretically, if he's too strong for me to take, chances are he turns the tables and breaches my mind instead."

Pryce shuddered.

She didn't blame him. It had only been yesterday that the Red King had carved the protective glyph off Pryce's chest and mind-jacked him to find out where she, Jarek, and Michael had gone. From what he'd told her, it had been brief and "painless," but having someone break in and root around in your head like that would be beyond disturbing. That kind of thing could probably leave psychological scars on par with the worst of traumas.

"And that would be super not good," Jarek said. "I get that much.

But what's the worst that happens? He sees some thoughts and memories before we throw the cloak back on and shut him down?"

"That," Rachel said, "and pretty much anything else he'd want to do. When you mind-jack someone, they basically belong to you. He could make me do a chicken dance, or, you know, unleash everything I have on the base before you even knew something was wrong." She watched Jarek, waiting for that to sink in. "Theoretically, if things went south, I'd be almost powerless to stop myself from blasting this place to embers and carrying him out of here. Unless you think you could stop me."

Jarek nibbled at his lip. "So you're saying it's complicated."

"Sure. We can go with that if 'potentially suicidal' doesn't have the right ring to it."

"Ah."

"Is there some way we can tip the balance?" Pryce said. "I'm assuming these mental engagements require careful focus, yes?"

She nodded, knowing where he was going and not the least bit surprised he'd figured it out. "Yes, laying the hurt on him would probably increase my odds, but—"

"Stumpy doesn't seem to be too put off by pain," Jarek said. "Although he does make noises when you chop his appendages off, so we could call that a maybe. What about hitting him while he's asleep?"

"Assuming he does sleep," Pryce said.

There was a creepy thought. He had a point though.

"Assuming he does," Rachel said, "I still don't think it'd be a good idea to attack a strong telepath like that. Tangling with sleeping minds can be pretty damn trippy."

"So it's complicated," Pryce said. He shook his head. "I would very much like to inspect this raknoth for myself at some point. Especially if he ever decides to talk."

"We need to get you glyphed up again first," Jarek said.

"I can do you," Rachel said and immediately regretted saying when Jarek turned a wolfish grin on her. "Oh, shut up. You know what I— oh, hey guys."

Lea and Alaric had appeared in the doorway, lingering as if they were afraid they might be interrupting something private or important, neither of which described the direction the conversation was heading.

"Hey," Lea said, stepping into the room, her eyes lingering on Michael's resting form. "Sorry to interrupt."

"Pretty ladies need never apologize for such things," Jarek said. "Old Resistance fighters, on the other hand…"

Rachel shot Jarek a dirty look. "Sexist."

Lea's golden-brown eyes twinkled with amusement.

Alaric paid no mind to Jarek's ribbing and sank into one of the chairs on the opposite wall with a tired sigh. "Hell of a show you put on back there," he said.

Rachel wasn't entirely sure who he was talking to until Jarek said, "Ah, didn't realize you were in there. Too many glares to sort through, I guess. Thanks for the backup, by the way. A word or two of praise from the father of the Resistance might've been helpful."

Alaric shrugged. "No one wants to hear this old man ramble. Seems to me like you handled yourself just fine."

"Clearly," Jarek muttered.

"So what's up?" Rachel asked as Lea came to stand at Michael's bedside.

Not that Lea needed a reason to stop by. She'd already been in to see Michael more times than anyone besides Rachel herself.

"Just stopping in to say hi." Lea carefully took Michael's hand and held it in both of hers for a moment. "Can I get you anything?"

Rachel gave her what she hoped was an appreciative smile and shook her head.

Lea's interest in Michael was clear enough, but Rachel was pretty sure they hadn't ventured beyond being anything more than friends. Knowing Michael, the Spongehead was probably entirely clueless about Lea's affections. Either way, Rachel was pretty sure she liked Lea.

She could only hope the girl would still get the chance to tell Michael how she felt if she hadn't already.

"Nelken also wanted us to ask you about cracking the Red King,"

Alaric said. He turned an amused glance at Jarek. "For some reason, he didn't seem to have much faith in your diplomatic skills."

"Ha," Jarek said. "Well Nelken can suck it, because we're already trying to figure out how to extract the juicy vampire secrets from Stumpy's thick skull. And since when did you become Nelken's errand boy? You building up steam to take back your old seat or something?"

Alaric waved away the question as if it were ludicrous. "He just asked. Why don't you tell us how your ingenious plan is coming along?"

"Oh," Jarek said. "Well…"

"We've got jack," Rachel said. "And plenty more on the horizon."

"Unless we decide to use our heads," Jarek said, giving her a pointed look.

Lea looked back and forth between them, her smooth, honey-brown forehead crinkling. "Wait, you can, uh, do that stuff too? To one of *them*?"

"It's an ongoing point of debate," Rachel said, still holding Jarek's stare.

She was thinking about adding that Nelken should probably come and ask her himself if he wanted her to stick her neck out for the Resistance, but Jarek broke their stare and turned to Lea first. "It'd be dangerous, though. Probably too dangerous."

"Which puts us more or less back at square one," Pryce said.

Too dangerous? That didn't sound like the Jarek she knew and tolerated. Was he baiting her? At second glance, she didn't think so. He really seemed to mean it. He'd heard her concerns and paid them heed.

It was kind of weird.

But too dangerous… She looked at Michael laying there, barely breathing, and wondered for the thousandth time what was happening in there beneath those spongy locks of his. Was he utterly unconscious? Dreaming?

Could hear them right now?

She'd been hoping so as she'd sat with him, whispering words of comfort, but now the thought struck something in her chest.

What if Michael was listening from some distant dark place? What if he could hear her agreeing it was too dangerous for her to take a crack at their best chance of finding out what was wrong with him?

She knew what he'd say. He'd tell her not to risk it. He would try to protect her no matter the cost to himself.

Which was exactly why she had to do the same for him.

There was no guarantee the Red King even knew anything that could help Michael, but she sure as hell wasn't going to find the answer sitting here, either. Maybe it was time to stop waiting for good news and go grab it by the stones.

Not that it'd be so easy.

The King's mind was stronger than anything she'd ever encountered. When he'd caught her by surprise back at the Red Fortress, he'd nearly overwhelmed her in the brief mental clash. And that had been a purely defensive challenge. She wasn't exactly a telepathic war veteran. She had no idea if she could really hope to pull off a successful attack on such a powerful mind.

But as she watched Michael's still face, she knew she had to try.

She looked up to find the others watching her.

"On second thought," she said, "let me at him."

CHAPTER THREE

As far as makeshift mind-jacking setups went, Rachel thought they hadn't done half bad.

Tiny didn't adequately capture the feel of the Red King's cell, which was nothing more than a simple cot-and-a-pot deal. She stood crammed into the tight space with Jarek, Lea, and Alaric. Pryce, lacking an intact cloak, had stayed back in medical with Michael. Rachel's own cloaking pendant—or her primary one, at least—was still adorning the Red King's neck from last night when they'd brought him in. The little trinket was the only thing keeping him from lancing out and taking over any unprotected mind nearby.

Rachel had whipped up a rudimentary spare to keep her own mind hidden in case any other raknoth should stray within a mile or two of HQ, but she'd left the good one on the King, in part because of its handy ability to be remotely controlled. Those controls, she'd handed over to Alaric in case they should need to abort the mission. Who better to have at the cutoff switch than a quick draw artist?

Jarek was kneeling beside the King with a long dagger in hand in case things managed to deteriorate further.

Lea, she supposed, was really only there for moral support, but given what she was about to try, she'd take as much as she could get.

The only part of their prep that had gone decidedly sideways was the "rest and recharge" bit. In hindsight, it had been stupid to expect she'd be able to get a wink of sleep with Michael lying in a coma and a no-holds-barred telepathic slug fest with the Red King looming at dawn. But they'd dragged out a cot for her right beside Michael and she'd hesitantly agreed to try anyway.

She'd needed the sleep, they'd been right about that. It was finding it that had given her issues all night.

At least they'd brought coffee this morning.

Now she stood there, half fried and half tweaking on caffeine, preparing to duke it out with the strongest telepath she'd ever met.

The Red King had been eerily silent since they'd entered. According to the guards, he'd taken neither food nor drink when they'd been offered. He hadn't spoken a word. They had him so thoroughly chained up it was a wonder he could breathe at all.

Assuming raknoth needed to breathe, of course. The soft, periodic jingle of shifting chains suggested maybe they did. As for Pryce's point, though, as far as the guards could say, the raknoth hadn't slept a wink.

He'd just laid there, regrowing the arm Jarek had severed with the Big Whacker at a rate that was spooky fast. The eye Jarek had taken with a lucky jab of a broken sword hilt (the blade of which the King had apparently snapped with his fist, no less) was already mostly regrown, the iris oddly muddled but intact. If the King were to do his red eye trick, she had a feeling the fledgling eye would come aglow along with its intact counterpart.

And all that healing in the absence of food or water. It was creepy.

Studying a raknoth would probably be a physiologist's wet dream. Or Pryce's.

Rachel was too anxious to get much amusement out of the thought. The Red King's steady stare didn't help. He cycled his gaze between their faces, every bit the predator looking for his opening.

They'd sorted all the details out before coming in, but he must've understood what they were about to do anyway, because his gaze finally settled on her.

He gave her a cold grin, and a faint hint of that creepy red glow crept into his eyes. "You think to challenge my mind, arcanist?"

"Holy shit!" Jarek said. "You remembered how to talk."

The King said nothing.

"Here's the deal, Stumpy," Jarek continued. "We need to know what the deal is with that nest of yours. Namely what it did to our friend and what you meant about the call for retribution. Are you familiar with the whole easy way, hard way spiel?"

The King ignored Jarek completely and continued staring straight at Rachel, his eyes flaming brighter. "I will break you, Rachel Cross. And then I will use you to break them."

Fear and doubt wrapped their heavy arms around her, and her reply stuck in her throat.

Jarek saved her the trouble. He punched the King in the face. The raknoth shook the hit off and growled. Jarek punched him again, then glanced back at her and winked.

"Looks like it's gonna be the hard way then."

Seeing Jarek seemingly in control of the raknoth made her feel a tad more secure, but the blows also had the unfortunate effect of starting the King's face shifting to that unsettling scaly green the raknoth adopted during battle.

Whatever. She wouldn't be looking him in the face during the action anyway.

She nodded to Alaric, who nodded back, jaw chomping steadily away at those leaves he chronically chewed, then she turned back to Jarek. "You guys know the drill?"

The King gave a growl-hiss of laughter. "You think these men can protect you? Jarek Slater who could not even protect his armor skin and Alaric Weston who could not protect his own wife and son?"

Knuckles cracked like old tree branches from Alaric's corner. He was glaring at the King with murder in his eyes, his perpetual chewing halted for the tight clenching of his jaw.

Lea put a hand on his shoulder. "Alaric." She held her other hand toward the comm he clutched. "Maybe I should—"

Alaric shook his head and fixed his determined gaze on Rachel. "I've got her covered."

Rachel believed him. She closed her eyes, preparing to work, then opened one to peer down at the Red King. "Just in case it wasn't clear"—she tilted her head toward Jarek—"Jarek Slater here is going to gouge your fucking brains out if I so much as give a weird twitch."

"That's right, Sir Stumpy." Jarek twirled the dagger around in his fingers and brought the blade to hover over the King's left eye. "And god help you, man, because"—he lowered his voice to a whisper—"she's got a lot of weird twitches to start with."

The King said nothing, but Rachel thought his leer looked a tad less certain. She cemented that fact in her mind and closed her eyes to focus.

As with most practices in arcanism, there were about as many ways to defend one's mind as there were arcanists in the world. Actually, probably a hell of a lot more, considering there weren't many arcanists running around.

When it came to channeling energy for telekinesis and other large scale physical applications, the laws of conservation were obvious shackles for an arcanist. Creative mental techniques could improve control and maximize efficiency in utilizing channeled energy, but there was no breaking the rules.

When it came to telepathic struggles, on the other hand, creativity and willpower were everything. There still must've been some energy exchange involved, it was just abstract enough—and apparently insignificant enough—that she'd never deemed it necessary to worry about. But maybe she was just a brute.

She knew some arcanists used subtlety and trickery to protect their minds, but that had never suited Rachel. She conjured her defense in much the same way as she constructed barriers to protect from physical attack, forging her will into walls of heavy, impenetrable steel. In this case, instead of channeling the energy to actually conjure a physical construct, she simply held her wall of will in her mental space.

Somewhere, a particularly adept arcanist was probably rolling over in their grave.

She added layer after layer of hard steel to her mental fortress, leaving a tiny way open like a kind of mental arrow-slit through which she could launch her own attack. Finally, when the mental construct was ready, she nodded. As immersed in her mental space as she was, the physical movement felt odd, and her voice sounded distant.

"Now, Alaric."

She didn't need him to tell her when he'd deactivated the King's cloak—no more than she would've needed someone to tell her she was going to get wet when she was already standing under a waterfall.

The King's mind crashed into her ramparts like a force of nature. She fought down panic and held her ground as the alien presence backed away then slammed into her again.

On the third surge, she formed her will into a spear and hurled it forth at the oncoming titan. It hit with all the potency of a wood tip on steel armor. She drew back to her defenses to regroup. In the distance, something cracked—was it her knuckles?—as she grit down and thrust her mental lance forward against the next attack.

The King's presence plowed through her attack and slammed into her defenses once more.

This wasn't working. She needed to do something. But what?

She might be able to stand her ground against the King's battery for a bit longer, but the only minds she'd ever invaded had been non-telepaths, which offered as much resistance as unlocked doors. The Red King was a ferocious predator. Even if she had the raw chops to go toe-to-toe with him, she sure as hell didn't have the experience. She might as well be a big lovable house dog trying to cross fangs with a wild wolf.

She might as well give up.

No. Not when Michael was lying comatose just down the hall. Not after all the pain they'd gone through in the past week—hell, in the past fifteen years. The raknoth had made a smoldering wreck of their planet. They'd hurt her and the people she cared about in more ways than she could count, and she had it in her to make the scaly green bastards pay for it.

If this son of a bitch had answers that could help Michael, she was going to take them.

Maybe she was a house dog trying to take on a wolf, but right now, that wolf was fucking with her family, and she'd be damned if she was going to run away with her tail between her legs.

She dropped her wall and surged forward with everything she had, vaguely aware that someone—was that her?—was crying out wordlessly in the distance as she did so.

The King met her head on in the telepathic analogue of a high-speed car crash. The constructs of their wills smashed together, deforming and twisting in upon one another. From there, the struggle morphed into something more akin to a wrestling match—intermingled tendrils of their wills struggling back and forth for control, clawing and scraping to find any weakness or purchase.

Rachel struggled for what might been five seconds or five minutes. There was no burning of tired muscles or aching of beaten body parts, only an intrepid, creeping decline in the speed and efficacy of each one of her mental maneuvers as their conflict raced from one bulging weak point to another. Attack and counterattack. Back and forth again and again.

At some point, there were voices in the faraway space of the cell, but she was too focused and too tired to hear them. She kept fighting and tried to gauge whether the Red King was tiring as she was. Given the fact that they were still going, she imagined he must be, but soon enough, she was too tired to even worry about that.

Minutes slogged by. The aches and pains and burning had definitely set in now. Or maybe that was all in her head. She couldn't tell anymore.

A part of her—and not a small part—screamed at her to call for Alaric to make it stop. She was contemplating listening to that part when the expansive pressure of the Red King's mind vanished. Gone, just like that.

She curled her mind into a defensive ball, reaching for her walls again, suspecting some devious trickery.

There was a voice again from outside and something… shaking her?

Slowly, cautiously, she eased partially out of her mental space and back toward her physical senses. When the King didn't come springing out of the darkness, she flung herself back into the confines of her body and shouted, "Cloak, Alaric! Now!"

Or tried to, at least. What came out sounded a lot more like a string of incoherent mumbles, but it was hard to tell whether that was due to her failure to get the words out or simply because of the blurring disorientation that engulfed her.

Darkness spotted her vision—or maybe it was vision that spotted her darkness—and her mouth felt like she'd just chewed an entire bag of cotton balls. For a second, she could barely move.

"Rachel!"

Jarek's voice. And there was something else.

The world resolved back into sense rather suddenly. She recognized the growl-hiss of the King's laughter. Lea's face hovered above her, upside down.

Upside down? Ah. Because her head was resting in Lea's lap—that was it.

"What—"

"It's okay," Lea said, squeezing her arm. "We pulled the plug. Alaric reactivated the cloak."

More laughter from the Red King, and then a thump and a growl—presumably Jarek punching him again.

Jarek appeared beside her. "Let's get her out of here."

"Hey," she mumbled, "I'm right here, you—hey!"

Jarek scooped her up as if she had all the heft of a cardboard box. She planted a palm on Fela's chest plate. "Put me down."

"You're tired," he said.

"You're a chauvinist."

He paused and lowered her gently to her feet. "You know I don't do so well with the big words."

She was too busy trying to keep from falling over to come up with any witty retort.

Lea moved to get the door. Rachel scowled down at the King as Jarek scooted her toward it. The raknoth stared back silently, eyes smoldering crimson.

"Arcanist," the King said just before she reached the doorway.

She traded a surprised look with Jarek and turned.

"The battle was well fought." The King didn't bother trying to look around at them from the cot as he spoke. "But your efforts are in vain. The rakul will come. None of us can stop it now."

"Rakul?" She glanced around at the others. "What's the rakul?"

"They are the harvesters," the King said. "The harbingers of our retribution."

Rachel glanced at Jarek to see if he was as confused as her. He rolled his hand in a *Keep him moving* gesture.

"And these harvesters are coming here? The nest called them? What about my brother? What did the nest do to him?"

That cold grin returned to the King's lips. "You need not worry about your brother. Or anything else. We will all be dead soon enough."

"Because of the rakul?" Rachel asked. "What are they? How much time do we have?"

The King said nothing to that or to the next dozen questions they all lobbed at him. Apparently he'd said all he intended to say. Jarek looked like he was thinking about trying to punch a few more answers out of the raknoth, but then he looked her over and changed his mind. "Let's get you back to medical."

She must have looked as bad as she felt, which was bad enough that she didn't argue.

Lea and Jarek hovered close to her as if worried she might collapse on the way. They explained how she'd fallen to her knees and cried out multiple times during the mental battle. In total, the whole thing had lasted only a few minutes, as opposed to what had felt like half an hour or more from her perspective.

The toll of her efforts must've still been noticeable by the time they arrived back at medical, judging by the once over Pryce gave her from Michael's bedside.

"Looks like we have a new patient to admit," he said.

"More like a fierce warrior princess," Jarek said. He ignored her half-hearted effort to push him away and saw her safely into her chair by Michael's bed. "She just bumped brains with Stumpy hard enough to get his creepy raknoth approval, I think."

Pryce gave her an impressed nod.

She leaned forward to rest her elbows heavily on her knees. "Moving on to more pertinent matters, anyone have a guess as to what the hell a rakul is?"

"They're the harvesters," Jarek said. "It's like you weren't even paying attention."

She glared at him.

"Rakul?" Pryce asked.

"Our champion earned us that cryptic tidbit from old red-eyes," Jarek said.

"He also said they were bringing our retribution," Alaric said.

Pryce stroked at his chin. "Cryptic with a side of vague, hmm?"

"Least satisfying meal ever," Jarek said. "Although he did also say we'd all be dead soon."

Pryce's fingers paused mid-stroke. "Oh."

Silence stretched between them.

"Is anyone else picturing a giant tentacled blob flying out of the darkness to swallow our entire planet whole?" Jarek finally asked.

Rachel frowned at him. "Well *now…*"

"I was veering the other way in terms of scale," Pryce said, "like a swarm of microorganisms sweeping over the planet and consuming all the organic matter it encounters. Or something. Just spit balling here."

"Lovely imagery, both of you," Alaric said, "but I think we oughta get a tad more information before you go thinking too hard. Meanwhile, we just keep an eye out for anything strange."

"Not a bad plan," Pryce said. He turned his thoughtful gaze on her.

"What are the chances our fierce warrior princess could extract more information?"

She shook her still fuzzy head. "I wouldn't count on it. I came at him with everything I had, all in, and it barely seemed to bother him." She scowled. "I just don't have the experience with this stuff. Maybe if I practiced, but..."

"I'd like to think I have a strong mind," Pryce said, "and the King punched through it like wet paper. You did exceptionally well. I wouldn't beat yourself up about it."

It wasn't the same. Pryce was gifted in his own way, but he wasn't a telepath. He'd never really had a chance once the King had ruined his glyph. She wanted to point this out, but if anyone else in the room already understood that, it was probably Pryce, and he was choosing to pay her the compliment anyway. So she shrugged and said nothing.

The low buzz of a comm broke the silence. Lea glanced at her wrist. "My mom," she said. "Be right back."

Lea stepped outside to take the call. The commanders had no doubt been eagerly awaiting news since they'd granted their little mind-jacking team access to the Red King this morning.

Hopefully they weren't expecting it to be the good kind. She sure as hell hadn't found any for Michael. That fact hung heavier on her head than any fatigue could.

She'd just have to try again. She probably wasn't going to take the King in a head-on fight anytime soon, but she could try talking to him again, and they could always try other ways. There was even the chance the universe could decide to be kind for once and Michael might just wake up on his own. She wouldn't hold her breath on that one. She'd just keep trying until she found some answers.

"Why did he say 'we'?" Jarek asked the silent room. "We will all be dead soon, he said. Not you. We. Like he was boned too."

"Maybe they pissed off these harvester things," Rachel said.

"That would fit with the warning the Reds broadcasted after you three escaped the Fortress," Pryce said. "It's a sound hypothesis given what little data we have."

"Great," Jarek said. "So we should be looking for the raknoth mob to come flying in for a planetary drive-by?"

No one jumped to offer an answer, and before they had much of a chance, Lea shuffled back into the room looking a few shades too pale.

"What is it?" Rachel asked.

"There's been a report." Lea directed her distracted gaze toward Alaric. "Strange activity. Down near Philadelphia."

"Strange how?" Pryce asked.

"There were multiple sightings of a weird ship around the area yesterday."

"And?" Jarek asked.

Lea snapped back from whatever funk she was in and looked around at them as if wondering why their jaws weren't touching the floor.

"They're saying it looked like something from another planet."

CHAPTER FOUR

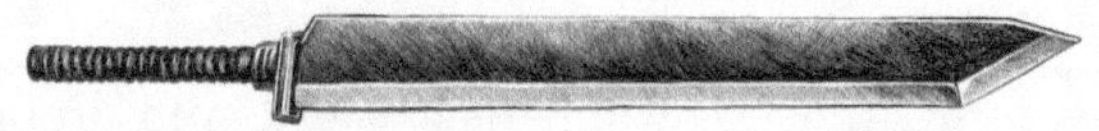

After fifteen years spent mostly alone and often in an exosuit, Jarek tended to see things differently than most. Take the news of a strange, possibly out-of-this world ship being spotted poking around Philadelphia, for instance. Where everyone else seemed to think it grave, ominous news, Jarek was mostly just glad to have a direction to go looking.

Sure, there was also the itty-bitty concern that this mystery ship could be harboring something that had a freaking raknoth ready to lay down and accept death. But it couldn't be much worse than sitting around HQ for another day, right?

"So…" He looked around at the others. "Everyone to the ship?"

Lea's forehead wrinkled in confusion. "You want to go?"

"What, you think I've been hanging around here for the company? I just wanna make sure my ass isn't gonna get eaten if I turn it around and saunter back to my little corner."

In truth, he couldn't quite say why he was so set on getting to the bottom of this thing. Self-preservation was one angle, that was true. But there was more to it. The threat of some dreadful impending doom had him captivated, like a horrific slow-motion car crash he just couldn't look away from. And on top of that, maybe he didn't want to see the people in this room get hurt.

Or maybe he'd just watched the old Star Wars movies one too many times and had delusions of grandeur floating around in his subconscious.

Could Jarek Slater be the one to save the world and restore balance to the Force?

Probably not. But if the shit was about to hit, he'd sure as hell rather face it beside Pryce and Rachel and the others than fly off and see what Catastrophe 2.0 looked like from a distance.

"This sounds like a wild goose chase to me," Alaric said.

"The Red King tells us these rakul guys are bringing the retribution and then a strange ship is spotted the next day," Lea said. "You don't think that sounds a little funny?"

"Sounds plenty funny," Alaric said. "But not like proof."

"Gee, sounds like someone should go have a look," Jarek said.

"Since when are you so gung-ho to get involved?" Rachel asked.

"You're telling me you're not chomping at the bit to go see the alien space ship… from space?"

"Maybe if we had even half a reason to believe this isn't just some made up bullshit." Rachel's gaze shifted back toward Michael. "But I can't really leave right now anyways."

That earned a sympathetic stretch of silence.

"I don't know about the goose chase," Alaric said, "but if you're set on going, I might trouble you for that ride back to Deadwood."

After a moment's irritation, Jarek inclined his head. "Guess a deal's a deal. What's a tiny detour across the country?"

Lea looked crestfallen. "You're not staying?" she asked Alaric.

Jarek was wondering the same thing, especially in light of the private conversation he'd had with the old Resistance legend on the way to HQ a couple days past—the one where Alaric had basically condemned himself for having run off to escape his problems in the first place.

Alaric didn't meet Lea's eyes, or anyone else's for the matter. "My people deserve an explanation."

It wasn't exactly an answer to Lea's question, but it also didn't have the air of finality. Jarek wasn't about to prod him for more. Alaric was caught in a tough choice between the town that looked to him for order and protection and a wayward son who'd probably rather kill him than talk at this point. More than that, though, he was a grown-ass man. And far be it from Jarek to question a grown man's prerogative to run screaming from his problems.

"The commanders are getting a team together to go investigate these reports," Lea said. "I'm sure you could talk to them about getting a ride back with—"

"Jarek's ship'll work just fine," Alaric said.

"Oh, yeah," Jarek said. "Make yourself at home. Definitely do that."

Alaric touched his fingers to the brim of an imaginary hat.

"Joke's on you, cowboy," Jarek said. "You have to come hunting aliens with me first. Do we know exactly who and where this lead came from, by the way?" he asked Lea.

Lea looked uncertainly between him and Alaric. "I could find out. If you let me come with you."

"Seriously?"

Lea spared a glance toward Michael before answering. "I don't want to be sitting around HQ if there's a chance I can help figure out what's going on."

"Sure, sure," Jarek said. "And the reason you can't go with your fellow Resistance team is…"

"She's not Alpha team," Alaric said.

Lea nodded. "And Mama Daniels is pretty careful about not bending rules for her daughter."

Jarek looked back and forth between them. "You guys have an Alpha team? What, do they get to carry the guns that are actually loaded?"

"We're not as toothless as you think," Lea said.

Jarek wasn't sure about that, but the look Lea was giving him sure as hell wasn't toothless, so he decided not to argue. He debated asking Rachel if she was sure she wouldn't reconsider stepping out for a day, but one look at her convinced him not to bark up that tree either. She wasn't about to leave Michael's side for anything less than a sure thing, and there was a fair chance Alaric was right about this being a wild goose chase.

"Well," Jarek said, "I guess if we're short one warrior princess…"

Rachel looked away from Michael to narrow her eyes at him.

"Okay!" Lea fairly bounced over to old hardwired intercom box on the wall. "I'll check with the guys over at comms, see if we have a name and location attached to the tip. Good idea, by the way."

"Don't encourage him," Pryce said.

"Hear, hear," Al added from Fela's speakers.

"C'mon, guys," Jarek said as Lea flipped a pair of intercom switches. "Maybe there's more to life than cracking skulls." He tapped the side of his helmet. "Maybe I should be cracking problems with what's in here."

"This is how the world ends," Al said.

Pryce's lip twitched. "Not with a bang, but with a thoughtful Jarek?"

"Yeah," Jarek said, "I think the raknoth kinda beat me to the punch on the whole end of the—"

"Communications here," a nasally male voice crackled out of the intercom box.

"Leo, it's Lea, I—"

"Oh hey, name twin!" Leo said. "What can I do ya for?"

Name twin?

Jarek shot Rachel a look, and despite everything, she had to visibly stifle a fit of laughter.

Lea gave Leo a laugh that sounded only a little forced. "I just needed to know who our source was on that ship sighting in Philadelphia."

"Phil-o-del-phia," Leo said in a sing-song voice. "City of brotherly love."

Guy clearly hadn't been to Philadelphia anytime in the past fifteen years.

Leo must've been working as he sang. "Looks like the name on the tip was—huh. That's interesting."

They all stared at the intercom, waiting. Finally, Lea said, "What's interesting, Leo?"

"Oh—uh, it's just that... Yeah, the name on the tip was John Carver."

Leo might as well have reached through the intercom and pushed Rachel off her chair for how violently she jolted. Lea looked nearly as surprised.

Jarek had just caught up to the reason for the ghostly pallor of Rachel's face when Leo's crackling voice continued, "But, uh, isn't that Michael's dad?"

CHAPTER FIVE

"This is a mistake," Rachel said. She could have elaborated on the statement by any one of a dozen routes. It was a mistake she'd left Michael to fly off to Philadelphia for the scant chance of finding out something about what had happened to him. If recent past was any indication, it was probably a mistake she'd done so alongside Jarek the trouble magnet.

More than anything, it was a mistake she hadn't told John about Michael as soon as she'd had the chance. The last she and Michael had spoken with John two days ago, they'd simply filled him in that Michael was indeed fine and that Rachel was helping him take care of some unfinished business. Worrying him with the details that they were trying to recover an alien artifact of unknown power and significance while being pursued by the Red King's army had seemed unnecessary, so they'd left it at that.

But once the nest had gone off and blown Michael into a coma…

She should have called the instant they'd made it back to HQ. She should have told him what they were up to from the start. She should have done a lot of things. But her fingers had frozen over the comm, and she'd simply gone on, waiting, hoping—in part for her and in part to spare John from the inevitable anvil to the heart. As bad as she felt for leaving Michael, she couldn't let someone else break the news to John.

It had to be her. In person.

Thankfully, Pryce had promised to stay with Michael and call her the instant anything changed. Granted, she'd only met Pryce a few days ago, but he seemed like a damn good guy, and that wasn't something she got to say often.

"It's gonna be all right," Jarek said from the pilot's seat beside her, drawing her attention back to the cockpit. "We'll be there soon, and we can get back just as fast if we need to."

That was true enough. If they'd been free to the open skies, the flight from HQ in the northwest corner of Jersey City down to Philadelphia would've taken less than twenty minutes. Of course, given that the Reds and probably the Overlord's forces as well would be on high alert trying to sniff out where their Red King had gone, they'd had to be sneaky skirting out of the city, and it had taken them closer to an hour to get here, but... "That's not the issue."

Jarek glanced toward the back cabin, where Alaric and Lea were hanging out for the flight, then he fixed her with a somber look. "I know. But the rest will be all right too."

His eyes lingered on hers, and his expression made her think he was seeing just a little too deeply. She looked away from him and out the windshield at bright clear sky.

"Why do you sound so sure about that?"

He shrugged. "Things always are on the other side of all the shit. It's just a question of how long you slog."

"Until it's not."

By way of answer, he laid an armored hand on her leg and gave it a soft pat.

She stared at the hand, not quite sure what to make of the fact that it was both Jarek's and resting ever-so-gently on her thigh. After several seconds' debate, she went with, "I feel like I'm being fondled by a robot."

"Shhh. You're gonna hurt Al's feelings."

Al affected a sniff. "Oh never mind that, sir. I'm just a robot, after all."

She almost felt guilty for a second, right up until Jarek's face split into a grin.

"Gah." She shook his hand off and crossed her arms. "You guys are the worst."

"We'll take it." He tapped at the console to pull up the map. "And on that note, if you could tell me where to land when we get there..."

She started to point out Unity, and then the ship cleared a herd of clouds and the crumbling ruins of Philadelphia stretched out miles below them. At that height, the city was little more than a mural of asphalt grays and barren, dusty browns, with no life—or brotherly love—in sight.

Rachel pinned their destination on the map, and once they'd passed over the heart of the city, they began to descend, headed west. The city ruins below gave way to slightly-less-demolished university campuses, which in turn were replaced by a long stretch of alternating commercial and residential areas. The density of the greenery grew the further they went, flying low enough now to clearly distinguish individual houses and cars.

Rachel wasn't used to seeing any of it from an aerial view, but it looked familiar enough all the same. There was John's old neighborhood, and there was the Home Depot they'd just about cleared out when he'd rallied the community with his ambitious vision and started work on transforming the abandoned shell of the Swarthmore College campus into what had eventually become Unity.

Normally, these sights would have conjured up some returning sense of home. Today, though, it was only dread she felt.

From what little she'd seen in her travels, Unity and the surrounding community were in far better shape than pretty much anywhere—Alaric's hometown of Deadwood being one notable exception. They seemed to have been luckier than most when it came to escaping the notice of roaming marauder outfits. Of course, it was just a tiny bit possible that could have had something to do with word spreading of Unity's dedicated defense force and the strange blond girl who could stop bullets and whip fireballs out of thin air.

Either way, none of it would have come together without John whipping them all into shape.

She caught sight of Unity's town hall through the trees, and a pang of anxious energy shot through her.

Home.

The ship slowed—presumably by Al's doing—as they approached the long chain-link fence that stretched all the way around Unity along the tree line.

Jarek let out an impressed whistle, staring off to the left, where several neatly organized fields stretched out, sporting a variety of crops. Dozens of people moved about them, picking, weeding, and otherwise tending.

Rachel directed Al to follow the line of grand historical buildings that separated the fields into two major divisions, toward the more densely-packed collection of twenty or so buildings at the heart of what had once been Swarthmore College.

She was uncomfortably aware that nearly every pair of eyes across campus was following them.

"I take it you guys don't normally see many ships around here?" Jarek asked.

"Not so much."

She suddenly felt idiotic for not having given them a heads-up. Myers would be racing out to see what the fuss was right now. Hoping to alleviate some of his tension, she instructed Al to set the ship down in a small, open patch of grass on the front lawn, well away from town hall.

"Home, sweet home," Jarek said.

"Don't take this the wrong way"—she looked over and met his eyes —"but could you just not talk for a little while?"

Jarek looked amused more than anything as he made a zip-the-lips gesture, stood, and waved her toward the back cabin, where it turned out Lea and Alaric were watching an old-as-dirt movie starring... was it Clint Eastwood? She couldn't remember.

"I'm just not getting it," Lea said to Alaric.

Jarek looked from Alaric to the thin screen and back again. "Really?"

Alaric powered off the screen, stood to check the mismatched pistols in his gun belt, pulled on his old battered long coat, and finally tucked an oily strand of long gray hair behind an ear before answering. "I know what I'm about, son."

Jarek pulled on his own gun belt, grabbed the gargantuan sword he too fondly referred to as his Big Whacker, and strapped the blade to the connector on Fela's back. "Guess that makes two of us."

Lea rolled her eyes but likewise checked her own sidearm before sliding it back into its concealed holster and pulling the fabric of her light jacket over it.

"Seriously, guys?" Rachel asked.

Jarek aimed a pointed look at the glyph-etched staff in her hand.

"Company outside, sir," Al said.

"Jesus," Rachel muttered. "Everyone keep their pants on. It's probably just Myers."

She slapped the hatch release and tried to calm her racing nerves as the boarding ramp descended.

It was indeed Myers, along with two of his finest and one of their greenhorns. Myers had his hand on the butt of his holstered pistol, his dark eyes wary and alert. The others already had their shotguns and rifles trained loosely on the ship. The weapons all dropped as soon as they caught sight of Rachel, even if much of the tension remained.

Jarek, unfortunately, saw fit to break the silence first. "Campus security?" He pointed emphatically at Rachel before putting his hands up. "She made me do it! Is that a freaking John Deere?" he added in a mutter as he caught sight of the utility vehicle Myers' crew had ridden in on.

For a second, Rachel considered telekinetically clamping his lips shut.

"Rachel?" Myers said, his hand dropping from the pistol grip. "Oh thank God. We weren't expecting… Who the hell is this guy?"

"Myers," Rachel said. "Guys. Good to see you all. This is, uh…" She glanced at Jarek and the others and decided introductions could wait. "Can we see John before we get into it?"

A frown fell over Myers' square face as he scanned the rest of her group. "Uh, yeah. Yeah, John's been worried sick about you two. He'll want to see you right away. Michael's still up with his people?"

She tried to keep her composure, but she must have failed.

"Oh God," Myers said.

"No, no." She shook her head. "He's not—He's alive. He's just not in good shape right now. I need to talk to John."

"Yeah. Of course." Myers glanced over his shoulder at his men and then back to Rachel's group, his eyes lingering on Jarek with his exosuit and his giant blade. "Your friends too?"

Rachel nodded, and Myers sent his backup off on foot to make room for them in the Gator.

"Thanks, boys," she called after them.

Alaric accepted the passenger seat with a surly look and an under-the-breath mutter. Rachel hopped into the Gator's bed alongside Lea. Jarek cautiously eased his armored bulk in behind them to both the groaning protest of the Gator and the clear displeasure of Myers.

"Can't you just run along beside us?" Rachel asked.

"And keep up with this bad boy?" He reached to pat the outer siding of the Gator's bed. "I don't think s—Oops."

Myers whirled in the driver's seat at the *thunk* of Jarek's pat. Jarek put on his best casual face and looked up at the sky as if trying to pretend the metal hadn't just dented. Myers scowled and stepped on the gas harder than he needed to.

Rachel knew the community tended to watch curiously when the Gator passed to see what was going on. Today, though, it was more than that. Everything and everyone around them practically froze. They stared, almost certainly wondering who the hell these odd newcomers were and why she'd brought them here.

Some of the looks were distrustful. Plenty more, though, were friendly. Acquaintances and familiar faces showed her smiles and waves, and a few even cheered her return. She did her best to return their smiles despite the deepening apprehension in her gut.

"I had no idea 'warrior princess' was such an apt description," Jarek mumbled beside her.

He met her dirty look with a grin and a shrug.

It was only a short ride to the regal stone hall at the head of the lawn.

"Unity, huh?" Jarek asked as they climbed out of the Gator bed.

She looked up at the great banner hanging from the town hall with the single, giant word painted in black.

"It's what John decided to call this place when it started becoming a proper community. Michael's flair for peace and good will didn't come from nowhere."

They made their way into the town hall under the watch of a small crowd outside. Inside, the building was rich with what most people called historic charm. To her, it had always just kind of looked old, but, like the rest of the campus, it was in good shape for its age.

Myers led them up the glossy marble steps and down the thickly carpeted hallway to John's office.

"So this is what it looks like when a place hasn't been pillaged and vandalized every other day for fifteen years, huh?" Jarek asked.

Myers favored him with a scowl.

"It's not for lack of trying," Rachel said. "Myers and his boys have chased off more marauders than we have citizens."

Myers stopped at John's door and grinned back at her. "I seem to recall having had a hand here and there."

She was too anxious to come up with any reply as Myers rapped on the heavy wooden door. John's muffled, "Come in," didn't do much to settle her nerves either.

They funneled into her foster father's office. With the exception of the gun safe in the corner, the room looked like a pretty typical college professor's office, which was appropriate given John's past life as a professor of biology.

Lines from years of accumulated worry and stress on John's dark umber face lit up with relief as his dark eyes sighted her. He rose to his feet and strode out from behind his desk. Like Michael, John was a large man with a powerful build, and he wasn't afraid to use that build when it came to death-by-bear-hugs.

Getting hugged by John was like being tucked under a lead blanket. It might've been borderline frightening if not for all the warmth and care that so clearly bled through.

These hugs had been a critical part of her path back to semi-sanity after John had found her, and it brought some comfort now.

"Oh bless me," John murmured. He squeezed harder and leaned back to take a closer look at her.

"I know, I know." She patted his back and disengaged from the hug. "You've been worried sick."

"It's a worrying world out there, Goldfish. There's"—his gaze drifted around the room to take in the others—"all manner of crazies."

"Completely agree," Jarek said. "Nuckin futz. Can't trust any of those bozos."

She rolled her eyes. "John, Myers, this is Jarek Slater."

"I assumed as much." John stepped forward to offer his hand. "Not quite enough world-class exos walking around to mistake the Soldier of Charity."

"Aw shucks," Jarek said, shaking John's hand.

"And you must be Lea," John said, moving down the line. He chuckled at her surprised look. "Oh, Michael told me something about a pretty young lady, couldn't get anything more than a first name out of him, though."

"Oh," Lea said, a shade of red creeping into her cheeks as she shook his hand. "Well it's, uh, nice to meet you, sir."

John smiled and turned to Alaric. "And you are?"

"Alaric Weston," Alaric said, gripping John's hand. "Pleasure to meet you, John. You raised a fine son."

Dammit, why'd he have to say that?

John's eyebrows had climbed up his forehead. "Well I'll be damned. Alaric Weston. Pleased to meet *you*, sir. Never thought to have the father of the Resistance visit Unity." He turned back to Rachel. "And speaking of that fine son, where is the Spongehead?"

Shit.

Adrenaline trilled through her chest, speeding her heart and casting a blurry filter over everything but John's questioning stare. The words she'd run over a hundred different times on the flight were suddenly nowhere to be found. There was only John's expectant look, waiting for her to tell him that everything was all right. And she couldn't.

John's face went ashen. "Oh God."

"He's alive," Lea said quickly.

John looked from Lea to Rachel. "What happened?"

"He's..." She swallowed and forced herself to meet his eyes. "Michael was standing next to some kind of raknoth device when it went off. He's in a coma."

"Oh God." John rocked back on his heels and stumbled back a step to lean heavily against his desk. "When?"

Rachel dropped her gaze to the floor, hot tears brimming in her eyes. "Two days ago. I should have called—I'm sorry—I just... kept waiting. Hoping. But when we realized you were the one who sent that tip up... I wanted to tell you in person. I'm sorry, John."

He was silent for a long time, his eyes half-lidded.

Finally, he moved forward to pull her into another hug. "It's okay, Goldfish. I just..."

"He's going to pull through," Lea said. Then, looking embarrassed, she added, "I really believe that."

The smile John tried to force only broke Rachel's heart that much more.

"Thank you, Lea," he said. "I know my boy's a fighter." He leaned back on his desk and looked around at them. "But you folks didn't come here to tell me about Michael, did you? You want to know about the ship."

"John..." Rachel said.

It was no mystery where Michael had learned his martyrdom from. But willing martyr or no, John didn't need anything else on his plate right now. He needed time to process and—

"We do," Jarek said. He ignored her sidelong scowl and traded a look with Alaric that made her wonder if they'd discovered their own form of telepathy.

"We're trying to figure out if this ship is connected in any way to the device that went off a couple nights ago," Alaric said.

John sat a little straighter. "The same device that…?"

Jarek and Alaric both nodded.

John considered that with a grave, distant expression. "Not sure how much help I can be there. All I have is a few accountings of a strange ship poking around Philly."

As sure as she was that John needed time to process the news about Michael, his reactions suggested he might prefer a distraction right now, especially one that made him feel helpful and in control. Maybe Jarek and Alaric had already arrived at that conclusion.

"If it is connected," Rachel said. "I'm hoping this ship might help us find out more about what happened to Michael. Maybe even how we can help him."

John gave a jerky nod. "Of course. I'll tell you everything I can."

"What was so strange about this ship?" Jarek asked.

"Well, one guy who claimed to get a good look at it said it had an odd purple hue to it. He couldn't seem to find the words to explain what he meant aside from saying it definitely looked like something from out of this world. He described it as being long, wingless, and mostly smooth, with big, uh, bulbous features."

"Was that not how he phrased it?" Rachel asked, sensing some hesitance.

John shook his head, and his somber expression cracked long enough to blow out a short chuckle. "No. I believe he said it reminded him of a giant ribbed dildo an ex of his used to have."

Well there was something you didn't expect to hear your foster father to say about a potentially alien ship.

"Well," Jarek said, "I think the possibilities just grew infinitely more terrifying."

"Was there, uh, anything else?" Lea asked. "Mentions of who the ship might've belonged to? Or a list of locations sighted?"

John shook his head. "We don't have much more on the details. But we do have an idea on its rough trajectory. The first reported sighting was in northwest Philly. Then again downtown."

"So how'd you hear about it over this way?" Rachel asked.

"That's the thing," John exchanged a concerned look with Myers. "We haven't noticed anything suspicious, but according to the last account, that ship was headed straight this way."

CHAPTER SIX

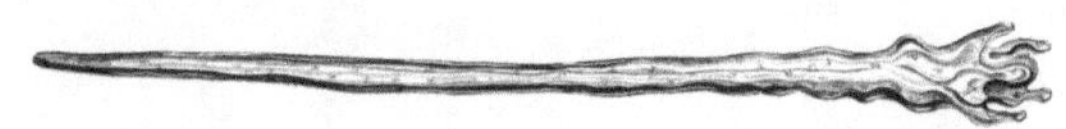

Rachel wasn't exactly expecting to see an alien ship looming just outside of John's window, but it didn't keep her head from whipping that way to check after the bomb he'd just dropped. "What?"

"Yeah, come again?" Jarek added.

Myers crossed his arms. "We've kept our eyes peeled all morning."

Rachel consciously refrained from rolling her eyes. Myers was a good guy, but he was quick to get territorial.

"It's been business as usual around campus," he continued. "Aside from you guys flying in unannounced, that is. No new entries other than that."

"Yeah," Jarek said. "You're probably right. There's no way anyone could have snuck over the big scary chain-link fence."

Myers positively bristled. "Look, pal, I—"

"Guys," Rachel said. "Not helping."

Jarek was absolutely right, but Myers already disliked him enough. So instead of saying anything else, Rachel switched off her substitute cloaking pendant and reached out to their surroundings, looking for anything amiss. Anything like, say, a raknoth-class telepath lurking nearby. Nothing immediately jumped out, but that hardly meant all of Unity was clear.

"Is there any reason to think this mystery ship would want to stop around here?" Lea asked. "We are dealing with hearsay, right? And even if we weren't, the thing always could have changed course or flown right past Unity."

John nodded. "I expect that's exactly what happened. Don't know what interest they'd have in a place like this."

"Might be hard to say without knowin' who 'they' is," Alaric said.

"Right on, cowboy," Jarek said. "And if this phallic monstrosity did just pass on by, that leaves us with a big pile of nothing in the way of leads."

"I wish I had something more useful to offer," John said. "And heck, maybe there's not even anything interesting about the ship, but when three separate contacts I only hear from once every month or two decide to call with the same story... Well, it seemed like it was worth passing on."

As much more obvious as his initial reaction had been to the news about Michael, it seemed like the weight was only now starting to fully settle on him. It might not have been obvious to everyone, but Rachel could see it in the weary distance of his eyes and the defeated set of his shoulders.

They'd talked enough for now. John needed time to process everything she'd just dropped on him. And regardless of what Myers might think, she needed to sweep Unity for anything otherworldly.

She was just about to propose they give John some time and go take a little tour of the community when Lea spoke up. "We truly appreciate the information, John. But we don't want to be in your hair too long." She looked pointedly at the rest of the group.

John, always the martyr, looked like he'd protest.

"I'll take them out to the market if you want a few minutes," Rachel said. "Show them the sights. Get some food." She hesitated. "Unless you'd rather me stay here."

"I could show them around," Myers said, finally uncrossing his arms.

John waved Myers back. "That's not necessary." He squeezed Rachel's shoulder. "You go show them around and we can meet back up for an early dinner?" He looked at the others. "Assuming you can all stay that long."

"I've never been known to turn down dinner," Jarek said.

"That sounds perfect," Lea said with a warm smile.

"Good then." John gave her one last lead blanket hug and bid farewell to the others.

Myers followed them back downstairs and out to the front lawn.

"You're good?" he asked, shooting one last frown in Jarek's direction.

"We're good," she said with what little smile she could manage. "Thanks, Myers."

He gave her an informal salute. "We'll see you in a bit then."

"So," Jarek said as Myers drove off in the Gator, "what's the plan?"

"I figured we could start at the market and find ourselves something tasty for lunch," she said.

"While you give the place the old Jedi mind sweep?"

She smiled and gave her best innocent shrug. "Maybe while I give the place the old Jedi mind sweep."

Jarek grinned. "That's my Goldilocks. Let's go then."

That could have been that, but then Jarek offered his arm to her as if he were some manner of fine gentleman.

She considered the arm, unsure how to react. Taking it was technically a possibility, but she couldn't seem to do anything aside from stare at it as if it were something from another galaxy. She met Jarek's gaze, aware of Lea stifling a fit of giggles behind them.

Jarek retracted the arm. "Yeesh. You look like you just saw a giant flying dildo or something."

She snorted. "At least it wasn't ribbed."

Jarek grinned. "Always the optimist."

Alaric coughed behind them, then cleared his throat.

"He raises a fair point," Jarek said. "Let's have the tour, princess."

She sighed and led them around Parrish Hall and past the slightly-less-majestic Kohlberg Hall to the crowded lines of tents and tables in the grassy quad beyond. The lingering tightness in Rachel's chest began to ease at the familiar sights, sounds, and smells of the market. Then people started to notice them, and a new tightness settled in.

The market served as both a food distribution system for those citizens of Unity like Myers who didn't already work in food production as well as a trading post for those within the community and those who visited from nearby. It had never been her favorite place on account of the crowd, and the prospect of sweeping her senses through that many minds sounded about as appealing as dancing naked through the busy quad.

But she needed to be sure, so she extended her senses and started for the far corner of the market, where her favorite vendor, sweet old Annie, would be posted with whatever stew or casseroles she'd concocted to see to it that the day's hungry traders had somewhere to barter their bellies full.

Most of the crowd continued bustling about its business as she moved into it with Jarek at her side, but a fair amount of people parted to let them pass, at least half of them just looking for a better opportunity to stare.

The four of them did make a strange sight, she supposed. Most of these people were probably used enough to seeing her with her extensively glyphed staff, but now here she was walking around with an old cowboy-looking Resistance fighter, a walking tank with a giant sword strapped to his back, and... well, Lea wasn't really odd in any way, but she drew plenty of stares—especially male ones—all the same.

Jarek and Lea looked almost as baffled by the spectators as the spectators were by them. It took Rachel a few seconds to realize that neither one of them was used to seeing this level of prosperity and peace between humans anymore.

Lea looked pleasantly surprised. Jarek looked at the place like it was already burning and all these good people just didn't know it yet.

Rachel swore she could see the wheels turning in his head. Maybe the marauders would finally attack with enough force to overwhelm them. Maybe some other disaster would leave them with the kind of famine that could make a community tear itself apart. Something terrible had to happen at some point, right?

Maybe she was simply projecting her own fears onto Jarek's convenient pessimism.

She followed Lea over to look at a few trinkets at one trader's table and half-heartedly exchanged what she hoped was pleasant small talk with the trader, whose name escaped her. Jarek and Alaric waited for them, silently watching the crowd.

Alaric looked far less flabbergasted by all of this, but that made sense. He'd been in Deadwood for the past five years, up in the mountains with his own little isolated community. His people had probably bartered and gotten along in much the same way. She didn't blame him for wanting to get back to it.

Lea indicated her curiosity was sufficiently scratched, and they moved back into the throng.

They were about two-thirds of the way through the market when she felt it: the flare of another telepathic mind, like a roaring bonfire in a field of tiny candles. And it was close.

She froze in mid-step, yanking her mental defenses into place.

There were no other telepaths in Unity—not since the two arcanists who'd helped train her for a short time had moved on. So who the hell was that?

With one hand ready on her cloaking pendant, she extended herself more cautiously this time, keeping her defenses tight, and scoped in on that bonfire to find out.

"What is it?" Jarek asked quietly beside her.

She was too busy scanning through the crowd of faces to answer. She allowed her senses to guide her eyes, dialing in on the telepathic presence.

Not him. When had the crowd gotten so thick? Not her. Maybe—

The blazing-bright presence disappeared completely and without warning.

A cloak? That was the only logical explanation, which meant she'd have to spot them the old-fashioned way, with—

There.

He was twenty feet away, standing completely still in the middle of the heavy foot traffic yet not seeming to be in anyone's way. He looked a few years younger than her, with mussed brown hair and the hint of a beard clinging to his sharp jawline.

More importantly, he was staring straight at her.

He turned away almost as soon as their eyes met and moved into the crowd, headed in the direction they'd come from.

"That guy?" Jarek asked. "Pretty boy?"

He really didn't miss much, did he?

She could give him credit another time. Right now, they needed to catch that kid.

"Get your running legs on," she said. "He's a telepath, and I don't know where the hell he came from."

"So much for that lunch," Jarek said, moving into the crowd beside her.

The market-goers, apparently sensing some urgency to their movements, gave them an even wider berth than they had on the way in. It should have been all they needed to make up ground on Pretty Boy, but he was working through the throng ahead as quickly as if it had been open field, moving with a dancer's grace as he weaved and wound through bodies and rogue limbs.

"He's gonna run," Jarek said. "As soon as he gets around the corner of that building ahead."

"How do you know?"

"Please. I know the look of someone who's about to run just as well as I know the look of someone who wants to be followed."

Ahead, Pretty Boy broke through the edge of the crowd and headed to the right of Kohlberg Hall.

"And you don't seem worried about either of these things because?"

"Mostly because I can top sixty in this bad girl and I'm not half bad at fighting my way out of hairy situations."

"You forgot your god-like powers of modesty," she mumbled as they broke the edge of the crowd and followed after the stranger. A quick glance back told her they'd lost Lea and Alaric, but there wasn't time to worry about that now.

The instant Pretty Boy disappeared around the corner of Kohlberg, Jarek surged forward to make up lost ground. Rachel cut right to get their target back in sight and broke into a run herself as Jarek tore across the open lawn.

Jarek, as he so often frustratingly was, had been right. Pretty Boy was running, and fast. So fast he almost didn't look human.

He glanced back as Jarek rounded the building after him, then he hung an early right, gathered himself, and leapt thirty feet straight up to the rooftop of the Lang building.

"Okay," she muttered.

That decisively closed the door on whether they were dealing with a normal human.

Jarek, aided by Fela and apparently not one to be shown up in a foot chase, launched himself up after Pretty Boy.

And there she was, she realized, just watching it all happen. She cursed herself and set off around the Lang building at a sprint. At the far corner, she hesitated, wondering whether they'd passed over the building or if they were duking it out on the rooftop.

A loud crack from the woods ahead answered that question.

The sound could have passed for a gunshot, but the subsequent stream of smaller crashes and rustling sounds identified it as a falling tree. Rachel readied herself to channel and scrambled down the small hill and into the trees.

Just past a fallen tree, Jarek was bearing down on Pretty Boy, who backpedaled through the foliage with eerily sure-footed grace, ducking and twisting clear of each grab Jarek made for him.

She loped after them, gathering her will.

"We just wanna talk, you little weasel!" Jarek said. "How the hell are you—Agh!"

Pretty Boy swept a hand through the air, and Jarek's feet swept out from under him as if a giant invisible broom had taken them.

So it was an arcanist they were dealing with?

"Tricksy little weasel." Jarek kipped back to his feet and lunged forward with a heavy punch.

Pretty Boy caught the punch with a bare hand.

Rachel had seen Jarek cave men's chests in with blows like that. She'd watched him wrestle with an uber-strong raknoth and throw grown men around like pillows. With Fela, Jarek was stupid strong. And this kid had just blocked his punch with little more than a grimace.

Jarek's faceplate was closed, but his shock was clear enough as he looked from Pretty Boy to their joined hands and back again. "Who the fuck *are* you?"

By way of reply, Pretty Boy drove an open palm into Jarek's armored chest. This time, Rachel's senses were extended far enough to feel the enormous pulse of energy Pretty Boy channeled.

Jarek, she could only assume, felt it even better when Pretty Boy let the energy loose in a telekinetic blast that sent Jarek rocketing through the air. He crashed into a tree twenty feet later.

Rachel leveled her staff and focused her will for her own telekinetic attack, banking on the fact that Pretty Boy would be too drained to do much about it.

He damn near wasn't.

As tired as he must've been, Pretty Boy was still attuned enough to sense the blast coming and fast enough to start moving. Just not fast enough to avoid it completely. The wall of force clipped him and threw his sideways dive into an awkward corkscrew. He hit the soft ground with a rush of expunged air, and Rachel wasted no time in preparing another blast.

"Ha!" Jarek cried from over by the tree he'd smashed into. "Ah, shit."

Rachel glanced Jarek's way to see what was the matter just in time to catch a man-shaped blur flying through the trees to crash into him. Only Jarek was ready.

He stepped with the rush, caught the arm of his attacker, and slammed the newcomer into the tree hard enough to crack through its trunk and plenty hard enough to kill any human. The glowing red eyes glaring at Jarek as the tree began to fall on them affirmed the attacker wasn't.

The raknoth pushed Jarek off and sidestepped out from under the toppling tree. Jarek mirrored him on the other side. A dozen smaller cracks rang out as the tree's branches caught their neighbors and dragged them down as well. The raknoth watched it happen, his back turned to Rachel.

She sprang forward before the fear could convince her not to and swung her staff at the back of the raknoth's head, throwing a full dose of telekinetic *oomph* into the strike.

Half a foot from the raknoth's skull, the staff slammed into thin air.

The raknoth rounded on her.

"Wait!" a strong voice called from behind.

The raknoth froze. And then Jarek slammed into him from behind, and the two crashed to the ground hard enough to leave a trail of torn earth.

Rachel spun around, staff at the ready. Pretty Boy finished pulling himself to his feet and raised his hands in peace. She watched him for a long few seconds, then spared a quick glance to see that Jarek and the raknoth were watching him as well. She traded a look with Jarek, and he scurried to his feet and back to her side. She kept her staff raised, and they backed up together until they could easily see both of them.

"Great," Pretty Boy said, hands still raised. "Thanks. I think."

The raknoth rose and went to stand beside Pretty Boy, the red glow bleeding out of his eyes until he looked like just another middle-aged man with salt-and-pepper hair—albeit a quite suave-looking one.

"Right," Pretty Boy said. "Uh, my name's Haldin"—he glanced over at the raknoth—"and this is Alton."

Alton the raknoth gave them a mirthless smile and a creepy little finger wave, and Haldin continued, "I think maybe we should talk."

CHAPTER SEVEN

In the tense silence that stretched between Jarek and Rachel and their mysterious company, the sounds of the Unity folk approaching the tree line were readily apparent to Jarek's exo-enhanced hearing.

"We've got company," he said.

Rachel pried her wary stare away from Alton the raknoth and Haldin the… whatever he was long enough to shoot him a *What the hell do we do?* look.

It was a good question. Talking it out with a raknoth and his buddy wasn't exactly at the top of Jarek's wise moves play list, but they'd come here looking for answers. If these two weren't connected to that strange ship everyone was talking about, there were either a hell of a lot more raknoth running around than Jarek had ever imagined, or some universal law of coincidence had been severely violated.

Judging from the volume of the voices at the tree line, though, they had about ten seconds to make up their minds before people started asking questions.

Talk now, he decided, kick asses later, as required.

Who said he couldn't be diplomatic?

"Let's hear them out," he said to Rachel.

"Okay." She glanced back toward the tree line. "We'd better move then."

"Sure," Haldin said. "Lead the way."

Rachel pointed over Alton's shoulder with her staff. "That way. You first."

Haldin shrugged. "Fair enough."

Alton turned and trekked off in the indicated direction without comment.

Jarek stayed close to Rachel's side as they followed the odd duo. Now that the skirmish had cooled, the two didn't seem to harbor any violent intent toward him and Rachel, but it never really paid to drop one's guard. Especially when one was dealing with a freaking raknoth.

"There's something odd about these two, sir," Al said quietly in his earpiece.

"No sh—"

"Aside from the obvious oddities, I mean."

Jarek didn't quite know what it was, but he didn't disagree with Al. The questions churning through his head were about as numerous as the leaves in the canopy above them.

This Haldin guy had definitely worked some telekinetic mojo on him during their fight. Jarek wasn't a doctor of arcanism, but that probably meant Haldin was gifted like Rachel, right?

Hell if he knew. And it still didn't exactly explain how the guy had managed to catch a punch that would've knocked a raknoth on his ass with a bare hand. Maybe it had just been a clever use of his abilities. Or maybe Haldin was something else entirely. Hell, maybe they were dealing with a raknoth arcanist. Was that a thing?

It probably would be in his nightmares now.

And, of course, there was one more possibility. Haldin—and maybe Alton too—could be one of these rakul the Red King had warned them about.

Without any way of knowing, Jarek's only real option was to keep on his toes and be ready to fight until he had damn good reason not to be.

If Haldin was human, that still raised the pointed question of what the hell he was doing running around with Alton the raknoth. Jarek, like pretty much everyone else on the planet, didn't know all that much about the raknoth, but he'd never heard tell of such a thing. Sure, the Red King and the Overlord had plenty of human cronies—thousands actually—but those men were more slaves than partners. Some had started as mercenaries. Some had been plucked from the streets. Most, though, seemed to have been tortured or otherwise mentally tampered with until they were loyal servants.

The relationship between Haldin and Alton seemed like something else entirely.

Beside him, Rachel called for a slight adjustment to their trajectory. About a hundred yards later, the woods opened into an impressive outdoor amphitheater.

A dark wooden stage—old but in good repair, like the rest of Unity—stood at the base of the semicircular basin. Opposite the stage, the amphitheater's seating rose along the incline of the basin in a series of large, grassy steps, each one lined along the edge with smooth gray stone to form natural benches. Four lines of neatly groomed trees separated the basin steps into organized sections, contained within sets of smaller stone staircases on either side. Clearly, someone—or multiple someones—put a lot of time into keeping the place pristine.

It was one of the most unnecessary things Jarek had seen in the past fifteen years.

It was also kind of cool.

Haldin and Alton followed the direction of Rachel's waving staff and sank down on the first stone step to the left. Jarek and Rachel remained standing. Jarek focused back the way they came with help from Fela's auditory sensors and decided the voices in the woods behind them didn't seem to be coming any closer.

For now, they were alone.

"Right then," Haldin said, hazel eyes shifting back and forth between them. "I'm sure you guys have a few questions."

No shit.

And now, on top of the other thousand, Jarek had to wonder why Haldin was expecting the questions to be unidirectional. Sure, a human/raknoth duo was weird, but between Fela and Rachel's abilities, it wasn't like he and Rachel were just another pair of everyday citizens. So why was Haldin's default assumption that they should be confused and intrigued by his and Alton's presence?

Maybe these two had simply been around and seen a lot of shit. Maybe they were just spectacularly self-centered. Or—and this seemed like the most likely option—maybe they were hiding something, and Haldin was self-conscious about it.

"What," Jarek said, "you think this is the first time we've just happened to bump into an arcanist, chase him into the woods, and get jumped by his raknoth sidekick? I call that a Tuesday. But now that you mention it, I guess there might be a few particulars, like who you are, why you're here, and, uh…" He tapped at the chin of his faceplate. "Oh yeah. Whether you happen to know anything about the weird ship that's been causing a stir around here. Word on the street is that it looks like a—"

"Let's start with the first two," Rachel said. "What are you doing here?"

Haldin glance at Alton. "We're looking for someone. It's kind of a long story."

Rachel looked less than impressed. "You're trespassing in my home with a raknoth. I think it's safe to say we have the time. So you can give me some fucking answers, or I can wipe these steps with you until they fall out."

Haldin watched her for a long stretch, his expression neutral and calculating.

Alton smirked, but his smooth baritone was only a hint condescending when he spoke. "We're not here to hurt anyone. We came here to help."

"To help who?" Rachel asked.

"Everyone."

Thank god they weren't going to be cryptic about it or anything.

Jarek rolled his hand in a *keep it coming* gesture. "You might have to use more than one word at a time if we wanna get somewhere today."

Alton's smirk only grew. "I thought you had the time."

With a careful mental command, Jarek opened his faceplate so the raknoth could see his eyes as he patted the hilt of the Big Whacker. "You know, I cut a raknoth to pieces with this thing two days ago."

"Okay, look," Haldin said, raising a hand.

He probably meant it as a pacifying gesture, but Rachel tensed and raised her staff in return.

Haldin dropped the hand. "This isn't necessary. We're here to help your peop—to help rid you of the raknoth before it's too late."

Jarek made a show of looking around at their surroundings. "Yeah. Did you miss the whole Catastrophe thing? It's already a bit too late."

"And why would you be looking to save us from your own people anyways?" Rachel asked Alton.

Alton's face was unreadable. "I have my own goals here, I admit. But they are synergistic with Haldin's, and with the ultimate good of the people of Earth."

"I know this planet's been devastated already," Haldin said, glancing at Alton for what had to be the hundredth time, "but it could get worse. A lot worse."

Worse as is rakul worse? He almost asked outright then decided it was better to keep them talking before playing what limited hand he had.

"You can imagine our skepticism about a philanthropic raknoth," he said to Alton. "Your kind don't exactly have a peaceful track record with ours. Frankly, I'm wondering if you didn't slam me through that tree back there and if I'm not just dreaming all of this right now."

"I could pinch you if you'd like." Alton held up his thumb and fore-finger with a disconcerting grin and sprouted a pair of wicked-looking claws.

"Not helping, Alton," Haldin said. "Look, I get it. My people have lost too much at the hands of the raknoth as well." A shadow of genuine pain crossed his face. "I've lost more than most fighting them. For a long time, I wanted to wipe them away from this universe, but it's not that simple."

The more Haldin talked, the more something didn't seem right about him. Something about the way he phrased things and the way he kept glancing at his raknoth pal—not to mention the fact that he had a raknoth pal at all—was just off.

"What do you mean, 'it's not that simple'?" Rachel said.

Haldin glanced at Alton. Again.

"Stop that," Rachel said.

Apparently the constant furtive glances were itching her heebie-jeebie button as well. A quick look at her expression, though, made him think something else might be afoot.

"What's up?"

Her eyes remained locked on Haldin and Alton. "They're talking."

It took a second, but it clicked. "Ah."

Telepaths. Tricky bunch.

"Granted, I'm not so good at manners," Jarek said, "but that seems pretty damn rude, fellas." To Rachel, he added, "What are they saying?"

"I can't hear them," she said. "I just feel the connection."

"Right." He shifted his weight, suddenly feeling like it wouldn't hurt to be ready to hack limbs off.

"Sorry," Haldin said. "You're right—it's not polite. Here." He pulled on a thin chain at his neck until a round pendant popped out from under his shirt. He turned a tiny dial on the pendant and looked at Rachel. "Better?"

Was that a cloak like Rachel's then? The weary nod she gave Haldin suggested so.

"What we're facing," Haldin said, "what we're trying to do, it's probably not going to be a wildly popular idea. We were just discussing how much we should be telling you."

"Well if that doesn't just scream trustworthy…" Rachel muttered.

Haldin raised his eyebrows, amusement twinkling in his eyes. "I realize this might be your home, but it's still kind of funny to hear that from the people who haven't told us the first things about themselves. Not to be confrontational, but we're talking in good faith right now, not because we're trembling at your power."

Rachel looked like she was deliberating whether to incinerate the pair of them or go for a record in the long toss. Jarek didn't blame her. It wasn't like he was a fan of people strutting their stuff in front of him, but he also had a certain amount of admiration for people who were cool under pressure. Plus, the fact that Unity wasn't his home probably didn't hurt either where keeping a level head was concerned.

"I'm Jarek Slater," he said, consciously shifting to a slightly less confrontational stance.

Haldin gave him an appreciative nod.

Jarek gave Rachel an expectant look.

"Fine," she said. "If it'll make this conversation less annoying, then fine. I'm Rachel Cross. Pleased to fucking meet you."

If Jarek hadn't happened to be looking straight at Alton, he probably would have missed the way the raknoth's brows twitched when Rachel said her name. Somehow, for some reason, that name meant something to Alton the raknoth.

Now what the hell was Jarek supposed to make of that? Alton's eyes shifted to meet his, cool and controlled once more. Next to him, Haldin's expression had gone somber. Did Rachel's name mean something to him as well?

"So there," Rachel said. "We're all great pals. Now why don't you tell us what's so complicated about wanting these assholes"—she pointed at Alton—"off our planet?"

Alton chuckled. "Oh, believe you me, we would love to leave this planet behind in a heartbeat if we could. But we can't. Your own people saw to that."

"I'm guessing there's an explanation in there somewhere?" Jarek asked.

"Long story short," Haldin said, "some of the people of Earth already tried to wipe the raknoth off this planet. They almost succeeded, even. But their actions had other consequences, ones I doubt they'd expected. What started as a mission to destroy the raknoth ended up being the accident that effectively bound our species' fates together."

Jarek traded a confused look with Rachel. "Say we don't follow exactly what you're talking about…"

"The blood," Haldin said. "You must've wondered why raknoth need to feed on human blood to survive."

Shit. That was actually a thing?

"Yeah," Jarek said. "Say we didn't really know about that either..."

Haldin raised his eyebrows. "Really?"

Jarek had heard the stories, of course. He'd also seen the Red King drink the blood of one of his own men, and then again with Pryce. Hell, he even knew some people had taken to calling them vamps, but he'd kind of figured it had all been a bunch of fear mongering and dramatic effect—or that the raknoth just happened to enjoy blood. There'd been no reason to think the whole requiring human blood to survive thing was anything more than another one of a thousand rumors floating around about the raknoth.

Before he could say any of that though, Rachel stepped in.

"It's not like we've had much time to swap diet plans what with them nuking the planet to shit and holing up in their big dark fortresses. How the hell do *you* know any of this?"

Haldin looked at Alton. "Well I learned some of it when I broke into one of his clan member's minds, but Alton's filled me in on some of the missing details since."

Granted, Jarek knew next to nothing about telepathy, but if Haldin had succeeded where Rachel had failed in invading a raknoth's mind, it seemed like a safe bet he was packing some serious artillery in that pretty little noggin of his. The fact that Rachel's hand had drifted to the pendant at her breastbone told Jarek she was having similar thoughts.

What if Haldin and Alton decided to throw a psychic double-whammy at Rachel right now? Would she be strong enough to get her cloak up?

If it came to that, it might be up to him to remove one of them from the equation before they could overwhelm her.

He tried to dispel the tension building in his shoulders. He'd deal with it if he had to, but his instincts told him that the two weren't about to try anything.

"Let's say we believe any of this," he said. "I still don't see how that lands you working with a raknoth. This all just sounds like more reason to want them gone."

Haldin nodded. "I don't necessarily disagree, but for two things."

"Enlighten us," Rachel said.

"Well for one, it's not really their fault."

"Bullshit," Rachel said. "They were the ones who decided to come prey on us in the first place."

Alton showed them a bitter smile. "Right, right. Except that we weren't. We came to Earth because we were made to."

"Which brings me to point number two," Haldin said. "There are worse things than the raknoth out there, and they're probably gonna come here someday if we don't stop them."

"Things like the rakul?" Jarek asked.

He might as well have stuck a cattle prod to each of their backs for how they tensed. They traded a shocked look, all hints of amusement and smugness draining away to be replaced by... was it horror?

Alton turned to Jarek, red embers awakening in his eyes. "Where did you hear that name?"

"One of your friends told us," Jarek said. "Why? What does it mean? Who are these harvester guys?"

"Impossible." Alton rose to his feet and took a step forward. "You don't even know of the blood bond yet one of my kin told you of the harvesters?"

"Back off, asshole," Rachel said, brandishing her staff.

"Alton," Haldin said, his tone calming.

"Something's happened," Alton growled at him before snapping his red-eyed gaze to Rachel. "Have you felt anything? A psychic disturbance?"

Rachel traded a glance with Jarek, and he was pretty sure she was thinking the same thing he was: a disturbance like that nest thing going off?

So much for this all being a made-up scare tactic of the Red King. Whatever the rakul were, they had Haldin and Alton shaking in their boots too.

The buzz of an incoming comm message yanked him back to the present. A second later, Rachel's buzzed as well.

That wasn't good.

The list of people who might be contacting him was short enough. The list of people who'd be messaging both of them at the same time was considerably shorter.

Something was going on.

"Message from Lea, sir," Al said quietly in his ear. "Oh dear. One word: help."

"Uh, can you guys just…" He held up a finger to Haldin and Alton. The look on Rachel's face told him she'd received the same message. "One second."

He slid his faceplate closed. "Message her back," he said quietly. "Find out what's—"

His wrist buzzed again, and this time the message appeared at the bottom of his in-helmet display: *Mosen here. Help.*

"Son of a bitch."

"Trouble?" Haldin asked.

Beside him, Alton straightened and began sniffing the air.

That didn't bode well. None of this did.

The Overlord's most dangerous errand boy just happened to be showing up right when they were sitting here talking to a mysteriously well-informed stranger and his raknoth pal?

Jarek looked at Rachel and wished he could beam his thoughts straight into her head. "We have to check on something. Don't suppose you two would be willing to stay put for a few minutes?"

Alton cocked his head and sniffed again. "I think we'd better not. I smell raknoth."

Rachel tilted her staff toward Haldin and Alton. "Friends of yours?"

"I doubt I have any friends left on this planet," Alton said, "but they are likely here because of us." He looked at Haldin. "We should leave."

Haldin stood without argument.

"Like hell," Rachel said, taking a step forward.

Jarek grabbed her arm and shook his head.

If Mosen was in town, they needed to move now if they didn't want to lose Lea and Alaric. Of course, he didn't really want to say that in front of Haldin and Alton. Storming off into a fight with two powerful unknowns at their back was bad enough without calling attention to the fact.

"This isn't over," he said. "But our friends might need us right now."

"I have a feeling we'll be seeing you again," Haldin said.

Then he and Alton turned and set off into the woods at a brusque pace.

"Dammit," Rachel hissed beside him. "Let's go."

Jarek watched after Haldin and Alton for a few more seconds, wondering if he and Rachel had been playing into some manipulative trap this entire time.

Either way, they'd made their choice. He nodded and turned to follow Rachel out of the amphitheater clearing back the way they'd come.

Out of all the questions whirling through Jarek's mind, one thing seemed sure enough: whichever way things panned out, their day probably wasn't about to get any less boring.

CHAPTER EIGHT

As unhappy as Rachel was to leave a strange arcanist and his raknoth buddy roaming free in Unity, the need to find Lea and Alaric was twofold.

For one, they were allies—maybe even friends—and she didn't want to see them captured, hurt, or worse. On top of that, though, if Seth Mosen was here, it seemed unlikely he'd be alone. He'd have brought plenty of reinforcements—Reds or the Overlord forces, it didn't really matter. All that mattered was that Seth Mosen was a wild dog and that his presence put the entire community at risk.

What was he even doing here?

Probably tracking them. They had captured one of his superiors, after all. The Overlord probably had half his army out looking for the Red King and the other half looking for her and Jarek. She hoped that was all there was to it. Because if it was something else, if the raknoth had learned about her and Michael's connection to Unity and decided to turn the screws by attacking their home…

She swallowed against a dry mouth. Baseless worrying wasn't going to help anyone.

Given that time was short, Rachel held the protest and stuck with a dirty look when Jarek moved to scoop her up into his arms. With

Fela, he could move more than twice as fast as a normal human, even while carrying her. In less than a minute, he was setting her down at the tree line of the quad. They stepped out of the woods and proceeded more cautiously toward the market, which was where they assumed Lea and Alaric still were.

And there they were, face-to-face with Seth Mosen and two other men. They were removed enough from the crowd that it wasn't hard to spot them, but that may have been mostly because the crowd was giving the tense little huddle a wide berth—not to mention a fair amount of nervous glances.

The sight of Mosen started the adrenaline racing through Rachel's chest and brought the unbidden, vivid memory of the crushing pressure of his hands on her throat. She focused on his two backup goons to clear her mind. One was short, with dark hair and a face that reminded Rachel of a toad and seemed immediately untrustworthy. The other was tall and narrow, right down to his slender face.

"We're just gonna walk up to them?" Rachel asked. "No plan or anything?"

"I can take Mosen with Fela no problem," Jarek said beside her. "But we need to be close to Alaric and Lea if the shit hits." He opened his faceplate and winked at her. "Guess we'll see what happens from there."

"This isn't a fucking game, Jarek. There are innocents everywhere. Good people. If he has reinforcements nearby—"

"We'll do what we have to." He glanced at her comm. "Might wanna get word to campus security in the meanwhile."

Shit. Why hadn't she already done that? She swiped at her comm and, quickly as she could, typed out: *Trouble at quad. Lock and load.*

She sent the message and looked up to see Mosen and his two goons watching them approach. Mosen's grin injected a hit of pure cold creepiness straight into her chest.

"Shit," she murmured.

Was it just her imagination, or had the toady goon grinned as she said it?

"We're good," Jarek said. "Deep breath, Goldilocks. We've got this."

The words might not have been particularly meaningful, but she had to admit she was glad to have him next to her right now. As off-beat and immature as Jarek could be, she couldn't think of anyone more capable of watching her back in a hairy situation.

They were about twenty feet away when Alaric and Lea followed Mosen's line of sight and saw them approaching. Both of them looked wired with tension, and Alaric was a few shades paler than normal. Understandable enough. How else could someone be expected to react when their son-turned-raknoth-slave-turned-matricidal-madman came calling?

"Here they are," Mosen called, hands splayed wide. "The wily arcanist and the Soldier of Charity himself."

Rachel drew up to Lea's side and placed a supportive hand on her shoulder. Jarek crossed in front of them and took position beside Alaric.

"Mosen," Jarek said. "How awful to see you here."

Mosen made a pouting face.

Rachel reached out with her senses to sweep for any lurking threats, starting with Mosen himself. Despite whatever the Overlord had done to him to grant him his exceptional strength and durability, she was pretty sure Mosen was still mostly human. His presence did feel a bit off, but she didn't linger on it.

"We were hoping to catch you closer to home," Mosen said, "find out what you've done with poor Al'Drogan."

That made Mosen's two thugs frown at him for some reason.

"With poor what now?" Jarek asked.

Mosen sneered. "Don't worry your pretty little head over it, Slater. We've got other business to take care of. Speaking of which, you didn't happen to notice anything odd on the way—"

Rachel missed whatever else he said as she reached her senses out to the two men behind him. The two men who were in fact not men at all. They couldn't be—not with minds that felt like that.

She yanked the tendrils of her mind in and bolstered her mental defenses.

Shit. This was bad.

Around them, over a hundred people continued their business about the market, blissfully unaware they were within easy throwing distance of a supercharged mad dog and his two raknoth comrades.

Could the four of them contain Mosen and two raknoth if—or probably when—it came to a fight? Hell, could they even survive themselves?

They needed to clear this place out before things got messy. She should have told Myers to evacuate, not to lock and load. It wasn't like him and his men would be able to do much against raknoth anyhow, aside from get hurt.

What she needed to do was warn Jarek somehow.

"—ame here for a pit stop on the way to drop off this old cowboy," Jarek was saying. "Didn't see any strange ships on the way in. You know, not that I'd tell you if I had."

"Really," Mosen said, his expression flat. "A pit stop."

Jarek shrugged. "Little out of the way, but where else can you find a community like this? Nice to remember there are still people being people on this planet."

Mosen sneered, looking around as if only now seeing the sprawling community around him. So maybe he and his raknoth masters didn't realize it was Rachel's home they'd come to. And if they'd come here looking for that confounded ship and not tracking her and the others, maybe they had no reason to hurt the people of Unity.

Of course, that didn't mean they wouldn't do it anyway.

"People are always being people everywhere," Mosen said. "It's just a little more interesting out there in the wild. Right, Pops?"

Alaric met Mosen's sneer with tired eyes for several seconds before he said, quietly, "You're not my son."

Mosen's eyebrows shot up and he place a hand over his chest in mock offense. "Well Jesus, I guess not with that attitude. Words hurt you know, Pops. No wonder I turned out this way."

Alaric's face was carved from stone, but his Adam's apple betrayed a hard swallow. "I believe he's still in there somewhere, my son. And I'll do anything I can to help him. But—"

Mosen shifted his weight, leaning closer to Alaric. "You have no idea what you're talking about, old man."

Mosen's voice was deadly quiet. Behind him, the two raknoth uncrossed their arms and prepared to move.

Mosen held Alaric's gaze for several seconds, then he rocked back and threw his hands up. "Enough with this touchy-feely bullshit! We have a job to do here. If you four haven't seen anything, I suppose we'll have to call in the troops to search the place and bring you home for proper questioning."

Shit. Shit. Shit. They needed to stop him, or distract him, or—

"Why don't we just tell him?" Lea asked.

Everyone looked at her, waiting.

Jarek turned a wary look her way. "I don't know if that's such a good—"

"Come on," Lea said. "I hate the raknoth as much as the next girl, but these are innocent people here. It's not like we're about to go chasing it down anyways."

"Chasing what down?" Mosen asked, leaning in like a dog at a dinner table.

"If you don't tell him, I will," Lea said.

Jarek looked at the crowd and blew out a short breath. "Fine." He narrowed his eyes at Mosen. "I lied. We picked up something on the scanners passing over Philly—something like I've never seen before. Couldn't spot it through the clouds, but it was headed down for south Jersey, or maybe Delaware." Mosen opened his mouth to say something, but Jarek held up a finger and added, "And this part's not important, but if you want to know why I lied, it's because I think you're a huge cock-hat."

Mosen crossed his arms and considered the four of them.

Rachel did her best to look the part of the weary traveler who was simply hoping Mosen and his cronies would fuck off and leave them alone.

It wasn't a hard act to keep up.

"We don't believe you," Mosen finally said. He glanced between Jarek and Rachel with a cold grin. "Where were you two just now?"

"You really need to ask why a man and a woman snuck off into the woods?" Jarek asked. "I think you need to get outta the Fortress more often, buddy."

"Well now I know you're lying, Slater." Mosen winked at Rachel then, and for a brief moment, his irises glinted with red light. "Girl like this needs a real man, not some wise-ass who hides behind his toys."

"You're only saying that because you haven't seen what I can do with my toys." Jarek waggled his eyebrows at Mosen. "Yet."

Myers chose that moment to pull the Gator around Kohlberg and into the quad. He had four of his men with him, all of whom had taken her lock and load advice to heart. Of course, she'd given that advice before she realized there were a pair of raknoth standing smack in the middle of a crowd, but it was too late now. Three more of Myers' men, also armed, were sweeping around the other side of Kohlberg on foot.

"Ah," Mosen said. "Sneaky little bastards."

Shit.

"Well," Mosen said, "we tried the nice way. Looks like it's time to call in the—"

Jarek sprung forward without warning and drove a fist into Mosen's face. The punch landed with a thud and a crack, and Mosen's head led his body through a short flight that ended with a hard crash to the ground several feet back.

Jarek was already grabbing the toad-looking raknoth and pivoting to slam him to the ground.

"Jarek, no! They're—"

Too late.

The raknoth's eyes came ablaze with red raknoth fire. She saw a flicker of surprise on Jarek's face before his faceplate whirred shut, and then the raknoth reversed Jarek's throw and hurled him ten yards across the quad.

Jarek turned through the air with a long cry of, "Shiiit!" and managed to turn his fall into a rough roll. "Rachel!" he shouted. "Raknoth!"

She was already channeling energy from the batteries on her belt into a hard barrier in front of her, Lea, and Alaric.

Just in time. The slender raknoth lunged forward and slammed to a halt against her invisible wall a few feet from Alaric. His toady friend turned his fiery gaze to Rachel and prepared to throw his weight into the assault as well.

She resisted the urge to blast them back to buy time. Aside from the fact that they were ridiculously strong and heavy, it wasn't really an option to launch a pair of angry raknoth into the crowd behind them—a crowd which was quickly beginning to panic as more and more people looked over and saw what was happening.

Rachel pulled more energy to prepare for the second raknoth's charge. Instead, though, the raknoth whipped his head around and rolled to the side. The next instant, Jarek slammed down to the soft earth, sweeping his ridiculously hefty sword through the space where the toad's head had just been.

Both raknoth leapt back with dual roars to square off with Jarek as he stepped in front of Alaric and Lea. The one with the slender face bumped into a market-goer hard enough that the guy hit the dirt as if he'd been struck by a low-speed truck. Luckily the raknoth were both focused on Jarek, and the guy's buddies grabbed him and dragged him off with the rest of the frantically dispersing crowd.

The sounds of rushing air and the low hum of electric motors rose through the din of the evacuation, capping the adrenaline-fueled pounding of Rachel's heart with a dose of cold dread. She met eyes with Myers, who was pushing toward them through the fleeing crowd, and they both turned their gazes skyward.

Ships.

Three of them, two larger carriers and one smaller ship about the size of Jarek's. They could have belonged to the Overlord or the Reds. It didn't matter. The victorious, bloody-nosed sneer Mosen shot her from the ground as he waved away his comm holo told her everything she needed to know.

Rachel tightened her grip on her staff, gathered her focus, and prepared to fight as enemy forces swept in from above to attack her home.

CHAPTER NINE

By Jarek's reckoning, facing unfavorable numbers in a fight pretty much boiled down to two options: refraining from direct engagement to buy time to enact a more clever plan, or focusing on a single target and attacking it decisively in hopes of leveling the playing field before things had a chance to get messy. Or dying.

Okay, so three options.

Jarek tended to fall into the reckless attack school of thought, so when he caught sight of the three ships descending with what he expected would be dozens of troops to join Mosen and the two raknoth in the Unity quad, he didn't hold back.

He picked the slender-faced raknoth on the left and leapt into battle with a wide horizontal sword sweep intended to drive both raknoth back and apart.

It worked, and Jarek followed up with a feinted lunge in the toady-looking raknoth's direction to drive him further away from his partner. As soon as Toady hopped clear of the feint, Jarek switched direction and darted toward Slender Face.

Slender Face dipped, rolled, and backpedaled with the best of them to keep clear of Jarek's flurry of sword strikes, his skin darkening slowly to scaly green battle-hide. The raknoth was quick, but that went without saying.

Jarek was about to reverse direction and rotate into another strike when Al cried out. "Roll!"

Jarek threw himself to the left without hesitation. Al was literally the eyes in the back of his head. When he said move, Jarek moved.

What felt like a hunk of steel rebar clipped the back of his legs as he went, and he came back to his feet in time to see Toady stumbling straight into Slender Face after apparently having tripped on Jarek's leg while trying to surprise him from behind.

"Good call, Mr. Robot," Jarek said, peddling back toward the others while he had a moment to breathe.

Gunfire cracked from overhead as the enemy forces—the Overlord's people, he was pretty sure—opened up on the four of them and the handful of armed Unity fighters approaching through the dwindling crowd. Jarek cringed at the lack of discrimination the shooters practiced for foe and fleeing innocents. A few town folk fell, along with one of Myers' men. The rest of the armed Unity guards hunkered down behind whatever they could and began returning fire.

A few shots pinged off Fela's armor. To the left, Rachel was dealing with the new threat in her own way.

A thin arc of spent lead slugs was accumulating a few feet in front of her, courtesy of that amazing bullet catcher of hers. Alaric and Lea were crouched behind her for cover.

A few more bullets slammed to a halt in mid-air a few feet from Rachel as Jarek watched. Alaric leaned around her and raised a revolver, his breath condensing in the air the bullet catcher had drained of heat to power its arcane function. Alaric fired twice, and a dark-clad enemy soldier fell from a transport above to topple lifelessly to the soft earth.

In response, the enemy fire picked up. The transports were pushing their way down to land in the quad when Toady and Slender Face, now both in scaly green raknoth mode, pressed in to renew their attack. Mosen joined them, and after that, things got hectic.

Jarek lost track of everything outside his immediate vicinity as he fell into a deadly dance with his three adversaries. He moved through sequence after sequence of attacks, dodges, and counters with trance-like focus. Kick there. Pivot. Swipe-dodge-riposte. Duck. Rising sweep. Take a hit. Give one back.

Don't stop.

Impossibly strong arms grabbed him from behind. Jarek dropped his sword, grabbed an arm, and dropped his hips back, pivoting as he went to flip Slender Face over his shoulder and slam him to the ground. He raised an armored boot to stomp down on the raknoth's head, then tensed as he caught sight of Toady charging in on his side.

There wasn't time to avoid the tackle. The instant before Toady hit, though, he was bowled off course by what could have been an invisible semi-truck.

Score one for Goldilocks.

Toady flew past Jarek instead of through him, and Jarek thanked his stars that he had a strong-willed arcanist watching his back.

By then Slender Face had rolled out from under him. Jarek grappled with an oncoming Mosen and managed to turn and throw him at a now-oncoming Slender Face, buying him a moment to scoop the Whacker back up from the ground.

The moment of peace only made him an open target to the enemy soldiers. Several bullets slammed into Fela's armor before Mosen and the raknoth stepped back within potential-friendly-fire range.

Jarek shook the shots off and brandished his sword at his three foes. "Bring it, bitches!"

"Not your finest work, sir," Al said.

"Guess I'll try to do better next time I'm fighting three—"

Slender Face lunged forward recklessly, as if he thought he'd caught Jarek with his pants down. Apparently he hadn't gotten the message that Jarek was a multitasker.

"—superhuman assholes!" Jarek cried as he darted aside, swinging his back leg around to leverage a hard overhand strike.

The blade cleaved Slender Face's right hand off at mid-forearm. Jarek followed up with a powerful sidekick to the stunned raknoth's ribs and a loud cry of, "Booyah!" He readied his sword, staring down Mosen and Toady. "Who's next for the choppy-choppy?"

"Jarek!" Rachel cried. "We've got a situation over here!"

"Sit-rep, Al." He couldn't afford to drop his eyes from his opponents, not when they could cover dozens of yards at a leap.

"Five of eight Unity men down, sir," Al said. "Enemy forces still unloading."

Well that was the opposite of good. And things weren't going much better in his own fight. As satisfying as removing Slender Face's hand had been, the raknoth was hardly incapacitated. The scaly bastard was already pulling himself to his feet. And—

A sound like a pride of lions roaring in perfect synchrony rattled the air.

"And there appears to be a third raknoth here, sir."

"Gee thanks, Al," Jarek said. "I hadn't noticed."

This was beyond not good. If they didn't do something to balance the odds—and do it quickly—things were going to go downhill fast once raknoth number three cut through Unity's meager forces and moved in on him and the others. Unfortunately, the raknoth decided to skip step one completely.

"Six o'clock incoming, sir!" Al cried.

The thudding impacts of the raknoth's footsteps had been warning enough.

Jarek reluctantly dropped his eyes from Mosen and Toady and whirled to strike at the new threat.

The rust-colored raknoth darted under the top-down diagonal cut with disturbing agility and delivered an open-palm strike to Jarek's lowered shoulder as he flew by. Even in passing, the raknoth's blow was substantial enough to send Jarek tumbling haphazardly toward Rachel and the others.

They managed to scatter before his armored bulk plowed into them. Alaric grunted in pain as a shot found him now outside of Rachel's protective barrier. Jarek scrambled to his feet and shielded the old cowboy with his armored body while Rachel and Lea closed back in tight. Jarek handed Alaric off to Lea and spun around, expecting to find a raknoth flying down on them from above.

Toady and the rusty-hided newcomer were both gathering themselves to leap when they jolted as if they'd received a strong shock. Behind them, Mosen and Slender Face were looking around, likewise confused.

The three raknoth whipped around in unison to face the woods where they'd tumbled with Haldin and Alton earlier.

Jarek realized the quad had gone quiet, and now everyone seemed to be following the gazes of the three raknoth.

There was a low hum from the tree line, steadily growing closer. Jarek eyed the nearest of the three raknoth, Rusty, and wondered if he should strike while they were distracted.

Before he could, the hum intensified—not really in volume so much as in the way it rumbled through Jarek's chest.

He glanced back just as a large, dark shape crested the tree line.

"Well I'll be damned," Jarek mumbled as the ship that was unmistakably the one they'd been looking for pulled into view.

It was fairly large, longer than it was wide, and its loosely cylindrical form rippled with fluid, bulbar shapes, as if the hull had been cast over top of an array of bubbles of varying sizes. What that hull was made of, he couldn't say, but it shimmered oddly from dark black to light purple at different spots and shifted fluidly as the ship glided smoothly forward.

"I don't believe that ship is of this planet, sir," Al said as the craft came to a resting hover overhead.

"No kidding."

The three raknoth ahead were statuesque, staring up at the ship with their fiery red orbs. Rachel, too, was looking in the general direction of the ship with a distant blank look, like she was otherwise engaged.

Silent tension hung in the air for several seconds, and then, without so much as a honk, the strange ship turned and shot off to the northwest with impressive speed.

Everyone seemed to snap back into their right minds as it went.

Jarek tensed, waiting for the fighting to resume and cursing himself for not taking his shot when he'd had the opening.

Instead of charging them, though, Rusty turned toward his ships. He didn't say a word, but enemy soldiers began funneling hurriedly back into the transports as if he'd roared the order.

Creepy.

"You too," Rusty said to Mosen and the other two raknoth, who were apparently his underlings. Mosen opened his mouth to say something, but Rusty silenced him with a crimson power glare.

Mosen looked at Jarek and behind him to Alaric with a snarl, then he fell in line behind his retreating raknoth allies.

Rusty watched them go before turning that fiery glare on Jarek.

Jarek had seen some scary looks in his day, but this one had to take the cake. Where Toady and Slender Face were mid-shift—hided but still human-ish in appearance—Rusty was in full-on raknoth mode: his smooth skin completely replaced by scaly hide and his human features dramatically shifted toward something more beastly and reptilian. He stood with all the confidence and authority of a fearsome warrior. The rust red color, like old, dried blood on his hide, only added to the effect.

"Next time we meet," he said, his voice low and strong, "I will take pleasure in ending you."

Jarek swallowed, glad for the cover of his faceplate, as the raknoth turned and strode to the smallest of the three ships.

He half considered going after him for a moment, trying to end the raknoth now that his allies were all loaded up. No. Better not to press their luck.

Whatever the hell had just happened between the raknoth and that strange ship, it looked like Rusty and his forces were willing to forget about Unity to go after the thing, and he wasn't about to give them reason to do otherwise.

Rusty hopped up to an open hatch, and all three of the ships promptly lifted up and rocketed off after the strange ship. Okay, hell, might as well just say it: after the *alien* ship.

They watched them go in silence, tension thick in the air as they waited to be sure the enemy forces wouldn't decide to swoop back and resume the assault.

The ships finally disappeared over the far tree line, and they all let out a collective breath.

"Okay," Lea said, eyes wide. "What the hell was that?"

"Well," Jarek said, "I don't know if it quite fit the giant flying dildo mold, but I'm pretty sure that was the ship we're looking for."

"Your friends from the woods?" Alaric asked, his voice strained.

"I have a feeling, yeah." Jarek moved to check on Alaric's wound, but the old fighter pushed him away and muttered something about it just being a graze.

Rachel was still staring after the long-gone ship with an utterly vacant expression.

"Hey." Jarek laid a hand on her shoulder. "What's up? We have wounded that need help."

At his touch, she snapped back with a sharp breath and turned a disoriented look over toward Myers and his men.

They started for the Unity fighters side by side, Lea and Alaric trailing along behind them. More people were showing up at the quad now, some only poking their heads out of nearby buildings, others rushing to Myers and the others to offer them aid.

"So much for Alton and Haldin staying put," Jarek said quietly to Rachel as they walked. "Guess we're back at knocking on doors to ask awkward questions if we want to find them again."

"Maybe not." Rachel gave one last disheveled glance in the direction the ship had disappeared before meeting his eyes with a grave look. "I know where they're going."

CHAPTER TEN

As heavy as the fighting had been, only four of Unity's people were dead.

It probably said something about Rachel's current mental state that the word *only* appeared anywhere in the proximity of the thought that four of her fellow community members had been killed in a pointless attack.

Maybe too much fighting and bloodshed in the past week had left her raw to it. Maybe she was half-comforted by dark thoughts of how much worse it could have been. Maybe—and if she was being honest, this one was probably the winner—she was just too stunned to process much of anything after what she'd just learned: the part that she'd left off when she'd told Jarek she knew where Haldin and Alton were going.

The part where Haldin had reached down telepathically from the hovering alien ship to tell her they knew what had happened to her mother and her family—and, more importantly, why it had happened.

It was a lot to process.

She looked around the quad in a daze, taking in the aftermath of their brief but furious battle. On top of Unity's four dead, several enemy troops had fallen as well. Plenty more from both sides were wounded, either directly from the engagement or because they were caught in the crossfire by freak misses and ricochets as the conflict unfolded. She stared at the swirling mass of noise and rushing bodies, thinking that she should do something to help, but no matter how hard she thought it, nothing seemed to happen.

At some point, John found her. She recognized him by the bone-crushing hug he wrapped her in. He exchanged a few words with Jarek. She was pretty sure she pitched in a few words as well, but when John left to help their people a minute later, she couldn't have said what they'd talked about.

She found her feet carrying her away from the chaos to a quiet corner. Jarek came to settle down next to her, followed shortly by Lea and Alaric, who was pressing a small cloth to the graze wound on his left arm. Lea was chock full of nervous energy in the wake of the battle. Thankfully, Jarek was willing to field her outpouring of questions. So Rachel sat there, only distantly listening as he recounted their meeting with Haldin the arcanist and Alton the raknoth.

The pair had been enough of an enigma on their own. Add in the stuff about the human-raknoth blood tie, Alton's decidedly ominous reaction to the mention of the rakul, and, most importantly, the question of how the hell her mom was connected to any of this, and it was too much to process in the aftermath of the battle.

Sometime later, when the wounded had been triaged and carted away and most of Unity had shifted their attention to talking about what the hell had just happened, John and Myers came to find them.

At John's suggestion, they left the quad and moved to one of the conference rooms in the town hall to talk. Shocked and/or tired and beaten as they were, no one saw fit to say much on the way over.

"Okay," John finally said when they were all sitting in the rich conference room around the long, glossy table. "Who were they, and why were they here?"

"Pretty sure they belonged to the Overlord," Jarek said. "Big scary raknoth who owns what's left of New York Cit—"

"I've heard of him," John said.

"Right. Well, I thought they were here for us at first, but it seems like they were looking for the same ship we were."

"That ship they all flew after?" John asked. "That... oh hell, that *alien* ship?"

Jarek nodded. "That's the one."

They all considered that in silence. Rachel had been thinking the same thing. She wanted to think the idea of an alien ship was ludicrous, but given the scaly green blood-sucking monsters who could shirk off bullets like flies, was anything really ludicrous anymore? If the raknoth really were from out of town, they had to have gotten here somehow, right?

Everyone else seemed to be reaching similar conclusions.

John leaned heavily back in his chair and blew out a long breath toward the ceiling. "I shudder to think what that thing was doing around here."

"They were looking for someone," Rachel said. "I'm not sure who, but..."

Haldin's last words rushed through her mind. *We can tell you what happened to your mom. Tomorrow. Her old lab. Stay safe, Rachel.*

And then they'd rocketed off without a backward glance.

Was it her they'd been looking for?

That idea sounded more deluded than alien ships and bulletproof space vampires. But why would they know about her mom?

John was watching her with deeply knitted brows. "They? You saw the ship's owners? You talked to them?"

She gave a weary nod and shot Jarek a look. He took her silent meaning and launched into the story of their meeting with Haldin and Alton, this time glossing over the detail of the rakul. By the end, John was leaning in with his elbows on the able, mouth half open and face half buried between his steepled fingers. Myers looked highly skeptical, and Lea and Alaric simply tired.

"How did a raknoth get inside Unity without us noticing?" Myers asked.

"Shit," Jarek said, "the raknoth masqueraded high enough up the totem pole to get access to nuclear launch codes before the Catastrophe, I don't think you should take it too hard if they snuck past your checkpoint. And as nice as your perimeter fence is, it'd have to be about five times higher and a thousand times stronger to have a chance at keeping one of those red-eyed bastards out."

Myers and John traded a disconcerted look. Rachel's insides squirmed right along with theirs. She had some inkling of what the raknoth could do—enough to know how woefully screwed Unity would be if it came to repelling a full-on raknoth invasion on their own. No matter what they did, how hard they tried, there were forces out there that could simply roll over them like bugs underfoot.

It wasn't fair. But that was probably why Michael had run off to join the Resistance and fight the bastards in the first place, wasn't it?

"I don't know how this would have ended up if you all hadn't been here," Myers said. "Hell, I don't even know if any of this would have happened at all. But I still feel like I owe you some thanks for having our backs today."

"Ah, it's no problem, guy." Jarek extended a fist across the table. "Put it here."

Myers eyed the fist dubiously then finally reached out to touch his own fist to it. Jarek retracted his fist and did a subdued victory pump.

"I guess there's a reason they call you the Soldier of Charity," John said.

Jarek made a face. "Ick."

John studied his reaction curiously. "Will you go after that ship? Try to find this Haldin person again?"

"Dunno about that one," Jarek said. "We've got some ominous warnings about our impending doom. We've got two guys running around out there who seem to know a whole hell of a lot more than we do, and apparently we know where they're headed too." He glanced uncertainly toward her and the others. "But I owe Alaric here a ride to Deadwood, and I can't speak for Lea or Rachel."

John turned questioning eyes on her. "What about Michael?"

Whether John meant them to or not, those three words cut like a hot knife. Because, as wholeheartedly as she'd set out on this expedition to help Michael, she couldn't ignore the new voice whispering in the back of her head, the one that told her she needed to find Haldin and do whatever it took to find out what they knew about her mom.

It was selfish. She knew that. Her mom was long gone. Helping Michael was infinitely more important. But none of that silenced the void her mother's disappearance had left. After fifteen years, the answers she'd been craving were suddenly dangling in front of her nose, and the void demanded she seize them, no matter the cost to her or anyone else.

But she couldn't say these things to John, who was still watching, waiting for her to tell him how they were going to make his son better again. So she shook her head, at a loss for words.

"We should bring him here if he's able to be moved," John said. "We can go as soon as things are stable here."

"I don't know how to help him," she said slowly.

The beginnings of a frown crinkled John's forehead. "We'll find a way. We'll do whatever we have t—"

"They knew about my mom."

John's frown deepened for a brief moment before it was swept away by shock. Around the room, everyone else turned to her with confused expressions.

She hadn't meant to say it out loud. Not really. Or maybe she had. Either way, it was out. She licked her lips and focused on John.

"I don't how or why, or who they were looking for here, but before that ship flew off, Haldin reached out to me and said they could tell me about what happened to her. And to my family too."

John watched her, one hand covering his mouth, his eyes wide with surprise and something else. Something she couldn't quite place at first but was somehow sure was out of place here and now. Was it worry? Guilt?

She wasn't sure, but her stomach turned when his features shifted to what was unmistakably his thoughtful face.

"Heaven have mercy," he mumbled.

Never mind uneasy. He might as well have punched her in the gut.

This was her mom they were talking about. Her mom who'd simply left for work one day and never come home. That had been precisely two days before a gang of thugs had broken into their house and ruthlessly ripped her family away from her. Two days before she'd lost nearly everything that made her who she was, and only seven more before the bombs had fallen and shattered the rest of the world.

And now here she was, telling John that some total stranger and his alien pal claimed to know what had happened, and all he had was a concerned look and an appeal to his almighty?

"What the fuck, John?"

What did he know? Why wasn't his jaw touching the floor right now?

He laid his hands palm-down on the table and took a deep breath.

A perverse torrent of emotions raged through her, murky streams of hope and dread viscously churning in her head and gut as she waited for him to speak. What was he keeping from her? Had *been* keeping from her all this time?

Finally, after the longest seconds of her life, he spoke.

"I've thought for a while now that your mother may have been involved in an early effort to stop the raknoth."

She waited, mouth open, forgetting even to breathe.

"I never knew anything concrete, but after what happened to your family..."

"What are you saying?" Her voice sounded oddly distant in her own ears.

He took another long breath and met her eyes. "It wasn't an accident I showed up so soon after those men attacked your house. I always told you I was coming to visit your mom when I found you, but... I was lying. She called me one day, about a week before she disappeared. Told me she'd done something with her colleagues, something to stop them. I didn't know what 'them' she was talking about. That was before most of us had any idea about the raknoth. And she wouldn't explain what she meant. She just told me things were getting dangerous and that she needed to let me know. She made me promise to check in with your father every day and to find you if anything ever happened."

He looked down, his eyes far away. "I only spoke with her one more time after that, when she called from a public console to tell me to find you and make sure you were safe. No cops. No questions. She was gone before I could ask them anyway."

Rachel felt like someone had wrapped her in a heavy wet blanket. She stared dumbly at John, mouth agape and heart thudding in some distant corner of her awareness as she tried to process anything through the dull buzz that dominated her mind.

"Why?" she finally whispered.

Why what? Why everything. With each passing second, another thousand of the infernal questions crawled into her mind. She grabbed one by the scruff and threw it out.

"Why didn't you tell me this sooner? Before…"

Before what? Before she'd come to know some modicum of peace living out her days protecting the people of Unity? Before Michael had run off to join the Resistance? Had she known what John had just told her, she probably would have gone with him.

Christ, had that been the reason Michael had gone in the first place? Had he known about all of this?

"It was a hard decision," John said. "One of the hardest I've ever had to make. But I didn't have any real answers. Just more questions. I couldn't see what good it would do you, especially when you were already fighting so hard to move past what had happened. It wasn't until the raknoth came walking out of the ashes of the Catastrophe that I even started to piece together what she might have been trying to tell me. And even then, it was only conjecture. I was only trying to do what I thought was best for you." He reached for her hand across the table. "I'm sorry, Goldfish."

The entire time he'd been speaking, what little space in her mind hadn't been rendered utterly numb with shock had been waiting for the inevitable explosion of indignant outrage. It didn't come. Not until John's hand settled over hers.

She yanked her hands back. They curled into fists of their own accord and slammed to the table, and with the impact came the flood of anger she'd been waiting for.

"You should have told me." She growled the words like a curse.

John pulled his hands back and held them up in surrender. "I'm sorry. I made a decision, and—"

She smacked the table again and was on her feet before she'd even thought about it. "And you were just trying to protect me? Bullshit! That wasn't your decision to make. I could have..."

She flexed her fists, uncertain as to exactly what she could have done and suddenly acutely aware of the way the others in the room were watching her, like she was a bomb ready to explode. All of them except Jarek, whose uncommonly stern gaze remained on John.

She'd nearly forgotten they were all there, absorbed as she'd been in her own thoughts. Now, though, she needed to get out of here. She needed a quiet place to think.

She turned for the door and went to find one, not bothering to stop when Lea called her name, or when John did the same.

She stomped up the stairs and through the halls toward her bedroom, lamenting the fact that she didn't have a raknoth to blow through the walls right now.

She'd nearly blown a gasket a few days ago when she'd realized Michael had lied to her about something that was only tangentially her business. John was pretty much the only other person in the world she'd thought she could trust. For him to drop this bomb on her...

It was too much, and she either needed to hit something or curl up in a ball and not come out for a few days.

When was the last time she'd even properly slept? Too long ago. That was for sure. But peaceful sleep seemed like the last thing she was about to find right now.

John's words played through her head on repeat, adding a new layer of hurt with each pass.

Maybe he had been wise—merciful, even—to keep these cryptic details to himself all these years...

No. Shit on that. He should have told her. Her mom, her burden to bear. And she needed to know—now more than ever.

She needed to find Haldin and Alton. They seemed to have far more answers than what John could give her anyway. Answers she couldn't turn away from now that old wounds had been reopened. Answers she'd probably always needed deep down. And maybe she could help Michael too while she was at it.

It was raknoth tech that had caused Michael's condition, and those two seemed to know more about the raknoth than anyone else she'd met. If anyone could explain what had happened to Michael, it might be them. The Red King sure as hell wasn't about to give them anything. Anything more than ominous scraps, at least. Haldin and Alton might even be able to tell them something about the nest and this business with the rakul.

The familiar comfort of her room turned out to be not so comforting. Certainly not like home should feel.

Had it really only been a week ago that she'd set out to find her missing brother? It felt like years. Too much had happened in that short time, and now... She wasn't quite sure what now.

But that could probably wait until she'd had a desperately needed shower and some decent sleep.

After that, she'd find out what happened to her mom all those years ago. She'd find out how to help Michael. She'd fix it all, and then she'd tell them and the rest of the world to shove it and go stick her head back in the sand where it was quiet and boring and the people she loved didn't keep things from her.

She just needed to talk to Haldin and Alton first.

And lucky for her, she knew exactly where to find them.

CHAPTER ELEVEN

Jarek raised a hand to knock on the door he was reasonably sure
was Rachel's. The hand froze, suspended a few inches from the
door by some insidious working of his own subconscious.

Why had he come here, again? It had sounded like a good
enough idea in the comfort of his own guest room just a few minutes
ago, but now that he was here…

"Oh, do go on, sir," Al said in his earpiece.

He shot a glare at Fela's empty form, which was parading obediently along behind him to the tune of Al's command, and bit back a
retort for fear of announcing his presence.

Mr. Robot could say what he would. He wasn't the one who had to
deal with all this… whatever it was. When the freaking blood-sucking
aliens told you trouble was on the way, what were you supposed to do
with that?

Get out of the way, maybe.

That was the easy answer. This was all getting too complicated too
fast. It had only been a few days ago that the Resistance had been fully
intending to take Fela from him, and now he was out here running
errands for them?

No. Not for them. He was here for himself. Looking out for

numero uno. If the sky was about to fall, he needed to know about it. It was a matter of survival. And given the way Alton the raknoth had reacted to mention of the rakul, it looked like Jarek may have been wise to stick around.

Of course, none of that really explained why was he standing outside Rachel's door like a damned nervous teenager right now.

A muffled creak from the other side of the door jolted him like an electric shock to the chest. Someone was coming. The doorknob turned with a rattle and a click, and the door swept inward before his startled brain could decide to bolt or put on his patented carefree grin.

He settled for jamming his hands in his pockets.

Rachel eyed him through the cracked door. "What do you want?"

"I…"

What *did* he want? World peace? Unlimited bacon?

Her?

Because that's why he was standing here, wasn't it?

He swallowed. "… wanted to check on you."

Flames might as well have blazed to life in her eyes. "If you think I need someone to come and—"

"Not because I think you need it," he said, holding his hands up in peace. "I just… Shit, I don't know. I was worried about you, I guess." He shook his head and turned to go. "So sorry for the interruption, princess. Won't happen agai—"

"Jarek."

He paused at the tone of her voice and waited for the heat in his face to drop a few degrees before turning to face her. She dropped his gaze after only a second, and silence stretched between them.

"You took the suit off," she finally said.

"Guy's gotta shower sometime."

"I didn't know Fela could follow you around," she said, finally pulling the door fully open.

She was wearing a comfy-looking pair of shorts and a Swarthmore College t-shirt. He'd never seen her like this. Barefoot. Dressed for comfort rather than kicking asses through walls. He'd been attracted to her since they'd met—doubly so after she'd laid the hurt on a couple rooms' worth of armed guards and knocked him on his own ass.

But the more he was around her—and now seeing her in all her irritated, pajamaed glory...

She was beautiful.

Jarek tore his gaze from Rachel to look at the exosuit, which his muddled brain pointed out had been standing out of Rachel's line of sight when she'd made the comment.

Stupid.

His own mind was warded from Rachel's senses, but he'd completely forgotten about Fela.

"I knew I was being quiet," he muttered.

The first traces of a smile tugged at Rachel's mouth. "I'm a hard girl to sneak up on sometimes. How'd you even lose her in the first place if she can move on her own?"

"Not on her own, ma'am," Al said from Fela's speakers. "And as for the how, I believe it boils down to bad decisions."

Jarek grimaced. "A lot of bad decisions."

"And copious amounts of alcohol," Al added.

"Yeah thanks, Mr. Robot."

"And that's not even to mention the particularly devious redhea—"

"I think she gets the picture, buddy."

Rachel shifted her moody stare back and forth between them. "Yeah, I think I get it all right."

Jarek clasped his hands together. "Fantastic. Let's skip the boring details, then."

She arched an eyebrow. "Boring, were they?"

He lingered with his mouth half open. "Is there a right answer to this question?"

"Only if you think I care."

"Ah. Then yes. Super boring."

She rolled her eyes and backed away from the door and into her room.

Jarek started to follow but lingered at the doorway. "I'm lost. Was that princess-speak for 'come hither'?"

She sank to the edge of her bed. "More like stay or leave, but just get out of the damn hallway whatever you do."

"Ah." Jarek glanced back and forth down the empty hallway and gestured to Fela. "After you, buddy."

Al dutifully marched Fela into the room and sank the suit quietly into the corner. Jarek followed and shut the door behind them.

"Well lucky me," Rachel said.

She was leaning back, propped up by her arms, with her legs crossed and—

Jesus, had her legs always looked that good underneath those jeans?

He forcefully raised his gaze and fixed her with what he hoped passed for a level look. "Do you wanna talk?"

She plopped back on the bed with a loud huff and waved a helpless hand. "What, because this is our thing now? We fight off the bad guys and then talk about our feelings to cope with the stress?"

"Hey, I'm perfectly amenable to destressing by more enjoyable means if the lady doth desire."

It was out of his mouth before he'd thought twice. Smooth as a fresh ream of goddamn sandpaper.

She raised her head from the bed just enough to show him an arched brow. "I thought you were into redheads."

He turned to look out the window at the fading hint of sunlight in the distance. "That was just a distraction."

Her voice was soft behind him. "And this wouldn't be?"

He glanced back to find her watching him with an indiscernible expression. The gaze deepened until Jarek broke eye contact and sank into a nearby desk chair to keep his heart from escaping through his throat.

Rachel sat up to face him. "You're kind of a walking contradiction, you know that?"

"Always keep 'em guessing. Tactics 101."

"You have me right where you want me, huh?"

He grinned. "I don't know if I'd put it that way."

"And on and on we go." She scooted back on the bed to sit cross-legged and lean against the wall. "So what did you wanna talk about?"

He shrugged. "You know. The Overlord attacking your childhood home. The coming doom. Michael." He hooked a thumb toward the door. "That itty bitty chestnut of life-altering news that spilled out earlier. We've got a few options, I guess."

She looked away, a shadow settling over her expression. "And what if I don't like those options?"

"Al tells a mean riddle when the mood's right."

A faint smile broke through as she glanced at Fela's collapsed form. "I bet he does."

"Come on, Rache," he said softly. "It's been a hell of a week. You don't have to hold it all in."

She considered him. "You don't really strike me as the listener type."

He smiled. "Can't say I'd know. But given the locale, I suppose I could give it the ol' college try."

She pursed her lips then shrugged. "Fine. I'm pissed."

"Ahh, yes. And how does that make you feel? Wait—wrong line."

She narrowed her eyes at him. "Ha ha."

"Seriously, though"—he crossed a leg and leaned back—"why are you pissed at John?"

She tensed. "What, you agree with him lying to 'protect' me?"

"Nope. Just asking to get you to talk. Read it in a book once."

She eyed him speculatively. "No you didn't."

He grinned. "I totally didn't. Let's try it anyway."

"Fine. I'm pissed because he lied to me. And because Michael did too, and now I feel like, I don't know. Like I'm not sure what the hell to do about any of it."

"I think I get what you mean," he said. He meant it too, as off-centered as he'd been by the events of the past week. "And I know how shitty it can feel to have your faith in someone let down like that, but… Okay, so you're not sure what to do. What do you want to do?"

"Find out what happened to my mom," she said without a second's hesitation. "And how I can help Michael." She cocked her head. "And maybe, if there's still time, we can try to figure out whether the shit's actually about to hit."

"See, I'd say that all sounds pretty reasonable. Responsible, even. That last part especially."

He couldn't blame her for wanting to learn more about her mom. And besides, getting that particular scoop meant talking to Haldin and Alton, which also happened to be their best shot at learning about this rakul retribution, and he was all for that.

And if it all just so happened to be accomplished as a "we" instead of a "he," that wouldn't be the worst thing in the world either, right?

"Truly, sir?" Al asked quietly in his earpiece. "That's all you have? Reasonable?"

Jarek suppressed the urge to tell him to shove a bolt in it and kept his focus on Rachel.

"I know that," she said. "I just... I don't know—feel lost I guess, like at some point I had a side, or some kind of equilibrium at least, and now it's just gone."

"Now you're really preaching to the choir, lady."

She shook her head as if she hadn't heard him. "When did any of this shit become our responsibility? I just wanted to make sure Michael was okay and now what? He's in a goddamn coma, Jarek. And now I'm out here chasing alien ships for fucking clues, and there's the rakul, and now my mom, and I—"

Her voice caught, and she visibly swallowed and reset herself with a deep breath.

"I just didn't expect this. Any of it." Her gaze snapped back from far away, and she focused on him with a wan smile. "Least of all to be talking it all over with the goddamn Soldier of Charity himself."

She could say that again, a thousand times over. The first part, at least. If he'd had his way from the start, the Resistance would have returned Fela to him as gracious payment for his rescuing Michael from the Red Fortress and he would've flown off into the sunset, fully armored and worry free.

But they hadn't, and he hadn't. The nest had activated, or

exploded, or ejaculated, or whatever the hell it had done, and now they had at least two raknoth forecasting big bad clouds of doom with just enough conviction that he couldn't quite bring himself to walk away and risk "retribution" falling down on his oblivious head.

"Goldilocks, if I've learned anything in the past fifteen years—and spoiler alert, I totally have—it's that shit doesn't go to plan out there. Pretty much ever. And granted, I might bring it on myself at times, but I really feel like the bigger the stick you walk around with, the bigger the problems life will whip out and slap you right in the face with."

"Does everything have to be phallic with you?"

"Everything."

She snorted. "So, what, you're saying I have a big stick?"

He glanced pointedly at the staff resting against the wall at the foot of her bed. "I mean, it's no Whacker, but yeah. You might just have the biggest stick I've ever seen. And, all things considered, I think you're handling it pretty damn well."

"You sure know how to flatter a girl."

A small silence stretched between them.

"What are you hoping you'll learn?" he finally asked. "About your mom, I mean."

Every part of her seemed to tighten at once, but she relaxed a degree or two before answering. "Well there's the obvious stuff. Where she went. Why she went. What she was up to. If she was actually trying to stop the raknoth before the Catastrophe... I don't know what I'd do with that, but I still wanna know."

"I get it."

"Maybe it's stupid. It's not like I'm the only one who lost family back then. Most of the goddamn world did. But I just need to know."

"I don't think it's stupid at all," he said softly. "Those kinds of open doors, they'll eat at you until there's nothing left."

Rachel only bobbed her head in absentminded agreement.

Jarek weighed his next words carefully. "After she disappeared..." Tension was creeping back into Rachel's shoulders, but he decided to push on. "What happened when those men came for your family?"

She looked down and studied her hands for a long stretch.

"They got them," she finally said. "My dad. My grams. They made me watch while..." She shook her head. "And then they started on me."

"How did you survive?"

"I don't know. I don't remember. The—whatever you wanna call it —the trauma, I guess, must have flipped the switch on my abilities. One minute I was there, terrified and about to die. I remember this feeling, like something had physically broken inside of me, and there was this sensation like I'd fallen into a whitewater rapid made of pure electricity. And then, next I knew, I was waking up in John's house so hurt and exhausted that he had to spoon feed me for a week. It was only years later, once I'd come to realize that sensation had basically been channeling overload, that John told me about how he'd seen two men fleeing the house when he'd arrived, and how he'd found two more inside, so battered he wasn't sure if they were dead or alive."

"Jesus. And you?"

"Passed out like a light the moment he found me, apparently." She shook her head. "I really don't remember any of it after Dad and Grams were..."

She stayed there, head gently shaking back and forth and eyes staring through the floor and off to distant horrible memories that she couldn't quite step away from now that she'd dredged them up.

Slowly, gently as he could, Jarek stood and crossed to her bed with tentative steps. Rachel's distant gaze held fixed to that same spot, and she said nothing when he sank carefully to the edge of the bed.

It was only when he laid a hand on the soft skin of her thigh that she stirred and met his eyes.

"I've never told anyone about this. Besides Michael and John, I mean."

"Us weary souls have to stick together, I guess." He patted her leg and withdrew his hand, suddenly feeling like the contact was somehow inappropriate for the moment, which in turn made him wonder when the hell he'd started worrying about that kind of thing. "I'm, uh... I'm glad you're telling me."

When he looked back up, she was still watching him. "I was wrong, you know."

"Oh yeah?"

She nodded, the beginnings of a soft smile in her eyes. "If someone had told me you were the guy I was going to be spilling my guts to back when I met you in that brig, I would have kicked them in the pants. But you're not so terrible at the whole listening thing."

He searched her face until her eyes inexorably drew him in. He couldn't have looked away if he'd wanted to. And he didn't want to.

"And how does *that* make you feel?" Somewhere beyond his thudding heart and his tunnel vision of those lovely hazel eyes, he recognized the voice as his own.

Then Rachel snorted and broke the spell of their gaze with a light push to his chest. "Like maybe we should get some sleep while we can if we're gonna keep walking around with these big sticks of ours."

"Yeah." Jarek glanced out the window for a distraction and realized it was dark now. "Never know what tomorrow's gonna bring, I guess."

"Answers, hopefully."

He gave a conciliatory tilt of his head and stood. "Hopefully."

She studied him thoughtfully. "So you're still in?"

"I came here, didn't I? You think I'm just gonna fly off now that things are getting interesting?"

"I kind of thought flying off was always the plan once you had Fela back."

Her and him both.

"Well, we know what happens to plans out there. I might have to sleep inside Fela with one eye open around the Resistance for, well, always, but we both saw that nest go off. We heard what few words Stumpy had to say about it, and then that thing with Alton… I've got a bad feeling about this, and I don't think it's going away until I get some real answers." He shrugged. "Plus, you know, maybe it wouldn't be the worst thing to see you get what you want too."

"Careful, mister. Any closer and you're gonna go making me think you care."

"Eh, we're all entitled to our opinions, I guess."

She gave him an indignant look and made a shooing motion toward the door.

He paused with his hand on the doorknob as something occurred to him. "So am I understanding correctly that John basically scooped you up and fled an active crime scene based solely on a pair of cryptic warnings from your mom? He doesn't really seem like the law-breaking type."

She gave a weak smile. "I guess my mom had sufficiently rattled his cage. He trusted her. I think he might have even loved her once upon a time, to listen to him talk… But yeah, if the Catastrophe hadn't happened a week later, he probably would've had a lot of explaining to do to the authorities at some point."

"Hmm. The shit hits in mysterious ways."

She smiled. "There's a bumper sticker if I ever heard one."

He opened the door and held it as Al dutifully marched Fela out of the room.

Jarek lingered at the threshold. "We'll find out what happened to her, Rache. Tomorrow. I'll beat it out of them myself if I have to."

She gave a slow nod, holding his gaze with a serious expression. "Thank you."

"Goodnight, Goldilocks."

When he pulled the door shut and turned for his room, Fela was waiting for him in the hallway with a hand raised high-five style.

"Seriously?" he whispered.

Al shrugged Fela's shoulders and switched from high-five to fist bump.

Jarek shook his head and bumped the exosuit's extended fist. "This is what you get excited for?"

"I can't help it, sir. Forgive me if I'm excited to see my human growing up."

Jarek huffed and started down the hallway. "Yeah, well, try not to get too excited until we find out what the hell we're dealing with. This could all turn sideways real fast."

"I believe that's exactly when having a reliable partner at your side comes in handy, sir."

Jarek didn't argue with that.

He couldn't decide what to think of the Resistance right now. If it turned out working alongside them was a good call, he might be able to stomach it. That being said, if HQ happened to go up in flames tomorrow, he wouldn't be shedding tears either.

Having Rachel's back, on the other hand... He didn't think he could go wrong there.

So tomorrow, they'd find their answers. And after that...

Well, he'd just have to see.

CHAPTER TWELVE

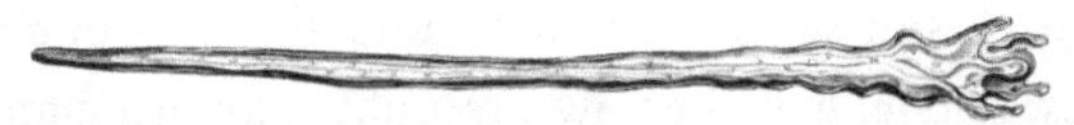

Rachel was surprised to see bright sunlight pouring into her room when she woke. As tired as she'd been when she'd laid down last night, it had seemed like a tall order to hope for anything resembling peaceful sleep with so much chaos going through her head. Apparently her brain had finally hit a tipping point and decided to say, "Fuck it," for the night.

She wasn't about to complain. As far as she could tell, she'd slept like a titanium brick, and she'd desperately needed it. Sleep hadn't worked miracles, really only graduating her from feeling like death to feeling like shit, but it was better than she'd had for too long now.

Jarek's visit had been unexpected. And unexpectedly not awful if she was being honest. The way he could slip from immature man-child one minute to caring, level-headed companion the next—not to mention the way he looked at her sometimes…

Whatever else she could say about Jarek Slater, he was always full of surprises—and not all of them bad. She was more than a little glad he'd stuck around and would have her back today when they met Haldin and Alton. Assuming those two actually showed at her mom's old lab.

She woke her comm to call Pryce for an update on Michael and saw he'd already left a message a couple hours earlier: *Still stable. No news is good news.*

Was it really, though? After what had happened to Michael, who knew?

She got dressed and went to find Jarek and the others. They were all awake and already eating when she arrived at the dining hall, with Fela standing at attention behind Jarek.

Mumbled good mornings—even chipper, in Lea's case—drifted her direction as she settled down to join them at one of the hall's several tables. Rachel gave her own mumbled greeting and dug into a bowl of oatmeal with a contented sigh. Across the table, Jarek was watching her with an amused look.

"What?" she asked, figuring it had something to with their talk last night.

He shook his head, doing a poor job of containing his grin, then looked pointedly at her bowl. "Oh nothing. I just thought the oatmeal was a little cold"—he bumped Alaric with an elbow—"but Alaric swore it was too hot. What do you think?"

She frowned at him and took another bite. "It's fine, what are you..."

Oh. Goldilocks. How hilarious.

She rolled her eyes. "Really?"

He shrugged and finally let that wolfish grin of his out in full. "You only get so many chances."

Rachel finished her breakfast as quickly as she comfortably could and suggested they hit the road (or sky, as Jarek insisted on pointing out). As much as she would have loved to go find a quiet spot to curl up and relax for a year or two, they had a raknoth and a strange arcanist to find, and too many time-sensitive questions to answer.

John came and, despite her protests, insisted on walking them out to the ship to see them off. Silence stretched between them along the way, uncomfortable as it was unusual. They'd rarely fought since Rachel had made it past her mid-teens.

Yesterday, she'd been plenty pissed, but now, after having talked things through with Jarek and gotten a good night's sleep, she wasn't rightly sure she was angry with John so much as at her lack of answers when it came to her mom. That being said, she was also hesitant to admit that to John, or that maybe she understood why he'd done what he'd done.

Tense as it was, the silence didn't stop John from taking one more crack at trying to smother her to death bear-hug style when they reached Jarek's ship and the others piled inside to give them a moment.

"I'm sorry, Goldfish," he said. "I know it doesn't change anything, but I had to say it before you left. You be careful out there. Whatever you might learn, just remember… well, you can't change the past, but you know you'll always have family here, right?"

Her stubborn defensiveness softened at that. "I know," she said quietly. She cocked her head. "And hey, if some of the other things we've been hearing have been even half true, we might have bigger things to worry about anyways."

"That doesn't make a father feel better about watching his girl fly off into the unknown."

She gave him a sad smile. "Hey, I never wanted to be a part of this either." She glanced at the ship. "But between Michael and all the doomsday talk, it's not like I could walk away and just pretend like everything's normal again."

John nodded and kissed her on the forehead. "I know. And I'm proud of you. For everything. Now tell an old man what he wants to hear."

Her lips pulled into a smile. "I'll be careful. And I'll see you again soon."

She turned and boarded the ship before either of them had a chance to get too emotional.

Their flight to the northwestern area of Philadelphia was a short one, and their conversation consisted mostly of Lea finding a dozen different ways to ask, "Are we really sure about this, guys?"

It was a fair question. If Haldin and Alton were so inclined to set a trap for them, they would be walking straight into it. Then again, if those two had wanted them dead and gone, they could have just left

Mosen to have at them along with his raknoth trio and their sizable contingent of armed men. She didn't trust the raknoth and the arcanist—not by a long shot—but she didn't think they were planning on trying to kill her and her friends. Not yet, at least.

More familiar sights began to stand out as they flew over what had once been the Main Line, up Route 1 and over the Schuylkill River. It had been a long time since she'd been up here, and she wasn't used to seeing it all from an aerial view, but that didn't stop waves of nostalgia and longing from rolling over her as she spotted an old restaurant here, or an old hiking trail there—reminders of the life that had been so violently taken from her.

Nostalgia morphed into cold dread and snaked its way around her gut as they soared over the rising hill of Midvale Avenue. She didn't want to look down at the rooftops of all those once mighty, pristine houses. She didn't want to spot the one that had been hers—the place where she'd lost everything.

An armored hand squeezed her shoulder, and she looked back to find Jarek behind her, having finished suiting up in the back cabin. He couldn't have known exactly what was going through her head, but he must've seen that something was up.

Rachel tried to give him a smile then turned back to direct Al to their destination as Jarek dropped into the pilot's seat beside her. Her directions weren't necessary, as they'd already marked the location on the map, but she pointed the way nonetheless.

A minute later, they were crawling over one last block of houses to look down at the open grounds and the large, C-shaped body of the Drexel College of Medicine.

Somehow, despite the Catastrophe and the fifteen years that had passed, the old building looked just as she remembered. Aside from the big alien ship sitting out in the front lawn, that is.

Al pulled the ship to a resting hover.

"Welp," Jarek said, "guess it's about time for strange encounters part two."

Rachel couldn't do much more than stare at her mom's old workplace. "I never thought I'd come back here," she finally said.

She felt Jarek's gaze linger on her.

"Not even to meet some weirdo arcanist pretty boy and his blood-sucking alien sidekick by their spaceship?"

The ghost of a smile pulled at her lips as she met his eyes. "So you think he's pretty?"

Jarek grinned. "Touché, Goldilocks… Touché."

"And spaceship?" she added.

"I mean"—Jarek waved in the ship's direction—"if the space shoe fits…"

"Yeah," Rachel said slowly, staring at the strange ship. "What kind of shit decisions did we all make to end up here?"

"Peyote," Jarek said. "Not even once."

He moved into the back cabin and reappeared shortly with guns and sword strapped on. "Everyone ready?"

Nods all around.

"Right," Jarek said. "Take us down, Al."

No one was in sight around the alien ship as they descended. Once Al dropped the boarding ramp and swiveled the ship around to face them toward the other ship, though, Haldin was sitting at the bottom of a slender staircase that had descended from the side of their ship.

He watched them from across the twenty yards that separated them and slowly raised a hand in greeting.

Alton appeared at the top of the ship's steps and descended behind Haldin as Rachel and the others deboarded and Al locked Jarek's ship up behind them. Haldin stood and stepped down to the patchy grass to clear the way for Alton, and the slender staircase folded in on itself behind them, moving with a kind of organic grace, until it merged smoothly with the ship's hull.

A few seconds later, the alien ship lifted silently from the ground.

At first, its movements seemed more clunky and awkward than the smooth flight they'd witnessed the day before when the ship had lured Mosen and his squad of assholes away from Unity. As it rose above Drexel, though, the ship stabilized and shot off northward.

"Guess there's more than two of them, then," Jarek mumbled beside her.

It seemed that way. As Alton and Haldin approached, though, the thought was quickly lost in a sea of more pressing questions.

"Oh hey, guys," Jarek called. "Fancy seeing you here. Long time and all that." He pointed skyward after the departing ship. "Didn't wanna introduce us to the fam?"

"Al'Krogoth and his ilk would have a much easier time finding us here with that ship sitting out front," Alton said. "The precaution seemed prudent."

"Right, yeah," Jarek said. "Good call. Al-who now?"

"Al'Krogoth," Alton said. "Zar'Golga's second-in-command, and the leader of the raiding party you confronted back at Unity."

"The brownish one," Haldin said.

"Ahh," Jarek said. "Rusty. Gotcha. Yeah, that guy was a dick."

Alton didn't seem to disagree. Haldin looked a bit amused.

"Why did you bring us here?" Rachel asked.

"You know at least part of the answer to that," Alton said, studying her curiously.

"My mom was a professor here, yeah. What does that have to do with anything?"

Alton gave her the kind of smile that was normally reserved for children who'd asked adorable but ultimately ridiculous questions. "Everything." He looked over his shoulder at the old building. "This is where it all started."

"Yeah," Jarek said, "which is drama-queen speak for…?"

Alton gave Jarek an amused look. "For 'this is where her mother started the infection that nearly wiped my people from the face of the Earth.'" Alton turned his smile on Rachel. "So maybe we should all step inside to chat."

CHAPTER THIRTEEN

I nside, the halls of Drexel felt more cramped and claustrophobic than Rachel remembered, but maybe that was just the lack of lighting talking, or the fact that she'd been smaller the last time she'd been here. The accumulated broken glass and debris left by what she imagined had been a steady stream of looters and junkies looking to find some fun shit in the big science labs didn't really help the place feel warm and welcoming either.

Most of those looters had probably been sorely disappointed, just like Rachel had been on the few occasions her mom had let her explore the lab instead of sitting around in her office, bored to death and wondering when they'd go home. Contrary to what the cartoons and movies had told her, it turned out most of the toys in real-life biology labs were little fun to play with and unbelievably expensive to break.

There was a muttered curse and a scuffling sound from the second floor overlook as they entered the building. The following footsteps headed steadily away, though, and they shrugged them off as those of a startled looter.

Tracing her way along familiar hallways toward her mom's old lab, the nostalgia returned in full force. In the reactionary map of her mind, this place was somehow clear of the stain of tragedy that would forever tarnish her childhood home. In her mind, this was still just the place her mom had worked.

Given what Alton had said outside, though, that perception might be about to change.

"What did you mean back there?" Rachel asked as they came out of the stairwell on the second floor and started for the south side of the building. "About my mom starting an infection, I mean."

"Exactly what I said," Alton said. "It wasn't just her, of course, but she was the one who put the"—he waved a hand—"*je ne sais quoi* into the virus that left us dependent on human blood."

"And why the hell would she do that?" She paused by the door to her mom's old lab, which Alton had passed by. "It's this one, by the way."

Alton looked at a door down the hall then back to her and shrugged. "Perhaps it was one of her collaborators' labs they worked in. It matters very little."

"Well if it matters very little," she said, reaching for the door handle.

The knob turned, but the door caught on a deadbolt, which was kind of surprising given that the building had clearly had its fair share of people poking around for goodies.

"Allow me," Alton said, a dim red glow springing up in his eyes as he stepped toward the door.

"Easy there, Red," Jarek said, stepping up behind Rachel. "I got it."

Rachel rolled her eyes, reached out with her mind, and applied the minute force required to slide the deadbolt open. She shook her head at them. "Neanderthals."

Haldin smiled at her while Jarek and Alton frowned at one another.

She held the door open for everyone but Alaric, who insisted she go first. She stepped through the door and straight into another afternoon of her childhood.

Everything was more or less as she remembered—shelves and

black bench tops all laden with scales, beakers, flasks, pipettes, and dozens of other instruments. Everything appeared to be in half-decent condition, aside from the light coat of dust that covered every horizontal surface.

Haldin and the others spread out through the lab space, inspecting this or that.

A tired sigh escaped Rachel as she turned back to Alton. "You didn't answer my question. Why would my mom want to make you…"

"Our dependence on human blood was not the desired effect," Alton said. "The virus was only intended to be lethal to us and benign to you. They succeeded at both of those goals, as well as at dispersing the virus across much of the planet's population. Many of my people grew horribly ill. Most of them died before we even understood what had happened. By the time we traced the malady back here, we'd ceased feeding, hoping to at least slow the disease's progression. No one had yet realized the blood that carried the curse was the only treatment for it as well."

"So you were already feeding before this all went down," Jarek said.

Alton inclined his head. "On occasion. It has been our way for millennia and for dozens of planets and species before yours. We are bred predators."

"That's all very poetic and guilt-free," Jarek said, "but it sounds like we were just being good prey, adapting to survive. And for that you blow up the damn planet?"

Alton wrinkled his nose. "That was not a democratic decision. The eldest of us at the time was already addled with the infection when he commanded the extermination of Earth, but the raknoth are a loyal people. Enough of them were desperate and afraid enough to listen."

"You make it sound like you weren't involved in any of this," Rachel said.

Alton glanced at Haldin. "I went elsewhere when the madness was unfolding."

"Convenient," Rachel said.

"Not for the people elsewhere," Haldin muttered.

Where the hell was this elsewhere? And, more importantly, "Why are you even telling us all of this? Let's say we decide to believe anything you're saying. What's your end game here?"

"In a word, peace," Alton said.

Jarek gave a bark of laughter. Lea and Alaric contained themselves but looked no less dubious.

"I think you've lost us," Rachel said.

"My people have no particular love for this planet—"

"No kidding," Jarek said.

"—but we cannot leave. As I said, for now, we're bound to the human race."

"Your food," Rachel said.

"More like our vitamins. The blood is required to keep the infection at bay, but it is not our sole sustenance."

"I don't understand," Rachel said. "That sounds like a fixable problem. One that doesn't require human lives."

"I don't disagree," Alton said. "Even ridding ourselves of the virus completely should have proved no more than a minor annoyance. We are quite adept at manipulating biological machinery to our will, and yet none of us have been able to crack the solution to whatever it is your mother created."

"Why do you think it was her?" Rachel asked.

"Because that's what her collaborators told us the day we showed up here," Alton said. "They only laid the groundwork. They didn't understand whatever change she'd wrought on the virus after the fact." A knowing smirk crossed Alton's features. "They said it was like sorcery."

There was a scary thought. Her mom had been talented in the same way Rachel was. If she'd decided to play dirty... was it possible she could have used her abilities to produce her very own designer virus? Rachel sure as hell wouldn't have known where to start with such a thing, but she also wasn't a virologist as her mom had been. With enchanting, after you got past givens like control and energy, you were really only limited by your own understanding and imagination. Was there any reason to think it couldn't work on a living organism as well as it did on, say, a staff or a pendant?

More importantly, would her mom really have done something like that? The raknoth were dangerous, vicious killers, true. But viral genocide? She wasn't sure she could believe that one.

But then why was her heart beating so fast right now?

"What did you do with them? What did you do to my mom?"

Alton held up his hands. "I didn't harm your mother. I was merely one of the small group that elected to try to fix our problem instead of taking the human race down with us."

"And I'm just supposed to believe that?"

"Believe what you will," Alton said, "but I never even saw her. When we finally traced the origin of the infection back here, she slipped out just ahead of our arrival." He glanced at her mom's corner office then back to Rachel. "I imagine she was trying to protect you and the rest of her family by leading us on a chase."

Something about the way he said it only deepened the nauseous feeling creeping into her gut. Jarek and the others were watching her as if she were a pressure-triggered bomb that Alton had just stepped on.

"And did you chase her?" she asked quietly, not wanting to hear the answer and at the same time needing to.

Alton watched her, weighing his next words. "The elder of our group sent four of our best hunters after her and…"

Nausea boiled up into her chest, threatening to spill over into rage. She said nothing, waiting for him to confirm something she realized now she'd always known deep down in her gut.

The attack that had robbed her of Dad and Grams, her mom's disappearance—none of it had been an accident. She'd always wondered, had always been suspicious. But now she knew. She could see it right there in Alton's eyes.

Her voice was a ragged whisper. "And?"

Alton dropped her gaze. "And he compelled a small group of common thugs to harass her home in an attempt to—"

Something snapped inside her, and raw, crackling power surged through her before she'd even consciously thought about the channeling. The only thought in her head was putting the motherfucker who'd helped destroy her family through the wall. And she did.

Alton struck the wall with a flash of red eyes and kept on moving, smashing straight through drywall, insulation, and brick with a thudding crash. He disappeared in a mess of flailing limbs, leaving nothing but the sound of a few late-falling bricks and the gentle pour of daylight through the ragged hole in the wall.

Over by the counters, Jarek was facing Haldin, hands half-raised in something like a boxer's stance.

Haldin stepped back, holding out his hands. "Easy, guys. We came to talk, not to hurt you."

Rachel ignored him and crossed to the new hole in the wall.

Below, Alton was picking himself up from the paved parking lot she'd blasted him into, his skin crawling with tendrils of scaly green around his glowing red eyes.

She jumped down after him, channeling energy off her fall and into the air around her so that she touched down lightly from her second story jump.

Alton regained his feet and raised his hands in peace, his eyes dimming and his skin shifting back to that of a normal human.

Rachel drew more energy from her batteries and hit the raknoth in the jaw with a solid telekinetic punch.

Alton jerked back a few steps at the blow but didn't drop his hands. "I'm not here to fight you, Rachel."

She didn't give a damn what he was here to do. Even if he hadn't been the one to make the call, he'd apparently stood by and watched his people destroy her family. He sure as hell didn't get to just decide they could have peace now.

She raised a hand and called forth the energy to lift Alton from the ground. He was heavy, heavier than any creature that size had any business being, but Rachel wasn't exactly in the mood to care. She squeezed her hand into a fist and closed the telekinetic walls in on him with enough force to crush organs and crack bones—on a human, at least. The raknoth made a face of discomfort but otherwise didn't flinch.

She slammed him to the ground with a growl. "What *are* you here for, you son of a bitch?"

He sat up but stayed on the pavement this time, hands still held up in a non-threatening manner. "I came to get my people off this planet before our masters come looking for us."

For a second, Rachel was tempted to see if she could concentrate bursts of heat well enough to burn those creepy eyes of his out of their sockets. With each second Alton remained docile, though, her curiosity regained ground on her anger.

"The rakul?" she asked.

Alton nodded. "As long as we're bound by your blood, we're all in danger."

"What the hell does that have to do with me? Why bring me here?"

"It may be nothing to do with you," Alton said, slowly rising to his feet. "It may be everything."

What the hell was that supposed to mean? If it was some arcane super-virus keeping them here…

"You want me to undo what my mom did?"

Alton said nothing.

"Are you fucking kidding me? You take my mom, my family, you nuke the fucking planet, and then you come to ask me for help? Do you have any idea what those sick fucks did to my family? You ruined everything in my life, AND NOW YOU WANT MY HELP?"

It was only in the following silence that Rachel realized she'd been shouting by the end. She whirled at a soft sound behind her, ready to blow something else through the wall, but it was only Jarek. Behind him, Haldin was touching lightly down to the pavement as she had.

"I'm not expecting you to change what your mother did," Alton said quietly. "But I had hoped that together we might try. Rachel, I… There's not much place for sympathy in our culture. But I wish now that we had handled things differently." His gaze shifted over her shoulder toward Haldin. "Many things."

Jarek stepped up beside her. "Hell of an apology, man. 'Sorry we blew up the planet and murdered everybody, guys, I almost feel bad about it.' Real touching stuff."

Alton's jaw tightened. "I can hardly be blamed for the collective actions of my people. The raknoth have wronged your kind, but it was not solely by my hand, and it was not so much worse than what you have done to species on your own planet in the past."

"Alton." Haldin's tone was reproving as he stepped around them to join the conversation.

"Regardless," Alton said, "there is more at stake here now, and if we do nothing, both of our peoples will pay the price for it."

"It always comes back to the vague doom-mongering with you guys, doesn't it?" Jarek asked. "Maybe you could give us something more specific, like who the hell these masters of yours are."

"You'd understand it's not mongering if you knew what we're potentially dealing with here," Haldin said

Jarek pointed at him. "That's not any less vague, for the record."

"We've answered many of your questions," Alton said. "I think the time has come for you to return the favor and tell us how you learned of the rakul."

The waning flames in her chest flicked back to life at his tone.

Return the favor? As if they owed this bastard anything after—

Jarek laid a hand on her shoulder and squeezed. "We'll tell you what we know as long as you explain what's going on," he said. "Right, Rache?"

She shrugged his hand off. "Fine." She looked at Alton. "Do you know about the nest?"

The tightness in Alton's expression answered for him.

"Right," Jarek said. "Well, we had a bit of a disagreement with a lovely fellow who calls himself the Red King, and long story short, the thing went kablooey."

Haldin turned a grave look on Alton. "Does that mean…?"

Alton didn't seem to hear him at first. He just stood there looking like someone had just told him his house had burnt down with his family inside.

"Alton?" Haldin said.

"Too late," Alton finally mumbled. "Too late. We're too late." He looked at Jarek and Rachel. "How did this happen? You were there? What was a nest doing anywhere near…" He shook his head, apparently at a loss.

Jarek shot Rachel an uncertain look. "One of our friends captured the nest from the Red King. No one knew what it was, and the King wasn't exactly helping matters what with trying to kill us and everything."

"How long?" Alton asked. "Since the nest burst."

"A couple days," Jarek said.

"Our friend was standing right next to it when it happened," Rachel said. "He hasn't woken up since."

If Alton had heard her, he made no sign of it, lost as he seemed to be in his own thoughts.

"We need to know how to help him," Rachel added. "It's important."

Alton snapped out of his funk. "Important? A single life? If a nest has burst, we're talking about the annihilation of every sentient being on this planet."

Rachel had almost been on the verge of feeling like she might have been overreacting to blow Alton through a wall—until he said that.

"This life is important," she said through clenched teeth.

The freaking stones on this guy. Or maybe it wasn't him. Probably, this was just how the raknoth saw humans—numbers and meals, not important, valuable people.

Alton looked at Haldin. "We need to call the others back. If they're coming… We need to visit the Zars and the other clans. We'll save Golga for last. He won't be—"

He broke off and cocked his head as if listening for something. Beside Rachel, Jarek did the same, looking off to the west.

Company?

Rachel was about to ask when Jarek said, "Same crew as before?"

"I believe so," Alton said.

What were they talking abou—

There. The rushing hum of a ship approaching in the distance. No, *ships*.

Jarek started back toward the building where Alaric and Lea were still watching from above.

"Time to go!" he shouted just as three ships crested the line of houses back by the main road, bound straight for them.

CHAPTER FOURTEEN

They didn't have time for this. Jarek waved up to Lea a second time. "Just trust me!"

Lea took one last look at the approaching ships, nodded stiffly, and jumped from the hole Rachel had blown Alton's scaly ass through. Jarek caught her, plopped her to her feet, and waved Alaric on next.

"We can't trust these two," Rachel murmured in his ear. "This might have been a trap all along."

She wasn't wrong, but they also only had about thirty seconds before they were drowning in Overlord troops, and Jarek's finely-tuned bullshit detector had been quiet enough through their interactions with Haldin and Alton that giving them the benefit of the doubt seemed the least of evils at the moment.

"Ship first," he said. "Trust talk later."

The fact that he said it quietly wouldn't matter. Alton would hear both of them with his freaky raknoth senses anyway.

Alaric was preparing to jump and looking none too pleased about it when he instead simply lifted from the ledge and floated smoothly down to join them on the ground below. He shot Rachel a wide-eyed look that still somehow managed to be surly.

"Let's go!" Jarek said.

No one argued. They set off across the paved lot for the front lawn, Haldin and Alton bringing up the rear.

"Al, be a dear," Jarek said.

Across the lawn, the ship's boarding ramp began to lower as Al powered up the ship.

It would be a tight one, but they should be able to squeeze out of there before the approaching ships landed any troops or boxed them in. He glanced at the group around him, running along as fast as their fleshy little legs could carry them. It was maddening to move this slow with enemies incoming. Alton probably could have matched his pace, but there wasn't much to do about the others.

Ahead, Al lifted the ship a couple feet from the ground, preparing to meet them halfway. Before he'd moved more than a few inches, the churning rush of what sounded like a jet engine swooped in from their right flank. The jet sound passed by overhead and was summarily drowned out by the chest-rattling roar of what Jarek could only assume was a freaking dragon of yore.

He followed the sound just in time to see a dark green figure crash down on Alton from above.

They punched into the soft earth with a low thud Jarek felt in his legs, and Alton's attacker raised a clawed hand to strike.

"Traitor!" he boomed.

Jarek jolted to a halt, reaching for his sword. Too late. He was too far to help.

The dark raknoth swiped for Alton's throat.

An invisible train of force plowed him off Alton just before his claws landed. The raknoth was quick, though. He managed to hook onto Alton with his claws and feet and drag him along for the ride.

Haldin produced a pair of long, straight daggers from inside his jacket and stepped after them.

"Jarek!" Rachel hissed from just behind.

Jarek didn't need to look to know what she was thinking.

They could still get away. They didn't know these people. Didn't owe them. One of them was a raknoth, for Christ sake.

Jarek drew his sword anyway.

He didn't trust Haldin, and certainly not Alton, but they couldn't very well run and leave them to die. A glance at the bitter resignation on Rachel's face told him she knew he was right.

Haldin, daggers in hand, pointed a finger and clubbed the dark raknoth with another invisible strike. The blow gave Alton enough of an opening to wriggle out of his hold and roll to his feet just as Toady and Slender Face thumped down to the ground behind the dark raknoth.

So much for making it out ahead of the crowd.

There was a soft whoosh of metal on leather to Jarek's right, then a pair of thunder-cracks. The two new arrivals staggered back as Alaric's first two shots found each of their foreheads. The small bullets didn't do much serious damage, but it never hurt to try, right?

Alton stumbled back to join Haldin as the dark raknoth rose to his feet, red eyes ablaze. Just behind the three raknoth, the three ships—no, four now—floated overhead, descending to bring the rest of the troops, which Jarek knew would include Mosen and Rusty or Al'Krogoth or whatever the hell his name was. One raknoth had been bad enough, but now four? Five?

"Are you guys multiplying or what?" Jarek asked. A glance told him Al had brought the ship close enough, but somehow he didn't think the three raknoth facing off with them would stand idly by while they shuffled aboard and made their escape. "How does that work, even?" he added, poking his two forefingers together. "Do you guys just…?"

The three raknoth ignored him, all staring at Alton.

"Zar'Golga," Alton said, tense and ready beside Haldin.

"Coward," said the dark raknoth—Zar'Golga, apparently—in a low, rumbling voice. "You dare speak to me?"

"You know what?" Jarek said. "He raises a valid point, Alton. It's clearly shameful." He swept the Whacker through a dramatic salute. "We'll just be on our way then, Mr. Zar, sir."

Zar'Golga finally spared Jarek a glance, his reptilian brow furrowed. Behind him, Rusty Al'Krogoth dropped down from the nearest ship, followed by Mosen.

"You will die," Zar'Golga said, his tone matter-of-fact.

"We will all die if the tidings are true and the twelve truly come," Alton said. "You know this, brother."

Zar'Golga bared glistening fangs. "You are no brother to me, traitor." To his posse, he added, "Leave the arcanist alive for questioning. Kill the rest."

The enemy raknoth all sprang forward without hesitation. Al'Krogoth, apparently eager to make good on his earlier threat, leapt straight for Jarek.

With little room for lateral movement and little desire to back up and let Al'Krogoth break their line, Jarek stepped forward to meet the raknoth with a diagonal sweep aimed at the neck. Al'Krogoth maneuvered under the strike with inhuman speed, the blade missing him by a hair's breadth as he charged on.

Jarek twisted out of the raknoth's way in time to avoid the worst of his sweeping claws, but at least a couple of them grazed the left side of Fela's torso with a cringe-worthy screech.

Jarek swept around, stepping after Al'Krogoth and into an overhead swing. Given how handily the raknoth had evaded his first swipe, he wasn't surprised when Al'Krogoth ducked under this one and turned into a neat roll. In fact, he was expecting it, which was why he was ready to nail the bastard with a one-legged mule kick as the raknoth came back to his feet.

"Score!" Jarek cried as his foot met what felt like a steel post. Luckily, he had Fela's strength behind him.

The kick sent Al'Krogoth flying over to crash into his dark green pal, Zar'Golga, who was busy trying to remove Alton's head from his shoulders.

If Al'Krogoth was a steel post, Zar'Golga must've been a lead one. The dark green raknoth barely budged when his rusty comrade slammed into him. Instead, he thrust Al'Krogoth aside with a rough elbow and plunged after Alton.

Next to them, Slender Face and Toady were having at Haldin and Rachel, but the arcanists weren't so easily had. Rachel smashed her staff into Slender Face's side baseball-style and must've added a little something extra judging by the way the raknoth went sailing halfway to the paved lot they'd come from. Haldin took a much subtler approach, twisting gracefully aside from Toady's grab and slamming the raknoth on the back of the head with a dagger pommel as he passed.

Jarek stalked after Al'Krogoth as the raknoth picked himself up. Sporadic gunfire barked to the right as what enemy troops had piled out began taking what shots they could.

It wasn't like they had to worry that much about hitting their bulletproof raknoth commanders, although Mosen was—

Shit, where was Mosen?

A cry from Lea answered that question.

Mosen was wrestling her into submission next to their ship's boarding ramp, where her and Alaric had taken cover. Alaric slammed the butt of his revolver into Mosen's back, which earned him little but the moment it took Mosen to release Lea and shove Alaric into the side of the ship like a paper doll. Jarek had to—

"Incoming, sir!"

Jarek spun around, sweeping his sword low. A rust-colored hand caught his leading arm. He ducked the incoming swipe aimed at his head and drove his left shoulder into Al'Krogoth's bulk, switching the Whacker into a reverse grip as he went.

Al'Krogoth got his feet planted and pushed back, their foreheads nearly touching. The raknoth bared gleaming fangs, crimson fire blazing in his eyes, and rumbled out a battle roar.

Jarek cocked his helmeted head back and slammed it into Al'Krogoth's snout before following up with another shove.

Al'Krogoth snorted and stumbled back a step, shaking his head. Jarek took advantage of the space for a rising reverse-grip sweep of his sword. It probably wasn't a strong enough blow to cleave a raknoth limb, but it managed to take a couple of Al'Krogoth's fingers as the raknoth tried to twist away.

At the top of the swing, Jarek switched his grip and whipped the sword around and back down, aiming for the rest of the arm. Most people would have been sufficiently distracted by losing a few fingers to sit there and get cut down like a good boy, but Al'Krogoth jerked back in time.

Straight into a telekinetic grand slam from Rachel's staff.

There was a low thrum of power, and Al'Krogoth took flight toward the Overlord's troops, most of whom were closer than Jarek had realized, apparently deciding to join the melee instead of watching from the sidelines and hoping to score a lucky shot.

And there were a lot of them.

Shit. Between the raknoth and that many men, even Jarek and Alton would be easily swarmed down. If Alton even had the chance to be. He'd gone full raknoth, his skin shifted to a light green hide and his facial features elongated under his red eyes. More importantly, he was also getting his ass handed to him. As Jarek glanced over, Zar'-Golga caught Alton with a one-two jab and stepped forward with a heavy haymaker only to be bowled off balance by a telekinetic shove from Haldin.

That done, Haldin evaded a grab from Toady and stepped straight into the path of Slender Face rushing in to tackle him from behind. Somehow, Haldin saw it coming, leapt a good ten feet in the air, and turned a neat backflip over the incoming raknoth.

"Help those two," Jarek said to Rachel. Not that Haldin particularly needed it, apparently.

Jarek turned for the ship in time to see Mosen slam Lea into the bulkhead at the top of the boarding ramp, one strong hand at her throat.

"Mosen!" Jarek cried, darting forward to stop him.

Thunder cracked from beside the ship, and Mosen buckled down to one knee and cried out in pain. Alaric stepped around from behind the ship, smoke still rising from the barrel of his revolver. Despite everything, Jarek felt a pang of sympathy for Mosen as he turned a shocked expression back toward his father and Alaric clubbed him across the temple with the butt of his gun.

Mosen sagged, not quite going limp, and Alaric clubbed him again. Mosen hit the deck. Alaric wasted no time in grabbing him by the collar and dragging him laboriously up the boarding ramp. An understandably rattled Lea pulled herself together enough to help him.

Satisfied, Jarek whirled to find Al'Krogoth stalking toward the ship. Off to the left, Alton was on his back again, desperately defending against Zar'Golga's attempts at his throat. Haldin was dancing circles around Toady and Slender Face, trying to come to Alton's aid, and Rachel was busy holding off the incoming troops, a visible pile of spent lead already piling up a few feet ahead of her.

They needed to get out of here.

"Foot soldiers on your six, sir," Al said.

They *really* needed to get out of here.

Jarek spun, indiscriminately sweeping his sword through a wide arc that cut clean through one man's neck and another's head.

"Back it up, motherfuckers!" he cried, a rare kind of panic clutching at him at the mass of bodies pressing in on him.

He was plenty used to being outnumbered, but not like this.

How many would it take to hold Fela down? Ten? Twenty? Whatever the number was, they had it. What he needed to do was pull his head out of his ass and start moving.

Something hit him from behind like a high-speed bulldozer before he could. He managed to land on his side and avoid impaling himself on his own sword, but strong, rust-red arms clamped around him like steel bands and kept him from doing more.

He clenched his jaw and threw his head back once, twice, three times, cracking the back of Fela's helmet into Al'Krogoth's snout with savage force. The raknoth's steel-band arms slackened just enough for Jarek to graduate to elbow strikes. He clawed his way loose and rolled free only for half a dozen men to throw themselves down on him.

More promptly followed, heavy, dark-clad bodies falling in on him from every direction until the sky was blocked from view and his world was reduced to claustrophobic darkness and a sea of strained grunts and constricting arms on every inch of his body.

Discipline broke. Panic took him, and a wild yell erupted from his throat as he punched, kicked, and kneed soldiers off, fighting his way toward freedom. Only there were more men to replace those. And more after that. And then there was Krogoth descending back down on him.

Shit. Shit. Shit.

A low, resounding horn blared somewhere above the pileup. For a moment, everyone on top of him was focused elsewhere.

Jarek exploded at the chance, kicking two distracted troops hard enough to send them bowling over a half dozen more men behind them, punching and elbowing his way into a sitting position. He grabbed the Whacker at his side, rolled backward, sprang to his feet, and beat a hasty retreat.

He glanced back at a second blaring horn, still backpedaling. The dark purplish form of the alien ship was lurching down to the lawn beside Jarek's ship. Two figures were already barreling down the ship's odd stairs: a girl with raven dark hair and a dark staff, and a guy with flaming red hair and enough firepower strapped to his person to level a few city blocks. As those two came, two more leaned out from the port above and opened fire on the swarming mass of Overlord forces. The soldiers responded in kind, and soon the air was full of gunfire.

Jarek whirled back to face Al'Krogoth as the raknoth plunged after him with an enraged roar. He kept backpedaling, dodging a few attacks and catching another on his sword.

When he'd nearly made it back to the ship, Jarek rapidly reversed direction and shouldered into Al'Krogoth, catching the raknoth by surprise. He followed up with a horizontal sword sweep that caught Krogoth across the chest, rending hide and drawing a violent shriek from the raknoth.

Jarek planted a solid sidekick into Krogoth's chest that sent him sprawling back into the pool of enemy troops, then he turned and sprinted for Rachel and the others.

Bullets pelted against Fela's armor until he drew up to Rachel and the frosty air of her busy bullet catcher's protective bubble.

"We gotta go!" he said.

"No shit!" Judging from the pallor of her face, Rachel had already slung more than enough energy around to leave her standing on shaky legs.

Behind them, the redhead and the staff chick had reached Alton and Haldin. Staff Girl stepped fearlessly into the fray and cracked a firm enough blow to Zar'Golga's head to get his undivided attention. Meanwhile, Redhead Rambo helped Alton to his feet and turned his attention to laying down fire at the enemy troops. Staff girl twisted, ducked, and twirled through an elaborate series of evasions as Zar'-Golga bore down on her. Beside them, Haldin did much the same to keep ahead of Toady and Slender Face.

"Al, fly low," Jarek said. "Keep those troops out of the ship."

The ship lifted off and yawed around until the boarding ramp was angled away from the Overlord forces. Jarek cringed when the movement drew enemy fire, but that was better than having their getaway hijacked by enemy forces. Assuming a lucky shot didn't end up crippling the ship completely.

"C'mon," Jarek said.

He charged into the raknoth melee, angling straight toward Slender Face's turned back. The raknoth heard him coming, turned to see Jarek's blade sweeping toward his neck, and dropped just fast enough to avoid losing his head completely.

The Whacker ripped a patch from the raknoth's scaly scalp, and Haldin swooped in on the opening Jarek had created. He took the raknoth by the throat and must have telekinetically swept Slender Face's legs out judging by the way the raknoth crumpled.

Haldin raised a dagger to Slender Face's eye, hesitated, and abandoned his clear kill shot to roll to the side and avoid an incoming Toady. Jarek pressed Toady back with a horizontal cut and aimed a hard stomp at Slender Face's head, but the raknoth was already rolling away.

"Elise!" someone cried. Redhead Rambo, Jarek realized.

Staff Girl—Elise—had either taken a hit or tripped up avoiding one. She was on her back, Zar'Golga stomping toward her.

Haldin rushed for the dark raknoth with a wordless cry. Before he got there, Alton flew in and landed on Zar'Golga piggyback style.

Zar'Golga growled and flailed for a hold on his attacker as Alton tore at his face from behind. Redhead Rambo, trying to help Elise up, took a wild backhand that sent him sailing ten yards across the lawn to land right under Jarek's hovering ship.

"Johnny!" Haldin and Elise cried in unison.

Ahead, Toady was hauling a scalped Slender Face to his feet.

"Rusty's coming back," Rachel said behind him.

"Goddammit," Jarek said, squaring off against the two in front.

"Get to the ship!" Haldin yelled off to the left.

"Where's Johnny?" cried another voice—Elise, he thought.

"Al," Jarek said, "bring the ship—"

Slender Face and Toady leapt for him, claws outstretched. He brought the Whacker up, bracing, and—

The dark prow of the ship yawed around and slammed into the two raknoth mid-leap, sending them careening violently off-course.

"Yeah, Mr. Robot!" Jarek cried.

That threat handled, Jarek spun to face Al'Krogoth beside Rachel.

"Get to the ship," he said, stepping forward to meet the rusty-hided raknoth's charge.

She didn't listen, but he paid that no mind.

All they needed was a second to get clear.

Jarek leapt forward and whipped his sword up for a heavy overhead strike. At the last second, though, he abandoned the feint and swept his arm around to catch a juking Al'Krogoth in a hard clothesline.

The surprise attack didn't quite knock the raknoth from his feet, but it left him too off balance to resist when Jarek dropped the sword, grabbed Al'Krogoth by the throat and arm, and hurled him back at the enemy troop line like an oversized scaly discus.

"Ship!" Jarek barked, scooping up his sword. "Now!"

Rachel didn't argue with him. They were clambering around the rear of the ship when Zar'Golga flew past like a dark green missile propelled by either telekinesis or a lucky hit from Alton.

They kept moving up the boarding ramp, and then Al was gaining altitude, hovering back toward the alien ship that had delivered their reinforcements.

Jarek realized with a jolt that Redhead Rambo—Johnny, was it?—was laid out on the cot. Lea, hovering over him, must have dragged the guy in with Alaric's help. They were at least twenty feet up when something landed on the boarding ramp with a light thunk.

Jarek spun, sword ready, to find Haldin prowling up the ramp. He glanced past Jarek at Johnny, then turned back toward the alien ship, where Alton and Elise had paused at the entry hatch.

Haldin made a skyward gesture, and Jarek got the impression there was communication happening that he wasn't privy to. Whatever it was, Elise and Alton looked less than happy about it as they ducked into the alien ship to escape the incoming enemy fire.

"Mind if we join you?" Haldin called over his shoulder.

The frequency of the bullets slamming into their hull eliminated any room to discuss the matter.

"Go, Al," Jarek said. "Get us out of here."

Al obliged, and Haldin hustled the rest of the way up the boarding ramp as it began to raise.

The cracks and dings of gunfire dulled marginally as the ramp sealed with a hum and a click and then faded off as Al guided the ship up and away. They hurried up to the cockpit to look through the cracked, bullet-riddled windshield as the alien ship rose beside them and jetted off to the east.

Al pointed them north and likewise gunned it, offering their soon-to-be pursuers the debate of deciding which ship to follow.

No one spoke for several minutes as Al took them through a series of course and elevation changes.

Finally, when it was clear they'd left their pursuit behind, the tension began to melt, and Jarek's single-minded battle-high relinquished control back to the ocean of questions swirling through the back of his mind.

Rachel collapsed into the copilot's chair, clearly exhausted and probably still in emotional shock from everything they'd just learned.

Jarek gave the top of her head an affectionate pat, earning himself a tired glare.

He felt for her. The raknoth, this freaking blood curse business… It was a weird enough lot to process even without the added family baggage—and that wasn't even to mention the ominous matter of rakul.

It was starting to look like a good thing he'd decided to stick around after all.

And lucky for them, they'd just gained a new crew member who seemed to know a whole hell of a lot about all of this.

"Well then." Jarek slid his faceplate open and turned to meet Haldin's weary gaze. "Welcome aboard, Pretty Boy."

CHAPTER FIFTEEN

"You're sure he's okay?" Elise asked, her concern showing even on the cockpit console's jittery holo.

Rachel looked back along with Jarek and Haldin, all of them craning their necks to peek at Johnny on the cot in the back cabin.

"Are you kidding me?" Haldin said. "I'm pretty sure this is one of his fantasies. He's probably having the time of his life."

Lea looked up from tending to Johnny long enough to cock an eyebrow at that.

Rachel couldn't see Johnny from where she was sitting, but she thought she heard him mumble something about beautiful women, and then a hand drifted into sight to give a thumbs-up.

Wonderful. Somehow they'd managed to pick up another Jarek. She shook her head and turned back to the holo.

"You're sure you're okay?" Haldin said. "And everyone else?"

Elise gave her own thumbs-up. "No casualties. Aside from Alton's pride, maybe."

"Yeah," Haldin said. "Well, that Zar wasn't exactly a lightweight."

"Zar'Golga," said a voice off screen. "Second eldest of the three

Zars on Earth, assuming nothing's changed since we left. I believe he's the one who's taken to calling himself the Overlord."

Alton came into view looking mostly human once again and in a foul mood. Coincidentally, seeing him immediately fouled Rachel's mood too after everything she'd learned about her mom and the attack on her family.

"That was the Overlord?" Jarek asked from the pilot's seat next to Rachel. "Huh. He was kind of a dick. But that seems to be a common theme with you guys. Also, Zars?"

"It's kind of like a raknoth social rank," Haldin said. "The lowest and youngest is Nan, then comes Al, then Zar."

"How about we skip the sociology lesson and get to brass tacks," Alaric said from the doorway behind.

He didn't look good, which was more than fair considering he'd just shot his own son in both legs and knocked him out with the butt of his gun.

Mosen was securely bound and dosed up with some tranquilizer in the back now. Rachel didn't know the first thing about having kids, but she'd be surprised if Alaric was managing to fly very high above the sanity line right now. That being said, he had a valid point.

After they'd managed to convince themselves they'd left any pursuit far behind, both ships had landed in separate locations to touch base and come up with a plan, and so far, that plan was sorely lacking.

"I think that's a wonderful idea," Jarek said. "Let's start with the basics. Like who the hell are you people?"

Haldin studied Jarek uncertainly.

"I think we're well past the need for secrecy," Alton said.

"Right," Haldin said. "We're, uh, Enochians, I guess you'd say."

Enochians? What the hell did that mean? Unless... No. That was crazy.

"Yeah," Jarek said. "Care to point that motherland out on the map?"

All at once, several tiny details clicked into place and drew Rachel to an impossible conclusion.

"Yeah…" Haldin scrunched his eyes. "We might need a bigger map for that."

It couldn't be.

That Alton had confirmed the raknoth to be otherworldly hadn't been such a shock. As far-fetched as scaly freaking space vampires had sounded just a few weeks earlier, it wasn't such a hard pill to swallow after seeing the raknoth in action.

Haldin on the other hand… Sure, he'd said plenty of odd things. And she had more than a few questions about how exactly he'd come to team up with Alton.

But a freaking alien?

It didn't seem possible. But it was. Somehow, she was suddenly sure of it.

"So," Jarek said slowly, "you're saying you're not from around here, then?"

"That's one way of putting it," Haldin said.

"Greetings, Earthlings," Johnny called from the back cabin in a strained voice.

Haldin fought a smile. "And that's the other way. He's been, uh, 'chomping at the bit,' I think it is, to use that one. Although we were kinda hoping for different circumstances."

"I take what I can get," Johnny called.

Haldin's gaze turned to Rachel, and she realized she was still staring at him like he was… well, like he was a freaking alien.

"Dude, what the…? How is that…?"

Haldin held up his hands in a gesture that said *I know, right?*

"So, Enochians," Jarek said. "As in those from Enochia? Is that a planet?"

Rachel finally managed to turn her stare on Jarek.

Why was his jaw not on the floor along with the rest of theirs?

Jarek met her stare and shrugged. "What? You know I love the *Wars*."

He said it as if the statement somehow fully explained his calm collectedness.

"Yeah, but—Never mind." She looked back to Haldin. "Is he right? You're from—"

"Enochia," Haldin said, nodding. "Or at least, that's what we called it. It's pretty similar to Earth, actually."

"Super convenient," Jarek said as if he were agreeing on something as pedestrian as the features that made for a good summer vacation spot.

"How... Where is it?" Rachel asked.

"About 70,000 light years across your Milky Way galaxy," Alton said from the console holo.

"Oooh," Jarek said. "Yeah, I've never been out that way. Explains that."

Lea emerged from the rear cabin looking incredulous. Even Alaric looked highly surprised, which were two words Rachel had never thought to attribute to the stoic Resistance fighter. Then again, as far as reasons to be surprised went, this one probably belonged around the top of the list.

When Haldin and Alton had first said something about coming "here" to help, she'd thought they meant coming to the freaking Americas or something.

"Okay," she said finally. "Aliens. Check. But you seem, uh, human. More than Alton does, at least." Her stomach turned as a disturbing thought occurred to her. "Are all of you like me?"

Haldin looked confused for a moment, but then understanding dawned in his eyes, and he shook his head. "No, very few Enochians are Shapers like you and I. And yes, we're human."

Shapers? That must be their word for arcanism. Or maybe it was an entirely different art, despite looking and feeling the same. The distinction didn't seem as important at the moment as some of the more basic questions like, for instance, how the hell there were humans on another planet halfway across the galaxy.

She was about to ask when Haldin added, "Our ancestors apparently came from Earth."

Surprise finally registered in Jarek's expression. Better late than never.

"Okay," he said, "well that's pretty mind-fucking."

"Right?" Johnny called from the back cabin.

Lea glanced back and began to protest about something.

"I'm all good." Johnny's voice was closer now. "Promise."

He appeared in the doorway a second later, his hair looking all the redder for the pallor of his face, which was clearly not all good.

"Just a few cracked ribs, I think," he added. "No reason to be a little girl about it." His eyes shot from Lea to Rachel to Elise on the holo. "No offense to our fierce tribe of warrior ladies, of course."

Rachel and Lea—and, Rachel had a feeling, Elise behind them—followed Johnny with critical stares as he sidled over and plopped down on one of the cockpit benches. "I'll just sit here then."

"So I don't get it," Jarek said. "What are you doing here, then? You have raknoth on your planet too?"

"There were seven of them." Haldin looked over at Alton's holo. "Only one left now."

"Does that come in non-vague speak?" Jarek asked.

"I got this," Johnny said, having regained a few shades of life in his pale face. "Check it out. So, basically, when shit was getting hairy here on Earth, Alton's old clan leader led his flock over to Enochia, where the raknoth had apparently stashed a bunch of humans like 1,500 years earlier for sport or whatever—gropped up, I know. Anyway, the seven who made it to Enochia went to work doing their thing. Infiltrating the world order, building an army of hybrids to replace their lost kin, cultivating the human population like livestock for blood to feed said army, you know how it goes."

"Sure, sure," Jarek said, though his intrigue was apparent enough past his casual tone.

"So, long story short," Johnny continued, "Hal and his mentor Carlisle caught onto the raknoth presence the hard way, got branded as terrorists trying to stop them, and basically kept kicking asses until Enochia got its collective shit together and helped finish the job. Once things were under control there and Alton had explained everything to us in full, we all signed up to fly across the galaxy and put an end to this crap before another army of raknoth or, worse, rakul decided to roll up on Enochia."

They all processed that in silence for a long handful of moments. It was preposterous. Outlandish. And yet…

Jesus. What had happened to the days when all they had to worry about were violent marauders?

"In other words," Alton finally said, "we were forthright about our intentions here from the start. Our two peoples share two common problems, and we came to address both of them."

"The blood," Rachel said.

"And the rakul," Lea added.

Alton gave a solemn nod. "But if the latter are already coming, I'm not sure what hope we have."

"What's the big deal?" Rachel asked. "You guys are bulletproof and stronger than anything on the planet. What could possibly be so bad about these rakul that you're all afraid of them?"

Alton showed them a mirthless smile. "The rakul, as far as we know, are the most powerful beings in the universe. They are the masters, the harvesters who reap what the raknoth sow."

"So, not good?" Jarek asked.

"Totally not good," Johnny agreed.

Alton pinched the bridge of his nose and squeezed his eyes shut in irritation.

"The raknoth we tried to interrogate," Rachel said, "the Red King—he mentioned something about retribution, more than once."

"They will visit that and much more on this planet," Alton said. "And likely soon if what you say is true."

"But why?" Rachel said. "Why are they coming here? What did we do?"

"You," Alton said, "like so many species before you, have done nothing to deserve their attention. It is simply in their nature to hunt and destroy. My kin and I, on the other hand, will have surely earned their fury once the messengers find them."

"What did *you* do?" Jarek asked.

Alton's expression soured. "We simply tried to live free from their reign. For millennia, my people have served the rakul. We have sought new places, new species, fresh prey throughout the universe, and we have cultivated them until they might prove a satisfactory hunt for the masters."

"Huh," Jarek said. "Well that's—"

"Gropped up?" Johnny asked.

"Yeah, that's…" Jarek frowned. "We can go with whatever that is." He looked back at Alton. "So what? You guys tried to make a run for it and hide out with the humans on Earth and Enochia?"

"We didn't have a choice after the sickness hit us. Our lives are tied to the fate of you and your planet now. If you die, we die."

"And that doesn't give us all a free pass with these masters of yours?" Jarek asked.

Alton shook his head. "There are plenty more raknoth across the universe who do not share our affliction. Even if we'd been honest all along, the rakul would not deny themselves a hunt and risk infecting our entire species only to spare a few dozen raknoth. Of course, now they will certainly kill us for having tried to conceal our continued existence on Earth from them, but we've likely only accelerated the inevitable."

Why couldn't the big bad aliens be on an intergalactic quest for hugs or something? But then they wouldn't be big bad aliens, would they?

"Man," Jarek said. "You guys need to unionize or something."

"This is no laughing matter," Alton said. "If a nest has been compromised, then the rakul will be coming. It could be next week or next year, but they will come, and they will destroy everything on this planet."

Jarek met Rachel's eyes, and somewhere beneath that practiced cavalier expression of his, there was concern and a deep weariness.

"What are we talking about in terms of numbers?" Rachel asked. "The rakul can't be that much stronger than your people, can they?"

Haldin and Alton exchanged a heavy look through the holo.

"There are twelve of them," Haldin said. "And they're pretty terrifying."

"You could show her," Alton said.

Haldin shot Rachel a questioning look and tapped the side of his head. "You comfortable with that?"

A trill of apprehension shot through her chest, unbidden and unpleasant memories of her telepathic struggle with the Red King leaping to the forefront of her mind.

She most certainly wasn't comfortable with that. Jarek spoke up before she had to say that, though.

"You guys can't just use your words and tell the whole class?"

"Oh there are plenty of words," Alton said. "'World' and 'ending' are two that come to mind. The twelve run the gamut from older and stronger than any living raknoth to absolutely ancient and quite possibly unstoppable. None of you will truly understand until you see them. And right now, Rachel is the only one in that ship who's equipped to do so."

"And what if I don't want to?" Rachel asked. "What if I'm hesitant to cross minds with an associate of the raknoth who helped destroy my family and doesn't seem to give a damn about my friends now?"

Haldin's brow creased. "I'm the one who's offering you free access here."

"So you say," Rachel said.

In truth, she didn't see any real reason not to believe Haldin. It was Alton she couldn't trust.

If these rakul were real—and it was really starting to seem like they might be—they needed to find out anything and everything they could about them. But now that she'd put it out there, she wasn't about to back down and pretend like Alton hadn't done the things he'd done. No answers were worth swallowing that pill whole.

So she let the tense silence stretch in the cockpit, refusing to take the bait.

"Your friend," Alton finally said. "The one who was affected by the nest burst. I did not intend to imply his life is unimportant."

She tried to hide her surprise at his acuity. Was she that transparent that he could see exactly which button to press to try to make this better? Maybe.

Or maybe Alton actually meant it.

"It's my brother," Rachel said slowly. "The—whatever, the nest burst—it put him into a coma."

Alton seemed to think about that. "I could see where that might happen, especially if he doesn't share your telepathic gifts."

"He doesn't. But he's heavily glyphed against telepathic influence. You're saying something got through those glyphs? That it was a telepathic attack that did this to him?"

"Not an attack," Alton said. "Probably more like an accidental overload. The messengers are not violent beings. They simply convey information over great distances."

"That's what that light was?" she asked. "These messenger things?"

Alton nodded. "The messengers' relationship with the spatial dimensions of the universe is… well, suffice it to say it's not like ours, so we use the nests to keep them tied down in one place until we have need for them. A bursting nest can be quite overwhelming for anyone who's nearby when the floodgates open, so to speak."

"So what can I do to help him?"

"Probably very little. I expect he'll recover on his own in time, but he…" Alton's expression was hesitant.

Rachel leaned forward. "He what?"

"It's possible he'll have been marked by that kind of exposure."

Her heart picked up. "Marked how?"

Alton thought it over for a span. "Well, after that much exposure, he may act as a sort of beacon for any other messengers that find their way here. If and when he does wake up, he may see and hear more than he wants to."

"Even past his glyphs?"

Alton gave a slow nod. "Possibly. Whatever protection you gave him is subject to your understanding of space. The messengers might have found unchecked paths we aren't even capable of processing, much less seeing. Worse, if those unseen pathways were traversed by messengers, they'll only shine out more brightly to their kin now."

Alton's words piled in and hit her like a slow-motion gut punch.

She said nothing, too occupied trying to consider what this might all mean for Michael. Assuming he woke up.

No. She couldn't think like that. And not that she could trust Alton, but she had a feeling the raknoth would have told her if he thought Michael was toast.

He would wake up. And after that…

"What do I do?" she asked quietly. "How do I keep my brother safe?"

"We could try to find some way to enhance his cloaking," Haldin said.

"Or we do everything in our power to convince the rakul this planet and its people aren't worth their time," Alton said. "At this point, it's looking like that might mean a fight, as terrible of an idea as that is."

"Fine," Rachel said.

Enough with the games. If it was a fight they were headed toward, it was time to see what the hell it was that had Alton and Haldin shaking in their boots.

"Show me." She gave Jarek and Alaric a pointed look. "Assuming you're comfortable with precautions."

Taking her cue, Jarek stood and faced Haldin. Behind, Alaric drew a revolver and trained it loosely at Haldin's back.

"Hey!" Elise cried from the holo.

"It's fine, Lise," Haldin said, holding his hands up peacefully. "We have to earn their trust if we're all going to do this thing together." He reached up to adjust the dial on his pendant. "Ready?"

Rachel stood to face him, reaching for her own pendant.

"You might want to stay seated," Haldin said. "These are going to be my memories of Alton's memories, so they'll probably come through a bit muddy, but it's still pretty intense stuff."

She ignored him and dialed her cloak out to encompass the entirety of the ship.

Haldin looked as if he'd protest but then shrugged and closed his eyes. She closed hers as well and reached out.

His mind was hard to miss, bright and powerful but also calm and gentle as they met in a kind of mental handshake.

"This might be kind of disjointed," Haldin's voice came to her. *"I'm not really used to doing this kind of thing."*

"You and me both," Rachel thought back. Then, remembering just how vulnerable Haldin was about to make himself, she added, *"I'll try to be gentle."*

Haldin's mind rippled with mild amusement, and the surface of his presence softened and slowly began to peel open.

Rachel braced herself and pushed into the opening, thinking gentle thoughts.

CHAPTER SIXTEEN

Rachel lay adrift in the stream of Haldin's consciousness, floating so closely to his thoughts and perceptions that they almost felt like her own.

An abstract spatial map of the cockpit was the first thing that stood out. Haldin knew exactly where each potential threat was, exactly how to move if he decided he needed to extract himself from the situation. Except he'd be hard-pressed to do that now that he'd surrendered himself to a perfect stranger, wouldn't he?

Was this the worst idea ever? Was it even going to work?

It had to work.

The somber weight of the thought reminded Rachel that it was Haldin's, not hers.

She needed to get herself centered before she got lost in here. And if the nervous fear radiating from Haldin's mind was any indication, she needed to brace herself for some horrific shit once the replay started rolling.

She'd watched the guy—Christ, the Enochian, she supposed—duke it out with raknoth and Fela barehanded. From what she'd seen, he could channel with the best of them, and he was apparently on par with a freaking raknoth in telepathic chops. Haldin was not someone she'd want to fuck with.

And while he wasn't quite quivering right now, he was clearly terrified of the rakul.

"Are you still okay with this?" she thought.

"I'm fine," came his voice. *"I mean, I kind of hate this. But you need to understand what we're dealing with."*

"Okay. We'll go back to when Alton first showed you the rakul, then?"

"You're in control more than I am right now."

"Right..."

They would go back to when Alton had first shared his memories of the rakul with Haldin.

Their shared mental landscape began to shift in response to her will, as if she were simply recalling one of her own memories. She caught flashes of a cityscape, similar in many ways to the pre-Catastrophe cities of Earth, yet decidedly different in the angles and features of the buildings, which mostly all looked to be formed from the same gray material.

Was this Enochia?

Yes, his mind told her, it was.

The foreign cityscape was beautiful, but there was something else hanging over the memory: a subtle background stain of pain and loss —Haldin's own personal pain and loss, she realized. He'd suffered. On Enochia, he'd lost more and conquered more tribulations than most would in five lifetimes.

"Best not to get sidetracked right now," Haldin's voice came to her.

Right. Alton's memories.

They flashed to a compound surrounded by a high perimeter wall —a military base of some kind. A Sanctum stronghold. Haven. Another flash, and they were inside the base, facing Alton through a thick window of what looked like bulletproof glass. Alton's cell. They didn't trust him. Not one damn bit. But they had to know. Hal leaned forward, pressing a hand to the window. He had to kn—

"It was a bit after this," came Haldin's voice in her head. *"Focus on the time Alton first actually showed me the rakul."*

Rachel did. Another flash, and they were in an odd, rather empty room with dark walls and... was this the raknoth ship? It was. She felt it. There were two others with Hal and Alton—a rugged man and an attractive woman she didn't recognize. Hal was reaching for Alton's mind. Reaching, reaching...

Another flash, and now the landscape was absolutely different than anything Rachel had ever seen. It was like a winter wonderland village on acid. Odd, globular buildings of some amber, translucent material lined the wide, snowy paths that stretched out before them. Big treelike plants reared out of sizable snow drifts here and there along either side of the paths, their tops draped with something like partially unraveled balls of psychedelic yarn rather than canopies of leaves.

As weird as the scenery was, it paled in comparison to the creatures that roamed the paths.

Her first thought was that they were kind of like sky blue versions of the Incredible Hulk. Then she got a better look at the wicked-looking horns sprouting from their heads and the dark, bony spurs protruding from their bulky forms all along the legs, arms, shoulders, and backs, and decided they were entirely more beastly-looking. Then the one whose eyes she was seeing through started off down the snowy path, and as her senses started to adjust, she realized how big they were.

They were goddamn frost giants. Or maybe frost demons was a better choice of words.

The scene was patchy and blurry in spots, and the more she watched, the more she realized things seemed to skip oddly here and there. That must've been what Haldin had meant about it being a memory of a memory.

Dozens of the blue giants tromped along the paths, groaning and grunting in strange, harsh language. Most of them were carrying boulders that must have been the size of trucks. Rachel's frame of reference shifted as her giant looked over its massive shoulder to where its fellows were hauling their loads: a great clearing where several more giants were busy at work erecting an enormous shrine to what could have been a god or a king of some sort.

"These are rakul?" she thought.

"No. Just another one of the species the rakul have exterminated."

"I thought you said this was Alton's memory."

"It is."

"But why are we in the head of one of these things?"

"The raknoth don't always walk around looking like humans. They take hosts from whatever planet they're currently invading."

"Alton is—"

"Was one of these freakishly strong giants, yes. About 2,000 years ago."

"I—What? 2,000?"

She watched in numb shock as their giant—or Alton, apparently—plucked one of the big psychedelic trees from the ground as if it were a small weed and proceeded to take a big bite right off its stringy top.

"I don't understand."

Was that how the raknoth had been able to so thoroughly wreck Earth from the inside? She thought of the raknoth they'd met—suave, dark-haired Alton and the square-jawed, sandy-haired Red King.

"So Alton and the others... Those were real humans before the raknoth, uh, took them?"

"Exactly," Haldin thought.

Well that was disturbing as all hell.

One of the giants bumped into his neighbor, who dropped his boulder onto another giant's foot. What sounded more like a foghorn than a cry of pain erupted from the injured giant's maw, then it whirled and clubbed the offender across the chest. The second giant staggered back, then caught itself and rushed its opponent in a full-on tackle. They hit the ground like a mild earthquake and tumbled around for position. One landed a solid kick, and its opponent crashed through the wall of one of the nearby amber buildings.

Around them, the rest of the giants only laughed as if this was all perfectly normal behavior.

"And what about the rakul? Where are they in this memory?"

"You're in control," he reminded her.

Right. She focused on what she wanted to see, and the scene shifted accordingly.

It was only a little later now. Several giants were still at work on the shrine, but much of the boulder-hauling crew were taking a break to chomp down on a hearty lunch of psychedelic tree yarn. Everything seemed peaceful enough at first glance. But then why was Alton so apprehensive? She could feel the nervous energy like a permanent stain on the memory.

A huge shadow passed over them, and she felt an inkling of her own dread join that of Alton's memory.

Around them, the giants were exchanging uncertain glances, a few of them rising wearily to their feet.

A ship descended into view and… No. Not a ship. Massive wings flapped once, twice, three times, and even from a distance, the air they displaced could be easily felt.

The thing that rode those gargantuan wings down to the ground… It was a dragon. That was the only word Rachel could use to describe it.

The mountain-sized quadruped slammed to a landing that shook the ground even from what she gauged to be a half mile away and kicked up an explosion of snow. Two fiery red eyes came to life, each at least the size of the huge boulders the giants had been lugging about.

Then the thing roared.

The sound was deafening. The psychic pressure that slammed into them was worse.

It hit like a tsunami of molten lead. Rachel gasped, reaching for her defenses and—

"It's okay," Haldin's voice came to her, his tone tight. *"We're okay here, remember?"*

The last thing Rachel felt right then was okay, but the sound of Haldin's voice at least jostled her from the memory enough that she could remind herself that nothing in here could actually hurt her. Psychologically damage her, on the other hand…

"What the fuck is that thing?"

"Kul'Naga, first and oldest of the rakul."

The giants were all on their feet now, some dipping into their big, amber houses and emerging with a variety of brutal-looking melee weapons. Kul'Naga watched them patiently as they grunted and groaned and prepared to make war.

Then one of the giants by the shrine plucked a boulder from the waiting pile and hurled it at the waiting rakul, and the chaos began.

It was a mighty throw considering the boulder probably weighed five or ten tons. Kul'Naga swatted it out of the air with massive forepaw and charged.

What followed wasn't a pretty fight.

The giants fought without fear, reigning blow after heavy blow on the enormous rakul. The attacks weren't without effect. Soon Kul'-Naga was oozing green fluid from dozens of ugly wounds, but the rakul took the punishment in stride and continued indiscriminately tearing his way through the giants' ranks with claws that must have been six feet long and sharp as razors. With each swipe, Kul'Naga hacked another giant to pieces like they were tissue paper.

The sky vibrated with their foghorn screams until Rachel wanted to scream herself. *"Okay! Enough!"*

The memory faded at her will, leaving the image of Kul'Naga standing atop a mountain of dead giants covered in blood burned firmly in her mind's eye.

"Jesus Christ. I don't... That thing... It's coming here?"

"I don't know. Apparently Kul'Naga only makes the trip for promising planets these days. But if word has truly escaped that there are raknoth hiding out on Earth, the rakul will come."

"They're not all the same?"

"They're more a collection of the top hits from all the species they've conquered."

She was wrapped silent in her own thoughts when she felt the pressure of Haldin pushing her gently away from the center of his mind.

"As much fun as it's been," he thought, *"I think you've seen what you needed to."*

For a brief second, she considered that she could feasibly delve deeper into Haldin's mind if she wanted to. She could validate everything he'd said from the start, learn anything and everything about him, and he'd be hard-pressed to stop any of it at this point. That was the danger of letting someone into your mind this completely.

But she couldn't do that—wouldn't. The only times she'd ever taken information from unwilling subjects had been matters of immediate life and death, and even that had bothered her. Plus, after seeing what she'd just seen, it wasn't hard to agree with Haldin: if something with even a fraction of Kul'Naga's power was coming for them, they needed to be able to trust one another when it came time to fight.

So she collected herself and withdrew slowly from his mind, thinking gentle thoughts on the way out.

Jarek wasn't used to feeling powerless. In fact, he'd pretty much ordered his life around never being in positions where he truly was. But when an until-then eerily still and silent Rachel had pulled a ghost act and blanched like a turnip, that's exactly how Jarek felt.

He whirled on Haldin and saw that the Enochian was likewise looking like he'd just sprinted a mile through hot desert.

"You might want to be ready to catch her," came Alton's voice from the console holo behind.

Jarek glanced between the two, utterly unsure what was happening, whether he should or could help Rachel. "I thought he was just showing her a memory."

"They're quite strong memories," Alton said.

Jarek was about to ask what the hell that was supposed to mean when Rachel's knees gave out.

He darted down to catch her and hauled her up in his arms. Her forehead was brimming with sweat, and Fela's sensors told him there was plenty more of the cold stuff plastering her shirt to her back and his arms. Light shivers trembled through her, but other than that, she made no sounds or movements.

Alaric was eyeing Haldin like he was trying to decide whether to kick him or be ready to catch him when the Enochian came to with a shudder.

In Jarek's arms, Rachel did the same.

"Rache…" He searched her face for any signs of panic or danger.

Mostly, she just looked rattled and disoriented.

"I'm good," she croaked. "We're good."

She reached toward the copilot's chair.

Jarek swiveled the chair around and set her gently down. "I take it you saw them?"

Haldin plopped down on the bench across from Johnny's. "We saw them."

"You're both okay?" Elise asked.

"Still mentally intact," Haldin confirmed.

"Just awesome," Rachel added. She snapped to and focused on Jarek. "They have a goddamn dragon."

"A… What? You're talking like Komodo, right?"

She shook her head, her expression grave and not the least bit joking.

"Bullshit," Alaric said.

"You showed her the World Ender?" Alton asked.

Haldin nodded, his expression equally grave, and the first cold tendrils of fear crept through Jarek's skepticism. "Holy crap. You guys aren't kidding, are you? How big are we talking?"

"Big," Rachel said. "He cut through an army of—well, I guess I'll just call them frost giants—like they were papier-mâché pygmies."

What in the everliving hell had Haldin showed her in there? Much as the idea of sharing head space freaked Jarek out, he wished he could have seen.

"A plus on the visual descriptions there, Goldilocks. And we've got a dozen of these freaking space dragons coming for us?"

"Only the one," Haldin said. "The rest of the twelve have chosen their own forms over the millennia."

"Nevertheless, you begin to see now how dire our situation is," Alton said—a statement, not a question.

Rachel nodded.

"So what the hell are we gonna do about these things if they're as bad as you all say?" Alaric said, still leaning by the doorway.

"We're gonna fight," Haldin said. "If it's too late to make sure they never come here in the first place, we're gonna fight the things that give the raknoth nightmares, and we're gonna win."

The lingering pallor in his cheeks and forehead weren't exactly confidence inspiring, but the Enochian at least managed to make it sound like he believed such a thing was possible.

"Well I'm glad someone has a plan, at least," Jarek said.

Haldin gave him a tired, forced smile.

"But for those of us who are more detail-oriented," Lea said, "how do we stop something the raknoth are afraid of when we're barely holding our own against the raknoth themselves?"

"The only way—" Alton said.

"—is to present a united front against them," Haldin finished.

"Raknoth and human," Alton said. "All of Earth standing together and ready when the rakul arrive."

Lea looked skeptical at best. Alaric looked like someone had just told him his only option for survival was to copulate with a goat.

"That's gonna be a tough sell for pretty much every human on the planet," Jarek said, "what with the Catastrophe and all. Maybe even tougher for your people. I don't know anything about raknoth culture, but it didn't look like the Overlord—or Zar'Golga or whatever—was trying to give you a hug back there."

"Zar'Golga is a problem," Alton agreed. "He is likely beyond convincing. And there are many other problems ahead of us, but the only option is to try. All other paths lead to destruction."

"What about Enochia?" Jarek glanced back at Haldin. "Do the rakul know about your planet too?"

"We're not sure," Haldin said. "It's possible they don't, but making sure of that is part of why we decided to come here."

"So, what?" Jarek said. "Five Enochians and a raknoth were all your planet could spare to help out your brothers from Earth?"

"There are more than five of us," Elise said from the holo.

"And we're, like, totally badass if that part wasn't clear," Johnny added, wincing at the effort of speaking past his injuries.

"I feel better already," Rachel muttered.

"We should get back to HQ," Lea said. "They need to hear all of this."

She was probably right about that. As much as Jarek didn't look forward to sharing any of this to Nelken's stone-faced stare or Sloan's openly derisive sneer, it was starting to sound like they'd be foolish not to start rallying the troops while they could.

The Resistance might not have been his first choice for allies, but it was the only serious manpower they were going to find that wasn't under direct raknoth control.

"We could probably stand to have another chat with Stumpy too," Jarek thought out loud. "See if he has anything to add to all of this."

"Stumpy?" Haldin asked.

"The raknoth we captured a few days ago," Rachel said. "The one who calls himself the Red King. Jarek started calling him Stumpy after he cut off an arm and a hand."

"Sweet Alpha," Elise whispered.

"Hey!" Jarek jabbed up a finger for pause. "While he was trying to kill me. Let's not leave that part out."

"Well that's a great start to human-raknoth relations," Haldin said quietly.

"Where should we pick you guys up?" Elise asked.

Jarek wasn't sure whether Johnny was gifted like Haldin or not, but he didn't need extra senses to identify the look that passed between the two Enochians. It was the look of two dudes who'd been through enough together to know exactly what one another were thinking.

"I was actually thinking we should stay with these guys and go have a talk with this Resistance," Haldin said.

"Hal…" Elise said, concern evident in the lines of her pretty face.

Haldin patted the comm on his wrist. "We'll only be a call away. And it's better this way. Something tells me things wouldn't go so smoothly if all of us came marching out of our alien ship at once and walked into the anti-raknoth base with our raknoth friend."

"He's right," Alton said. "Our presence would only cause friction, if not an outright battle, and we need to move quickly if the rakul could already be on their way." He frowned at them through the holo. "In a perfect world, I would have sent Franco along instead of Johnny—"

"Hey!" Johnny said.

"—but we'll just have to work with what we have."

"I could grow a mustache and act all sophisticated too if I wanted," Johnny mumbled.

"You're welcome to try," came a smooth voice from somewhere off camera.

Elise's lips twitched, but her expression sobered as she focused back on Haldin. "Promise me you'll be careful."

"C'mon. When have I ever not been?"

Elise arched a dark eyebrow at him. "I love you."

"And I you," Haldin said. "We'll talk soon."

With that, the Enochians ended the call.

"Nice." Jarek turned and offered a closed fist to Haldin.

Rachel rolled her eyes.

Haldin eyed the fist dubiously and finally reached out to give it a tentative shake. "Uh, thanks?"

Johnny shook his head. "You're such an Enochian, broto."

"Whatever," Haldin said, a slight flush creeping into his cheeks. "Shouldn't we get moving?"

"That we should." Jarek sank into the pilot's chair beside Rachel and shot her a wink as he powered up the ship's motors. "Time to go save the world from the big scary monsters, right?"

The troubled look she gave him left him wondering if it was a blessing or a curse he hadn't been there to see just how monstrous those big scary monsters were. Not that it really mattered.

One way or another, he had a bad feeling he might be finding out in person soon enough.

CHAPTER SEVENTEEN

"I think you're going to have to run all of that by us one more time," Commander Nelken said. To his right, Sloan was staring at them like they'd all escaped a psych ward, and on the other side of the council room table, Commander Daniels' eyes radiated grave concern.

Jarek shifted in his chair, more out of impatience than discomfort. He couldn't really blame them, he supposed. It was a lot of crazy to try to process at once. He still wasn't entirely sure he believed it all himself, but he at least trusted that Rachel had seen something terrible in Haldin's little flashback cinema, and that was enough for now.

Beside Jarek, Pryce looked more rigorously pensive than Jarek had ever seen, which was really saying something when it came to Pryce. Given the controversial—not to mention mind-blowing—nature of the information they'd brought back, the commanders had agreed to meet immediately and without the full council in attendance.

Judging from their faces, that last part had been a good call.

Lea looked down their line hopefully. "Anyone else want to chime in?"

No one seemed to be overly surprised when Jarek leaned forward to speak—go figure.

"What's there to be hung up on?" he asked. "We found that strange ship, and it just happened to be manned by some humans from another planet who came here to cure the raknoth of their human blood addiction and let them move on before their rakul overlords come calling. Fight the power. Isn't that kinda your guys' thing? C'mon."

Sloan rolled his eyes. "Every bit of this story is ridiculous. Humans from another planet? Evil space-faring conquerors coming to bring hell on Earth?"

Jarek bobbed his head. "You're right. It's almost as ridiculous as scaly green vampires running around with glowing red eyes, sucking blood and shirking off bullets like Nerf darts, right?"

Sloan turned his wide-eyed gaze down the table to Nelken and Daniels. "You two don't seriously believe any of this, do you?"

Nelken looked like he was having a serious internal debate on that matter.

Daniels met Sloan's gaze with steely ice in her eyes. "I trust my daughter, and you should too. When's the last time you left this base, Richard? How would you even know what's happening out there?"

Sloan visibly clenched his jaw and sat back to cross his arms and pout.

"I understand how hard this all must be to process," Haldin said from over beside Lea, "but it's crucial we begin preparations as soon as possible. I've only seen scattered glimpses of the rakul, but it's enough to convince me it's going to take everything on this planet fighting together to stand a chance. My planet—"

Sloan gave an obnoxiously loud snort. Nelken frowned at him. Pryce just kept watching Haldin like a dog waiting for another scrap of food to fall.

"—was slow to admit to even the threat of the raknoth, and it almost cost us everything. From what I've seen of Earth, it cost your world much more. But what's coming now is far worse."

"We appreciate your candor, Mr. Raish," Nelken said, "but it is, as you say, quite hard to process. Not to be rude, but how can we responsibly believe any of this? Do you have any way of proving, for instance, that you are indeed from this… Enochia?"

"There's probably hundreds of ways we could determine that," Pryce said.

It was the first time he'd spoken, and it earned him frowns from Sloan and Nelken.

"But since most of Pryce's methods will probably go straight over our heads," Jarek said, "why don't you just go check out the guns your people so rudely asked my man Johnny to leave at the door then come back here and tell me those things are from Earth."

Pryce looked like he wanted to argue but then tilted his head in concession.

Nelken wordlessly flipped a switch on the intercom in front of him.

"Armory," came a gruff response.

"Rodgers," Nelken said quietly, "please bring the weapons we're holding for our new guests to the council chamber."

"Uh, yes, Commander. Right away."

Nelken gave a thanks, clicked off the intercom, and tilted his head toward Jarek.

Jarek gave a hesitant nod in response. That was twice Nelken had surprised him by being… well, not a dick. It was a little disorienting.

"This is bullshit," Sloan mumbled in Nelken's ear. "Who gives a crap if they have fancy guns?"

It was quiet enough that no one else should have heard, but Jarek had Fela's sensors on his side.

"It's far from perfect," Nelken muttered back, less quietly, "but it's something." He turned back to Lea and Haldin. "In the meantime, let's continue hypothetically. If these rakul were really coming to Earth, what would we do about it? As Mr. Slater would gladly tell you, we're limited in our ability to handle the raknoth. What do you propose we do against something stronger?"

Jarek joined the others in looking to Lea, who'd been the first and loudest to voice the obvious: the Resistance—the rag-tag organization formed with the sole intent of breaking raknoth control on their planet—was not going to like their answer to that question.

Hell, they didn't even like it.

After the day's events, Alaric had been too pissed or frustrated or whatever boiling stew of instability he currently was to even come to this meeting. Rachel was only a hair better, sitting next to him in a dark, gloomy haze.

Still, if they were even going to think about it, it had to be said, and Lea was the only one who had even a scrap of a chance at being taken seriously.

"If it's all true," Lea said, "then we might need to start thinking about an alliance."

Pryce audibly swallowed, but his head bobbed in agreement. He understood.

Commander Daniels' expression grew more troubled.

Nelken raised his eyebrows half an inch. "With?"

Lea chewed on the thing she so clearly didn't want to say. Finally, quietly, "With the raknoth, sir."

Sloan gave a yelp of laughter.

Nelken looked like he might rebuke Sloan, but before he could, Lea spoke in a firm voice.

"I don't want to be telling you this any more than you want to be hearing it. You sent us out to find the facts. This is what we found." She glanced at the Enochians and back to the commanders. "I want solid proof as much as you, but in the meanwhile, we need to at least be having the conversation."

Nelken and Daniels shared a somber look, both of them ignoring Sloan's indignant shuffling and huffing. Together the two commanders turned back to Lea and gave slow nods.

Sloan's eyes went wide. "You can't be serious."

"It'll be a cold day in hell before I willingly align with the raknoth," Nelken said, turning a sober look on Sloan. "But if we turn up solid evidence that a cold day in hell is indeed what's coming, we'd be fools not to consider our options."

"Well said, Commander," Pryce said.

Commander Daniels nodded her agreement.

Sloan stared at them all for a handful of seconds, mouth agape, then he recrossed his arms and went back to sulking.

"This conversation stays in this room," Daniels said, looking at each of them in turn. "What we're talking about here is an apocalypse scenario. It could tear this place apart."

Jarek figured that went without saying.

Much as pre-Catastrophe society had tried to convince itself it had moved beyond bigotry and into a free-range field of sunshine and open minds, he was pretty sure it hadn't. At least not to the extent that the men and women of the Resistance would be open to making peace with the raknoth after the whole worldwide nuking thing.

These soldiers wouldn't care when they learned that the raknoth had been victims themselves in a way, or that not all of them were involved in or even in support of the actions that had led to the Catastrophe. It wouldn't matter.

Jarek wasn't sure he cared so much either, but he'd seen enough people doing enough atrocious things to one another in his life to be sure about a couple things.

Thing one: people—human or raknoth—didn't do bad shit because they were evil. They did it because they had desires, dreams, and more often than not, a long history of trying circumstances that had chipped their concepts of right and wrong down to the ground.

Thing two: humans were every bit as vicious and shitty as the raknoth. Maybe more so. They were just less well-equipped to exert those savage wills.

It wasn't that Jarek wasn't upset about the raknoth blowing the world's ass off, or that he didn't share the others' profound discomfort at the thought of working with the scaly bastards. It was mostly just that he wasn't too far up his own ass to see that both sides had pulled some cheap shots and that these indignant humans might have done the same damn thing to the raknoth had their positions been reversed.

And if this fresh hell was ready to descend on them, he certainly wasn't about to shit on humanity's only decent hope of survival out of pride or principle. Because that's what this was about, right? Survival? That's what he'd been telling himself all along.

But whose survival? If he was really so far above it all, why worry about whether all these petty a-holes pulled through? Why not take Pryce and Al and go find themselves a nice quiet rock to hide under until the world stopped burning for a second time?

He hadn't registered he was staring at Rachel until she turned to meet his gaze with lovely hazel eyes and an expression that said *Dude, what the hell are you staring at?*

He couldn't help but smile at her unspoken snark. When she saw it, Rachel's expression softened and turned more genuinely curious, and the look between them deepened until the sounds of Nelken's and Daniels' voices receded to nothing but dull background buzz, and Jarek forgot where he was and what they were doing there and why anything even really mattered beyond those golden locks and—

The hard knock on the wooden doors at the back of the room hit him like a splash of cold water straight to the giblets.

Jarek rocked back in his seat and composed himself as Nelken called out for the ill-timed knocker to enter.

So what? Maybe Jarek wasn't humanity's biggest fan. And maybe he wasn't some paragon of selfless service.

But this connection he felt sometimes when he looked at Rachel… The rest of the Rachels and Pryces—and maybe even Als—who might be in danger out there…

If those things weren't worth fighting for, Jarek wasn't so sure there was a reason to keep rolling out of his cot every morning.

The double doors parted, and a stout man with a buzz cut— Rodgers, presumably—entered the room carting a tray laden with Johnny's odd-looking guns. A pang of guilt shot through Jarek as he recognized Rodgers' bulldog face as the same one that had been on duty when Michael had busted him into the armory a few days ago to reclaim Fela.

Rodgers carted the tray forward, perfectly business-like until he caught sight of Jarek and gave one of the darker, angrier scowls Jarek could recall having ever received.

Jarek scrunched his face in his best *oops* expression and waved.

For some reason, Rodgers didn't wave back. He only gave the commanders a curt nod to acknowledge their thanks, shot Jarek one more hard glare, and turned to leave.

The commanders rose and came to inspect the Enochian hardware along with everyone else.

At their core, the weapons all looked to follow the basic point-and-shoot design of Earth's own firearms—some manner of grip or butt with a barrel that pointed toward the things you wanted to kill. Beyond that, though, details like feeding and firing mechanisms, magazine placement, and pretty much everything else varied, some slightly, others radically.

One thing was clear: none of them—aside from Johnny and Haldin, of course—had ever seen firearms like them. Actually, looking at the series of tiny coils along the barrel of one handgun, Jarek wasn't even sure they could all be properly designated as firearms.

After a minute's inspection, Nelken finally looked up at Johnny. "Why were you carrying this many weapons?"

Johnny squinted at Nelken. "Is that a rhetorical question? Or..."

Haldin nudged him with an elbow.

"What?" Johnny said. "Sometimes you just gotta get the lead out." He glanced around the room. "Am I using that one right?"

Jarek grinned and gave Johnny a thumbs-up. "A for effort."

If anyone else understood the reference, they weren't amused enough to show it.

Once they'd satisfied their curiosities, the commanders returned to their seats, their expressions a few degrees more unsettled than they had been a few minutes ago. Everyone else sat as well, aside from Pryce, who remained at the cart, inspecting every nook and cranny of every weapon with machinelike precision.

"This obviously doesn't represent hard proof of anything," Nelken said, "but it is… odd. I think you should tell us what you came to say."

Haldin launched into a rundown of his rather extensive knowledge of the raknoth. A lot of it was rehashing what Lea had already explained: the roll the raknoth served under the rakul, the origin and aftermath of the manmade infection that had rendered the raknoth dependent on human blood for survival. Rachel perked up beside Jarek during that part, but Haldin elected to leave any mention of her mom out of the story.

The commanders took it all in silently, their expressions shifting slowly from skepticism—or outright disbelief in Sloan's case—to slack-jawed awe as more and more pieces of the puzzle fell neatly into place.

Jarek knew how they felt. As outlandish as the story sounded, it was hard to completely ignore the way it aligned what little they knew of the raknoth into a cohesive whole. It might not all make "sense", but it didn't *not* fit.

As Haldin talked, Jarek picked up several tidbits that he hadn't known.

For one thing, there were somewhere around eighty raknoth feasibly still on Earth, which was at once a terrifying thought and a hopeful one if they were truly going to count on their strength to survive the rakul.

For another—and this one was a freaking doozy—they learned what the raknoth actually were.

The epiphany came when Daniels held up a hand to pause Haldin and asked, "But why do they look like us when they're not walking around as green monsters? If they've really moved from planet to planet and infiltrated all these different alien species... Are they"—she wrinkled her brows, clearly struggling to believe she was seriously asking this—"shapeshifters or something of the like?"

It was a good question, now that Jarek thought about it. After witnessing the Red King and Alton Parker going full-raknoth mode, he'd kind of just accepted that it happened, but he hadn't paused to think about the endless possibilities of the other species they'd encountered in the past if Alton's stories were to be trusted (which, according to Rachel, they were).

Haldin scrunched his face. "Sort of. The raknoth are, for lack of a better word—"

"Parasites," Pryce said, finally looking up from Johnny's hardware. "They must be small enough to integrate with or replace our brains. Or at least small enough to exert telepathic influence from within one of your cloaking fields." He tapped at his chest where Haldin and Rachel wore their pendants.

Jarek didn't need to wait for Haldin to nod in agreement. Of course Pryce had figured it out, the clever old bastard.

"The real raknoth are fleshy, tentacled things about the size of a human brain," Haldin said. "But they don't walk around like that by choice. Mostly, they find a host of their target species and, uh, well, invade." He glanced at Pryce. "That's an impressive deduction."

Pryce shot Jarek a discreet wink as he returned to his seat. Jarek was less surprised by Pryce's intuition than the others, but only because he expected Pryce to be brilliant by default and because he knew the hypothesis was merely one of a couple dozen Pryce had already constructed about the raknoth. He must've eliminated the others based on what he'd heard today.

Daniels' eyes were wide. "You mean the raknoth we've seen… used to be people?"

Haldin nodded. "But as far as I've seen, the host ceases to be anything more than a vessel once a raknoth moves in. Usually, at least."

There was a thought to make your skin crawl. Judging from their looks and uncomfortable shifting, the others were having similar thoughts—aside from Johnny, who waggled his eyebrows at Lea and generally seemed to enjoy watching their reactions.

"And the rakul?" Nelken asked once they'd all taken a sufficiently long moment to ponder the horror of tiny alien octopuses crawling into their heads. "What can you tell us of them?"

"Not as much," Haldin said. "They were like the raknoth once, a long, long time ago."

"In a galaxy far away?" Jarek mumbled under his breath.

Rachel gave the world's smallest snort next to him.

"How long ago?" Nelken asked. "You said the raknoth had been serving the rakul for millennia. How old are they?"

"Sorry, guess I forgot to mention that part." Haldin swept his gaze around the room. "The raknoth are immortal."

CHAPTER EIGHTEEN

In hindsight, Rachel was pretty sure she should have picked up on this one already. Haldin had outright told her the memory they'd re-experienced together had been both Alton's and 2,000 years old. Clearly, the raknoth was old. That didn't make him an immortal, necessarily, but she probably should have seen it coming. Then again, she had been a bit distracted by the mountain-sized World Ender, Kul'Naga, and the maelstrom of his psychic fury.

"Immortal," Jarek said. "As in, those who don't die? Like ever?"

"Not until you poke them with pointy objects, at least," Johnny said.

Christ. They really were freaking space vampires, weren't they?

How had she missed this? Somehow, she'd thought the talk of the raknoth serving the rakul for millennia had been historical, a recounting of generational heritage, but… "Alton didn't mean they'd served for hundreds of generations, did he?"

"I think new raknoth trickle in as needed," Haldin said, "but no, most of the raknoth are thousands of years old."

"Alton?" Sloan asked.

Rachel immediately realized her misstep. The commanders would have to learn about Haldin's raknoth buddy at some point, but right now probably wasn't the ideal time—not when they were still trying to convince them there was even a rakul threat to begin with.

"One of my crew," Haldin said. "The one who helped us find Earth."

Sloan leaned forward like a jackal sensing vulnerable prey, stark green eyes narrowed. "And how exactly did he know how to do that, I can't help but wonder?"

Everyone who knew the answer tensed. Everyone but Haldin, who calmly held Sloan's stare. "Because he was among the seven raknoth who came to my planet from Earth fifteen years ago."

Sloan was halfway to his feet before Haldin finished his sentence. He slapped a long-fingered hand to the tabletop. "You see?" he cried, turning to Nelken and Daniels. "Who else would propose an alliance with those monsters except their own agents? The raknoth sent them here with this ridiculous story." His glare shifted to Lea then to Rachel and Jarek. "And you fools fell for it. We need to lock these—these 'Enochians' up. We need to—"

"Calm yourself, Commander," Nelken said, his expression stern.

"And watch your tongue while you're at it," Daniels said, cold fire in her eyes.

Sloan sneered. "Just because your daughter believes this idiocy doesn't mean—"

"Richard." Nelken's voice fell like a gavel, and Sloan jerked back, green eyes smoldering with indignant fury. "We'll hear the full story before we determine what is to be done with our guests."

"Fine." Sloan waved a hand at Haldin and crossed his arms. "What in god's name is your excuse?"

"Believe me," Haldin said, "I didn't take to working with one of them lightly. The raknoth took everything from me. They killed my parents, my mentor. They came within an inch of enslaving my entire world. There was a time I wanted to wipe the entire raknoth race from the universe."

"And yet you joined them," Sloan said.

"And yet I decided to work with the guy who showed me how and why it had come to that, and how he planned to redress their wrongs."

"And you trusted this Alton?" Daniels asked.

Haldin shook his head. "It's not a question of trust. I don't think I ever could have decided to trust Alton Parker after the things he did on my planet. But I've been inside his mind. I've seen beyond his words and straight into a place where he wasn't capable of lying to me. I know what he wants as well as he does."

"And what is that?" Nelken asked.

"To save his people, from the rakul and from their dependence on our blood."

"And why should we trust any of this?" Sloan asked. "Even if we did trust you—which I don't, by the way—how can you be so sure this raknoth isn't playing you?"

"I told you: I've been in his mind. He belonged to me. I scoured every corner of his being for a scrap of dishonesty, and I found nothing that didn't support what I just told you. Rachel can tell you how powerful that evidence is."

Heads turned toward her.

"It's true," she said. "Once a telepath's in your head like that, there's no hiding anything, no lying. You belong to them until they choose to release you. And despite all that danger"—she looked at Haldin—"he opened his mind to me today to show me the rakul."

She weighed her next words carefully. If she'd pushed deeper into Haldin's head, she could have told them with certainty whether or not he was to be trusted. Instead, she'd decided to respect his openness and leave most of his stones unturned. Maybe her impulse to do that was all the answer she needed.

Or maybe Michael's naivety had finally rubbed off on her.

"We can trust Haldin," she finally said. Maybe she didn't mean it at the deepest level—Christ, she didn't even trust the Resistance that much, and especially not Sloan, the slimy bastard—but it was what the commanders needed to hear right now.

Haldin gave her a small nod, and she returned it, feeling a sense of warm camaraderie with the Enochian.

Then Sloan mumbled, "And who's to say we can trust you?" just softly enough to paint the illusion he hadn't meant it to be plainly heard, and her warm feelings evaporated in an instant.

"Look, Dick," Jarek said, "I know your Commandership is *super* valuable to the Resistance and everything, but maybe, in your infinite wisdom, you could find it in your shriveled old heart to stop being an insufferable little bitch to the people who are doing your work for you. Or you could get off your ass and do the fighting yourself if you're not happy with what we're doing out there."

"Oh, but I thought it wasn't fighting that you're suggesting," Sloan said. "I thought it was laying down in bed with the monsters who destroyed us. Do you people hear yourselves?" He was on his feet now, voice rising. "We're sitting here talking about humans from other planets. About teaming up with the fucking raknoth so that we can stop an enemy we have no actual proof even exists, much less is coming here to—"

Pryce shot to his feet, drawing their collective attention. At first, Rachel thought he was about to lay the verbal smackdown on Sloan, but he was looking at his comm like something was wrong.

Her heart picked up.

Could it be Michael? She'd basically left Pryce as his caretaker and barely had a chance to poke her head in the door before being swept into the council chamber on their return. Would Pryce be the one they contacted if something had changed with her brother?

She realized she was already halfway to her feet.

Pryce's gaze shot from the comm straight to her, confirming her fear before he said a word.

"What is it?" she whispered. "What happened?"

"He's awake," Pryce said.

They should have been good words—great words—but the way Pryce said them... And why did he look so tense?

"We need to get over there," he said. "Now. Something's not right."

She turned without a word and made for the door, ignoring the voices behind her. She broke into a jog. Terrible scenarios played out in her head, a garbled reel of worst-case scenarios, complete with gut-wrenching sensations that narrowed her vision down to a hazy tunnel directed toward Michael and nothing else.

She threw the door open and took the hallway at a run, vaguely aware that Jarek and Pryce were following her, heart pounding in her throat now, shoving past the two oblivious Resistance agents she encountered.

Was this it? After everything they'd been through, everything she'd done to protect him, was this how it would end?

She ran on, trying her best to shut the insidious whispers out of her head.

The shouts and wordless growls told her something was seriously wrong before she'd even made it to the first of the two medical rooms. When she burst into the second room, it was to the sight of Michael violently convulsing on the bed, eyes wild and limbs flailing. A stream of incoherent gibberish poured out of his mouth, punctuated by a few audible words.

"Traitors! Treachery… punished… forgotten… void."

The attending doctor and her assistant were at work on both sides of the bed, muscling Michael's free arm and leg into leather restraints like the ones they'd already bound his other limbs with.

Rachel watched in a stupor, feeling ill.

This wasn't how it was supposed to happen. Michael was supposed to emerge peacefully from his coma. She was going to find him lying in his bed, groggy and disoriented, but awake. She'd run her fingers through his spongy hair and ask the lazy-bones how his nap had been.

The tortured scream that erupted from Michael's throat ripped that delusion asunder.

Rachel shook herself out of her frozen horror and rushed to the bedside to help. Before she could, Jarek stepped up beside her, calmly caught onto Michael's free limbs, and pressed them firmly to the bed. The doctor and her assistant jumped on the opening, securing the bindings without a word. That done, the doctor scrambled to the cabinets in the corner of the room to grab something.

"What's happening to him?" Rachel cried over Michael's persistent ramblings.

Across from her, the assistant only clenched his jaw and shook his head, apparently unsure how to answer.

The doctor returned a few seconds later with a battered injector, which she promptly placed to the side of Michael's neck and triggered with a sharp click-hiss sound. She withdrew the injector, and Michael's struggles slowly grew less insistent until he gave one final, full-body jerk and collapsed back to the bed, slack and subdued.

He looked weakly around the room and finally locked eyes with Rachel.

"They're coming," he whispered.

Then he slumped back to the bed, completely limp.

After a stunned moment of silence, the doctor's fingers shot to Michael's throat.

Rachel leaned in, thundering heart threatening to escape her chest with each beat. "Is he…?"

"Stable." The doctor glanced at the bedside displays. "I just gave him a sedative to keep him from hurting himself. Or us."

"Okay," Rachel heard herself say. Her heart took a few steps away from the ledge. "Okay."

"So what the hell was that?" Jarek asked.

The doctor glanced between them. "I don't know."

"I think," came Haldin's voice from the doorway, "that was a tele-pathic broadcast."

The others were there with him: Pryce, Johnny, Lea—even the commanders.

Haldin's eyes found hers. "Did you feel it?"

She was about to point out that she'd been cloaked, but now that she thought about it, maybe she had felt something—a whisper of a whisper at the edges of her senses. Or had she? She'd been too distracted to be sure.

"Maybe," she said. "I don't know." She looked back to the doctor. "Is he gonna be all right?"

The doctor pursed her lips and glanced down at Michael's now peaceful form. "I can't say with any real certainty, but his waking up is a promising sign, at least. He should be down for at least a few hours with the sedative, probably more, but with any luck, he'll wake up under control after that. For now, we just have to wait and see."

Rachel swallowed against a dry mouth and nodded her thanks. After another minute of monitoring, the doctor moved to the front room to give them some privacy. Rachel stared numbly at Michael as the others filed in closer.

What was happening to her brother?

Slowly, the adrenaline bled out of her system, leaving behind little but the heavy reminder of just how damn exhausted she was. She turned at a movement to find Haldin telekinetically lowering a chair into place behind her. She gave him a tired nod and sank gratefully into the chair.

"So if it was a broadcast," Nelken said, "who was it from?"

"Three guesses," Jarek muttered.

"Not many other possibilities," Haldin agreed. "Even world-class telepaths can't range more than a mile unless—"

"The messengers," Rachel said. "That's what the raknoth and rakul use them for, right?"

"Among other things, yeah."

"Wait," Lea said. "Like the same messengers from the nest?"

"Maybe not those exact same ones," Haldin said, "but yeah."

They watched Michael's gentle breathing in silence as they considered the implications.

They're coming, Michael had said. They'd all heard it. And no matter what anyone wanted to say, they all had a pretty good idea who the "they" was.

She looked at Haldin. "You're sure you felt something?"

"You're not?"

She settled her chin onto the bridge of her hands and said nothing. She wasn't sure what she'd felt. There'd been too much going on. But if Haldin was sure…

Alton and the Red King were both pretty convinced the rakul were coming. And Alton had said Michael's exposure to the bursting nest might have opened him up to see things he'd rather not.

What other explanation fit all the pieces?

"Could the broadcast not just as easily have come from one of the raknoth?" Pryce asked.

"I can think of at least four that are hungry for our asses," Jarek said. "Maybe they're trying to shake you guys up."

"I think I would have felt the difference," Haldin said, "but I guess we can't be sure what Michael just experienced until we can ask him. Unless…" He turned a questioning look to Rachel.

She shook her head. "I'd rather not burn his glyphs just so we can try to meddle in there. For all I know, it could make things worse for him."

Haldin held back whatever it was he seemed to want to say. "Then I guess we wait."

Rachel rested her hand over Michael's and was settling in to do just that when the base's orange alarm lights pulsed to life—thankfully without the obnoxious buzzing sounds she'd heard them make in the past.

Maybe they weren't going to have to wait that long after all.

They all shared a concerned look. Nelken and Daniels both looked entirely too surprised for her liking.

"Sloan." Nelken said the word like a curse.

It was only then Rachel realized Sloan hadn't followed his fellow commanders here.

Daniels strode briskly over to the intercom. Before she touched the small box, it went live with a crackle and what sounded like a microphone being jostled or handed off.

There was a brief silence, and then Sloan's voice sounded from the speakers, steady but urgent.

"Attention: we've received reports that Newark and Jersey City have fallen under bombing runs by Overlord forces. The commanders ask that you proceed to the main commons for an emergency briefing. Please do not panic. So far, reports indicate that these attacks appear to be minor. Briefing begins in five minutes. That is all."

The box gave a sharp click and went silent, leaving them all staring at each other in quiet shock.

"Is it just me," Jarek said, "or did Dick just go rogue?"

CHAPTER NINETEEN

Even without the annoying alarm lights and the panicked Resistance agents scampering to and fro as Jarek and the others emerged from medical, Jarek would have known something was wrong solely by the tension in the guards' stances outside of the Red King's cell down the hall.

He gave them a courteous nod as he neared the cells with Rachel and the others on his tail. The guards were too preoccupied to notice, chattering as they were about why a disheveled Nelken and Daniels had stormed out of medical a minute *after* Sloan had made a critical announcement speaking for them.

It all smelled a bit like the beginnings of disorder in the ranks.

"You got anything, Al?" Jarek murmured.

"Scanning what local chatter there is," Al said in his earpiece. "It doesn't sound good, sir."

Jarek stepped aside to let a few desperate looking scramblers claw past him in the narrow hallway and took the moment to check on the others behind him.

The Enochians were calm, ready. Neither Haldin nor Johnny could've been much older than twenty, but they'd clearly seen their share of tense situations. Pryce looked considerably more fidgety, but that wasn't so unusual for him. Rachel, on the other hand, looked like she was moments away from either catatonia or a violent explosion, which was understandable enough.

She didn't need this right now, not while Michael was still in the woods. Then again, if Sloan's message had been any indication, they might all be finding themselves right back in those woods alongside Michael shortly.

The traffic cleared, and Jarek squeezed between the guards only to nearly run into Alaric as the old Resistance fighter lumbered out of the cell two doors down from the Red King.

Alaric wasn't exactly a spring chicken on the best of days, but he looked a couple decades past his normal surly stoicism as he turned his back to the wall and slumped down to his haunches.

It wasn't a great leap to figure why. That cell must've been where they were keeping Mosen, the epitome of wayward sons (if by "wayward" you meant homicidal maniac).

Jarek pulled to a halt beside Alaric. "You guys go on. I'll catch up."

Haldin continued on without complaint, Johnny and Pryce on his tail. Rachel met his eyes and hesitated. He wanted to say something witty or comforting, but she dropped his gaze and moved on before he could think of a single useful word.

Jarek turned back to Alaric, who resolutely avoided looking his way.

"You coming to the team meeting, old timer?"

Alaric gave a disinterested grunt.

Jarek looked at the door beside them. "Is he awake?"

Another grunt, possibly one of confirmation. Then, "Is Michael?"

"He was. It wasn't pretty, but he's tranqued for now. You got a plan for Seth?"

Alaric finally met his eyes with a hard, tired stare.

It went on silently for several seconds before Jarek finally looked away. "Right..."

He tried a few times to add to the statement but couldn't find the right words.

What was there to say? *Sorry Zar'Golga the Overlord twisted your son into a total psychopath until he was willing to kill his mom—your wife. Maybe he'll be super happy you stole him from his evil master and you two can be best friends forever now.*

Yeah. Right.

Jarek wasn't sure why he felt the need to say anything at all. Sure, he didn't like to see Alaric suffering, but since when had he been the one to help people with problems that didn't involve marauders in need of a cold sword through the heart? If anyone in their ragtag band was qualified to be dolling out psychological aid, it sure as well wasn't him.

But here he was, and something told him that before the day was over, they might be needing Alaric the Father of the Resistance instead of Alaric the slumping sulk. He was about to say something to that effect when Alaric spoke up.

"Guess I won't be making it back to Deadwood after all."

He suppressed a reflexive *Well not with that attitude, you won't!* as well as the following urge to tell Alaric that maybe he would make it and who knew?

Now wasn't the time to coddle. Alaric Weston didn't need coddling.

"Look, you heard what Sloan said. I think the shit's about to hit, and I think it's gonna paint the walls in here just as shitty as the ones out there."

Alaric's brow crinkled, and his lip might have even twitched. "Your point?"

"Let's try caution this time, sir," Al said quietly in Jarek's ear.

Jarek dropped on his haunches beside Alaric to speak more quietly.

"You missed out on today's lesson with the class, so I'll give you the highlights. You've already heard how dangerous these rakul are. You won't be surprised to hear the commanders are a bit skeptical and more than a bit upset at the idea of joining hands with the raknoth to fight an enemy they have no real reason to believe even exists."

"And we do?" Alaric asked.

It was a fair question, but also one Jarek had asked himself more than enough times in the past hours to know his answer.

"I trust Rachel. And what you don't know is that Michael just had some kind of telepathic episode and told us that 'they' are coming. Three guesses on who 'they' are, but hell if Sloan is gonna listen. Whatever's happening out there, things are about to get a whole lot tenser around here, and I'm pretty sure he has zero intention of not Dicking up any attempt to prepare for what he figures are fairy tale monsters."

Alaric was watching him closely now. "Your point?"

Jarek spread his hands. "My point is that you're Alaric Fucking Weston, man. You're the last guy in this rat maze anyone would expect to even think about buddying up with the raknoth, and you're probably the only guy they'll be willing to even consider hearing it from." He pointed in the direction of the common room where the troops would be marshalling now. "I know this is a shitty time, but those people are going to need someone to rally around when the cat gets out. They're gonna need Alaric Fucking Weston, and the sooner the better. So what do you say? Let's go see what the fuss is out there."

Alaric's gaze had shifted to Mosen's cell door as Jarek spoke, and now he refused to meet Jarek's eye. He said nothing, but something had changed in his expression. Good or bad, Jarek wasn't quite sure, but Alaric had clearly heard what he'd had to say at least.

Jarek rose from his haunches. "You do what you gotta do, old timer."

Alaric said nothing, and Jarek didn't wait around to see if that would change.

"Surprisingly tactful, sir," Al said as Jarek turned down a now mostly empty hallway toward the common room.

And yet unsuccessful.

He got it—Alaric was going through some heavy shit—but that was exactly why Jarek was hoping the old cowboy would giddyup and take control of his life. He needed the Resistance, and the Resistance needed him. Couldn't Alaric see that?

"You tried, sir," Al said as if reading his mind.

"Yeah. The diplomat. That's me."

"Alaric may yet come around, sir. And it's going to take more than diplomacy to get these people on board with an alliance," Al said. "If this is Zar'Golga's work, he couldn't have picked a worse time. Or better, depending on your perspective."

That was for damn sure.

Al hadn't found anything meaningful in his scan of local broadcasts, but Jarek thought the message was clear enough: *Come out and let us kill you, or we'll just reboot the Catastrophe and finish killing everyone else instead.* Do what we want or we'll hurt people: the operational foundation for any bully or dictator worth their salt. How could anyone say no to that?

But why now?

If Zar'Golga wanted to flush the Resistance out, why hadn't he resorted to these measures in the past? As far as Jarek had seen, the raknoth had treated the Resistance with all the caution one gave an irritating fly—swatting it away and forgetting it existed until it bothered them again.

Maybe it wasn't the Resistance Zar'Golga was after at all. A pang of guilt down his throat, into his chest. What if it was him and the others Zar'Golga was after? What if this was his retaliation for their slipping through his fingers back in Philly that morning? Or maybe it had something to do with Alton confronting Zar'Golga about the rakul.

It didn't matter. They'd survived, and if the crazy bastard wanted blood for it, all they could do now was try to stop him.

Ahead, the common room was a dull buzz of voices. When he entered, the space was teeming with enough activity to give even someone who'd spent his life in a skintight exosuit a twinge of claustrophobia.

It didn't take long to spot Rachel, Pryce, Lea, and the two Enochians in the far corner, padded from the rest of the crowd by a few feet of space and a liberal handful of wary stares. And there was Sloan, standing at the open center of the crowd like a shepherd gathering his flock.

Nelken and Daniels were at his flanks, speaking to him with tense expressions. There were too many voices in the room for Fela's sensors to pick out what they were saying, but Sloan resolutely avoided their eyes and looked ahead at the gathering crowd, his expression smug and supreme.

"Looks like things are off to a great start," Jarek mumbled as he began scooting, shuffling, and—here and there—pushing his way through the dense crowd toward the reject corner, doing his best to ignore the several dozen open stares and murmurs that followed him along the way.

"No Alaric," Pryce said when Jarek joined their corner huddle.

"We'll see." Jarek reached over to pat Rachel's back.

She looked anemic, and when he touched her, she jumped as if she hadn't quite noticed him there.

He gave her what he hoped was a reassuring smile.

It had been a long, long few days for all of them.

Sloan seemed content to wait as Daniels and Nelken continued their whispered one-way conference with him, which either meant that the attacks had paused for now or that Sloan was more concerned with this little game of his than he was with the innocent civilians dying out there for no reason.

The gathered Resistance members waited, anxiety eroding their obedience until it felt like the room would detonate at one wrong word.

Was that what Sloan wanted?

Finally, Nelken ceased talking to Sloan and held up a hand for silence, which fell almost immediately.

"As Commander Sloan has already informed you," he said in his best commander's voice, "there have been multiple bombings reported in our nearby cities. Overlord forces appear to be working together with the Reds to systematically cover Newark and Jersey City."

"What're we gonna do?" came a voice from the crowd.

"What can we do?" another voice cried.

Daniels and Nelken traded a glance that said they were wondering the same thing. Sloan only waited.

"The attack has paused at the moment," Nelken said, "but it seems likely they'll return. So far, it's been limited to low-potency IEDs dropped from passing ships. Assuming they aren't holding anything more lethal in store, it will take them a long while to cover a large enough area to threaten widespread casualties."

"We'll start by deploying more scouts to better establish the enemy's trajectory," Daniels said. "From there, we'll decide where we can most effectively deploy our forces to intercept. You all know as well as we do that we have limited means to deal with aerial attacks, but we'll use what we have to the best of our ability. More importantly, we'll do anything and everything we can to help our people out there."

Murmurs.

Nelken stepped forward to take the lead. "Whether or not we're able to counter these attacks, it falls to us to support those affected however we can. At nightfall, we'll send out teams to help survivors and potential targets alike find shelter, and—"

"Shelter where?" someone called. "Where's left to hide?"

Several more questions and protests followed on the back of that one, blurring together into a jumbled mess of voices as the tangible, frantic energy slithering its way through the crowd grew, strengthening its hold on the room.

Nelken and Daniels called for quiet. Behind them, Sloan was still silent. The little weasel looked like he was thinking about doing something stupid or underhanded. Probably both.

"The situation is dire," Nelken said, nearly shouting now to be heard over the persistent murmurs and whispers, "but we *will* keep our heads and get through it. We're Resistance, remember? We're here to fight the hard fights, to stand up to those no one else will stand up to."

"Is that what you're doing?" Sloan asked, his nasally voice not as strong as Nelken's or Daniels' but loud enough to be heard through the room nonetheless.

Nelken and Daniels looked back at their counterpart. Nelken's back was to Jarek, but the look on Daniels' face was that of someone who'd just realized the pet snake perched behind them was in fact a venomous viper that had no qualms whatsoever with striking them dead.

"Sloan—"

"Because earlier," Sloan said, "it sounded an awful lot to me like you were thinking about standing beside those alien bastards, not against them."

More whispers rippled through the crowd, pressure building like a sealed pot of boiling water.

Sloan watched his fellow commanders smugly. The slimy Dick had finally found a spine. Too bad it'd had to happen right when it was liable to cause a riot.

"Richard," Nelken said, his voice low enough that most of the crowd wouldn't hear and that Jarek would have missed it if not for Fela's sensors. "Now is *not* the time for—"

"That's right," Sloan called out to the crowd that was suddenly about a light breeze away from a collective conniption. "You've probably all been wondering what we were meeting about in private this afternoon." He strolled around Nelken and Daniels as he spoke, putting himself between them and the crowd.

Nelken looked to be very seriously considering closing Sloan's mouth with his clenched fists. He must've realized doing so would only worsen the situation, though, because he, along with Daniels, only glared at the back of Sloan's head as the rogue commander pointed a finger toward Jarek and the others.

"We were hearing from them. From the two freaks who wrecked our base just three days ago and their newest batch of alien freak friends."

"Whoa!" Jarek cried. "Who knew you were such a closet bigot, Dick?"

Rachel kicked his leg in what was presumably a signal for him to shut the hell up, but too many heads had already turned.

Sloan just sneered at him. The man wasn't a complete idiot. He knew the damage was already done.

Jarek looked from the mass of heads watching him to Nelken and Daniels, who looked as unsure as he was about how to catch the live impact grenade Sloan had just lobbed them.

Nothing to do now but eat it.

"Look," he said, turning to face the bulk of the crowd, "we've seen a lot of shit today. The kind of shit that two-thirds of your commanders thought might be worth thinking about and"—he waved a hand—"I don't know, *verifying* before we decided to induce a base-wide stroke epidemic."

"What's he talking about?" voices asked the commanders.

"Who are those two kids?" others called. "What are they doing here?"

"As Mr. Slater so eloquently put it," Daniels called over the crowd, "we've learned a good deal of new information about the raknoth threat this afternoon. Perhaps most importantly, we've learned that, after the incident with the nest device three days ago, the raknoth themselves may no longer be the greatest threat this planet faces."

"Yes," Sloan said, a kind of frantic fervor burning in his eyes now. "The rakul! The conveniently absent monsters that a pair of aliens"— he pointed at Haldin and Johnny—"learned about from their own raknoth friend. What's not to trust?"

Dozens of suspicious eyes turned to study Haldin and Johnny.

Shit. Jarek needed to say something, anything to disrupt the manic idiot. But there was too much. Too much to explain, and too little patience left in those accusatory stares.

He was about to try anyway when Rachel stepped up.

"I've seen them," she said, projecting her voice in a way he wasn't used to hearing from her.

That gave a few of them pause. More heads turned, waiting, listening.

Rachel looked around the room, meeting their eyes. Finally, she pointed to Haldin. "None of you will like what I'm about to say, but I've been inside his head, seen his thoughts and memories."

She'd been right. The wave of distrust that swept through the crowd was practically tangible.

"And what I saw…" Rachel continued, raising her voice to be heard. "Look, none of you are going to want to hear this, but the raknoth aren't the biggest bads out there. They have bosses too, and those bosses are coming for us."

More murmurs.

Most of the crowd was still eyeing their entire corner with distrust, but a few expressions had turned doubtful, questioning.

Apparently Rachel had one of those trustworthy faces.

"Lies and hearsay," Sloan called, drawing the crowd's attention back to him. "We cannot stand for this. We will not allow this organization to be commanded by those who'd listen to the word of alien sympathize—"

Alaric Weston pushed his way wordlessly out of the crowd. Sloan recoiled at the look in his eyes, then fist met bony cheek with a smacking thud, and Commander Sloan fell to the concrete with a yelp.

In the wave of gasps that rushed through the room, Jarek managed to bite back his cry of delight and settle for a satisfied grin. It served the bastard right.

The only question was whether Alaric's gambit would pull the crowd into order or convince them to lose it.

"You crazy…" Sloan muttered from the floor, his hand clutched to his cheek and his nauseatingly green eyes wide and wild as he looked up at Alaric. "How dare y—"

"Shut your mouth." Alaric didn't say it particularly loud, but there was enough surly weight in his tone that Sloan froze mid-word, tensing as if Alaric were about to strike him again.

Behind them, Nelken and Daniels looked almost as shocked as if Alaric had hit them too.

Before anyone could push past the hurdle of their surprise, Alaric turned to face the crowd.

"You all know who I am, what I've done." He swept the crowd with his gaze, letting the silence stretch. "You've all heard stories about why

I left. Some might have been accurate, others probably not. But here's the one bit of truth that matters: I left because I was afraid. Not afraid for my life. Not afraid we were going to lose."

The room hung on a silent string, waiting, watching the confession of their founding father with mouths agape.

"I was afraid to face the truth that was looking me square in the eyes. I was afraid to face the son the raknoth took from me, the boy they twisted and prodded until he was able to kill his own mother."

The outpouring of whispers Jarek expected didn't come. Only silence.

When Alaric spoke again, his voice was a shade rougher. "Turning away from that truth was the only way I knew to keep my sanity. But it was wrong. I left my son to the Overlord, let that bastard claw his way deeper into Seth's head while I sat on the other side of the country pretending I was doing something good." He shook his head and glanced back at Nelken and Daniels. "Well no more."

He looked back out to the crowd, his eyes regaining their usual steel. "You know who I am. You know I have as much reason to hate the raknoth as any of you. And after everything I've seen, I'm here to tell you that if Rachel believes there are worse than the raknoth out there, then I believe it too, and no amount of indignant yapping on our parts will change the facts."

Silence, broken only by the shuffling of Sloan pulling his gangly self to his feet behind Alaric.

"Touching," Sloan said. "But seeing as you just struck a Commander of the Resistance—"

"Oh please," Alaric said. "This isn't some royal court. My hands'll stay attached to my wrists, and I'll shut you up again if I have to. I mean to keep these people safe, no matter what that means, and right now, you're not helping."

Sloan's nostrils flared, his lip quivering with a barely contained snarl. "You left, Weston. This isn't your Resistance anymore."

Alaric shook his head. "This has never been my Resistance, Dick. It's *ours*. And I'm back now."

Sloan's stare shifted from Alaric to the crowd. "Are you all going to stand for this? For runaways who waltz back in telling us to listen to the enemy, to trust them?"

"Carmichael," Nelken said. "Simmons."

Two of the men on guard duty, or two who were geared up and toting shotguns, at least, stepped forward.

"Take Commander Sloan back to his quarters, and see to it he stays there for the time being."

Sloan whirled on Nelken, emerald eyes wide. "You can't." He turned to the approaching guards. "Hold that order, soldiers."

The two barely paused to trade a glance.

Sloan gave one last, low, "I am your Commander," to the two Resistance guards.

They took his shoulders.

"This isn't over," Sloan snarled at Alaric and the other commanders.

Then he clenched his jaw and shuffled silently off with the guards, electing to maintain what little dignity he had left by not struggling.

CHAPTER TWENTY

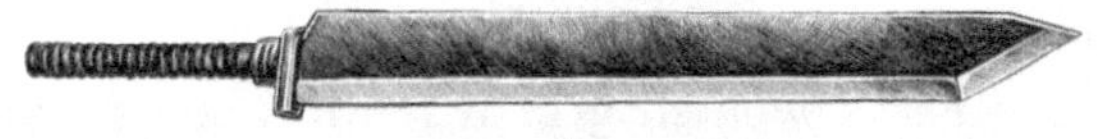

"The Resistance must have at least a few anti-air measures to work with," Pryce said, looking away from his inspection of Johnny.

"A few old launchers, from the sound of it," Jarek said, fighting down a smile at the look on Johnny's face.

As bleak as things seemed right now, it was hard not to be a little amused at the side show going on beside Michael's bed in medical.

When Pryce had asked Johnny if he minded him taking a closer look, Johnny had only reluctantly agreed.

"As long as all ten fingers stay outside of me," he'd said. "I know how it is with you people and aliens and probes."

Jarek had pointed out that the probing typically went the other way around, and Pryce had begun his inspection on a thoroughly uncomfortable Johnny. Mercifully, he'd abided by Johnny's single condition as he poked and prodded, checking pulse, pupillary reflex, something with the fingernails he was pretty sure had to do with circulatory function, and about fifty other things Jarek wasn't really sure about.

"The problem," Jarek continued, "is trying to cover two entire cities with a handful of ground-deployed weapons."

"This outfit really doesn't have a few ships to whip up and go harass them with?" Johnny asked.

"Just the two," Jarek said. "And neither of them is armed as far as I know. My ship's barely holding together as it is." He glanced at Rachel. "You got any clever tricks tucked up those magical sleeves, Goldilocks?"

She shrugged. "I might be able to knock a ship or two out of the sky if you got me close." She looked at Haldin. "What about you? Ever tried scrambling electronics before?"

Haldin gave her a wolfish grin that for some reason scratched Jarek's irritation button. "Once or twice, maybe."

"All right then," Jarek said. "Maybe we should go see about commissioning one of those ships and having you two run interference."

It wasn't much, but it was something.

Alaric's theatrical reentry to the fight had helped halt the momentum of the unrest creeping through the ranks—at least enough that Nelken had been able to delay the ticking time bomb that was the Resistance membership right now by promising to hold full council to discuss facts and future plans as soon as the bombing runs had been dealt with.

Of course, resetting the clock and actually disarming the lingering riot bomb were two different things. That was a problem for after they'd dealt with Zar'Golga, though.

They didn't have much to work with, but if they didn't want to watch the Resistance fall into disorder, they needed to throw a monkey wrench into the Golga's bombing operation, and they needed to do it fast.

If someone had told Jarek a couple of days ago that the Resistance was fixing to implode, he probably would've given them a solemn thumbs-up and continued on with not giving a rat's ass. But now...

"Ow!" Johnny jerked a hand back from Pryce, who must have pinched his finger.

The doctor on duty poked her head in at the sound, frowned at the lot of them, then disappeared back to the front room. She seemed less than thrilled that Michael's bedside had become their unofficial meeting spot.

"This is really the part of our story that got the most of your curiosity?" Haldin asked Pryce.

"Oh, I assure you," Pryce said, "I am thoroughly intrigued across the board. But this is the only part of the story I have any ability to assess for myself. Talking about space-faring, world-destroying aliens, I have no real point of reference by which to draw reasonable conclusions. You two, on the other hand—"

Pryce abruptly abandoned his inspection of Johnny's teeth and clapped his hands in Johnny's face with a wordless cry.

Johnny jerked back, hands raised defensively.

"—appear to be perfectly human upon rudimentary inspection," Pryce concluded. "Which tells us nothing about the validity of your claims, but is quite astounding if you truly came from this Enochia."

Jarek cleared his throat.

"Right." Pryce stepped back from Johnny and shoved his hands in his pockets. "Not the most important thing to be talking about when we have the Overlord bombing the city and a race of intergalactic conquerors on deck."

As if on cue, the alarm came silently alive in the corner with a rhythmic pulsing of orange light.

"Another bombing run?" Haldin asked.

The light strobed four more times then died.

"Probably." Jarek shook his head. "Bastards."

"We should contact our people," Haldin said. "They can help us handle this."

That was probably true, but they'd have to be careful about involving the other Enochians, and doubly so about Alton. Inviting any outsiders into the fray right now would only breed more distrust in the Resistance. God forbid word got out that one of them was a raknoth.

Haldin brought his comm holo to life just in time to show an incoming call from Alton.

"Speak of the devil," Jarek mumbled.

Haldin answered the call and turned so the rest of the group would be in frame. After a few seconds of idling, the holo floating over Haldin's arm resolved into an image of Elise, Alton, and a third man Jarek didn't recognize—older, maybe in his early fifties, with jet black hair, an eloquent-looking mustache, and sharp olive green eyes.

Jarek gave a jovial wave. "Howdy, gang."

"Sorry we didn't check in sooner," Haldin said. "It's been a hectic day."

"Earthlings putting you to work?" Elise asked.

"That's one way to put it," Johnny muttered, eyeing Pryce.

"Any news?" Haldin asked. "We're kinda dealing with a situation over here."

"The bombings," Alton said.

So they were watching from somewhere. Hell, they were in a spaceship. Who knew what they could be doing and seeing from that thing?

"You saw," Haldin said. "Good. We could probably use your help, actually." He glanced back at Jarek and the others. "Assuming the good folks here at Resistance HQ don't riot at the thought of us freakish alien types pitching in."

Jarek shrugged. "I've always been more of the save bacon first, ask questions later mindset anyways."

"Engaging Golga's forces head on is unwise," Alton said.

"No disagreements here," Jarek said, "but letting them bomb out the few poor bastards they didn't get fifteen years ago isn't really an option either."

Alton inclined his head. "I understand, but meeting brute force with more of the same will do nothing but widen the already considerable rift between our peoples. We can't let that happen if we hope to prepare for the rakul in time."

"Well I'd try to go hug them into submission, but something tells me that's not gonna pan out so well. That Golga guy didn't seem like he was up for talking."

"I think Alton's suggesting more of a surgical strike," Haldin said.

Alton nodded. "Much as I would like to make everyone see reason here, Jarek is not wrong. Golga was not willing to listen before, and I see no reason to believe we could ever convince him to change his mind."

"But why?" Rachel asked. "If you and the Red King are so sure the rakul are gonna toast you guys too, why isn't he? Why wouldn't he want to fight for his life?"

"Many of my people would rather kneel at the feet of the rakul and beg forgiveness than resist them and invite certain death. Zar'-Golga is no coward, though. He's nearly as old as the youngest of the rakul. If they truly respect any of the raknoth, he was among them before we fell from their graces. And if he truly believes they are coming now, I imagine he's hoping he might curry favor by laying waste to us before they arrive. He won't stop until they are here or we are dead."

"Which brings us back to the whole 'gotta fight to not die' conundrum," Jarek said.

"Indeed," Alton said. "But perhaps we can adjust the scale of that fight to something more favorable."

"A challenge?" Haldin asked.

Alton nodded. "A challenge."

"What," Rachel said, "the raknoth have some kind of warrior's honor code or something?"

Alton scrunched his face. "Not precisely, but most of my kind do take fierce pride in their worth as warriors. I've rarely seen one of my people refuse a duel, and never a Zar."

"Right on," Jarek said. "So we cut off the head of the snake, and then what? Hope we can replace it with a slightly less douchey head?"

Silence and a few shrugs.

"Al'Krogoth might be reasoned with," Alton said. "Or perhaps this Red King."

They all turned that over in silence. Deposing one ruthless bastard to clear the way for a slightly more agreeable dictator to take his place? Who said America was dead and gone?

It wasn't a flawless solution by any means, that was for damn sure. But the more Jarek thought about it, the more he was sure that it was the solution they needed—the one way he might be able to stop an army in its tracks with his lone sword.

Because now that the possibility was out there, he couldn't turn away from it, could he?

Hell no, he couldn't. Not after everything they'd been through in the past few days. Not after all the shit he'd spewed to Alaric about stepping up to the plate, about taking control.

Not when he had it in his power to save this many people.

This was bigger than him. Bigger than the dick-measuring politics and the cult-like institutional loyalties that had kept him steering clear of outfits like the Resistance for the past decade.

For the good of the tens of thousands of defenseless civilians in the area—and possibly even for the long-term survival of humanity—Zar'Golga needed to be stopped. And whether you wanted to call it fate or destiny or sheer damn bad luck, it had fallen to him to be one of the few people on the planet capable of single-handedly doing something about it.

Call it ego or recklessness or good ol' delusions of grandeur, but, somehow, in that moment, Jarek knew what he had to do.

It was his turn to step up to the plate. This was how they won.

"Even if we can bait Golga into a fight," Haldin was saying, "we still have to beat him."

"He is quite formidable," Alton said.

"Look who you're talking to," said the guy with the dark hair and the mustache.

Alton gave the slightest roll of his eyes but then added, "Hal does have a better chance than I do."

Jarek was barely listening to them.

"Al," he whispered, quietly enough that no one heard, "be a dear and open a local broadcast."

"Sir, I know what you're thinking, and I think you should take a moment to—"

"Just do it."

"You're certain?"

"I am."

Al let out a somber sigh. "Very well, sir. Opening a local broadcast now."

Jarek ran through a basic outline in his head, then put on his best showman's grin and spread his hands wide, even though it was only his voice transmitting.

"Attention! To any pricks arrogant enough to call themselves the Overlord with a capital O."

Understanding dawned in Rachel's and Pryce's widened eyes at the same time.

Rachel reached a helpless hand toward him. "Jarek, wait."

He almost listened. But he couldn't stop now.

"Jarek Slater here. Couldn't help but notice you decided to put on your giant douche hat and start dropping bombs after we gave you the slip down South. Seriously, man? I mean, I might act like a five-year-old sometimes, but I'm only off by a couple decades. What's your excuse, you immortal man-child?"

Rachel didn't look happy about any of this. Haldin, on the other hand, wiped the surprise off his face and rolled his wrist as if to say *keep it moving*.

"Anyways," Jarek continued, "let's get to the point. You done crossed the line, Zar. So here's the deal: I challenge your scaly ass to a duel. I can't say it's for the city, or anything like that. Those stakes aren't mine to give. But what I can say is that if you don't fight me, you can be damn sure every one of your red-eyed underlings are gonna know that the mighty Zar'Golga refused to duke it out with a sad little human. Oh, and the rakul, too. I'll be sure to let them know before they rip this planet to shreds. How much favor do you think you'll be currying after that?"

Pryce had gone a few shades paler. Haldin gave Jarek a thumbs-up as if Jarek was simply delivering a good bout at debate club rather than poking the meanest, strongest bear on the planet. Rachel ceased glaring at Jarek only long enough to skewer Haldin with the same look.

Almost done. Just one more thing.

"So what do you say, Zar? You wanna come play with my Big

Whacker?" He drew a deep breath and pushed through the adrenaline-tinged fear. "High noon tomorrow. Port Newark, round two. Let's go, you son of a bitch." Then he allowed the fear to spill over and mix with the anger into something manic as he cried, "Toodles!"

Al cut the line.

"What the hell did you just do?" Rachel asked.

Jarek blew out a long breath, tension bleeding out of his body and leaving him feeling drained in more ways than one. "Saved the day, with any luck." He tried to conjure a grin with the words, but couldn't seem to find one lying around.

Rachel held him on the point of her stare until he felt like he'd shrivel. Then she whirled and stalked out of the room, cracking her staff forcefully into the floor with each step.

When she'd gone, Haldin clapped him on an armored shoulder. "That was well done." He cocked his head. "I think."

There were a few murmured assents. Pryce finally closed his gaping mouth.

"Yeah," Jarek said quietly, feeling a lot less confident than he had a minute ago. "Go me."

CHAPTER TWENTY-ONE

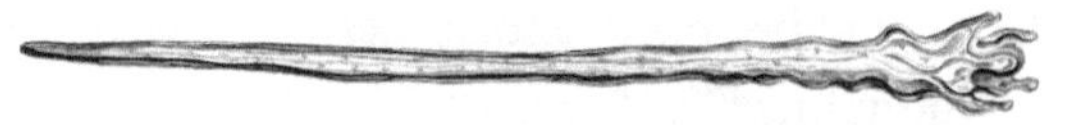

After she'd had a few minutes to cool down in the hallway, Rachel decided Jarek's stunt wasn't the worst solution to their otherwise untenable problem. Taking Zar'Golga on directly was far better than trying to meet his forces in the field, and especially better than doing so without crippling either side of the engagement and leaving them worthless to fight the coming rakul. And if anyone was certified for a one-on-one deathmatch with the world's most dangerous space vampire, it was probably Jarek.

Or her.

No. On paper, her abilities might qualify her for the job. She could smack a raknoth around with the best of them. But stepping into the arena for a fight to the death with the Overlord? She wasn't built for that like Jarek was.

She couldn't help but wish someone else—maybe Haldin, but anybody really—could have stepped up. But she understood why Jarek had taken the hot seat, why he'd decided to take the weight of the world on his shoulders. It didn't make her any less pissed he hadn't thought to at least stop and talk about it, but she got it.

Because deep down, underneath the layers of devil-may-care showmanship and general wise-assery, beyond his distrust of all organized establishment, Jarek Slater was the guy who'd fight to his last breath to protect the people who needed protecting.

It was probably why she... what? Liked him? Did she *like* Jarek? She leaned her head against the cool cinder block wall and sighed.

Of course she liked him. She was a master of sticking head in sand, but she wasn't quite good enough to deny that one. He was a child, and he drove her more than a little crazy at times, but he also made her smile—consistently. That was no small feat. She'd never felt safer knowing someone had her back, and sometimes, when he was looking at her, she even thought...

Jesus, what was the world coming to? And why was she lurking in the hallway like an angsty teen when there were people dying out there?

She needed to do something.

Jarek had played his hand, there was no stopping that now, but she'd be damned if she was going to let him waltz into that stadium and die alone tomorrow. The chances of Zar'Golga showing up seemed decent enough. The chances of him doing it in good faith and giving Jarek a fair fight seemed drastically slimmer.

So she'd go. She'd make sure Jarek's back was clear while he cut down that savage monster, and then, with any luck, they could breathe long enough to turn their attention to other things—like the second coming of the apocalypse.

By the time Jarek and Haldin emerged from medical into the hallway, Rachel was actually feeling half okay about the plan.

Jarek eyed her as if she were an armed explosive device. "We're gonna see if Stumpy has any useful input if you wanna come."

His wariness only grew when she nodded wordlessly and gestured for him to lead on.

Approaching the Red King's cell felt less intimidating this time around. After everything they'd learned, the raknoth were no longer the mystery-shrouded monstrosities they'd seemed just days ago. Still monstrosities, maybe, but it made a difference, understanding some of the hows and whys that had brought them to Earth and led them to do what they'd done to the planet.

Twisted and barbaric as their actions had been, on some level, the raknoth of Earth were still people—or beings, at least— that just wanted to be free.

Or maybe that was only Alton Parker.

Zar'Golga certainly didn't seem to have any qualms about indiscriminately killing humans. Understanding that the raknoth were operating on more than pure evil was one thing, but it didn't change the fact that humans were basically a resource to them and that most of them seemed intent on keeping it that way. That was unforgivable.

And then there was the other tiny ember burning her straight in the eye: the matter of what the raknoth had done to her family.

From what awful scraps her mind hadn't wiped blank, the home invasion had always seemed like just that: a brutal but ultimately run-of-the-mill crime. People had been doing that since forever. She'd always wanted to believe it had been something more—meant something more—but John had eventually convinced her that if the answers had ever been out there, they'd been wiped clean when the bombs had fallen.

Slowly, she'd started to come to terms with it. Only to find now that there *was* more to it, that all the horrible events of her life really were connected, and that the raknoth were sitting at the center of it all.

She wasn't ready to forgive that either—probably never would be. At some point, her and Alton were going to have a long, potentially painful talk about it. But for now…

She'd seen what was coming for them—in far more detail than she'd needed.

When the rakul arrived, they'd be needing all the help they could get, no matter how bitter the pill she'd have to swallow. So she kept her mouth shut and paraded after Jarek, thinking neutral thoughts.

As usual, three Resistance troops were standing guard outside the Red King's cell.

Jarek nodded to them. "Gents." Then, toward the cell door, "Stumpy. I know you can hear me in there, buddy. Didja miss me?"

The guards traded *is this guy nuts?* glances as they unlocked the door and parted to let them through. Jarek winked at the one with the key, pushed the door open, and led the way into the cell.

Inside, the Red King's cell was exactly as they'd left it, with the one exception of the raknoth himself, who'd regenerated an alarming amount of tissue. His marred hand was now whole again, and the arm that had been removed from near the elbow wasn't so far behind.

"Looks like you're gonna have to rethink your brilliant nickname," she muttered toward Jarek.

"Maybe so," he said, "but he'll always be Stumpy in my heart."

The Red King's limb lengths weren't the only things that had changed. Inky black lines had appeared, crawling their way up along his neck from underneath his shirt collar and down along the length of his fresh limbs in patterns that reminded her of spiderwebs.

He looked ill.

"He needs to feed," Haldin said quietly.

The Red King looked at Haldin, took a few curious sniffs, then went back to staring at the ceiling.

"That's what those lines mean?" Rachel asked.

Haldin nodded. "He needs blood. The same thing happened to Alton when we, uh, first took him prisoner a while back."

"Alton?"

Rachel nearly jumped at the sound of the Red King's voice. He was watching them again with a feeble crimson glow in his eyes.

"His true name is Braka," Haldin said.

The King gave a growl-hiss of laughter. "Al'Braka? Was he not one of the fools who ran off to die with Zar'Faenor?"

"The only one who didn't die," Haldin said. He looked at her and Jarek as if asking permission to continue.

She shrugged. He could knock himself out. If it got them anywhere, she didn't really give a crap.

"He came back here to try to cure the sickness so your people can move on," Haldin said. He reached inside his jacket and produced a small plastic blood bag he must've nabbed from medical. "But now it looks like we've got a rakul problem to worry about first."

The King licked his lips at the sight of the blood and eyed Haldin with renewed interest. "What do you know about the harvesters, human?"

Haldin telekinetically slit the top of the bag with a wave of his finger and shrugged. "Enough to know we're all screwed if we don't pull our heads out of our asses and start getting ready for them."

Another growl-hiss of laughter. "There is no 'getting ready' for the rakul, human. There is submitting, and there is dying. In our case, they are one and the same."

"Well aren't you just a chatty ray of sunshine today?" Jarek said. He looked at Haldin. "He must like you."

The King looked like he might reply, but Haldin lowered the blood bag close to his mouth and began pouring, and for several seconds, the raknoth did nothing but slurp down mouthfuls of the dark, viscous fluid with a series of appreciative grunts.

"Well now you're just cheating," Jarek said. "Also, gross."

Rachel couldn't argue with the second part, even if the King did deserve a point or two for how tidy he managed to be in downing what must've been a pint of blood.

"What's your real name?" Haldin asked when the bag was nearly empty. "I'm Haldin Raish."

The King finished his thick drink and licked his lips clean before answering. "I am Al'Drogan," he finally said. "Thank you, Haldin Raish."

"Drogan," Haldin repeated. "You're welcome."

"Doesn't have the same ring as Stumpy," Jarek said, "but hey, maybe it'll grow on me. What if we told you that we know what's coming, Drogan? And that we're ready to consider setting everything else aside for the time being so we can all fight for our lives and live to kill each other another day?"

The King—Al'Drogan—considered Jarek. "If you plan to stand and fight," he finally said, "then I would wager you do not truly understand what is coming." He inclined his head toward Jarek. "You are a passable warrior—"

"Coming from the guy who lost his arms to me," Jarek said.

"—but the weakest of the rakul would crush you like a petty insect—"

"Not the first time I've heard that."

"—and even if you wish to make this foolish stand," Drogan continued, an irritated growl slipping into his words, "the Overlord will never think to stand with you. He would sooner see this world burn than align himself against the masters alongside your kind. He may even think to burn it himself if he believes it will return him to their favor."

"Yeah," Jarek said. "That's actually why we came to talk to you, buddy. You might have already heard in here with those creepy little ears of yours, but Golga's out there wrecking any shot we have at making this whole Earth alliance dream team happen. We need to stop him."

Drogan took in each of them anew, scrutinizing, measuring. "You are serious about this."

"Guilty as charged," Jarek said.

"You do not know what you speak of. The rakul—"

"I do know," Rachel said. "I've seen them."

Drogan's eyes widened, pulsing brighter.

"In memories," she added, more quickly than she needed to.

Why did she care if she gave the bastard a literal or figurative heart attack?

"We both have," Haldin said.

Drogan's eyes dimmed. "Then you both understand how hopelessly doomed this planet is."

"Oh, don't be such a drama queen, Stumpy," Jarek said. "You guys could learn a thing or two from humans if that's all it takes for you to lay down and take it. Where's the raknoth fight, man?"

"It died with the last raknoth clan that thought to shirk the masters' rule."

Jarek looked a shade less certain. "There have been revolts before?"

Drogan gave a growl-hiss of laughter. "Of course there have, you imbecile. Do you truly think my people would willingly go on like this for millennia without attempting to break free?"

Rachel resisted the urge to ask about the details of how and why the revolutions had failed. "It doesn't matter now. We don't have a choice here. The rakul are coming. You must've felt their message, even through that cloak." She looked at Haldin. "I know we did."

Drogan drew a sharp hiss of breath through his teeth. "Cursed void, I prayed I had only imagined it."

"My brother was affected when the nest went off. He had some kind of seizure when the message came."

For the first time, Drogan wriggled against his chains. "You must release me! It may only be a matter of days now."

"Michael's okay now, by the way," Jarek said. "Thanks for asking."

"What concern is the life of one human when the entire world sits on the precipice? Fools! We must move now."

Jarek traded a surprised look with Rachel. "Just like that, huh? One hint that these guys are on their way and suddenly you're on board with this thing you say can't be done?"

Drogan ceased his wriggling and gave an indignant sniff. "I do not shirk from the thought of an honorable warrior's death. But that does not mean I wish to die. I am still young, and I do not relish being a servant of the rakul any more than the rest of my people."

"So help us," Jarek said. "Help us hand them back their own asses when they get here. Help us get the rest of your pals on board to do the same."

Rachel expected the raknoth to laugh or scoff, but he didn't. He just laid there in silent thought.

"The Overlord must be removed first," he finally said. "Zar'Golga likely would have ascended to Kul in the next millennium had our mission here went as planned. He will destroy any who think to resist the rakul in the hope of securing his future."

"Ten steps ahead of you on that one," Jarek said. "I challenged the a-hole to a duel."

Drogan looked at Jarek like he'd just confessed he thought the Earth was flat. "That was exceptionally foolish, even for a human."

Jarek raised his hands. "Hey, don't hold back, Stumpy. Tell me how you really feel."

Drogan blinked. "I was not being facetious, Jarek Slater. You nearly fell to me. Zar'Golga is far stronger, faster, and more experienced in combat. Much as it shames me to say, better you attempt to catch him unaware or in the chaos of a larger engagement. Face him one-on-one, and he will kill you. An honorable death, to be sure, but not one that promotes our survival."

"If I didn't know any better, I'd say it almost sounds like you're worried about me, Stumpy."

Drogan scowled. "Ridiculous. I merely recognize you as one of the few humans who may be of any use if we are to attempt this madness."

Jarek grinned. "You're gonna go and make me blush now."

He could play it off all he wanted. Rachel didn't miss the traces of uncertainty hiding beneath that grin.

Drogan let out a hissing sigh and fixed Jarek with a level stare. "You came here for my counsel, yes?"

Jarek tilted his head in acknowledgment.

"Now you have it," Drogan said. "Do not go through with this plan if you wish to live."

Jarek frowned, thought about saying something, and turned for the door instead. "Helpful, Stumpy. Real helpful."

"Zar'Golga does not have a weakness to exploit," Drogan said.

Jarek paused, hand halfway to the door.

"If you do this," Drogan continued, "you must not underestimate him. And do not dare show him mercy. Zar'Golga may not be as old and powerful as the rakul, but he is the most cunning warrior I have ever known."

Jarek held the raknoth's gaze for a length, then he pulled the door open. "See you tomorrow, Stumpy. Maybe I'll bring you back a souvenir."

Drogan might have actually cracked the faint beginnings of a smile. "Fight well, Jarek Slater."

Rachel glanced between Drogan and the open doorway Jarek had disappeared through, her earlier confidence in the plan crumbling.

Zar'Golga wasn't easy prey, or prey at all, really—they'd seen that clearly enough this morning. If it hadn't been for their interference,

Golga would have killed Alton half a dozen times during the fight. But to hear Drogan talk about Golga now…

Jarek was tough, but they were talking about a creature who'd probably conquered more planets than Jarek had scars.

And while he clearly wasn't oblivious to the fact, Jarek didn't seem nearly rattled enough about it.

"I need a drink," he said when they joined him down the hallway outside medical. He glanced at Haldin. "Is that a thing with you guys, or—"

"I need to talk to you." Rachel was caught off guard by her own tone, and a part of her burned with satisfaction at the look it put on Jarek's face, like a part of him had just shriveled up. "Alone," she added.

Haldin shot Jarek a slightly pitying look, nodded to Rachel, and shuffled off to rejoin the others in medical.

Rachel grabbed Jarek by the arm and tugged him around to an isolated corner in the next hallway. Even before counting Fela, Rachel probably weighed about half of Jarek. With the exosuit, he could have lifted a dozen Rachels and held them all at arm's length. Despite all that, he didn't resist.

"You're angry," he said.

"You're an asshole." He held up a finger and started to say something, but Rachel silenced him with a look. "You just get to decide you're gonna waltz off on your big suicide cock fight, and fuck whatever the rest of us have to say about it?"

"It's not right, I know." For a second, he actually looked apologetic. Then his big stupid mouth won out. "I mean, a suicide cock fight—what does that even mean? Are the cocks suicidal, or—"

She thrust a hand toward him and let her frustration flood out in a wave of telekinetic force.

He staggered back a few steps and raised a hand. "Okay, okay! Jesus, Goldilocks…"

She maintained her weapons-grade glare and tried unsuccessfully to blow a strand of hair out of her eyes.

Jarek, to his credit, didn't say a thing about the failure. "Look, what do you want me to do? Tall, Dark, and Ugly's gotta go, and someone has to do it. I took Stumpy, I can take Golga too."

What she wanted him to do was to drop the tough guy act for five seconds and tell her that he understood he wasn't invincible. That he could die tomorrow. That just because Golga needed to go didn't mean he was going to do it quietly—or at all.

"You heard Drogan in there," she said. "This isn't just another fight. You can't keep acting like this is some fucking game you can't lose."

Jarek shrugged. "It's my neck."

She ground her teeth. "Fine. You're a grown man, you can do whatever the fuck you want—good for you. But you don't get to make that call then expect us all to care."

His face furrowed into a dark frown, but she wasn't done.

"Is that what you want? You want me to plead for you to stay, to not throw your life away like a fucking crazy person?"

He said nothing and held her stare with maddening calmness. Only it wasn't calmness, was it? There was tension there in the line of his jaw. Tension that bled slowly into guilt in the dark depths of his eyes. Seconds ticked by, his mask wavering a millimeter at a time. She thought to look away, but her eyes didn't move.

Freefall. That's what the stare felt like. Only gravity had reoriented, and…

And when had he stepped so close? Or had it been her who'd stepped closer to him?

She caught his hand midway to her cheek out of reflex more than anything. He moved closer, eyes darting across her face now, uncertain, vulnerable. They settled on her lips.

Her voice came in a soft whisper. "What the fuck are you—"

He kissed her.

Her breath caught, and her chest jolted with alarm and shock and… warmth. It flooded in, starting at his lips and spreading through her like a roaring fire on a rainy day. She shuddered, and he pressed in closer. Her eyelids drifted closed, and she let him.

It was a good kiss.

He pressed against her, strong arms circling around her waist as his lips found the shape of hers, warm and soft beside the sharp, scratchy stubble of his chin. His scent surrounded her, not pleasant, necessarily, but unmistakably alluring. She flicked her tongue lightly at his, and—

She sucked in a sharp breath and shoved him away. "What the fuck, dude?"

Her head was spinning. She hadn't consciously thought about it, but she must've added a few ounces of telekinetic oomph to the shove, because Jarek was on the other side of the hallway now, looking nearly as shocked as she felt.

He opened his mouth to say something, then he caught himself and shrugged. "You gave me a look."

"Like hell." Right? The words left her mouth before she had a chance to think about it, and they sounded much more certain than she felt.

Jarek gave her a grin that did irritating things to her insides. "So you're saying you didn't like it, then?"

"I…" She shook her head. "Can we just get back to the point here?"

"If I knew what the point was."

She rolled her eyes. "The point is that you're a dick. And that I'm coming with you tomorrow."

That sobered him right up.

"Whoa, now. Let's not get ahead of ourselves. It's bad enough risking one of us on a gamble. And Michael might need you here. Hell, everyone might—especially if…"

There it was—the crack in his bravado as he failed to finish the thought.

Especially if Drogan was right and he'd made a life-ending mistake.

"See how it feels when people go and make these decisions without thinking about their friends?"

The fear and the doubt hung on his features a few moments longer. Then he swallowed and met her eyes again. "So you're calling me your friend now, huh?"

"Bite me."

He stepped closer. "Gladly."

She forced out a snort and pushed off the wall to shimmy toward medical before he could close her in. "This is a terrible idea, you know. There's no way that scaly prick will play fair if he thinks there's even a chance he could lose."

He shrugged, suddenly looking tired. "Of course it's a terrible idea. But Golga's the linchpin to this whole thing, and it's still the best way to get a shot at him."

She gave a slow nod. "I think you're right. But that doesn't mean you should risk everything alone. I'm coming with you."

He took a deep breath and set his jaw. "Okay, Goldilocks."

She turned to leave before either of them could take it any further than that.

She didn't want to talk about the kiss, didn't even want to think about it right now. This entire situation was already plenty fucked without adding another steaming pile of feelings on top of it.

When she entered Michael's room in medical, Pryce and the Enochians all looked up and then away too fast for them to have been talking about anything other than her. The guilt plastered on their faces didn't help their case either.

"All right, peanut gallery." She waited until they all dropped the act and met her gaze. "We need to start talking about a plan B."

CHAPTER TWENTY-TWO

"Oh, I do like her, sir," Al said in Jarek's earpiece as Rachel vanished around the corner.

Jarek stood there for a long moment, mired in a curious mixture of gut-deep dread at the thought of tomorrow and light-headed excitement at the lingering taste of Rachel's lips.

"Yeah," he said finally, setting off down the hallway. "Yeah, I think I do too, buddy."

Just one more itty-bitty reason he needed to make sure he didn't get her killed. It was a hell of a lot easier pulling the trigger when it was only his neck.

Which was exactly why he wasn't planning on taking Rachel to the stadium tomorrow.

His neck, his decision, right? Definitely.

So then why did he feel so shitty about it right now?

Maybe he really was an asshole.

"An asshole who's gonna save the damn day," he mumbled.

"You tell 'em, sir."

Jesus, he needed a drink.

His talk with Al'Drogan had been less than productive. He'd wanted a weak point to attack, a flaw to exploit, but no. He was about to fight the freaking invincible Achilles of raknoth—except no, bad example, because Zar'Golga sure as hell wasn't going to have a cranky heel to hold him back.

Drogan had seemed sincere enough about wanting to save his own skin from the rakul. The fact that Drogan was agreeing Golga's demise was a crucial step in that process and yet still warning Jarek off his current collision course with the warlord only made that warning all the more disheartening.

But it wasn't like Jarek had any great alternatives.

Their chances at putting an end to the bombing runs with their measly two-and-a-half ships and the Resistance's handful of heavy weapons weren't stellar. And even if they managed to pull it off, it wouldn't fix the root of the problem.

As long as Zar'Golga was alive, the outlook on the whole raknoth-human alliance idea went from shitty and highly improbable all the way down to completely unimaginable.

One way or another, the Overlord had to go, which meant someone had to do the deed. As confident as he'd felt in the moment he'd decided to issue the challenge, though, he couldn't help but wonder now if he'd made a mistake.

Maybe. Probably, even. But it wasn't like they had a list of candidates standing by.

Alton had only barely survived Golga's attack back in Philly with constant help from Haldin. He wouldn't last in a one-on-one. Haldin, on the other hand, was clearly faster and stronger than any human Jarek had ever encountered. He assumed the Enochian had his arcane abilities to thank for that, seeing as Johnny exhibited no such super-human talents. All things considered, Haldin might actually be a match for Jarek. Maybe more than a match.

Hell, Rachel probably could be too if she really wanted to roll her sleeves up and get dirty.

But he never could have stood aside and watched either of them step out to fight Zar'Golga on their own.

Rachel was right. He'd acted selfishly, without forethought. He'd defaulted to habits gained from working, living, and fighting on his own. And at the end of the day, he didn't feel badly about taking this fight for his own.

But whether he liked it or not, he wasn't alone in this fight anymore. He'd always had Pryce and Al, but now he had Alaric, Lea, the Enochians, maybe even the Resistance.

And he had Rachel.

Rachel, who'd stood beside him at every turn, who'd already saved his bacon more times in a week than anyone save for Al. Rachel, who was decidedly on his side and fierce and strong and increasingly sexy as all hell.

He hadn't meant to kiss her, really. Wanted to, sure, but the actual execution had unfolded seemingly of its own accord, like watching natural law in motion. The kiss itself—the way her surprised breath had tickled his lips, and the way her initially resistant lips had given way to hot, urgent need, if only for a moment…

He shook his head clear as he passed by a pair of Resistance soldiers who were eyeing him distrustfully.

Good thing he wasn't wearing sweatpants right now. Then they really would've had something to stare down.

Al cleared his throat at the development and snapped Jarek back to more appropriately doomy and gloomy thoughts, which he had in spades.

He probably wouldn't have admitted it out loud without several drinks and a damn good reason, but facing down Drogan at Pryce's and then again at the ports easily ranked among his top five most pants-shitting moments, right near the top of the list.

Fighting marauders and the rest of humanity's most deplorable wasn't a bucket of giggles, but at least Fela's protection gave him a safety margin when tangling with humans. As long as he didn't screw the pooch too hard, there was almost always a way out of any tricky situation he'd find himself in.

On top of that, he understood humans. Intimately. Take the most depraved sicko you could find, and Jarek could at least marginally understand what made them tick—enough to anticipate how they would react in different scenarios.

When it came to fighting raknoth, though, all of that flew out the window. On a basic level, he was coming to understand who the raknoth were and what drove them, but that didn't really dull the shock of their ferocity in battle. They were vicious predators: brutally strong, uncannily quick, and damn tough to take down.

He'd fought plenty over the years who'd fancied themselves hard men, savage men. Several of them had been. But none of them had held a candle to the savagery of a raknoth.

Every fight he'd had with the raknoth had been quietly if not overtly terrifying, and now he'd consigned himself to fighting the worst of them.

That drink was starting to sound more like an antidote than an indulgence.

As far as he'd seen, HQ didn't exactly have a bar on its premises, which was kind of surprising, given how hopeless their fight had been over the years, but someone had to have booze around here.

Alaric.

Alaric seemed like a guy who wouldn't wander too far without knowing where to find some whiskey—especially after the day he'd just had.

Jarek was about to turn for the council chamber where he figured Alaric might be when he spotted the grizzled old Resistance fighter through the open doors of the mess hall. Or at least what the Resistance members called a mess hall. It was fairly identical to every other room in HQ: low ceilings, bland, emotionally oppressing cinder block walls. The only things that set it apart were the couple dozen tiny tables spaced around the room and the serving counters over to the right.

It was past common dinner hours already, and only a few people remained in the hall. Alaric sat in a far corner, dispassionately spooning some manner of stew into his mouth.

Jarek paused at the door and contemplated retreating to the ship instead. He was pretty sure he had half a bottle squirreled away somewhere, and now that he was here, he wasn't so sure he felt like talking.

He was about to turn around when Alaric looked up. He caught sight of Jarek, seemed to have his own internal debate, and then settled with a look that suggested he had something to say and little interest in actually saying it.

Ah, hell with it.

Alaric went back to his stew and didn't look up as Jarek approached, but he did raise a boot and push the plastic chair opposite him out from under the small table.

Jarek considered the chair and gingerly settled his and Fela's combined bulk down. "Word has it there's a new sheriff in these here parts."

Alaric scowled at his stew. "Real funny."

"Almost as funny as that bit where you slugged Sloan in front of half the Resistance."

A faint smile touched Alaric's mouth. "Best feeling I've had in years."

"I was hoping we could celebrate with a drink."

Alaric swallowed a bite and shook his head. "Don't touch the stuff these days. Don't know as there's much to find around here anyway."

Well so much for that plan.

Alaric finally looked up, his eyes measuring. "I heard what you did, by the way."

"I bet you did. If this outfit spent half as much time fighting the raknoth as it did gossiping, we'd probably be in the clear already."

"Can you take him?"

Jarek tapped idly at the tabletop. "Theoretically, yes."

"And practically?"

"He's stronger, faster, and apparently a whole lot more badass than any of the raknoth I've faced." He shook his head. "I dunno, when the freaking Red King acts like he might be concerned for your well-being, you have to wonder what it is you just signed up for."

"Maybe he's trying to rattle you, keep you from giving his master the same treatment you gave him."

"Maybe. But I don't really think so. I think he's scared, Alaric. About what's coming. Seems like Alton and our Enochian friends are too. And thinking about what would scare the monsters—not to mention Rachel... Well, that's pretty damn scary, right?"

Alaric shrugged, studying him closely. "About as scary as flying into what's probably gonna be a trap to face what's probably the most vicious bastard this planet's ever scene in a one-on-one duel."

"Yeah, well... Someone had to do it."

"Did they?"

Jarek didn't say anything. It did feel an awful lot like he was preparing to fight an uphill battle just to buy the right to fight another bigger uphill battle, and another after that. Thinking about the entirety of the work ahead made him want to go find a dark, quiet corner to hide in.

But people were dying out there, and a lot more were going to join them if someone didn't find the stones to keep putting one foot in front of the other. Not that that was about to quell the stream of icy dread flowing through his guts or anything.

"He's broken inside," Alaric said quietly after some time.

It wasn't hard to guess who he was talking about. Jarek just wasn't sure what to say to that.

"Seth was a good kid once, you know," Alaric continued, not seeming to notice or mind Jarek's lack of input. "Wanted to be a painter for Christ sake. 'Course the Catastrophe put a damper on all of that, but you never would have known it to look at him—not at first. It got harder in the first couple years, watching the world degrade and never rebound. You know how that felt. Hell, I can only imagine what you got up to back then."

"Yeah..." Jarek rubbed the back of his helmeted head. "Mistakes were made."

The ghost of a wan smile crossed Alaric's face. "They most certainly were. Starting the Resistance, leaving Seth and his mother to fend at a homestead for months at a time... I thought I was doing a good thing for the world, but... Well, mistakes were made. I don't think that bastard Golga ever meant to find Seth. His people were always sweeping through here and there back then, grabbing up fresh recruits—willing or no." He shook his head. "They found my son by sheer shitty luck. Golga must've realized who Seth was when he got into his head to do whatever it was that…"

Alaric ran a hand over his scraggly gray beard.

"No use speculatin' now. The point is that I've been moping in Deadwood all these years, thinking the reason that bastard was able to get Seth to… do what he did was that I'd opened the door. That I'd failed him as a father, failed to protect him and his future. Hell, everyone's future. The future of the world. But I was wrong." He fixed Jarek with a haunted look. "You know what he told me today?"

Jarek shook his head, not entirely sure he wanted to know.

Alaric clenched and unclenched his jaw several times before he managed to speak again. "He told me he wishes he'd had the chance to kill me too. Wishes he could have cut my throat while I slept."

"Jesus."

Alaric took a shaky breath and shook his head. "Not an easy thing to hear, you can imagine, but it did help me see something."

"What's that?"

"The way he said it, that evil glow in his eyes… Golga didn't just play with my son's head. I'm sure of that now. He didn't just twist his thoughts and fears around. He broke Seth's mind completely, smashed it to bits, then he told him who he was gonna be and what he was allowed to think and believe. My boy could have hated me—probably would have after everything that happened. He might have even wished I was dead." He shook his head. "But never like that."

Jarek had seen far too many people slide down the insidious slope from well-meaning to monstrous to think anyone was truly above the risk of going bad in terrible circumstances, but he wasn't about to say that to Alaric right now.

Besides, maybe there really was more to it than that. Golga had clearly done something to Mosen. Probably a lot of somethings, considering the eyes and the ridiculous strength and resilience. It wasn't hard to imagine the transition from Seth Weston to Mosen the psychopath had involved a good deal of mental reprogramming, possibly of the creepy alien telepath variety.

In the end, Jarek wasn't sure it really mattered.

Maybe there was some piece of Alaric's son left in Mosen. Maybe he was even redeemable. Jarek hoped so for Alaric's sake.

But even if that were the case, it didn't make Mosen any less dangerous right now, and he wasn't about to pretend otherwise.

"I'm sorry, Alaric."

Alaric fixed him with a grave stare. "I'm not telling you any of this for sympathy, son. I'm telling you because that son of a bitch Golga needs to die." He stood, gathering up his bowl. "I'm still not sure the rest of his kind shouldn't join him, but if these rakul are coming... Well, maybe an alliance is the only way. But not with him. When we face him tomorrow, I want you to remember that."

"We?"

"Nelken told me to pass along his thanks if I saw you before he did. And to let you know you have the full support of the Resistance in taking that bastard down. Surprised he didn't track you down yet. They're putting together an escort team for you."

That was unexpected. He'd mostly been counting on another attempted chastising from Resistance command, complete with phrases like "loose cannon" and "reckless behavior."

"And you didn't think to tell him that's a terrible idea?"

"Nope. Just told him I'd lead it. Nice call on high noon, by the way."

"What? It's not enough to send a whole team into a potential trap? They need to send a commander too?"

Alaric frowned down at him. "I'm no commander."

"Are you sure? Because you punched one out and used the words, 'I'm back now.' I might need to brush up on Resistance bylaws, but I think you might be a command—Hey!"

Alaric was already striding off to deposit his bowl in the receptacle by the kitchen. "Get some rest, son," he called, flicking two fingers over his shoulder in something between a salute and a wave. "Big day tomorrow."

"Yes, sir, Commander, sir," Jarek called. "Good talk, man. Great closure. Yeah, don't let me keep yo—"

Alaric disappeared through the doorway.

"Yep, he's gone," he mumbled. "Jesus. For people who question my decisions, they sure are eager to all jump in on the suicide cock fight."

"Astounding," Al agreed. "It's almost as if they care about you, sir."

He huffed a light chuckle. "Rachel, maybe. Alaric probably just wants to make damn sure Golga ends up properly dead tomorrow." He hesitated, too uncertain about his next words to even speak them to Al at first.

"Too bad neither of them will be there."

Al was silent for a stretch. "You know you don't have to do this, sir," he finally said. "There are several alternatives that might feasibly enable us to remove Zar'Golga from the equation."

"Got any we can pull off by tomorrow that don't involve hundreds of innocent people dying?"

Another silence. Then, "Excluding miracles, sir?"

He smiled a tired smile. "I sure hope not, buddy. But I guess we'll find out soon. You pulled Stumpy's comm info, right?"

"I did sir, but—"

"Send the message, Al." He stood to leave. "Tell that bastard there's been a change of plans."

No one could try to stop him if they didn't know where he was going or when he'd be there. And if it was time to step up to the plate, he might as well do it right.

"Tell him I'll see him bright and early at Yankee Stadium."

CHAPTER TWENTY-THREE

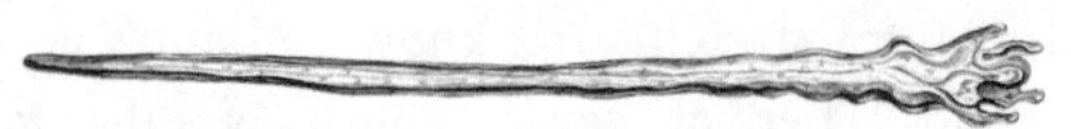

Rachel took yet another deep breath and reminded herself that it was, in fact, *not* creepy as all hell that she was sitting here waiting in the dark cabin of Jarek's ship. It was only practical. Because despite what might have come out of his mouth, Rachel had bought Jarek's agreement to bring her along to the duel about as readily as she'd have bought a lightly used roll of toilet paper.

He had no intention of letting her fly into harm's way with him tomorrow.

She wasn't sure about that, of course. It was only a strong hunch. But the fact that Al had unlocked the ship and let her on board with only minimal fuss supported said hunch. Al had actually seemed kind of relieved to see her.

It had been a little bizarre, talking to Al here at the ship even as he was simultaneously speaking with Jarek in HQ. She'd offered to wait until Al had wrapped up his conversation on the other end, but he'd insisted it wasn't a problem. One of the perks of being a digital construct, apparently.

Once she'd gotten on board and settled into Jarek's raggedy but comfortable brown recliner, though, Al had mostly left her to sit with her own thoughts, which was just as well. She had what felt like a few years' worth of mental processing to catch up on, and out here, it was dark and quiet and almost peacefu—

"Here we come, ma'am," Al said quietly from the cabin speakers.

Well, it was dark at least.

Her heart picked up as half a dozen scenarios played through her head. Would he be angry she'd sneaked aboard? Should she even care? If he was, he could shove it. He didn't get to pull a fast one and then get upset just because she'd seen through his crap. Right?

Yeah. Assuming he actually was pulling a fast one. She could be getting ahead of herself. And if he wasn't... Oh god, he was totally going to think she'd come here to see him because of that stupid kiss, wasn't he? Of course he would. Jarek was probably categorically incapable of comprehending that a female didn't want him.

Because she didn't, right?

The boarding ramp gave a few clacks and began to descend with a low hum.

She watched it go, insisting to no avail that her stupid heart get its shit together and slow down.

The ramp touched down to the pavement outside, and the first two boot steps sounded up its length. It was dark out there, but she could just make out Jarek's silhouette as he paused near the bottom.

"Say," he said quietly, "you have something you forgot to tell me, Mr. Robot?"

She thought about waiting to see if Al would say something out loud but decided the jig was already up. Knowing what little she did about Fela's sensors, she wouldn't be surprised if Jarek had heard her breathing or her heart or something, and he could probably see her sitting in the dark right now if he was using his helmet display.

"He wanted to tell you you're an asshole, but I thought I'd take the honor."

"Them's fightin' words, Goldilocks." He strode up the ramp and slapped the switch to close it behind him. Once it had closed and locked with a few clicks, he brought the cabin lights on and slid his faceplate open. "Do I at least get to know what I did this time?"

"It's more what you're planning to do. Namely without me."

He studied her seriously for several seconds, then closed his eyes and sighed. "What the hell, Al?"

"I tried to tell her no, sir," Al said from the cabin speakers. "She just sat down against the ship to wait. I couldn't let her stay out there!"

"Oh yeah? You tried, huh?"

"Well… I didn't say I tried *hard*, sir."

"Dammit, Al, I—"

"Don't blame this on Al," Rachel said. "He's the only one in there acting like a responsible adult."

Jarek leaned against his dresser and drummed lightly on the edges with armored fingertips as he watched her.

"What?"

He opened his mouth, thought better of it, and then went for it again. "I don't suppose you'd be willing to go back to HQ and just pretend like this didn't happen?"

"Seriously?"

He shrugged.

"Yeah, sure," she said. "Just as soon as I get you to sign this I-promise-I-won't-throw-my-life-away-taking-unnecessary-risks-and-trying-to-be-a-hero form I brought."

His lip twitched upward. "Did you just call me a hero?"

She narrowed her eyes. "I said *trying*."

"Right." He glanced around the cabin as if checking for additional stowaways. "This coming from the lady who committed light home invasion to put herself in place to do the same thing."

"How hypocritical of me. I must be spending too much time around the wrong people."

"Uh-huh." Jarek considered her for another few seconds and shrugged. "Well, if you insist on staying…"

There was a pop and a series of clicks running down the length of Jarek's body, and Fela began to unpeel from him, starting at the chest and branching out to the arms and down the torso, which was—it turned out—completely bare. As was the rest of him.

"Dude." She averted her gaze as he turned his pasty but well-muscled backside toward her and rooted through the top drawer of his dresser. "What are you doing?

"Putting on my pajamas. Like a responsible adult." He paused and shot her a grin over his shoulder. "Unless you'd rather I didn't."

"Yeah, I think I'm all good, thanks. I don't date albino alopecia patients."

He shrugged and tripped his way into a pair of dark sweatpants. "You try keeping tan in there. Or hair."

She wrinkled her nose at him. "Ick."

In truth, the pastiness didn't bother her so much, and the relative lack of body hair actually did pretty flattering service to his well-built torso—in the few spots the extensive scars didn't distract the eyes at least. But she wasn't about to say that right now. Not when it was just the two of them alone in a small ship in the dark night. And especially not when he'd just tried to sneak out on her.

At least he hadn't tried to bullshit her once she'd called his bluff. He got a few points of credit there, but that was trivial next to everything else.

And he seemed to sense it as he pulled on a forest green t-shirt and settled on the cot a few feet away.

"I guess you'd probably like an apology," he said.

She bit back the *Goddamn right, I would* and forced a deep breath before speaking. An apology would be nice, sure. And she was definitely still pissed at him. But the more she thought about it, the more she realized she was pissed at herself too. And at Zar'Golga. And Alton Parker.

When it came down to it, she was pretty much pissed at the whole world. And she was through with not doing anything about it.

"You're not doing this on your own," she said.

He studied her until she finally looked over to meet his gaze.

"Okay, Goldilocks. If you're sure you want in, you're in."

There wasn't a hint of joking or dishonesty in his face or tone. Unless he was hiding a whole other level of lying skills behind those dark eyes, he really meant it this time.

"When were you really planning on going?"

"Al sent a message. Duel's at dawn. Assuming Golga shows."

"Why wait until tomorrow?"

He rubbed at the back of his head. "You wouldn't?"

She shrugged. "I'm asking you."

He looked down at his hands. "Well, I guess the honest answer is because fighting him in a dark stadium sounds like pretty much the most pants-shittingest thing I can imagine. Plus, I dunno." He waved a hand. "Space vampires, sunlight… Couldn't hurt my chances, right?"

And there it was. Out here, removed from his suit and his public image and alone but for her, he was ready to admit it. Jarek was every bit as afraid as he should be.

The remainder of Rachel's anger bled out of her, and she reached over and took his hand. "Neither could letting someone watch your back with a big stick." She fixed him with a serious look. "I won't let it end like that tomorrow. I don't give a shit what the deal of the duel is. We're taking Golga down, and then we're getting the hell out of there. Together."

He searched her face as if he were only now truly seeing her for the first time. "I, uh… Thanks, Rache. I'm sorry I tried to leave. I was just—"

"If you say trying to protect me, so help me, I'll use the staff."

He grinned. "I was gonna say falling back to old habits, but I guess I'm open if you're into that kind of thing."

She tugged her hand free from his and rolled her eyes but failed to keep her mouth from pulling into a smile.

"Nelken wants to send a team with us," Jarek said, his expression sobering once more. "Alaric's planning on leading it."

"Maybe we should let him. The more the merrier, right?"

"Oh, sure. Until they decide to just bomb the stadium with us in it. There's a reason I was hoping to keep the number of necks risked down to one here. If we're doing this thing, it's you and me."

She didn't argue—maybe in part because she didn't totally disagree, but mostly because she'd already taken the liberty to arrange her own plan B in case things went sideways. Instead, she just nodded. "Fine. You and me."

He reached out and brushed a loose strand of hair from her forehead. "You and me."

She caught his wrist and gently pushed it away.

"What?" He sized up her frown. "Are you telling me this isn't the part where we totally make out?"

Try as she might, she couldn't manage to halt the heat flowing into her cheeks. "It so isn't."

She dropped his gaze while she still could, but not before she caught the wolfish grin spreading across his mouth.

Thankfully, he rose without another word and tromped up toward the cockpit.

"We'd better get moving, then," he called over his shoulder.

"Now?" She stood and followed after him.

"Might as well get over there and get settled while it's dark," he said as she plopped down in the copilot's chair beside him. "That way Al can watch for funny business through the night."

"Both outside and inside the ship, sir," Al said.

"Yeah, yeah," Jarek said. "Just plot the course, will you, Mr. Robot?"

"Already plotted, sir. Are we all sure about this?"

Jarek turned a questioning look to Rachel. "There's still time to bail, Goldilocks. Judgment free. Even by my standards, this is kind of a bold move. If Golga decides to play dirty—"

"You'll need someone watching your back," she finished. "What do you think I'm here for, the good company?"

"I mean, it's not bad, right?"

She broke their gaze and looked out the banged-up windshield to hide her smile. Once she was facing the thick darkness outside rather than Jarek's infernal grin, though, her smile died quickly enough.

"I'm not leaving."

"All right then," Jarek said. "You know the drill, Al."

"Assuming this thing can still fly," Rachel muttered as Al powered up the ship's motors.

The ship had taken more than its fair share of gunfire that morning.

Jarek frowned at the beaten windshield. "She'll hold together." He winced at the protesting groan that accompanied their liftoff. "Right, Al?"

"At this point, I don't know if we would survive a collision with a pigeon," Al said, yawing the ship around and easing into a careful acceleration, "but yes, sir. The ship is more or less capable of making the trip."

Jarek met her dubious stare. "See? Totally golden. As long as we don't end up needing to make a hasty getaway."

She arched an eyebrow. "Yeah. 'Cause when has that ever happened before?"

Jarek patted the control console. "She'll hold together. I might need to recruit Pryce for some serious repair work once we make it back. But she'll hold together."

Even with their creeping speed and excessively cautious route, the flight didn't take long. Thirty minutes later, they were closing in on Yankee Stadium from the northeast. According to the map, at least.

The only real visual landmark was the glow of Zar'Golga's New York base of operations several miles to the south. Directly below, though, by the stadium, it was too dark to pick out much other than the occasional light or fire here or there.

Al brought them to a quiet landing in what the map proclaimed had once been Joyce Kilmer Park and cut the engines. Without the steady hum of the engines and with nothing but darkness outside, the silence pressed in on them extra heavy, right along with the apprehension—at being in enemy territory, at what they were fixing to do tomorrow.

At being utterly alone in the dark night with Jarek Slater.

She felt more than saw him watching her. Not that there was much to see. Al had killed the lights in the cockpit and dimmed those in the back cabin enough to keep the cockpit windshield from acting as a well-lit *Come kill us here* sign.

"What?" she asked, the heat in her cheeks actually making her grateful for the cover of darkness.

The Jarek-shaped silhouette shook its head. "Nothing. We should get some sleep. You take the cot, I'll—"

"Take your cot." Rachel gingerly plodded through the dark and laid down on one of the benches at the rear of the cockpit. "The prize fighter needs his beauty sleep. I promise I'll survive."

He hovered nearby for a second, seeming like he'd say something, but then disappeared into the back without a word. There was the padding of bare feet and a few shuffling noises, then a series of faint mechanical whirs and more decisive clicks and snaps.

Jarek entered the cockpit again, his silhouette enlarged with Fela's added bulk.

"What're you—"

He bent down and scooped her up into his arms.

"Hey!" she cried as he maneuvered them into the back cabin.

"Shh," he whispered.

"Might I remind you both that loud noises are currently inadvisable?" Al said quietly from the cabin speakers.

"See?" Jarek said.

"Yeah, well maybe you shouldn't go around snatching people up like Tarzan."

The dim lighting in the cabin was just enough for her to make out his face as he stopped at the cot and studied her.

"You gonna put me down, or do I have to give you a banana or something?"

He smiled and set her gently down on the cot. "Rewards are welcome but not required."

He lingered over her, holding her gaze, and for a long, breathless moment, she thought he'd kiss her again. Worse, she wanted him to. But thankfully some corner of her sane mind managed to squeeze out, "Head in the game, Tarzan. Big day tomorrow. Eye on the prize and all that."

He cocked a brow. "Isn't it?"

She forced a snort, trying to ignore the rest of the feelings swirling through her. "I never really took you for a cheese ball, but…"

"Oh, I'm just full of surprises." Finally, mercifully, he stood back up and broke some of the tension between them.

"Where are you gonna sleep?"

By way of reply, he sank to the deck and stretched out beside the cot.

"Seriously?"

"Bedding is kind of redundant when you have an exo with perfectly formable internal padding," Jarek said. "Al knows how I like it."

"Is it too much to ask to be left out of your innuendos, sir?"

"You know it is," Jarek said. "Now can you be a dear and get the lights?"

Al affected a sniff in response, and the cabin lights cut out, leaving them in nearly complete blackness. She couldn't even see Jarek now.

"Thanks, buddy," he said quietly. Then, after a pregnant silence, "Guess I'll see you bright and early, Goldilocks."

The fear that she'd been holding down since first boarding the ship to wait for Jarek began to creep out now, writhing its tendrils around her in the dark and weighing her down until she couldn't move, couldn't breathe.

Tomorrow. What was going to happen tomorrow, she couldn't say, but there was no option that sounded anything less than terrifying—short of Golga simply not showing up, of course. Something told her that wasn't going to happen, though.

Slowly, almost timidly, she reached out in the darkness and found Jarek's hand already resting on the edge of the cot, waiting for hers. She gripped it tightly, wishing she could feel the warmth of his flesh instead of the cool smoothness of his armor.

Jarek must have had a similar thought, because he wordlessly released her hand, and after a pair of clicks and a faint whir, a warm hand found hers and squeezed.

She squeezed back, half a dozen thoughts hanging on the edge of her tongue. For a long time, she hung there in limbo, wanting to talk, to cry, to run. To do anything but lie there and wait for the inevitable.

Jarek held her hand all the while, and she held his back until the silent darkness finally took her.

CHAPTER TWENTY-FOUR

Form-adaptive, supportive internal membrane and gallant chivalry aside, when he woke, Jarek certainly didn't feel like it was a TranqFoam mattress he'd been sleeping on. The aches and pains in his hips and back weren't so bad next to the discomfort radiating—or *not* radiating, as it were—from his right arm, which was numb as a brick.

His eyes showed him what his hand should have been able to feel: even after he'd finally managed to fall asleep, Fela had kept his arm raised up to the cot side, and his fingers were still intertwined with Rachel's. He probably had Al to thank for that, the romantic devil.

Thoughts of romance faded from thought as Jarek untangled his fingers from Rachel's and peered up at the glint of dawn sunlight poking in from the cockpit windshield. The blood red glint.

"Well that can't be good," he muttered, trying to shake some semblance of life back into his arm. "Talk to me, Mr. Robot"

"A single ship did enter the stadium, sir," Al said in his earpiece. "Roughly three hours ago. But it left quickly enough. It only appeared to be sweeping the area."

"Appeared to be?"

Beside him, Rachel stirred with a moody groan.

"That's a lot of concrete for the scanners to see through, sir. Perhaps if you'd been more open to a certain party's protests, I could have properly pointed out the potentially confounding detail."

Shit.

"Point taken, Mr. Robot. Maybe I'll let you have a vote next time I challenge the lord of the space vampires to a deathmatch."

"That would be most appreciated, sir."

"What is it?" Rachel asked, taking a crack at manually wiping the bleariness from her eyes. "What are you guys talking about?" She seemed to remember where they were at all at once and sat bolt upright. "Are they here?"

"Easy, Goldilocks." Jarek rolled to his feet and stretched his arms overhead. "Someone came and went in the night, but we're like fifty percent sure they didn't leave a trap for us. Maybe even sixty, if Al's feeling cocky today."

"My sincerest apologies," Al said. "Next time I'll get my act together scan harder, sir. It's not as if the equipment has technical limit—Oh."

Jarek tensed. "What?"

"Lone ship inbound for the stadium, sir. A fairly small craft. No larger than ours."

"Oh." Jarek traded a somber look with Rachel.

Double shit.

Technically Golga's arrival—assuming it was indeed Golga—was good news. But somehow it didn't make Jarek want to do the happy dance.

"Okay." He hefted the Big Whacker from its hanger on the side of his locker. "Game time, then."

He strapped on his sword and gun belt as he had a thousand times before, taking what comfort he could in the familiarity of the process. Then he turned to Rachel, who was checking something on her bullet catcher.

She met his eyes, looking tense but steady, and Jarek decided he was damn glad she'd called his bluff. As much as he detested inviting her neck to the chopping block beside his, having her here at his side was about the most reassuring thing he could have asked for.

"Ready?" she asked.

"Let's do it." His lip twitched. "And then we can go save the day."

She spared him a long moment's stare then turned and headed up to the cockpit.

"Rain check," he called after her. "Got it."

"That ship is setting down in the stadium, sir."

"Right. Take us up, Al."

Jarek stepped into the cockpit as the ship crested the adjacent buildings and the wide shape of Yankee Stadium came into view. From what he could see through the scuffed, cracked windshield, the stadium was still largely intact but for the caved-in southwestern corner, which had probably been caught in the same blast that had left several of the nearby buildings in ruins.

Like a lot of structures these days, its walls were coated with a healthy growth of moss and beginning to crumble in places.

Al pulled the ship to a hovering halt over the worn pavement of the parking structure across the street while they assessed the scene ahead.

"Always wanted to see a big game here," Jarek said.

Rachel gave him a tired smile. "No you didn't."

"No." He smiled and shook his head. "I really didn't. How's it looking, Mr. Robot?"

"I'm seeing some movement down on the ground level, sir. Looks like reinforcements."

"Not exactly unexpected," Jarek said.

"Comforting," Rachel said, popping an earpiece over her left ear. "In case we get separated," she added, tapping the earpiece.

"Good call. Al, can you—"

"I've already linked us, sir," Al said. "I'll open the channel as needed."

"Thanks, Mr. Robot." He gave Rachel one last questioning look, and she nodded, mouth set in a firm line. "All right, then. Let's take the field."

The ship crept forward with a quiet groan. Rachel half closed her eyes, and he realized she must be scouting with her senses

They crested the eastern edge of the stadium, just over the scoreboard, and there was the ship—a sleek dark number, built for speed—and a lone figure in front of it with pin points of fire for eyes.

Zar'Golga.

Jarek's stomach churned with apprehension and dread even as a trill of excitement shot through his chest.

The ship drifted into the stadium.

Rachel's eyes snapped open at the same time Al spoke.

"Oh dear. Not good." The ship lurched to the left. "Not—"

A thunderous boom shook the cockpit, and the next thing Jarek knew, he was flying across the cockpit toward Rachel.

She smacked into the bulkhead ahead of him, and he just managed to get his hands up in time to catch himself before he smashed into her. His outstretched hands left dents on either side of her head.

"Son of a bitch," she groaned.

The ship veered wildly downward, rolling back and forth, console alarms blaring all the while.

"Starboard motors out," Al called over the racket. "Stabilization limited." The rear hatch popped open and began to descend. "Recommend you abandon ship, sir!"

Jarek gathered himself and steadied Rachel. "Jumping legs, Goldilocks. We gotta bai—"

The ship bucked, and he slammed a hand into the bulkhead to keep them from spilling over. "Go, go!" he barked, pushing Rachel through doorway to the cabin and stumbling along behind her.

The ship rocked downward, and Rachel staggered into the cot ahead.

No time. There was no time.

"Hold on!" he shouted. Then he scooped her up, took a few running steps, and leapt for the open rear hatch.

They cleared the ship, and open sky stretched out around them, leaving nothing below them but thin air and the rows of stadium seats rushing by too quickly forty feet below.

The upward momentum of Jarek's leap died just as they cleared the seating and made it over the grassy field. Then they were properly falling.

Jarek was preparing to toss Rachel upward as best he could to buy her an extra second or two when their flight inexplicably slowed. Or maybe not so inexplicably.

"Jesus Christ, you're heavy," Rachel growled against him.

He could have kissed her. He'd been fully prepared to take a heavy landing for the team, but even with Fela's significant mechanical aid, the shock of impact wouldn't have been pretty.

Instead, they drifted down at a manageable pace and touched down jostled and disoriented but uninjured.

Jarek drew his sword, scanning the surrounding stadium. A group of dark-clad men were emerging from the tunnels at one side of the field. Back where they'd flown in, a pair of guys were looking down at them from a perch by the scoreboard, one of them holding some manner of rocket launcher.

"Traitorous bastards shot us down," Rachel said behind him.

He was about to commend her on her astute observation when Al cried, "Geronimo!" in his ear.

He whipped around to see the ship buck drunkenly downward, still cruising forward with considerable velocity. It hit the field with a bone-jarring crash and a wrenching of strained metal and skimmed fifteen yards across the grassy field, bound straight for Zar'Golga and his dark ship.

Golga gathered himself and sprang into a ridiculously high leap that carried him over the incoming ship-shaped missile. The raknoth landed twenty yards away from Jarek and Rachel, eyes alive with scarlet fire, and began stalking toward them, not even bothering to turn back as their ship's prow smashed into his vessel with another sharp crash.

"Right," Jarek mumbled, taking in Golga properly.

The Overlord wore no clothes, his entire body covered instead in the dark forest green scales of his raknoth hide, and he held a giant, gnarly mace leisurely over one shoulder.

Movement to the right drew Jarek's attention, and he glanced over to see another half dozen men emerging onto the field, led by their old raknoth pals, Toady and Slender Face.

Jarek stepped forward to plant himself between Golga and Rachel while she faced Golga's posse.

This was bad. But they weren't dead yet.

"I'm starting to get the impression you might not plan on playing fair, Golga," Jarek called.

The raknoth stopped ten yards from them and studied them with those glowing red eyes, his reptilian expression unclear.

"You have a strong history of fleeing from our engagements," Golga said. "If we are to duel"—he hefted the giant club from his shoulder—"I will not have you scampering away from death when it comes."

Gulp. Jarek wanted to scoff at Golga's choice of weapon, but the thing was huge, and the ease with which he was waving it around… How strong was this bastard? It didn't matter. It was a fight. It was just another fight.

"And you couldn't just let us land first?" he called. "Dick move, man. And what gives with the backup army?" He glanced at Rachel. "Mine was a stowaway. What's your excuse?"

"They are here to prevent foul play on your end."

"Foul play like shooting an arriving party out of the damn sky?"

"They will not interfere, only prevent the arcanist's interference as they observe your demise," Golga said.

"Oh yeah? And what happens when I kill you? I don't suppose they're just gonna say 'cheers' and be on their way."

Golga bared a few gleaming fangs in what had to be the creepiest grin Jarek had ever seen. "They will observe your demise without interference."

Right. Because Zar'Golga the freaking Overlord himself was clearly not even entertaining the possibility that a puny mortal like Jarek Slater could end his ancient existence.

It was arrogant, sure, but the weight behind that arrogance was like a mountain, and it settled firmly on top of the already substantial trepidation in his gut.

This creature had conquered entire planets. He was thousands of years old. He was stronger, faster, more powerful than Jarek could ever hope to be.

Jarek looked at the dark metal of his sword and reminded himself that no matter how strong and fast the bastard was, he was still flesh and blood. He could die just like the rest of them.

He glanced back at Rachel. She clearly liked this even less than he did, but there wasn't exactly an abundance of choices left. It wasn't like they could get in their ship and leave.

He gave her a small nod, and she returned it after a second with a look that assured him she wasn't about to lay down and let either of them die, no matter what happened. It melted some of the apprehension clutching at his chest as he turned back to Zar'Golga and that giant studded club of his.

Flesh and blood, he reminded himself.

Scaly, strong-as-hell flesh and blood.

"All right then, big guy." Jarek slid his faceplate closed, took several distancing steps away from Rachel, and pointed his sword at the raknoth. "Let's see if you know how to use that thing."

The scarlet fire of Zar'Golga's eyes blazed brighter. Then he lowered the mighty club from his shoulder and charged.

CHAPTER TWENTY-FIVE

As it turned out, Zar'Golga did know how to use that thing.

The raknoth tore across the thick grass between him and Jarek in an unnervingly fast sprint instead of the wild leap he'd been expecting. Golga's first swipe was entirely too fast for the massive size of his club, but he managed it all the same. Jarek scooted back and barely shifted out of the club's path in time.

Jarek nearly shat himself on the spot when he parried Golga's follow-up strike and got a better feel for just how damned heavy that club was—and again when Golga pulled the deflected club back under control as if it had all the heft of a plastic wiffle bat.

He aimed a counter at Golga's head, but the raknoth was quick, and Jarek was rattled. Golga easily stepped under the strike and spun to deliver a horizontal club sweep that probably would have left Jarek's torso a broken mess, Fela or no. Jarek didn't wait around to find out.

He leapt backward a good ten yards, buying himself a moment to breathe. Or trying to, at least.

Goltha followed at a tireless sprint fast enough that Jarek had to tuck straight into a roll upon landing to avoid another heavy club sweep. He barely had time to think before he righted himself and found an overhand blow descending on him.

He twisted aside, clearing the club's path by a hair's breadth, then drove Golga back with his own diagonal cut. The raknoth wasted no time pressing back in.

Jarek turned through a mind-numbingly fast series of steps, twists, attacks, and counterattacks, reacting on pure, hard-wired reflex. No matter how fast he moved, Golga was already there at the next step. Jarek needed a second to reorient, to breathe.

But Golga pressed on, raining blow after blow with no noticeable sign of slowing.

Jarek was off-center now—had been from the start—and was slipping further with each exchange. He couldn't keep this up.

Zar'Golga could.

The raknoth fought on like a tireless, ferocious animal. If Jarek didn't get his shit together, and fast, one of these tiny slips was going to end up snowballing into Golga knocking his head off with that ridiculous club.

He had a brief image of Rachel watching him pummeled to a bloody mess by this red-eyed monster, her hands outstretched, her face frozen in a soundless scream.

If Jarek didn't get his shit together—if he gave into the tired voice telling him it was already over—then it wasn't just his life. It was Rachel's. It was Al's. More likely than not, it was the Resistance and all those poor bastards getting bombed out of their homes for a second time.

And fuck that.

Never mind that Rachel never would have stood by and watched him die without throwing in. Never mind that he was tired and outmatched and afraid.

They'd come here for a reason. They'd risked their lives and everything else for a shot at this vicious bastard. Between the ship going down and the shock at Golga's raw power, Jarek had lost focus on his purpose here, but now it snapped back, clear and crisp.

He'd come here to put down this animal before Golga destroyed them all.

Jarek gritted his teeth and stepped into Golga's next attack. The raknoth, having been hammering at him mercilessly for nearly a full minute, hadn't expected that. Golga reacted quickly enough, dropping a hand from the club to reach for him, but Jarek plowed a lowered shoulder into Golga's side before the raknoth could grab him.

Golga hit the ground with all the mass of a full-grown grizzly bear, rocking the earth beneath Jarek, but bounced back to his feet with barely a moment's pause, club in hand.

Jarek was already coming down on him with a series of cuts that put the raknoth momentarily on the defensive. It didn't last long. With each strike, Golga regained some control, simultaneously dulling Jarek's fleeting momentum.

Jarek pressed on with everything he had, but soon enough they were back on even footing, circling each other cautiously for the first time in the fight. When Golga changed his pacing, Jarek tensed, but the raknoth only drew to a halt and showed him an unsettling, fang-filled grin.

"HQ is calling, sir," Al said in his earpiece. "Urgently. Multiple channels."

Jarek could continue pressing on with everything he had all he liked. What he had wasn't enough, simple as that. Golga was as fast as he was strong, as cunning as he was vicious. With the likely exception of potty humor, the raknoth outclassed Jarek in every way he could think of.

But none of that meant that Jarek couldn't win. All he had to do was shift his definition of the word.

"Tell them they don't need to worry anymore, buddy. I'm taking care of it."

The whole challenge of close-quarters combat with deadly weapons boiled down to one thing: hitting them with your deadly weapon while avoiding theirs. Simple, sure, but not easy—especially against a freakishly strong and fast blood-thirsty monster with count-less years of fighting experience.

What was far easier was to remove the second half of the fundamental equation of battle.

Even the best fighter was intrinsically more vulnerable in midstrike. Of course, that vulnerability was normally countered by the fact that, if their opponent valued their life, they'd be busy blocking, dodging, or otherwise not dying.

But if that opponent decided he was going to take a motherfucker down with him, no matter the cost—and hey, maybe he could even survive the hit he'd take anyway—that was another matter entirely.

And as long as Golga died, Jarek won.

So he didn't hold back when Golga charged him with all the power of a rampaging bull and the control of a time-tested warrior. He didn't plan for counters or evasions. He focused on the spot where he was going to cleave Golga's head from his shoulders, and he charged to meet the raknoth in kind.

The strike Golga threw would not be reckless. He was too good for that. But Jarek would make him pay for it all the same. He wouldn't waste his energy trying to save his own skin. He'd trade blow for blow with the vicious bastard. He'd end Zar'Golga, end this fight. Even if it killed him.

He only wished he'd said goodbye to Pryce. Told Al he'd been the best friend he could have asked for. Given Rachel one last kiss.

A wordless battle cry ripped out of his throat as they closed in. Golga's eyes flared brighter as he began to swing his club. Jarek swept his sword up for the killing blow and—

Golga reversed direction with impossible speed, ducking under Jarek's cut and spinning around with an upward diagonal sweep. Time seemed to stretch, and yet Jarek could only watch in horror, powerless to avoid it as the club rose toward his face.

Then it hit.

<hr>

Everything was dark, and Jarek couldn't remember why. Then he blinked open his eyes to... blue sky? And grass. He was lying in thick grass. Al was crooning something in his earpiece. Fiery pain was blossoming across his face. His back and shoulders ached from some recent impact, his comm was buzzing steadily, and—

"Jarek!" a voice cried. Female. Worried.

Rachel.

Jarek sat bolt upright—or tried—and nearly vomited from the swirling nausea the movement brought on.

"Careful, sir," Al said.

Zar'Golga stood over him, giant club resting lightly over his shoulder. When his addled brain caught up, Jarek realized he was looking at the raknoth with his own eyes, not his helmet display. His faceplate, he realized from the warped edges of his helmet, had been torn clean off by the blow that had landed him here.

Golga watched his disoriented inspection with pulsing red eyes and emitted a low, amused growl. "You have played your part marvelously, Jarek Slater."

Played what part? What the hell was he talking about? And why was Jarek's comm buzzing with a third call now?

"I'm taking Alaric's call, sir," Al said quietly in his ear. "I have a bad feeling about this."

"Yeah," Jarek said, hoping Golga couldn't hear Al. "I've been told I'm quite the character."

He glanced around, hoping to find the Whacker within grabbing distance, but no—there it was a few yards behind Golga.

It wasn't like Jarek had any shot of moving fast enough to catch Golga by surprise right now anyway.

"I was merely hoping you and the arcanists would come rushing to protect the city when the bombs started falling," Golga continued, "but this worked out far better."

"Get up, Jarek," Rachel's murmured voice came through his earpiece. "Get up, dammit."

Toady and Slender Face had posted themselves between her and Jarek, and Golga's soldiers were eyeing her with itchy trigger fingers, but she looked like she was contemplating making a push for him anyway.

Golga must have heard her murmur across the field. He brandished his club in Jarek's face. "Both of you stay. I insist."

Jarek met his red-eyed stare as evenly as he could. "So is this the part where you tell me you've been waiting a thousand years for someone to grant you a true warrior's death or something? Because if so, you should probably get to the point while you still have a head to do it with."

Golga watched Jarek for a long moment, massive club held at arm's length like a cheap plastic toy. Then he tilted his head back and laughed.

What was the bastard waiting for? Screw it—it didn't matter. Whatever the raknoth wanted, Jarek wasn't going to sit here and be toyed with. He might as well make a move, any move.

Golga finished laughing and spoke before he could. "That your kind would think to stand against the rakul when you are the mightiest of their warriors..." He laughed again and poked at Jarek with the tip of his club.

"Sir, it's HQ."

The tension in Al's voice was like a punch to the gut on its own. But then he said the words.

"They're under attack."

Over to the right, Rachel tensed like she'd heard Al's message too.

"You see?" Golga asked, baring fangs in a sneer at their reactions. "It is over for you and your friends. You have meddled in affairs beyond your comprehension, and now the time has come to pay the price."

"How—"

Jarek stopped himself as the pieces fell into place. It was obvious, wasn't it?

Golga must've been tracking Mosen somehow. They'd had enough sense to ditch Mosen's comm and make sure his mind was cloaked like Drogan's. They'd even rooted through his clothes and gear. But they could have missed something, and even if they hadn't, there were other ways. Golga could have implanted Mosen with a tracking chip for all he knew.

It didn't really matter how Golga had found HQ. What mattered was that Jarek had played straight into the bastard's hands. Golga had wanted to draw out their heavy hitters so he could roll over HQ with minimal resistance. That's what the bombings had been for.

Only Jarek and Rachel hadn't just stepped out to deal with the pests on their front yard. They'd done Golga one better. They'd flown off on this half-cocked idiocy he'd called a plan and managed to leave both themselves and HQ that much more open to attack.

And now they were stuck here at the mercy of the strongest, most ruthless creature Jarek had ever encountered—without a ship, surrounded by Golga's posse. HQ was about to burn if it wasn't already doing so.

And Golga was raising his club.

No time.

Jarek coiled and prepared to throw himself at the raknoth to punch, kick, bite, and otherwise fight to his last breath.

Golga was faster.

The raknoth's foot slammed into Jarek's chest and stomped him to the grassy earth like a pneumatic press. Even through the armor, it knocked the wind out of him.

Jarek clawed at Golga's foot and tried to pry himself free, but the raknoth was too strong.

"I can smell it on you," Golga rumbled. "The fear. The defeat. And now, Jarek Slater, at the height of your folly, you may prepare to die."

That said, he swung the club.

A hundred thoughts exploded through Jarek's mind: defensive maneuvers. Twists, turns, and crotch shots. Cries of terror and rage. Every single thing he could have done in that last moment.

And yet, somehow, he couldn't seem to do a goddamn thing but lay there waiting to die.

Then Golga's club jolted to an abrupt halt halfway through his swing.

For all of a single second, the raknoth looked as flabbergasted as Jarek felt. Then it dawned on both of them.

Rachel. God bless her golden locks.

For that single second, hope swelled in Jarek's chest.

Then Golga gave a terrifying roar and heaved at the motionless club, and a shaky-looking Rachel fell to one knee.

"Kill the arcanist!" Golga bellowed.

Toady and Slender Face loosed a pair of roars and darted forward to honor his orders.

"Rachel!" Jarek screamed.

He had to move, had to help her, had to—

Golga raised his foot and stomped Jarek's chest hard enough to reduce his awareness to a breathless mess of dark spots.

For one morbidly blissful moment, Jarek nearly forgot where he was and what was happening.

Then his world cleared, and Zar'Golga's club began its descent toward his head.

CHAPTER TWENTY-SIX

Jarek had never bought into the whole "life flashing before the eyes" thing. For one thing, he'd never experienced such a phenomenon, and god knew he'd given his poor brain enough opportunities to engage the *Oh shit, this is it* button.

Maybe it was simply that none of those situations had been his time. Maybe he'd somehow always known deep down inside that it wasn't the end just yet, that the way out was only a grunt, a strain, and —more often than not—an excruciating pain away.

Maybe this time it would be different.

But right now, all he saw was a giant freaking club speeding down to crush his skull to pulp. Rachel had two raknoth at her throat. HQ was under attack.

And Jarek sure as shit wasn't about to wait around for that trip down memory lane.

He was cocking back to throw the mightiest crotch shot he could manage when Golga jerked in mid-blow. The raknoth's club slammed down next to Jarek's head, kicking dirt into his face, and Golga staggered back with a choked roar.

What in the—

A small pop split the air.

Golga jerked again, and this time, Jarek noticed the fine trail of dark ichor that exploded outward from his torso, painting the grass in a thin line just as a second pop reached them.

A sniper?

Stunned as he was, Golga gathered enough of his wits and power to throw himself thirty yards through the air toward the combined wreckage of their two ships for cover from Jarek's friendly sniper angel.

Assuming they were friendly—whoever the hell they were.

"Jarek!"

Rachel's cry sent a blast of panic through his chest.

He kipped to his feet, snipers momentarily forgotten, and took off for Rachel at a dead sprint.

She was on the ground, hands outstretched toward Toady and Slender Face, who seemed to be caught in mid-lunge by whatever defenses Rachel had scrambled together. Without a clear line of fire, Golga's soldiers were approaching to pitch in with fists, knives, and batons.

A wordless cry erupted from Rachel's throat, and her eight nearest attackers rocketed backward on the wake of a soft boom. Rachel collapsed forward onto her hands but started woozily fighting her way to her feet.

The two raknoth regained their feet far quicker. Toady closed on her first and grabbed her staff. Rachel thrust her hand in his face and sent the raknoth stumbling backward with a flash of brilliant white light.

Rachel turned her staff on Slender Face, but he was pressing in too fast.

On a good day, when he was particularly motivated, Jarek's sprinting speed with Fela could flirt with sixty miles per hour. Watching those red-eyed bastards closing in on Rachel, he was beyond motivated. He broke sixty, no question, and he didn't slow down except to lower his shoulder at the end of his charge.

Sixty wasn't the only thing he broke.

Jarek's shoulder slammed into Slender Face's narrow chest with a wet cracking sound. The impact felt a light breeze shy of removing Jarek's shoulder from the socket, but it had the intended effect. Slender Face went sailing a good ten yards backward and would've continued for another five if he hadn't bowled into two of his own men.

Jarek clenched through the pain of the impact and stepped into a one-handed sword sweep at Toady's neck.

The raknoth had apparently recovered enough of his eyesight to see it coming, and he leapt back to regroup with his partner.

Jarek stepped back toward Rachel, still facing their foes, until he felt her hand on the back of his shoulder.

"We need to get out of he—"

The wrenching screech of torn metal yanked Jarek's attention back to the ships to find Zar'Golga hefting a large metal section of...

"Motherfucker," Jarek mumbled.

Golga had torn off the end of one of the stubby wings of Jarek's ship and was now charging across the field, toting his giant club in one hand and holding the torn section of wing to his right side as a shield from their mysterious sniper friend.

"Goldilocks, I think it's time to run."

"I've got it covered," Rachel said behind him.

"Unless you've got a ship tucked between those lovely cheeks, I think we might—"

The blow of a deep horn rumbled his core, and a shadow rose up behind them, accompanied by the sound of rushing air. He spared a glance over his shoulder and gave a delighted, "Ha!" at the long, dark bulbous shape of the Enochians' ship.

"You can blow up one ship," Jarek cried, rounding back on Golga, "but—shit."

Golga was closing too fast. He'd be on them before their reinforcements could hope to land, and this time he had Toady, Slender Face, and a handful of wary troops on his side.

Sniper fire pelted at Golga's shield with a series of sharp smacks and delayed pops. A couple of the shots tore through the metal, but

Golga didn't slow. Rachel tensed behind him, and a glance her way told him Toady and Slender Face were on the move again.

A few steps into their charge, though, Slender Face jerked to a halt, spewing thin trails of dark blood-stuff.

Jarek spun back to face Golga's charge. "Whoever's watching our asses up there deserves a cookie."

"You can see to it he gets one when we all get out of here alive," a voice said in his earpiece—not Rachel, but definitely female.

He didn't have time to ask who, what, or why. He darted forward to meet Golga's charge where the aftermath of their impact wouldn't spill back and roll over Rachel.

It felt a little bit like stepping up to butt heads with a runaway semi-truck.

At least he could buy time for Rachel to make it safely aboard their miraculous getaway ride.

Jarek brought his sword up as they closed the last ten yards between them.

A shadow flicked over Golga. The raknoth's stride faltered, and he raised his shield just as Alton Parker slammed down on him in a double-footed drop kick from on high.

Alton kicked off of Golga's raised shield like a springboard and sent the dark raknoth stumbling back several steps as Alton turned through a tight backflip to land in front of Jarek.

Golga was still recovering when a second figure dropped down between them. A thrumming pulse of pressure swept through the air as Elise touched down, long, dark staff in hand, and Golga's backward stumble turned into full-on flight.

They both turned to Jarek, Alton's eyes alight with raknoth fire and Elise's brimming with a kind of battle lust that sent a jolt of strange feelings through his anatomy.

Elise's tone was calm and commanding. "Get to the ship."

"Not without my Goldilocks!" Jarek cried as he spun to see Rachel blasting Toady up into the stands a good twenty-five yards away. It wasn't without a cost, though.

Even without the wobbly knees, the pallor of Rachel's face was enough to know she'd already channeled more than enough by now.

Gunfire barked from the descending ship overhead, scattering Golga's troops as they sought cover to return fire.

A furious roar from behind announced Golga was back on the war path.

"The ship," Jarek shouted at Rachel. "Go!"

She didn't argue. She turned and jumped, bolstering the effort with enough arcane juice to land her on the unfurled ship stairs twenty feet above. The burly balding guy laying down fire from the ship's hatch reached out a hand to pull her in.

"You next, metal man!" Elise shouted. "Up you—"

"Incoming!" Al cried.

Jarek whipped around in time to see Golga winding up to hurl his massive shield at them from fifteen yards away.

Jarek leapt over Elise and Alton and touched down with the Whacker raised in a two-handed cross guard, angled to deflect.

The wingtip hit with an awful grinding crash and the momentum of a small car, but Jarek was firmly planted. He managed to hold his ground. By some minor miracle, the Whacker held its own as well, and the hunk of metal smashed off and went spinning up and over Jarek's left shoulder, twirling through the air like a giant skipping stone.

Golga was still coming, his charge shaking the ground beneath Jarek's feet.

Jarek stepped back, preparing to turn aside another savage blow from that giant club.

Elise slipped past him at the last second, quick and fluid, and dropped to plant one end of her staff to the ground, aiming the other at Zar'Golga's chest. As she moved, the tip of the staff flipped open to reveal a long, dark spearhead.

It was a perfectly timed surprise attack.

Golga twisted his way wide with that uncanny speed anyway.

Only, before he cleared the spearhead, Golga ran into an invisible wall of thin air. His red eyes flared almost white hot, and then he crashed onto the spear full-tilt. As fast as he was moving, the narrow spearhead punched clear through his hard hide and plunged far enough that it must have emerged from the other side.

It wasn't enough to stop him.

Golga bellowed a roar and aimed a club swipe at Elise's raven-haired head.

She flattened herself to the ground with startling agility, evading the sweeping club by a hair's breadth.

Jarek sprang forward and swept his sword at Golga's neck.

Golga ducked the strike so narrowly that the broad side of the blade scraped his scaly scalp.

Before either of them could recover, Alton flew past Jarek's left and planted a devastating front kick right beside the spear in Golga's chest.

The kick must've been on par with, if not beyond, anything Fela could manage, because it sent Golga sailing across the field like a dark green missile. Elise reached a hand after him, and her spear tore free of Golga and flew back to her hand.

"Ship!" she cried, whirling around. "Now!"

That sounded like a plan.

Elise was the first to take her own advice, leaping to the hovering ship just as Rachel had done. Alton was barely a second behind her. Jarek, seeing Toady approaching from the stands and Slender Face picking himself up from his bad date with their guardian sniper, wasted no time in following on their heels.

"Got 'em," the burly guy said in a low rumble of a voice when Jarek reached the hatch. "Get James."

The ship banked to the right as four or five hands unnecessarily grabbed Jarek and yanked him through the open hatch and into a corridor whose walls resembled the dark, purplish material of the ship's hull. Alton scrambled off down the odd corridor. The bullets thudding against the ship's hull sounded distant and ineffective as the ship veered around in the rough direction Jarek had pegged the sniper to be firing from.

"Well." Jarek looked between Elise and Rachel, who he'd narrowly avoided smooshing into the corridor wall when they'd pulled him through. "I'd say that went swimmingly."

Rachel's hard eye-roll was interrupted by the ship's sudden dip and deceleration.

A few seconds later, a small, tweaky-looking blond guy came scrambling through the hatchway toting a long, silvery rifle that was clearly of Enochian origin. Suddenly those odd pops Jarek had heard in place of normal gunshots made marginally more sense.

"I'm in!" cried the sniper in a frazzled tenor. "Go, go, go!"

Whoever was at the ship's helm complied with gusto.

Everyone braced against the ship's acceleration. The sniper, who was the only person without a handhold, a staff, or an exosuit to keep himself stable, stumbled and nearly fell. Jarek reached to steady him, but the little guy pulled it together on his own.

Finally, the acceleration eased off, and the thud of bullets on the hull ceased, leaving only tense silence hanging in the corridor until they all collectively unclenched at once.

"Thanks for the assist back there," Elise said.

"Oh, you know," Jarek said, waving his free hand and sheathing the Whacker with a practiced motion. "I like to think I do it for the children."

"Yeah…" A small smile tugged at Elise's mouth. "I was talking to *her*, actually."

Jarek glanced at Rachel, who showed him a smirk.

"I probably would've been trampled to paste back there if Rachel hadn't kept Golga on the rails."

"Uh, right." Jarek rubbed at the back of his head, playing back the moment in his mind. "I knew that. Totally."

"I think what he means to say is that we should be the ones thanking you," Rachel said.

Jarek inclined his head. "Also that. Wait…" He narrowed his eyes at Rachel. "You knew they were coming. That's who you were talking to when we hit the ground back there."

Rachel shrugged.

"Tricksy little arcanist," Jarek muttered.

"People were worried you were gonna run off all half-cocked into a trap for some reason," Elise said. "Crazy, I know, but we figured it couldn't hurt to be nearby just in case."

Jarek opened his mouth and closed it. There wasn't much to say to that.

"We need to get to back to HQ," Rachel said.

"Already headed that way." Elise fiddled with her staff, which compacted rapidly down from five feet to about half that. She tucked the half-staff into a sling on her back and set off down the corridor. "Come on."

Jarek followed the group down the corridor, which he now noticed looked so odd thanks in part to its smooth lack of ninety-degree angles.

"This is James and Phineas, by the way," Elise said, pointing first to the wiry blond sniper and then to the burly, balding bear of a man.

James gave them a nervous wave. Phineas gave a deep grunt from behind his dark beard without really looking at either of them.

"Nice shooting back there," Jarek said, inclining his head toward James' otherworldly rifle.

"Oh!" James said. "Uh, thanks."

They arrived at what appeared to be the cockpit in short order. The room was similarly devoid of sharp angles, and the front half of it was... transparent? No, something else.

He could see outside to the Hudson river below and the buildings of New York City off to the left, but he wasn't simply looking through a large, semi-spherical window. The image bent in odd, subtle ways here and there, following the curves of where the room's walls would have been, like the wall was projecting the view from outside.

"Neat-o," Jarek mumbled.

The sight of the landscape rushing by, coupled with the lack of any clear window panes, display edges, or wind created a strange, slightly unnerving, sensation in Jarek's head and gut. He shook it off and focused on Alton and the man with the dark mustache—Franco, was it?—over by what looked like a control console.

"We still need a way inside," Franco was saying to Alton. "We can't very well expect to be much use heckling their army from behind."

Jarek was just about to point out that the main entrance was concealed and that said army might still be standing around with their thumbs up their asses when a section of the weird wall-screen zoomed in across a miraculous distance to show a swarming mass of armed, dark-clad figures rushing about the lot above HQ. A fleet of transport trucks and a few ships were arrayed behind them among the shipping containers.

One small group of dark figures all turned to jog away from one section of the lot. A few seconds later, there was a flash of fire, followed shortly by smoke and dust. Explosive charges.

Son of a bitch.

They didn't need to find the entrance. Not when they could just blow the lot to pieces until they found something interesting.

As the dust and smoke began to thin, Jarek saw they already had.

A section of the lot had caved in to a tunnel or room below. Golga's forces surged forward, plunging down into the opening a couple men at a time.

"Shit," Rachel muttered beside him.

He couldn't disagree.

"There must be a back door," Alton said. He turned, his eyes now devoid of raknoth fire, and directed a questioning look at Jarek and Rachel.

"There's an underground garage entrance," Rachel said, "but I doubt we could land anywhere near it without bringing that whole horde down on us."

There had to be another way.

That was a big army down there, and right now the Resistance's only saving grace was that Golga's forces were being funneled by the size of their entry point. Once they'd blasted a few more entryways, though, things were going to get ugly fast.

"Sir, I've got it," Al said in his ear. "A back door."

"How—"

"I'm on the comms," Al said. "For some reason, they seem rather willing to share sensitive secrets with allies right now."

"Well Jesus, Mr. Robot, share it with the class!"

"Right, sir," Al said, speaking through Fela's external speakers this time.

The Enochians stifled their confused looks and listened along with Jarek and Rachel as Al rattled off a series of directions. Alton's gaze became distant as Al spoke, and the ship veered gently starboard, changing course to take them around Golga's army to Al's secret entrance in the old park northwest of HQ.

Alton's eyes drifted shut, and Jarek's stomach confirmed the wallscreen's story as they dipped low to the ground.

He wasn't sure how the ship's hull would fare against modern scanners, but they were close enough now that Golga's men could have visually spotted them if they happened to be looking in exactly the right spot. Fortunately, they seemed rather occupied with their full-on assault.

A minute later, Alton slowed the ship at Al's instruction and descended to land in the grassy clearing beside what looked like an old sewer outlet set into the hillside at the park's edge.

"We can't leave the ship unguarded," Alton said as they made their way back to the hatch.

Given the look James and Franco exchanged with each other and then the others, that was shorthand that the two of them should stay behind.

"We have it under control," Franco said, disappearing into a nearby room behind Phineas. He emerged a second later, sporting a sleek weapon that looked something like an assault rifle. Phineas came behind him, laden with several new weapons in addition to the rifle he'd carried in.

"What about you?" Jarek asked Alton. "I can't imagine they'll be too excited to see red eyes popping in through the back door. You got a pair of shades or something?"

Alton frowned. "I'll try to keep it under control."

"Splendid," Jarek said. "What could possibly go wrong?"

"Let's move," Elise said.

The back door was unsurprisingly locked, but the code Al's panicked contact had provided opened it without issue. The hallway beyond was dark and, like the rest of HQ, cramped.

"How far are we from HQ exactly, Al?" Jarek said.

"A little under a mile, sir."

"Awesome," Rachel muttered.

"Well." Jarek gave Alton a meaningful glance. "Guess we better give you guys a ride then."

Rachel narrowed her eyes at him but hopped into his waiting arms with no additional protest.

"Come on." Jarek waggled his eyebrows at Elise and turned in invitation. "You know you wanna."

"Is he always like this?" Elise asked as she planted her hands on his shoulders and hopped onto his back piggy-back style.

It couldn't have been the most comfortable mount, especially considering the enormous sword strapped across his back, but she managed.

"Always," Rachel confirmed with a nod.

"Alpha save us," Elise mumbled.

Beside them, Phineas gave Alton a long, hard look before finally raising his arms and allowing the raknoth to scoop him up in a bridal carry.

Elise shook against Jarek's back with silent laughter.

"Tell anyone about this," Phineas grumbled, glaring at Alton, "and I'll kill you."

Alton stowed his smile and tilted his head from Jarek to the dark hallway beyond. "After you."

"All right, ladies," Jarek said as he stepped into the darkness and Al flipped on Fela's external lights to illuminate the way. "Get ready for the ride of your lives."

CHAPTER TWENTY-SEVEN

Back at the stadium, when the ship had been going down and they'd had to bail, Rachel had been scared. Scared, but not terrified. She'd had an ace up her sleeve. She'd known that the Enochians wouldn't be far away and that they'd be waiting to swoop in if things went wrong—as they most spectacularly had.

Now, though, plunging through the dark, dank hallway toward HQ, a growing terror tugged harder at her heart with each fluid step of Jarek's inhuman pace.

Some of that terror was for herself. They were charging into what amounted to a large deathtrap, after all, where enemy forces would literally be raining down on their heads.

Part of the terror was for Jarek and the rest of her friends, for similar reasons.

When Jarek had nearly fallen to Zar'Golga back at the stadium… Ace up the sleeve or no, she'd felt a moment of true terror when Golga had scored that hit, when she'd thought maybe Jarek was already dead.

But he'd pulled through as he always seemed to, and now most of her terror was free to focus on Michael, who, for all she knew, was still lying helplessly unconscious in the med rooms, probably defenseless but for Pryce. Assuming the older man was even still with him.

The report of a distant explosion reverberated through the darkness ahead, fanning the flames of terror in her heart.

This was bad. Worse than bad.

And this time, her sleeve was woefully devoid of aces.

It was hard to tell what was ahead by the shaky light as they charged forward, but she thought she saw the suggestion of an end to the hallway in the far reaches of the light. Jarek couldn't have been running for more than a minute. Even with her in his arms and Elise clinging to his back, Jarek could really haul ass, she'd give him that—even if Fela deserved most of the credit.

The ride was surprisingly smooth, too, considering. She wasn't sure whether Elise could say the same back on her perch, but Jarek managed to keep Rachel steady enough in his arms that she almost could have forgotten she was being carried by a running man if she closed her eyes and tried.

The things he could do in that suit were impressive. Maybe not impressive enough to turn back an army and save the Resistance, but she could hope, right?

No. What she could do was stand right beside the big wise-ass and turn the tide with him—maybe even while making sure neither of them died in the process.

The darkness ahead gave way to Fela's external lights and resolved into a door that looked old and heavy and rusted around the edges. Muffled shouts and a few gunshots came through the door as Jarek drew to a halt and gently lowered Rachel to her feet.

Alton pulled up behind them and deposited a very disgruntled-looking Phineas to his feet.

Elise hopped off Jarek's back, shifted uncomfortably, and pulled her staff from the sheath on her back. "We should make you a saddle."

"Pryce would have a field day with that one," Jarek muttered.

Al must have provided the code directly to Jarek's ear, because he tapped in five digits without hesitation.

The gnawing fear in Rachel's stomach was paralyzing as Jarek pulled the door open and stepped into the sounds of chaos. She found her focus through sheer force of will and followed after him.

HQ was in tumult. That much was immediately clear, but at least she didn't hear any gunfire at the moment.

The back door emerged into a tiny side hallway that fed directly into the common room after a single turn.

Rachel spared a glance back to make sure the others were through and the door was shut behind them—and, maybe, to double-check that Alton's eyes weren't glowing raknoth red—then she moved into the common room on Jarek's flank.

Large chunks of rubble were piled in one corner of the common room along with several dark-clad forms, still and lifeless on the concrete floor. The corner had apparently caved in, but it looked like the Resistance had somehow patched the ceiling. It wasn't pretty, but at least it wasn't open to the lot above. For now.

Resistance troops lined the perimeter of the room, most of their weapons trained toward the corner despite the lack of any immediate threat. Alaric and Nelken stood with them, each holding an assault rifle. Alaric bent to say something to Haldin, who was sitting cross-legged on the floor beside him, eyes closed and back resting against the wall.

Haldin seemed to rouse marginally. Rachel felt a tendril of his mind brush lightly against her own. He said something to Alaric, and Alaric's gaze shot over to them, followed by Nelken's. Nelken beckoned, and they hurried over to join the commanders.

"Hell of a party you've got here," Jarek said when they were close enough to speak quietly.

Above, the boots stomping across the lot were numerous enough to be plainly heard over the whispers in the room like the falling of some obscenely thick rain on their humble shelter.

"The Overlord?" Alaric asked.

"Still alive," Jarek said. "And probably not far behind us. They must've tracked Mose—Seth to find this place."

Alaric gave Jarek a look that might have been frustrated or accusing, then he gave a conciliatory nod. "Figured the same."

"What's going on up there?" Rachel asked.

"Haldin's giving them hell, as far as we can tell," Nelken said.

A pair of detonations above shook the room and punctuated his remark, kicking loose a shower of dust in the process.

Elise crouched down by Haldin and put a hand on his shoulder, her own eyes drifting shut.

"He sealed up the first breach they managed," Alaric added. "Not really sure how, but it's still only a matter of time before they punch through."

"That's a lot of men up there," Jarek agreed. "Raknoth too, I'm guessing. Not sure how we're getting out of this one."

Alaric scowled at Jarek. "Well I reckon killing their Overlord would've been a good place to start."

"You're right." Jarek jabbed a finger at Alaric. "I'll let you have at him next round, cowboy."

"Gentlemen," Nelken said, "I think we have more pressing matters at hand."

Matters like making sure Michael was alive and safe—or as safe as he could be right now, at least.

"I'm going to medical," Rachel said. "I need to check on Michael."

"I'll come," Elise said, rejoining their huddle. "I need to find Johnny."

Rachel nodded at her and the commanders. Her eyes lingered a moment longer on Jarek's.

"Be safe," he said.

"Yeah," she said, "coming from you."

He shot her a wink, then his helmet gave a whirring groan, and he frowned at the dented edges where his faceplate used to be. "Shit. Forgot I was flying without protection. Pretend that was dramatic."

Rachel turned and set off down the adjacent hallway, praying that wouldn't go down in the books as their last interaction.

She did her best to work through the ranks without too much pushing. A glance back confirmed Elise was with her.

Of the two roughly equidistant routes leading to medical, the hallway straight ahead past the council chamber was far more congested with armed Resistance traffic, so Rachel cut right down the less crowded hallway. Halfway down its length, three—no, four—explosions rocked the base from the direction of the common room, shaking more dust loose, right along with Rachel's resolve.

Her step faltered. She traded a worried glance with Elise and saw her own question reflected in Elise's wide blue eyes.

Did they go back?

The explosion that boomed from the other side of HQ a second later jolted them back into action.

Jarek, Haldin, Alaric, all the others—they were big boys. They could handle themselves better than most, in this base or otherwise. Definitely better than Michael, who very well wasn't even conscious right now.

They rounded left at the next junction, moving at a hard run now. Gunfire erupted from ahead, or maybe it was from behind. Worse, it might have been from both directions. The network of looping hallways made it hard to tell for sure.

At the corner, Rachel darted across the hall and into the cover of medical's doorway before peering down the next hallway.

Resistance troops were likewise taking what cover they could in doorways. Further down, Commander Daniels herself was leading the way in returning fire on the dark-clad men fighting their way out of the cells they'd apparently breached at the end of the hallway.

Rachel turned to see Elise peeking out from the corner she'd just skipped over from, holding a dark pistol at the ready.

Elise inclined her head toward medical, and her voice entered Rachel's head though her lips didn't move, *"Go."*

Rachel only thought about arguing for a split second before she nodded and hurried to the back room.

Michael's bed was empty.

Her stomach went into free fall. Then a flicker of motion caught her eye, and she turned, staff flying up to point down the raised barrel of a handgun, and—

She sucked in a breath then blew it out, tension bleeding from her chest and shoulders as she lowered her staff.

On the other side of the pistol, Michael did the same and lowered his gun. Beside him, Pryce lowered his own pistol and patted at his chest over his heart.

"Jesus, Rache," Michael said, "you scared the—"

She stepped briskly forward and pulled him into a hard but brief hug. He returned her squeeze, and she pulled back.

"Good to see you on your feet, Spongehead." She turned to Pryce. "Thanks for sticking with him."

Pryce opened his mouth only to be cut off by another wall-shaking explosion close by.

"We need to get out of here," Pryce said. "Is Zar'Golga—"

"Alive," Rachel said. "We barely made it out ourselves."

"Out of the frying pan…" Pryce said, looking around as if plotting potential escape routes.

"I need to go help them," Rachel said.

"We've got your back," Michael said, shuffling forward.

"Michael, you've been unconscious for the past—"

"We'll be safer with you anyway," Michael said.

"Plus," Pryce said, "if you happen to decide it's time to abandon ship, I'd rather not be squirreled away back here."

Rachel wasn't so sure abandoning ship was even a remote possibility at this point, but they raised fair points either way, and they didn't exactly have time to argue. For all they knew, Golga's men could breach through right above their heads at any moment.

"Okay. You've got your bullet catcher, Spongehead?"

Michael patted the spot where the device must've been clipped to his belt beneath his shirt.

"All right then." She paused by the door back to the hallway. "Cover our asses, Spongehead. Pryce, you stay between us so—"

"Catcher fields," Pryce said. "Overlapping. Got it."

She almost smiled despite herself. "Right. Let's go."

Elise was nowhere in sight when Rachel stepped into the hallway.

Commander Daniels had been pressed back toward medical, and at least four of her soldiers had fallen, but those who remained fought on grimly.

A few of Golga's troops shifted their fire from the Resistance forces to Rachel, apparently expecting an easy target.

Bullets slammed into the edge of her catcher's field, each one tearing to a halt and falling harmlessly to the floor until she was treading over a trail of spent lead through suddenly frigid air.

She raised her staff and threw a column of telekinetic force at the densest group of enemy soldiers. Another soldier yanked out a grenade and pulled the pin. Rachel reached out and telekinetically swatted the live grenade from his hand before he could throw it.

Everyone who saw it threw themselves out of the hallway and into the nearest available rooms, but the blast still caught a few enemy soldiers. Even with the gunfire ringing in her ears, the explosion was nearly deafening in the small hallway space. A wave of hot air slammed against the barrier Rachel had erected, peppered with bits of shrapnel.

A triplet of gunshots barked just behind her, and she glanced to see more dark-clad troops rounding from the hallway behind them. Spent lead fell to the ground at Michael's feet as the catcher did its work. Too much lead. Michael and Pryce's breaths steamed out of their mouths in the frigid cold the catchers inflicted on their patch of hallway.

The breeze of equilibrating air swept at her hair as she shifted her staff around, aiming to disrupt the worst of the attack on their flank.

She was drawing energy for her attack when a vast telepathic presence swept through the hall, parting around her as if she were a tiny boulder in the middle of powerful river.

Rachel froze, pulling her mental defenses tight around her. That presence wasn't human—she was sure of that much.

With her defenses as arranged as she had time to manage, she rechecked their surroundings, expecting to find enemy soldiers closing in on them from both sides.

Golga's men were frozen in place along the hallway, standing at attention with eerie, silent precision.

"What the f—"

At a creak from behind, Rachel spun, staff raised.

Given that they were the only serviceable cover in the hallway, all the cell doors had been thrown open during the firefight. All but the two doors guarding Seth Mosen and Al'Drogan. And now, the closer of the two doors was opening with a groan of creaky hinges while Golga's troops looked on in absolute stillness.

Daniels watched with a tight jaw, and the remaining Resistance soldiers looked around in fear and confusion, most of them probably wondering whether they shouldn't just gun their oddly still foes down while they had the chance. Rachel couldn't say she wasn't wondering the same thing.

The cell door finished opening, and Elise emerged. Al'Drogan strode out behind her, completely unchained, fiery-red eyes sweeping the hallway.

Some gasped. Others cursed. And every Resistance agent in the hallway pointed their weapons at Drogan.

Elise patted the air with her hands. "It's okay, everyone."

"Easy, guys," Johnny added as he stepped out of the room behind them, holding the odd assault rifle he carried in as non-threatening a way as possible. "This isn't what it looks like."

"Are you crazy?" one of the Resistance soldiers demanded, keeping his rifle trained on Drogan while trying to simultaneously keep a wary eye on the creepily still enemies at his back. "That bastard will—"

Commander Daniels silenced him with a raised hand, glancing around at Golga's unmoving troops with only a tad more confidence. "You'd better explain yourself quickly then," she said to Johnny. "Because it certainly looks like you're attempting to spring the Red King from custody."

Johnny held up a finger then gave a conciliatory nod. "Okay. It's exactly what it looks like. But! The King here is the only thing keeping these guys"—he gestured at the frozen troops—"from going all shooty-shooty-stabby-stabby right now. You don't have to call him buddy, but he's on our side right now."

"Bullshit," the Resistance soldier said.

Daniels didn't look like she necessarily disagreed.

"Those are his friends attacking us out there," another added. "I say we kill the bastard while we can."

Elise bent an eyebrow at Rachel. *A little help here?"*

Rachel swallowed, recalibrating her shocked tongue.

"Johnny's right," she said, putting as much weight and authority behind the words as she could.

Several eyes shifted toward her. No one here but Daniels probably much cared what she thought, but some of them had seen what she could do, and they knew that she'd fought for them in the past.

Hopefully it was enough.

"Look, our asses are too far in the fire to argue right now."

The sounds of nearby gunfire and shouting added credence to her words, as did the blood-curdling roar that tore out from the direction of the common room.

Shit. They needed to get back to the others. And if this was really happening, maybe Drogan could even help shut down the rest of Golga's forces.

She looked at Drogan, then back to the men and women watching her. "I've been closer to this raknoth's mind than anyone here." She shook her head. "He's not my friend. But right now, he's not my enemy either, and if we don't take all the help we can get, we're all gonna die down here."

No one spoke for a long tense moment.

Then Michael barked, "Let's move, people!"

Heads turned to Daniels, who gave a solitary nod. "You heard Carver, people. Let's move."

Uncertain stares slowly gave way to bobbing heads.

"We need to get back to the common room," Rachel said. "Shut them down before—"

A sound like a choir of roaring lions spun Rachel back to Michael's side of the hallway. Down by medical, Golga's men began to unfreeze and promptly parted to clear a path.

Al'Krogoth stepped in view, rusty hide fully intact and crimson eyes blazing, a low growl rumbling in the back of his throat.

"Fuck," Rachel said.

Too late.

CHAPTER TWENTY-EIGHT

After Rachel and Elise departed for medical, things actually seemed rather dull to Jarek—for all of one whole minute, at least. Judging from the focus etched on Haldin's brow and the fact that Golga's forces weren't currently blasting down on their heads, the Enochian was still at it with his little mischievous arcanist act, which left them with little to do but sit and wait.

At least until Alton bristled up and quietly announced that Haldin was under attack. The raknoth didn't specify beyond that, but the sudden sheen of sweat on the Enochian's forehead gave Jarek a decent guess as to what he meant.

There had to be at least one raknoth topside—probably several—and it looked like they must be taking it upon themselves to disrupt the arcanist who was currently HQ's main defense.

"Can you help him?" Jarek asked quietly.

"I am." Alton's tone was flat, his gaze distant. "There are several of them nearby."

Several raknoth topside. Fantastic. At least Alton hadn't accidentally called them his kin out loud. He was already drawing enough distrustful stares as it was.

Jarek reached over his shoulder for the Whacker but thought

better of it. The common room was the most spacious place in HQ, but even here, the ceiling was too low to easily swing a giant sword around, and that wasn't even to mention the risk of catching a friendly with this many Resistance forces around.

For a second, Jarek considered asking Phineas to borrow one of his snazzy assault rifles, but the stoic bear-man didn't look eager to part with any of his ordnance. Instead, he strode over and scooped up a carbine one of the first batch of Golga's men had carried in before Haldin sealed the breach. However the hell he'd managed that one.

Pound for pound, he wasn't sure who was packing more power between Rachel and Haldin, but he had to admit the Enochian was devilishly crafty from what he'd seen. As tenuous as their arrival had been, Jarek was glad the Enochians were on their side.

In addition to the rifle, Jarek plucked two loaded mags from the soldier's vest and tucked them into his gun belt before checking to ensure his current mag was full enough. The weapon wouldn't take down a raknoth, but there were plenty of men ready to kill them up there too. Jarek might as well be useful until it was time to let the Whacker out.

When he turned to cross back to the others, Haldin looked markedly worse than he had a minute ago.

That was when things went to shit.

Haldin's eyes snapped open, wide with alarm. "Take cover!" he cried.

Jarek almost listened. Then he lunged toward Alaric, Nelken, and Haldin on impulse and nearly punched a hole through the wall breaking his momentum.

Behind him, the ceiling exploded inward with a violently loud pop and a stream of crumbling sounds. A thick wave of dust and larger particulates swirled through the room.

Jarek shoved a protesting Nelken and Alaric down next to Haldin and stood over them, arms planted against the wall to shield them as best he could.

It wasn't much, but it was all he could manage before the next blast hit.

Jarek barely had time to register there had been a blast at all until after the rapid series of violently abrupt impacts that left him drifting in a murky haze of disorientation.

He blinked and tried to move. It hurt.

Somehow, he'd ended up on the ground, something was on top of him, and it was… He blinked again.

It was dark in the room?

Impossible, said his sluggish brain. It was still daylight outside. Which meant…

Another explosion rattled Jarek's insides.

"We're buried, sir," Al's voice crackled in his ear. "In case you hadn't noticed."

Jarek coughed and tasted something suspiciously similar to blood. "Rock and a hard place, huh?"

He tried his arms and found his left arm pinned and his right only marginally more free and, thanks to Fela's iron grasp, still gripping his commandeered carbine.

He was about to make an awkward attempt at heaving his way out when the slab over his face shifted with a sound of grinding stone and then flipped explosively off him.

Daylight poured in, revealing Jarek's rescuer to be Alton Parker.

The raknoth spun toward the source of a pained cry and disappeared to go help someone else.

The common room was a devastated mess, strewn with heaping piles of collapsed asphalt and debris ranging from the size of golf balls to kitchen tables. Much of the ceiling was gone, and—more importantly—dark-clad figures were swarming around the edges of the now-open pit that was the common room.

More importantly still, several of those men were pointing guns at Jarek's unprotected face. And he was still too pinned to move anything but his right arm.

He ripped his stolen carbine free from the rubble, praying it hadn't been too badly damaged, and pointed it at the nearest soldier.

The weapon jolted in his hand, barking out shot after shot. The closest of Golga's troops fell back to use the lip of the room as cover. The rest of them returned fire.

Jarek turned his head away from the worst of it. Bullets smacked down around him, several cracking and twanging off the bits of his armor that were exposed from the rubble pile.

Luckily, he didn't need to see with his own eyes to aim.

"A little help, Al?"

"I can barely see anything, sir!"

Shit. He hadn't even thought about that. Most of Al's sensors had gone with the faceplate, and half of the others were probably buried right now.

The incoming fire intensified, and the itchy fingers of claustrophobic panic clutched harder at Jarek's chest.

His heart beat faster, almost as fast as the bullets were pouring down all around him now. He needed to move, needed to—

"Jarek?" someone called from somewhere near his feet.

Haldin?

"I could use a big strong robot hand over here!" the voice said.

Definitely Haldin. And he needed help. Jarek's help. The thought centered him.

Jarek tossed the now-empty carbine aside, twisted as best he could, and reached his right hand across to the large hunk of debris on his left shoulder. In comparison to what Fela could technically lift, the piece pinning him probably wasn't so heavy, but he didn't have the position or leverage, and god only knew what else was stacked on top of it.

He pushed those thoughts aside and pushed with all his and Fela's combined might. With the grating rumble of stone on heavy stone, the rubble slid back inch-by-inch. Another inch or so and he'd be able to—

Something slammed into the side of his helmet hard enough to render thinking temporarily problematic—a bullet, he realized.

"Move, sir," Al's voice said somewhere in the back of his foggy brain.

His ears rang. Another inch or so to the right and that bullet would've—

"Move!" Al cried.

Jarek snapped back and gave the rubble one last heavy shove. There.

He ripped free of his rubble-strewn confinement. Once his torso was up, his legs came easily enough. He stood, drew his left pistol, and fired a few barely aimed shots to keep Golga's men cautious as he stepped over to the slab of collapsed ceiling he thought Haldin's voice had come from.

"Hal?"

And shit, where was Alaric? And Nelken?

"Back here," came Haldin's voice.

The enemy fire was dulling down, largely thanks to the fifteen or so Resistance soldiers who'd remained alive and unpinned through the ceiling collapse. They'd rallied behind rubble piles, hallway mouths, and other cover, and were returning fire now. A few more were fighting their way in from the uncollapsed sections of HQ.

In the one corner with a mostly intact ceiling, Phineas was directing a particularly heavy stream of deadly lead (or whatever Enochians used in their bullets) at Golga's troops from behind a large pile of rubble.

Jarek got a grip on the thick slab in front of him and heaved. The thing was heavy, but he managed.

He was wondering if Haldin couldn't have moved the slab himself when it toppled away from the wall to reveal the Enochian had been busy with other matters.

Haldin was hunkered down beside Alaric. Nelken was wedged against the wall beside them, trapped by rubble all around, including the small mountain of debris inexplicably floating over his head.

The instant Jarek's slab fell off them and cleared the way, the floating pile shifted and toppled clear after it, and Haldin slumped back against the wall.

Jarek rushed forward to help Alaric pull Nelken out from under the looming pile.

Nelken roused as they handled him, reaching up to clutch at Jarek's arm and trying to cough something out of lungs that were probably half full of dust. They only moved him a few inches before it became clear his legs were still pinned, and it looked like they were going to have to move some serious weight to get him out.

Jarek bent to grab the slab that looked to be the primary culprit.

"Behind you!" Haldin snapped.

Something landed right near Jarek's vulnerable ass with a thump and a shifting of rubble.

Haldin sprung into motion before Jarek could stabilize his slab enough to aim a mule kick backward. A second later, there was a sound of crushing stone and a furious roar.

Apparently the raknoth had joined the party.

Amid the dwindling gunfire, he heard the thuds of multiple impacts around the room. More raknoth? Or Golga's soldiers moving in?

Either way, not good.

He set his feet and heaved the slab higher, lifting and then pushing until the slab passed the tipping point and fell aside to the floor with a heavy boom. Below, Nelken grunted in alarm or pain. Yanking him out like this without understanding what was pinned where was probably a monumentally bad idea, but they didn't have time to do it right, and an injured leg was better than a dead commander.

Jarek scrambled to clear a few more easy pieces then reached for the next large piece obstructing Nelken.

Alton appeared to beat him to it and yanked the heavy slab aside to reveal two more Resistance fighters, a man and a woman, huddled together beneath, looking harrowed but relatively unharmed.

For a split second, their expressions shifted to profound relief. Then they caught sight of Alton, whose eyes had gone red somewhere between his exertions and the bullets slamming into his back, and their expressions twisted to pure terror.

The woman produced a pistol and pumped four rounds into Alton's chest before Alaric hurled himself over to pull her gun arm down.

"He's trying to help, you dimwits!"

Before either of them could respond, a second pair of fiery-red eyes dropped down behind Alton, and a pair of scaly green arms clamped around his torso and chucked him across the room, where he smashed into the opposite wall like a sack of bricks.

The enemy raknoth turned back to them just in time to catch Jarek's front kick full-on in the chest.

The kick launched the raknoth across the room, bouncing from one pile of rubble to the next.

Alaric was waving the two stunned Resistance troops to action. "Wipe those dumb looks off and help me get your commander out of here!"

They snapped to and complied, and Jarek turned to follow his raknoth foe, reaching for the Whacker as he went.

He hadn't drawn his blade—hadn't even made it two steps—when what might have been a six-hundred-pound gorilla came down on him from behind. He did his best to tuck and roll with the thing's considerable momentum, but there was only so much he could do with his attacker stubbornly riding him all the way down.

They bounced across the uneven ground in a series of messy rolls that ended with Jarek on his side and strong, scaly arms trying to wrap their way around his torso and neck.

He threw a pair of vicious elbow strikes back at his faceless opponent and was rewarded with a wet cracking sound and a low growl. A violent backward headbutt changed the growl to a screech, but the impact left Jarek's own head ringing. He bucked against the raknoth's steely grip all the same and managed to slip free in the distraction.

In a single second, he was on his feet and aiming a hard stomp at the raknoth's head.

Not fast enough.

A second raknoth—the one he'd kicked he realized—came out of nowhere to catch him in a low shoulder tackle, and he didn't stop there. The raknoth pumped his powerful legs, driving Jarek back, back, back, until they slammed into the wall they'd excavated Nelken from. Luckily, Alaric and his helpers had shuttled Nelken out of harm's way by then.

Lucky. Right. Because now all Jarek had to contend with was the raknoth pinning him to the wall and his buddy who was rising from the rubble to come help tear Jarek's head off.

Across the room, Alton was tangling with a new raknoth now. To the left, Haldin stood over his fallen raknoth opponent with a pair of long, simple daggers in hand, one of which was coated with dark raknoth blood.

A hard punch to the stomach drove out what little air remained in Jarek's lungs and yanked his attention thoroughly back to the raknoth at hand. He replied with a hard knee of his own and brought his closed fist down on top of the raknoth's thick skull.

It was about as pleasant as punching a vault door, but Jarek gritted his teeth and threw another punch into the side of that reptilian head, and then another. He got in two more good punches before the raknoth he'd failed to stomp to its end lunged over, caught Jarek's raised fist, and slammed his arm to the wall.

For a few seconds, the three of them struggled furiously.

Then another raknoth dropped into the room, and everything seemed to freeze.

When he got a look at the newcomer, Jarek realized why.

Even if he hadn't been carrying that obscenely large club of his, Jarek would've recognized the raknoth by the dark green of his hide and by the sheer animosity that radiated off him like a deadly miasma.

Zar'Golga had arrived.

CHAPTER TWENTY-NINE

"You've gotta be shittin' me," Jarek muttered.

The two raknoth holding him thrust him harder into the wall as if demanding silence, and across the room, Zar'Golga showed him that bone-chillingly murderous raknoth grin of his.

Fighting Golga one-on-one had been bad enough. And somehow, Jarek didn't think things would work out better with an entire army and god knew how many raknoth at Golga's back.

Golga appeared to feel similarly as he pointed his club toward Jarek. "This time, there will be no esca—"

Half a dozen shots rang out from the right, and Golga jerked back, spattering the wall behind him with dark ichor. Jarek followed the shots to Alaric and Phineas, who were both sporting sleek Enochian rifles. Then all hell broke loose.

Raknoth roared. Golga's forces renewed their fire on anyone who wasn't in close proximity to the raknoth below. Haldin sprang across the room and drove a hard boot into the side of Golga's head.

Jarek needed to get free and help Haldin. The Enochian was good, he'd give him that, but he doubted Haldin fully appreciated what he was getting himself into fighting Golga one-on-one.

Jarek bucked against his captors, kicking and stomping. He broke his left hand free just in time to catch a clawed hand on its way to his exposed face.

Ahead, Haldin twisted and turned past a rain of Golga's blows with grace and speed that should have been well outside the limits of a human being. He moved as if he knew what would happen before it did, like a machine built for the sole purpose of dancing smoothly around a rampaging raknoth.

While Jarek struggled to keep one raknoth from gouging his eyes out, the other came to the realization that Jarek's hands were tied and his neck vulnerable.

A strong hand clamped over his armored throat and tugged him forward only to slam him back into the wall. And then again.

Jarek's vision swam with oddly-colored spots from the impact, and he was fighting a losing battle for breath. But at least the raknoth's new hold freed up one of his legs.

He kicked the raknoth's right knee before he could give Jarek another slam. There was a gristly crunch, and the raknoth hobbled back but didn't fall. Instead, he gave an angry roar and started forward again, ready to end Jarek.

His buddy held Jarek in place, content to let his kin have the honor.

Or did, at least, until Phineas came charging in and planted an earth-shaking punch right on the side of the raknoth's head.

The punch should've broken Phineas' hand. Only it wasn't his hand, Jarek realized, but a prosthetic.

Jarek's captor stumbled aside from the hit and released his grip on Jarek to aim an angry backhand at Phineas. The blow caught the big guy in the chest and sent him sprawling into the wall, but Phineas' distraction wasn't wasted.

Jarek threw a shove into the raknoth's chest, hard enough to buy himself a moment as the raknoth with the bum knee closed in on him from the left.

In one continuous motion, Jarek tore his sword free and stepped in a high to low sweep. The giant blade caught the incoming raknoth at the left knee joint and ripped through, tearing more than cutting.

The raknoth fell with a screech, and Jarek pivoted straight into his next strike, maintaining the blade's considerable momentum and steering it into a rising sweep at the spot where the second raknoth would probably be lunging straight for his exposed back.

Claws ripped at his left shoulder armor as he completed his turn, and then the raknoth came into view and Jarek's blade connected with his upper arm. Between the angle and the raknoth's proximity, the strike didn't have the power to remove the arm, but judging by the sound and the feel of the impact in Jarek's hands, it at least broke something.

Jarek darted back just in time to avoid a wild backhand. The raknoth lunged after him. He spun, dropping his left hand from the hilt, and brought the Whacker around in a high horizontal sweep.

The sword kicked in his hands, and the raknoth fell to Jarek's side, the top half of his head torn open. Jarek caught a glimpse of something wriggling in the dark fluids oozing from the open head wound, and his stomach turned. Then a roar to his left wrenched his attention away.

Across the room, Haldin's daggers shot up to meet a tremendous blow of Zar'Golga's club. Jarek tried to cry out. Too late.

What was the crazy bastard thinking, trying to catch that thing with those tiny—

The club smashed off thin air as if it had hit an invisible, immovable post a few feet from Haldin's daggers. Jarek's horror turned to shocked admiration as the force and leverage of the impact proved sufficient to jolt the weapon free from Golga's grip.

Haldin, apparently expecting the large weapon to come spinning out of Golga's hand, had already ducked to the side to avoid its wild trajectory. What he hadn't expected was how seamlessly Golga reacted.

The raknoth abandoned the club as if throwing it away had been his intention all along and whirled to catch Haldin by the throat. Haldin dropped his daggers and managed to catch Golga's hand with both of his and avoid getting his throat torn out, but he couldn't do a thing to keep Golga from driving him down to his knees and yanking him in for the killing blow.

Jarek sprang forward, aiming an overhand strike at Golga's left elbow. The raknoth saw him coming and leapt backward, releasing Haldin to avoid Jarek's attack. Jarek planted his feet and turned, raising his sword as he tracked Golga.

There was a gasp of air and a choking cough from behind, and then Haldin stepped to Jarek's side, daggers at the ready.

Behind Golga, Alton stood wearily from an unmoving foe and began to skirt the edge of the room toward them.

Two raknoth dropped down from above to bar his way—Toady and Slender Face, Jarek registered.

Another pair of raknoth dropped down behind Jarek and Haldin, low growls emanating from their throats. Jarek didn't realize how silent the battle had gone around them until shouts and gunshots picked up from somewhere down the hallway behind them.

Jarek waited until Golga himself turned to inspect the racket, then he took a quick glance. He cursed at what he saw.

Rusty-hided Al'Krogoth emerged from the hallway, not ripping and tearing his way through the Resistance troops there but merely pushing through them as if treading through a field of tall wild grass. One of the stunned troops pointed his pistol at Krogoth and pulled the trigger, and the raknoth simply swatted him aside.

Behind him came Drogan, another raknoth, and... Johnny? And Rachel, Elise, Daniels, and another dozen Resistance soldiers.

Jarek traded a confused look with Haldin, expecting any one of the several raknoth in the room to spring at them at any moment. He followed Haldin's gaze around the lip of the common room pit and realized most of Golga's soldiers were watching the scene in eerie silence, their weapons lowered to their sides.

What the hell was going on?

"Stop them," Krogoth said.

Jarek tensed as the raknoth beside Krogoth prepared to spring, but he leapt well over them and Golga and landed squarely on Toady's stout form.

Roars erupted from every direction.

"Traitors!" Golga bellowed.

He lunged at Jarek and Haldin.

They split apart. Jarek aimed a swipe at Golga's leg as he streaked in between them, but the raknoth stepped aside from the attack.

The two raknoth who'd dropped down behind Jarek and Haldin were moving in to help their master, but Drogan and Elise cut them off.

Golga rounded on Jarek and charged, deigning to leave Haldin unchecked at his back.

Jarek pedaled backward, sweeping his sword around, and used his last step to leverage a heavy diagonal cut at the oncoming raknoth.

Golga went aerial and spun in parallel with the strike, and Jarek nearly shat himself when the raknoth's scaly hand shot out and clamped onto the dull back edge of the Whacker.

Golga touched down from his aerial maneuver and pulled, and between Jarek's surprise and the raknoth's unbelievable strength, Jarek stumbled forward, off balance. Golga roared in Jarek's face and smacked the base of the blade with his free hand hard enough to tear the hilt from Jarek's hands.

Jarek let out his own battle cry, lowered his head, and drove into Golga as hard as he could.

Golga was already scrambling to gain control over Jarek when they hit the ground. Jarek wrestled with the raknoth, throwing knees and elbows where he could. Golga made a grab for Jarek's vulnerable face, and Jarek grabbed the raknoth's wrist. Too late.

He growled a curse as hot lines of pain lanced across his face. He clamped down harder on Golga's wrist and struggled against the raknoth's superior strength as warm blood ran down his face, forcing his left eye shut.

Then Golga flew backward as if struck by an invisible cannon ball.

Jarek spit blood from his mouth, pushed down his body's pleas to slump to the floor and never move again, and kipped to his feet.

Rachel was there at his side, staff raised in the direction of Golga's flight. Haldin faced them from Golga's flank.

Golga leapt back to his feet and started forward. Only something was off. The raknoth moved like he was trapped in a pool of thick syrup—or thick concrete maybe, given how freakishly strong he was.

"We've got him," Rachel said beside him, her voice tight.

Across from them, Haldin's expression was just as strained.

No time like the present, then. Jarek darted forward and threw a hard kick into the side of Golga's head. The raknoth spun and crashed to the ground. He struggled against his telekinetic shackles to push himself up toward Haldin. Jarek snaked his arms under Golga's armpits, locked his hands behind the raknoth's skull, and hauled him to his feet.

Golga struggled against his hold, but Jarek had the leverage now. A moment later, the raknoth's arms were both tugged straight out to his sides and held immobile by unseen hands. Rachel and Haldin again, Jarek assumed.

Haldin appeared at Jarek's side, grabbed the back of Golga's head in one hand, and planted the tip of a dagger in front of the raknoth's eye with the other.

Behind him, Rachel slammed her staff to the ground, and a low, thrumming boom swept through the room, drawing all eyes to them.

"That's all she wrote, folks," Jarek cried, the taste of his own blood only adding to his frantic battle high. "Now if you'd kindly lay down your weapons and claws and get the fuck out of here, we have some stern words to exchange with this club-happy ass-hat."

"Surrender," Haldin said to Golga, his expression grim and his dagger hand steady.

Golga ignored him.

Krogoth stalked across the room toward them. Haldin's dagger hand stayed perfectly stable as he glanced back at the rusty-hided raknoth. Finally, he gave a small nod and took a step to the side, allowing Krogoth to approach Golga directly.

"Traitor," Golga said, his voice a low rumble. He wasn't struggling anymore. "You would join these pathetic meat sacks? Rebel against the masters?"

"I would fight for my life," Krogoth said, "rather than lay down to the masters' fury like a sheep to the slaughter." The scarlet fire in his eyes dimmed in a manner that seemed almost remorseful. "You will not stand beside us?"

"Fool. I will tear you to pieces myself if you—"

Krogoth clutched wordlessly at Golga's throat and wrenched with a clawed hand. Jarek's stomach turned at the horrible wet sound and the airy screech that pierced through it.

Twin voices demanded at equal intensities in Jarek's mind that he stop Krogoth and that he stand aside and do nothing. The latter won by default.

In front of him, Haldin and Rachel looked like they were experiencing a similar moral paralysis.

Meanwhile, Krogoth calmly pushed through the gurgling screeches and methodically clawed his way through Golga's throat until the raknoth's body went limp in Jarek's arms.

He stepped back, feeling like he might puke. Jarek was no stranger to violence, but this was disturbing on a whole new level.

Krogoth took a firmer grip on Golga's spasmodic head, and Jarek looked away.

There was an awful ripping sound, and Jarek slowly looked back to see Krogoth holding Golga's disembodied head high for all to see.

Having apparently made his point, Krogoth spiked the head to the ground and crushed it with one tremendous stomp.

Thick, awful silence hung in the air, broken only by the groans of the wounded and the sound of someone retching over to the left. Jarek crept slowly over to recover the Whacker from the floor, then he turned to face Krogoth, sword at his side.

"The rakul are coming," Krogoth finally called to the silent assembly. He swept his fiery gaze around to each of the raknoth in turn. "You have all felt it. There is no choice now. There will be no mercy for us." His gaze drifted to the huddles of Resistance soldiers around Alaric and Commander Daniels. "We must protect the blood, lest the sickness take us. We must fight, lest the masters do it instead. If any of you wishes to challenge me in this, step forward now and face me."

None did.

None except Alaric.

He set his rifle down and shuffled out from behind cover with a limp he must have obtained in the fight or the cave-in. One of the Resistance troops moved to support him, but Alaric waved him off.

Daniels pushed out from her party and met Alaric halfway.

Krogoth watched them approach calmly, his eyes dim and his posture bored.

"If what we've heard about these rakul is true," Alaric said when he and Daniels stood in front of Krogoth, "it might be we need to set aside the hatchet to survive. For now." He shook his head, his stare that of pure, immutable stone. "But don't think for a goddamn minute that means that hatchet's buried. We're not your blood bags to be used and discarded as you please, and we'll never forget what you did to our planet—the destruction you bring even now. We'll kill these rakul, and then you and I are going to have words about your future here."

Krogoth stared at Alaric for a good fifteen seconds before he finally turned his gaze to Daniels.

She only returned his stare with her own brand of stony stoicism, silently acknowledging her support of Alaric's claims.

After what felt like another five minutes, Krogoth gave an almost imperceptible nod and leapt out of the common room pit to the lot above. "Your champions may be formidable," he called back down, glancing at Jarek, Haldin, and Rachel. "But that does not put you in a position to make such demands. Be happy we leave while some of you still stand this day."

With that, he turned and stalked out of sight.

The rest of the raknoth in the common room looked around at each other uncertainly and then vaulted up to the lot and followed after their new leader. Golga's—or Krogoth's—troops helped each other in clambering up after them, then they obediently marched off as well.

Drogan was the last to leave. He eyed his captors of the past few days for a long spell before finally fixing his gaze on Jarek and taking a few sniffs.

"Your wounds suit you," he said.

Jarek swallowed, resisting the urge to wipe at the blood still trickling lightly down his face, plastering his left eye shut. Maybe he was tired—maybe just creeped out—but he couldn't decide what to say to that.

Drogan leapt out of the common room before he had to.

The raknoth turned back only long enough to give a perfectly creepy wave of his partially regrown fingers. "Until we meet again, Jarek Slater."

Then he strode off into the midmorning sun.

Jarek turned his one-eyed gaze to Haldin and Rachel and forced his best nonchalant smile. "I think he likes me."

He must have looked garish, because Rachel just cringed.

"C'mon." She walked over and squinted at his closed eye before pulling him off toward medical. "Let's get you cleaned up before you bleed everywhere."

Around them, people were beginning to move again—checking on ignored injuries, looking for fallen friends, and carting the wounded back toward medical. Haldin and Elise stood together in one corner, their arms tightly wrapped around one another.

"Yeah," Jarek said, allowing Rachel to drag him across the rubble-strewn ruins of the common room. "I mean, we wouldn't want to go and make a mess of this place."

CHAPTER THIRTY

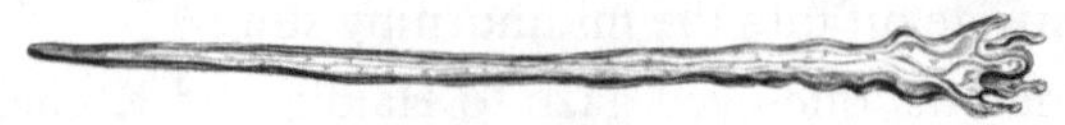

Rachel had never considered herself particularly squeamish, but, then again, she'd never realized just how much a few face wounds could bleed either. As far as she could tell, Jarek's wounds weren't all that deep, but they'd stubbornly bled on as she'd done her best to mop up the mess and seal up the damage with the wound glue she'd nabbed from medical.

In light of the dozens of critically wounded Resistance soldiers, the doctors hadn't protested when she'd offered to clear out of medical and see to Jarek's wounds herself. In fact, she wasn't certain they'd even heard her.

To say HQ was in shambles was putting it lightly. So they'd trekked outside and found a quiet corner in the shipping container yard.

"Everything considered," Jarek said, thankfully managing to not move his face too much, "I think—"

"If you say you think things went swimmingly"—Rachel paused from her work to wave her wound glue swab in front of him—"I'm going to lobotomize you with this swab."

"—think," Jarek said, holding a finger up for pause, "that it was a hell of a day." His face split into a grin—just a tad too far. "Some medical professional you are."

"Annnd now you're bleeding again."

His grin started to widen. "Ah, you're just giving me the busin—Ow."

Rivulets of blood welled at three more points as her work cracked under the load of his insistent grin.

"Dammit, hold still." She leaned in closer to dab the blood away and reapply the glue where needed.

As she worked, she idly wondered whether the wounds would leave some horrific scar raking from his left brow down to his right cheek. It'd be a shame, but, all things considered, it was probably a small enough price for surviving an ambush, an invasion, a bombing, and two fights with Zar'Golga. At least his eyes were both intact.

Plus, knowing Jarek, he'd just think a scar was badass anyway.

Focused as she was on the task, she almost forgot how close her face was to his—at least until she noticed the way he was watching her. Once she noticed, though, she couldn't seem to unnotice.

His eyes bore into hers with solemn intensity, and she felt a pull that was becoming familiar.

"Rache, I—"

"Don't."

She hadn't thought about saying it—wasn't even sure why she did —but it popped out all the same. And, for some reason, Jarek looked less surprised about it than she felt.

He gave a shrug and slipped on one of his nonchalant masks. "I just wanted to say thanks."

She should say something. Apologize. Explain.

But explain what?

She was hardly sure herself, so she followed Jarek's lead in limping away from whatever had just happened.

"Thanks?"

Well played, Rachel. Smooth.

Jarek's smile didn't spread to his eyes. "I mean, I think we can both agree I'm good—amazing, even—but I'm not sure I would have made it through today without you."

She dropped his gaze in favor of the pavement. She didn't want to see the fragility in his smile knowing that she'd put it there. Part of her wanted to reach out to him, to tell him all the terrible shit that had gone through her head in the moments she'd thought she was about to lose him, when Zar'Golga had stood over him, club raised. But she couldn't.

"Jarek, I didn't mean I—"

"I get it," he said. "It's hard. We almost died today. Either one of us could finish the job tomorrow. And even if that weren't the case…" He looked into the distance and shrugged. "It's hard. For people like us, I mean."

"That's not…"

Not what? Not true? It's what she wanted to say.

But it was true. And Jarek knew it. And the fact that he knew it only made her feel all the worse for feeling the need to distance herself.

But she didn't have a choice. Did she?

Because Jarek was right: either one of them could be dead tomorrow. She didn't need to look any further than the chopping block of Jarek's face to remember that.

They'd won the battle, but they'd barely even made it to the beginning of the war. The rakul were coming, and the thought of getting close to someone just to lose them—to lose *him*…

It was ridiculous. More than ridiculous, it was stupid.

She'd had more than enough loved ones ripped away for one lifetime. And she'd be damned if she was going to let either of them end up in a position where they let their emotions pull them into doing something stupid.

She almost laughed despite herself.

As if that wasn't what led both of them here in the first place. Hypocrisy, thy name is Rachel.

But this was different. This could be managed.

This could be business. Slay the rakul and save the day first. Everything else later. Simple. Easy. Manageable.

So why couldn't she get that stupid kiss out of her head?

She needed to say something. The silence had already stretched too long between them.

"So what's next?" she finally asked.

Jarek didn't seem to begrudge her the awful segue. A few ounces of amusement even crept back into his expression.

"Next, I suppose we pull ourselves together the world's first human-space vampire alliance and start preparing to slay ourselves a space dragon. Assuming you're still game."

The last bit took Rachel by surprise.

"How could I not be? It's not like we really have a choice anymore."

The rakul wouldn't be keeping a list and sparing the innocent when they arrived. It was all hands on deck. Fight or die. And even if it weren't, she still had questions that needed answered—why her mom had done what she'd done to the raknoth, what had actually happened to her in the end. It might not change anything, but she needed to know. And sometime soon, Alton Parker was going to tell her.

Jarek sighed and stood to offer her a hand. "We always have a choice, Goldilocks. Always."

Christ, how did he do that? Switch from carefree wisecracker to somber philosopher at the drop of a hat?

But he was right. Rachel had a choice, and she was going to see this thing through to the end—maybe even find some justice for her mom along the way.

She took his hand and allowed herself to be hauled to her feet. "Well, in that case... Wanna come save the world with me?"

Jarek showed her his first genuine smile since the tension had started. "I thought you'd never ask."

As rough as the entirety of his day had been, Jarek had to say that reflexive little whammy of rejection from Rachel might have been the most brutal part.

Okay. In fairness, taking Golga's club to the helmet had probably been a bit worse. And then there was the aching bloody mess of his face. But then it was definitely the rejection.

Maybe he should put down the sword and start writing bad unrequited love songs. Not that this was… that—the cursed L word. Absolutely not.

He enjoyed being around Rachel. That was it. Maybe he kind of wanted to do it more. Maybe without all the pesky clothes, he decided as Rachel strolled up the steps to the Enochians' ship in front of him.

So sue him. Add it to his bill. He'd settle up after they dealt with the intergalactic assholes coming to rain on their parade. Assuming there was anyone left to settle up with at that point. Or a planet to do it on.

It still didn't feel quite real, the coming doomsday via space dragons and god knew what else. But then again, it didn't sound wildly less believable than a bunch of immortal space vampires invading Earth's population and blowing it to smithereens after the humans gave them a crafty super virus, which had totally happened, so "real" was probably out the window at this point.

Inside their ship, the Enochians were gathered in an oddly angle-less lounge room, most of them seated on a pair of cushy blue Enochian couches—which turned out to be more or less just like the couches on Earth, go figure—Haldin and Johnny on one couch, with Elise in between them, and Franco and James on the other. Alton Parker was standing, and Phineas sat in one non-corner of the room, slumped heavily against the smooth, vaguely purple wall.

Michael and Pryce had beat Jarek and Rachel on board too, and were seated in a pair of chairs by one couch, probably all too happy to step out of the chaos of HQ for a few minutes. Pryce looked harried but unhurt. Michael looked like he might fall out of his chair from exhaustion at any moment.

They all turned when Jarek and Rachel walked in.

"Broto," Johnny said, "that's gonna make one badass scar."

"Right?" Jarek said with far more enthusiasm than he felt.

He wasn't exactly excited about the disfigurement Golga had left him with. He was hoping it might manage to heal without leaving a garish mark. But if he did have to come out of this with facial scars, at least they probably would be pretty badass.

And he still had both eyes. Hard to complain about that.

"So what's up, guys?" Jarek asked. "Are we celebrating a victory well won?"

"You call that well won?" Alton asked.

"Hey, someone's gotta give us credit for the day's victories," Jarek said. "Zar'Golga? Problem solved. Surprise attack on HQ? Averted. Necessary evil alliance with the raknoth?" He wiggled a hand in a *so-so* gesture. "Eh. Progress was made. Not bad for a day's work."

"And the unstoppable force coming to destroy this world and everything on it?" Alton asked.

That silenced everyone for a solemn few seconds.

"I didn't say it was a perfect day," Jarek finally said. "Jesus, guys, small victories."

Haldin's lip quirked in a small smile.

Johnny pointed at Jarek. "Him. I like the way he thinks."

"That makes two of us, guy," Jarek said, raising a solitary fist in Johnny's direction.

Johnny raised his own fist to meet Jarek's long-distance fist bump.

Franco stirred as if suddenly remembering something. "You two sit," he said, beginning to rise. "I'll bring more chairs."

Jarek raised a hand and plopped down against the smooth wall with a contented sigh. "No worries, man. All set here. Unless…"

He glanced up at Rachel, but she settled down against the wall beside him with a contented sigh of her own.

"So where do we stand, Captain Buzzkill?" Jarek asked Alton.

The raknoth frowned at him. "The humans will never trust my kind. Or any humans who freely choose to work with them, I imagine."

Jarek searched the vaults of his cavalier chipperness for something to defuse the troubling sentiment. But that vault was empty—had been all along, really. He was tired, and he hurt, and at the end of the day, Alton was right.

No matter what monsters might be coming for them, humans and raknoth wouldn't be holding hands and skipping into the sunset anytime soon. The only thing they'd really managed to do today by ending the fight "peacefully" was probably to alienate most of the Resistance. And ensure everyone would stay alive long enough to be available for bountiful slaughter once the rakul arrived on Earth.

Small victories, right?

"They don't need to trust the raknoth," Haldin said. "Not at first, at least. If everyone can just make it to tolerating one another"—he cocked his head—"and if we don't all die off the bat, trust can come later."

The look that passed between Alton and Haldin gave Jarek the impression that Haldin was speaking from experience after whatever had transpired between them on Enochia. It was easy to forget, and still pretty hard to believe, that these people had fought to protect their own world from the raknoth only to fly across the galaxy with one of them to do it all again.

"We probably could have gotten a better start," Rachel said. "This is a two-way street, and Krogoth didn't exactly roll out the red carpet of friendship to the Resistance back there."

Haldin nodded. "We have a lot of work to do."

Johnny made a face. "Ah, diplomacy. Our greatest strength."

Haldin smiled and pointed at Alton and Franco. "That's what we brought these two along for."

Franco arched a decidedly sage eyebrow at Haldin from over steepled fingers, a small smile pulling at his mouth as he received the compliment. Alton looked less flattered.

"We wouldn't happen to have any idea how long we have to do this work, would we?" Pryce asked.

Alton shot a speculative glance at Michael and shook his head. "Not with any real accuracy. At any time, the twelve could be scattered well across the galaxy, and possibly beyond. Depending on location and just how furious they are, we could be looking at anywhere from days to years." He gazed through the deck, thinking. "If the nest ruptured three days ago, judging from what little I felt of Kul'Gada's message yesterday, my best guess is that we're only looking at a few weeks before at least he arrives."

"Kul-whadda?" Jarek asked.

"Kul'Gada."

Beside Jarek, Rachel tensed at the word.

"Am I correct in assuming 'Kul' is a fourth title?" Pryce asked. "Above Zar?"

Alton nodded. "It is the title of the rakul and the highest station of our people, though a Kul can only loosely be called one of us. If we translate to your years, Kul'Gada, the youngest of the twelve, is well over 10,000 years old."

Jarek processed that for a few seconds. Across the room, Pryce's mouth cycled open and closed half a dozen times as probably three hundred times that many questions fought to escape his head.

Jarek raised a hand.

Alton stared at him for several seconds before he finally shook his head and extended a hand to Jarek in invitation.

"I have a feeling I'm not gonna like the answer to this one," Jarek said, "but, uh, has anyone ever actually taken down one of these rakul guys?"

Tense silence stretched, the earth crew all leaning forward in anticipation. The way the Enochians' gazes all dropped to the deck gave Jarek all the answer he needed.

"Only once," Alton finally said. "By the oldest of my kin."

"And what happened to that guy?" Rachel asked.

Alton's smile was utterly devoid of humor. "He became Kul'Gada."

"And I take it that meant no sympathy for the little folk anymore?" Jarek asked.

"Not so much," Alton said. "In fact, it's the opposite, if anything. Ascensions to Kul clearly don't happen every day. Or millennium. I would imagine Kul'Gada feels the need to prove himself even now. He's certainly acted like it over the past 2,000 years."

"Sounds like a swell guy," Jarek said.

"But at least he demonstrated it's possible to kill a rakul," Pryce said.

"It is most certainly possible," Alton said. "For all their power, the rakul are flesh and blood. On the inside, at least."

That raised a few eyebrows.

"And on the outside?" Jarek asked.

"It varies," Alton said. "Some have become amalgamations of the many species we've conquered over the millennia, strengthening their bodies over time while we are forced to start fresh with each new species we infiltrate."

"Right…" Rachel said quietly.

"Creepy," Jarek agreed.

"It's one of the ways they've kept us subservient all this time," Alton continued. "By the time any of my predecessors thought to first question the way of things, the rakul had already grown too strong."

"Double creepy," Jarek said.

"But killable," Haldin said.

"Right," Johnny said. "All we gotta do is unite a bunch of scared humans and the blood-sucking monsterrr—umm, guys who blew their planet to ashes and get everyone ready to rumble with a dozen alien warlords who've basically never suffered a loss."

"So yeah," Jarek said slowly. "A bit of work to do, then."

"Who doesn't like a good challenge?" Elise asked.

"Well," Pryce said, glancing from Alton to Haldin, "as our resident experts, what do you believe to be our best shot from here out?"

"We'll begin reaching out to the other raknoth on Earth," Alton said, looking to Haldin and Franco for confirmation. "There are several clusters of my people scattered across the planet. We'll try to convince them the only hope is to join forces and rally here to face the rakul together."

Jarek looked at Rachel. "Guess that means we should focus on getting the party started right with Krogoth and Drogan."

Maybe they could even get Mosen to help them bridge the gap with the raknoth, provided the ruthless bastard had any pull with

Krogoth's new regime—and especially provided Alaric didn't shoot Jarek in the face for even suggesting such a thing.

Maybe he'd wait to mention it, at least until he had a functional faceplate to protect him after word got to Alaric.

With Fela's missing faceplate, his thoughts turned to his wrecked ship, sitting abandoned in the middle of Yankee Stadium.

He and Pryce—and mostly Pryce if he was being honest—had some heavy-duty repairing to get to. A lot of work to do indeed.

Jarek sighed and leaned back to rest his head against the wall. When his shoulder brushed against Rachel's, he paused, waiting to see if rejection would strike again and she'd withdraw from the contact. He felt more than saw her uncertain sideways glance. Then, quietly, she shifted and settled more comfortably against his side.

So it was gonna be like that, then.

Jarek met Michael's soft frown with an easy smile then settled in to take a few deep breaths and enjoy the contact while the others continued talking plans. Then his comm decided to buzz and ruin everything.

"Call from Alaric, sir," Al said in his earpiece.

Jarek scooted around so the others would be behind him and in frame. "Share it with the class, Mr. Robot."

Jarek's comm holo sprang to life to reveal a battered-looking Alaric standing in the council chamber, which was empty but for the muffled bustle of voices and activity that carried through the doors.

"We've got rubble," Alaric said without preamble. "The kind it'd be handy to have a big strong exo to clear out."

"Well don't beat around the bush, Alaric," Jarek said. "Was there something you wanted?"

Alaric scowled. "Get down here and help unless you all have something better to do." His hard stare shifted over Jarek's shoulder to the others. "What are you all doing, by the way?"

"Just trying to save the world," Johnny called. "You know how it goes."

"We were discussing our best next steps in facilitating a human-raknoth alliance," Haldin added. "We're happy to move the discussion to HQ as soon as everyone's ready."

Alaric shook his head, his scowl deepening. Jarek half-expected him to give a strong *Hell no*, or something of the sort, but when he spoke it was with defeated acknowledgment.

"I can't believe it's come to this."

No one in the room seemed to disagree with the statement.

"Not that I'm particularly excited to suggest it," Alaric continued after a stretch, "but the logistics of this half-assed alliance might at least be a touch easier now that we have a Resistance Commander on board."

Jarek studied the stoic expression beneath Alaric's grizzled beard.

"You?" he asked finally.

Alaric nodded.

"Can't imagine Sloan approved that decision," Jarek said.

And he had a feeling he knew why.

"Sloan is dead," Alaric said. "Enemy forces breached into his room from above. Looks like the blast took him."

That earned a moment of silence, which Jarek willfully refrained from breaking with something along the lines of *Good riddance.*

"He wasn't the best man we lost today," Michael finally said.

"No," Alaric said. "He wasn't."

Jarek had never seen Alaric look so tired. For a second, he thought about asking if Mosen had made it through the fight safely in his cell, but that wasn't liable to do Alaric's mood any favors.

"All right." Jarek stood and showed Alaric a casual salute. "I'm on my way, cowboy. We'll get HQ squared away and then worry about the end of the world. See you in a few."

Alaric looked a shade surprised, but he stifled it quickly enough, said a gruff, "Thank you," and cut the call.

Jarek looked back at the others. "Anyone up for strengthening alien goodwill with a bunch of twitchy Resistance fighters?"

They shared a look and all rose to their feet. Jarek pulled Rachel to her feet, and, together, the party began the short trek out of the ship and back to HQ.

As they went, Jarek found himself wondering where along the line things had changed to the point that he was the one leading the march to go help the same Resistance that had been willingly hiding Fela from him not even a week ago.

Sideways, apparently.

Or maybe not. Maybe it *wasn't* the same Resistance they were marching to the aid of right now.

Because everything had changed, hadn't it? For now, at least.

And all it had taken was the threat of extinction.

Jarek wasn't about to paint a big red R across his chest, and he sure as hell wasn't about to thoughtlessly toe the line and give any of them the *Sir, yes sir*, but there was no denying it anymore. After years of trying to do the right thing from a distance, he'd finally picked his side. He was as much a part of this now as any of the soldiers scrambling around in the tunnels below.

He was still his own man, and always would be. But for the foreseeable future, being his own man meant fighting for the Resistance—and for the rest of Earth too.

Tomorrow would bring new struggles. In the weeks to come, there would be squabbles and fights. Friendships would be shaken, alliances forged and broken. Most likely, people would die—maybe a lot of them. And even if everything went to plan and raknoth and human somehow came to stand together without friction or animosity in a few short weeks, at the end of it all, they still had to face their retribution.

The rakul were coming.

But for today, at least, they were alive. And it was time to do something about it.

END BOOK TWO

AUTHOR'S NOTE
THE "META NOTE" EDITION (UPDATED SEPTEMBER 6TH, 2020)

What would YOU do if, tomorrow, all of our world leaders sprouted red eyes and started launching nukes without warning?

That, Dear Reader, was pretty much the question I was asking myself as I sat down to start writing The Harvesters Series. Or so I tell myself in hindsight.

In truth, this series really began more as a protracted byproduct of my procrastination than anything else.

See, before that big glitzy apocalypse question really grabbed me, I was already elbows deep working on another book—the first book I'd ever written, in fact. A lengthy tome that was in fact starting to look like the beginning of an epic sci-fi trilogy. But there was a problem.

I had this cool, action-packed alien invasion story going down on this world called Enochia.

I had this neat-o idea about how these events were all tenuously connected back to this ancient world called Earth.

I even knew the broad strokes of what had happened back on poor ol' Earth.

(*SPOILER ALERT: It involved world leaders one day sprouting red eyes and launching many, many nukes without warning.*)

What I *didn't* have was a totally firm grasp on WHY Earth had been devastated, or WHAT happened next. And boy, did I need to know the answers to those questions.

In fact, I needed to know SO MUCH that, much like a man trying to change a light bulb in a house of loose shelves and squeaky drawers, I chucked the tome of my Enochian work-in-progress aside to go focus on these new, *totally* important sidetracks.

(In my defense, they were oh-so-shiny and exciting.)

I meant to spend an afternoon at the drawing board doing some worldbuilding to satisfy my curiosity.

I ended up writing the four-book Harvesters series (plus two prequel novellas and multiple short stories) instead.

And while it all started with a simple questions (*what would YOU do when the nukes started flying and all the rules went out the window?*), I was pleasantly surprised to find a much more interesting story quickly taking shape before my eyes.

A story about two outcasts finding each other in a world gone horribly sideways. (And, yes, ALSO a story with LOTS of action, bloodthirsty aliens, and explosively snark-tastic shenanigans, too. But mostly the "outcasts" thing.)

And it didn't end there, either.

Because the more I watched Rachel and Jarek come to life struggling against the raknoth and their bleak post-apocalyptic settings in these books, the more I needed to know WHY they were the people they so clearly *were* under the surface.

Why was Jarek so bitter about the world when he so clearly wanted to do good?

Why was Rachel so closed off when her powers allowed her to see the world with a depth that few of us could shake a wizard's staff at?

Sure, I had workable ideas. Broad strokes. Loose, hand-wavy things.

I knew the general flavor of the story pie. I even had a decent idea of what most of the ingredients were. But I didn't have the full recipe.

We'd come full circle. Turtles all the way down.

Again, I found myself needing to know.

So I rolled up my sleeves and went to work, reverse engineering exactly how one ends up with one wise-cracking, sword-slinging, exo-suit-wearing Jarek Slater, and a chop-busting, magic-slinging Rachel Cross to match.

I had a blast finding my answers via the prequel novellas, *Cursed Blood* and *Soldier of Charity*. More importantly, I think you will too.

(And better yet, you can grab 'em both for free.)

All you have to do is go to *lukermitchell.com/hell-to-pay-signup* to join my mailing list and download your free copies of *Cursed Blood* and *Soldier of Charity* today!

In addition to occasional behind-the-scenes notes like the one above (which was actually adapted from one of my Sunday newsletters), as a member of the list, you'll also get access to free books from all of my other fictional worlds—as well as discounts and short stories you won't find anywhere else.

(Rachel's origin story *Cursed Blood*, for instance, is only available in the box set or to my mailing list readers.)

Sign up at the above link to grab both Harvesters novellas free today, and enjoy!

And if newsletters and email shenanigans aren't your bag, no worries. You can always visit *lukermitchell.com/books* to find the complete list of my published works—and to grab *Reaping Day* (Book 3) and continue the series today!

Whichever way you go from here, I just want you to know that I really do appreciate you coming along for this ride. I sure hope you've enjoyed it, and here's hoping you enjoy the next one even more! Thanks so much for reading. We'll see you on the other side.

Cheers,
Luke Mitchell

ABOUT THE AUTHOR

Not a llama. Mostly human.

Luke is a storyteller whose dreams include learning the ways of the Force, becoming a sentient robot, and maybe even one day growing up. Also, lots of zombies… Don't ask.

Oh, and that "growing up" bit? That was a lie.

After studying engineering science at Penn State and neuroengineering at Drexel, Luke finally decided to throw in the towel on building a working Iron Man suit and opted instead to simply make things up and write them down. Boy, is he having more fun now.

When he's not holed up in his writing cave trying to string words together, he can often be found powerlifting, video-gaming, reading, and/or drinking the darkest, most roasty beers he can get his mitts on. Sometimes all at once.

But you know what? That's enough about Luke. He's really not that interesting. Still, if you'd like to say hi to him for whatever reason, he'd probably be glad to hear from you!

Go to **lukermitchell.com/hell-to-pay-signup** to join the mailing list and grab your free copies of *Soldier of Charity* and the list-exclusive *Cursed Blood*!

Additionally (as you wish)…

Follow me on BookBub for new release alerts
bookbub.com/authors/luke-r-mitchell

Browse the rest of my published titles
lukermitchell.com/books

Join the Patreon team for digital copies of ALL of my work (past, present, and future) — and much more!
patreon.com/lukermitchell

Thank you for reading!

www.ingramcontent.com/pod-product-compliance
Lightning Source LLC
Chambersburg PA
CBHW061606190726
48288CB00007B/2194